'And could I h
soda while I wa

'Fine,' Leo said, irritate~~d~~ ~~bent over.~~

'And—'

'Good God, what else?'

'Just that it's Gary's birthday. So if there's a special dessert or something…?'

'Yes. I. Will. Send. Out. A. Special. Dessert. Now, are you all right for socks and undies, or do you need me to get you some of those too?'

'Actually, I never wear socks.' Sunshine smiled serenely. 'And I'm not wearing undies tonight—not under *this* dress!'

Leo could feel his eyes bug out of his head. 'Thanks for that mental picture, Sunshine. Anything else you'd care to share?'

'Well…'

'Yeah, hold that thought,' he said, and made a bolt for the kitchen. Where he leaned against the wall and burst out laughing.

His sous chef looked at him as if he'd grown a gigantic unicorn horn.

Clearly it had been a long time since he'd laughed.

Dear Reader

Food is a great passion of mine—in fact I'm in love with about a dozen celebrity chefs. So I wasn't exactly surprised to find myself becoming fixated on the idea of a chef as a hero…and Leo Quartermaine was born.

My other great passion is shoes. Oh, my goodness, the *shoes*! So…hello, Sunshine Smart.

And, of course, I'm partial to a nice romantic wedding.

HERE COMES THE BRIDESMAID gave me a chance to combine all three things in a setting always irresistible to me—my hometown, Sydney—as best man Leo and bridesmaid Sunshine are put in charge of planning the perfect wedding for two absent grooms.

Leo is driven, grumpy and serious. Sunshine is quirky, perky and enthusiastic. They have different takes on love, on life, on relationships—not exactly the easiest working combination to plan a wedding reception. Add in an inconvenient sexual attraction, and things get even trickier.

But HERE COMES THE BRIDESMAID is more than a story about opposites attracting—although the clash of personalities in Sunshine and Leo's case *can* lead to some eye-popping conversations! It's also about being jolted out of your comfort zone and opening yourself to everything that's in you, and finding the one you thought you'd never find—ready-or-not-here-I-come.

And there's nothing quite as romantic as being taken by surprise by love.

I hope you enjoy HERE COMES THE BRIDESMAID.

Avril Tremayne

XXXX

HERE COMES THE BRIDESMAID

BY
AVRIL TREMAYNE

Published in Great Britain 2014
by Mills & Boon, an imprint of Harlequin (UK) Limited,
Eton House, 18-24 Paradise Road, Richmond, Surrey, TW9 1SR

© 2014 Belinda de Rome

ISBN: 978-0-263-24680-3

Harlequin (UK) Limited's policy is to use papers that are natural,
renewable and recyclable products and made from wood grown in
sustainable forests. The logging and manufacturing processes conform
to the legal environmental regulations of the country of origin.

Printed and bound in Spain
by Blackprint CPI, Barcelona

Avril Tremayne read *Jane Eyre* as a teenager and has been hooked on tales of passion and romance ever since. An opportunistic insomniac, she has been a lifelong crazy-mad reader, but she took the scenic route to becoming a writer—via gigs as diverse as shoe salesgirl, hot cross bun packer, teacher, and public relations executive. She has spent a good chunk of her life travelling, and has more favourite destinations than should be strictly allowable.

Avril is happily settled in her hometown of Sydney, Australia, where her husband and daughter try to keep her out of trouble—not always successfully. When she's not writing or reading she can generally be found eating—although she does *not* cook!

Check out her website, www.avriltremayne.com, or follow her on Twitter, @AvrilTremayne, and Facebook, www.facebook.com/avril.tremayne

HERE COMES THE BRIDESMAID
is Avril Tremayne's debut book
for Modern Tempted™!

This title is also available in eBook format
from www.millsandboon.co.uk

Dedicated, with thanks, to my husband and @kder
for absolutely everything.

To the astute, eagle-eyed Americans Lisa McNair Palmer
and Melinda Wirth for knowing what's good
and what's definitely not.

And to each and every one of my marriage-minded friends!

CHAPTER ONE

TO: Jonathan Jones
FROM: Sunshine Smart
SUBJECT: Bridesmaid meets Best Man
Darling Jon
I've met Leo and I adore him!

We are on the same page, so fear not—your wedding reception will be everything you ever dreamed of!

Wish we could have the actual marriage in Sydney too, but hooray for enlightened New York!

Hugs and kisses to Caleb.
Sunny xxx

TO: Caleb Quartermaine
FROM: Leo Quartermaine
SUBJECT: WTF??????
Caleb
What are you doing to me?

Sunshine Smart cannot be a real name. And she wants to friend me on Facebook! NOT JOKING!

Despite being dropped in it with the lunatic, I will ensure the dinner doesn't turn into a three-ring circus.

Can't wait to meet Jonathan—but please tell me he's nothing like his bridesmaid.
LQ

SUNSHINE SMART WAS looking forward to her second meeting with Leo Quartermaine. *Despite* their introductory meeting two days ago, lasting just ten minutes and ending with him declining her request to be Facebook friends.

She loved Leo's restaurants—well, what she'd read about them. Because she'd never actually eaten at one... which she was about to remedy.

She loved him on TV—tough but fair, judging those reality TV would-be chefs, and *dreamy as* when fronting *Cook It Up With Leo.*

She was predisposed to love anyone whose brother was smart enough to marry her best friend Jonathan Jones.

And she just—well, *loved* him. In that *Isn't he adorable?* way of loving people who were just so solid and serious and a teensy bit repressed.

But his hair—or lack thereof—was a problem. There was no *reason* for Leo to shave his head. It wasn't as if he had a comb-over issue. He could have a full head of hair if he wanted! Lush, thick, wheat-blond. She'd seen the 'before shaved head' photos on the internet. And the start of the regrowth at their first meeting. She'd read a comment in an article about it being easier in the kitchen without hair—but she wasn't asking for a ponytail!

Anyway, that could be fixed. There was time for him to grow it. She would just drop a word in his ear.

Sunshine checked her make-up. Her new red lipstick looked fabulous. Her eyes...well, what could you do? The grey eyeshadow was heavily layered; mascara so thick each lash look like a tarantula leg—make-up intended to distract people from her ocular weirdness. About which there was nothing she could do—unlike Leo Quartermaine's hair!

She got out of her car—a bright yellow 1970s relic—and walked purposefully towards Q Brasserie.

* * *

Leo Quartermaine heard Sunshine approach before he saw her.

He associated that tap-tapping rhythm on the polished concrete floor with her, despite only having met her once before.

He was betting she was wearing another pair of ankle-breaking high heels.

To be fair, she *was* a shoe designer. But shoe designers made flats, didn't they? Like those ballet-slipper things. Not that he could picture Sunshine Smart in ballet slippers. Or trainers—crikey!

'Leo!' she called out, as though he were a misplaced winning lottery ticket, suddenly found. He was starting to think 'ecstatic' was her default setting.

'Sunshine,' he said, managing not to roll his eyes. *Sunshine!* How had her parents put that on the birth certificate without gagging?

'So!'

He'd already clocked the fact that she often started her utterances with 'So!' As though an amazing revelation would be out of her mouth on the next breath.

'News!' she said, tap-tapping towards the window table where he was sitting.

And, yep, six inches of spike on her feet. In electric blue patent leather. God help his eyes.

She stripped off her trench coat as she made her way across the floor, causing her long necklace to swing. He'd noticed the necklace last time. Pretty. Three types of gold—a rose gold chain, with a yellow gold sun and white gold moon dangling from it.

Miraculously, her dress was an understated colour— pale grey-blue. But it fitted her like a second skin and had one of those things—pellums? Peplums? Whatever!—that dragged a man's eyes to a woman's waist and hips. She had a hell of a figure, he had to admit. Curvaceous, like the hourglass pin-up girls of the 1950s.

Leo got up to pull out a chair for her on the opposite side of the table. She took the opportunity to kiss him on the cheek, party-girl air-kiss style—except it wasn't like any air-kiss he'd ever had—and he'd had plenty. It was a smacking, relishing kiss. *Not* the kind of kiss to slap on a person you barely knew.

Oblivious to his momentary shock, Sunshine tossed her trench coat carelessly onto a nearby chair, sat, and beamed up at him. 'Did you hear? They've set the date. October twentieth. So we've got two months. A spring wedding. Yay!'

Yay? Who the hell said 'yay'? Leo returned to his seat. 'Not much time, but doable.'

'Oh, it's *oodles* of time,' Sunshine assured him airily. 'So! I've made a list of everything we need to do, and now we can decide who does what, give each task a deadline, and go from there.'

'List?' Leo repeated the word, apprehensive. He liked lists. He worked well with lists. The haphazard approach to life of his wastrel and usually wast*ed* parents had made him a plan-crazy list junkie. But this was a simple dinner he could organise with his eyes closed while he whisked a chocolate soufflé.

For once in his life he *didn't* need a list.

'Yes.' She reached down beside her to where she'd dumped the silver leather bag she'd been swinging when she walked over and pulled out a dazzling chartreuse folder. She removed some paper, peeled off two pages and held them out to him. 'Your copy. I'm actually not really into lists,' she confessed—*surprise, surprise.* 'So it may need some work.'

He looked at the first page. At the big, bold heading: *The Marriage Celebration of Jonathan and Caleb, October 20th.*

Seeing the words was like a punch to the solar plexus. It was real. Happening. Imminent. His baby brother was getting married.

What were the odds? Two Aussie guys who'd never met in their own country moved separately to New York, met at a random party, and—bang!—happy-ever-after.

It didn't matter that Leo didn't know Jonathan, because Jonathan made Caleb happy. It didn't matter that the ceremony was taking place on the other side of the world, because the place was just logistics. It didn't matter that their marriage was only going to be legally recognised in a handful of countries, because *they* knew what it meant wherever they were.

Leo wondered if he would have had more luck meeting the love of his life if *he* were gay. Because it sure wasn't happening for him on his side of the sexuality fence. The succession of glossy glamour-pusses who seemed to be the only women that came his way were certainly lovely to look at—but they didn't *eat*, and they didn't occupy his thoughts for longer than it took to produce a mutual orgasm.

He wanted what Caleb had. The one. Someone to get into his head, under his skin, to intrigue and dazzle and delight him. Someone who burrowed into his core instead of bouncing off his shell. Someone to belong to. And to belong to him.

He thought back to his last failure—beautiful, talented singing sensation Natalie Clarke. She'd told him on their second date that she loved him. But nobody fell in love in two dates! Nope—what she'd loved was the concept of Leo the celebrity chef. She'd wanted them to be part of 'the scene'. And who said *'the scene'* with a straight face? He couldn't think of anything worse than 'the scene'…except maybe her predilection for snorting cocaine, because apparently *everyone* on *'the scene'* did it.

In any case, she was a relentless salad-with-dressing-on-the-side type. And she liked playing her own cheesy love songs in the bedroom *way* too much.

With a repressed shudder he brought his mind back to the present and ran his eyes down the list.

Budget
Wedding Party
Master of Ceremonies
Venue
Menu
Alcohol
Guest List
Invitations
Flowers
Lighting
Music
Cake
Clothing
Shoes
Hair and Make-up

What the hell...? Why did *that* need a subheading?

Gift Registry
Photographer
Videographer
Wedding Favours
Order of Proceedings
Toasts and Speeches
Printing
Seating Plan

Each item was bullet-pointed with a little box that could be ticked, and accompanied by questions, comments and suggestions.

Good thing she wasn't into lists!

Sunshine must have noticed the stunned look on Leo's face, because she asked, 'Have I screwed it up?'

'This is…' he started, but words actually failed him.

'Exciting?' Sunshine suggested, looking as if she were about to celebrate Christmas, her birthday *and* the wedding all at once.

'Comprehensive,' Leo corrected. He ran a hand across his scalp. Her eyes followed his hand. She was frowning suddenly. He wondered what was going through her mind.

She opened her mouth. Closed it. Opened it. Closed it. Sighed.

Then, 'So!' she said. 'The venue is the first thing. Because it's bound to be tricky, securing somewhere wonderful with only two months' notice.'

'It may have escaped your notice, but I am a restaurateur,' Leo said. 'I *have* venues. I *am* venues. *And* menus. And *booze*.'

Sunshine seemed startled. 'Oh. I just assumed we'd be too late to get a large group booked into one of your places. That's why I've suggested somewhere like the hotel on—'

'My brother is *not* celebrating his marriage in a hotel.'

'Okay. Well, there's that lovely place that used to be a stately home in—'

'Or in an old house.'

'Then perhaps the new convention space—which is not as tragic as it sounds. In fact it has a—'

He slammed his hand on the table. 'No!' He stopped, reined in the spurt of annoyance. 'No.' *Better. Calmer.* 'We have a perfectly…' *Reaching, reaching...* 'Perfectly perfect…' *hmm, thesaurus required* '…private room in this restaurant.'

The only sign that Sunshine had noted his ill-tempered hand-banging incoherence was a tiny twitch at one side of her mouth. He feared—he really feared—she was trying not to laugh.

'Which seats…?' she asked, her head on one side like a bird, with every indication of deep interest.

'Seats?'

'How many people does the private room seat?'

'Twenty-five.'

Sunshine crossed her arms—seemingly unaware of how she was framing her rather spectacular breasts—and looked at him, apologetic. 'See? Me and lists! I got the order wrong. "Guest List" should have come before "Venue". So! Let's take a step back. I have Jon's invitation list. Do you have Caleb's?'

'It's coming today some time.'

'Because there are seventy-five people on our side.'

He stared. 'You are not serious.'

'I assure you, I am. And that's with a savage cull.' She shuddered theatrically as she uncrossed her arms. *'Savage.'*

'Caleb wants an intimate dinner.'

'That's not my understanding, but I'll tell you what—you check with Caleb overnight, and we can reconvene tomorrow.'

His eyes narrowed. 'I hate it when people try to soothe me.'

Sunshine bit her lip. 'Oh, dear, and I was *trying* to sound like I was keeping an open mind. But…okay. I'll tell you straight out, if you prefer: there is no way this is going to be a dinner for twenty-five people. And there's no use getting in a snit about it—it's just the way it is.'

'I'm not in a snit.'

'If you say so.'

'I do. Say so.'

'All right.'

'I'm *not.*'

'All *right.*'

Another mouth-twitch. She was *definitely* trying not to laugh.

And Leo had had enough. 'I have to go,' he said, despite not being needed in the kitchen for fifteen minutes.

'Yes, I can see everything's getting under way here. I love the buzz of restaurants. Jon and I used to try a new restaurant every other week. I miss him. He's so...so important to me.' Her voice wobbled the merest fraction as she added the last bit.

Uh-oh, tears. Leo didn't do tears. He felt himself shrink back. Wanted to run.

But her face morphed into something tortured, right before his eyes, and he froze. It was as if a layer had been ripped off her in one half-second. Her eyes were strained and yet also vacant, as if she were seeing...emptiness. Her lips trembled. Her skin looked ashen. Every trace of happiness was obliterated. The contrast with her normal exuberance was dramatic—almost painful to see.

All this because her best friend had moved overseas and she missed him?

Huh?

Leo wanted to touch her. Pat her hand or...something. Say...something. He who never touched, never comforted, because he didn't know how. His hands fisted uselessly.

Then Sunshine blinked. Shook her head—tiny, tiny movement. And in another half-second everything clicked back to normal and Leo breathed a silent sigh of relief.

'Um...' he said. Yep, he was super-articulate today.

But she was smiling blindingly, as though that moment had never happened, so he did the sensible thing and shut up.

'We haven't got far down the list,' she said. 'What about if I shortcircuit a few things? You know, invitations, et cetera.'

'What do you mean, "shortcircuit"? And "et cetera"?'

he asked, still a little shaken. Everything about her was throwing him off kilter.

'I'll get some options together for us to look over tomorrow. Nothing scary!'

She was completely back to normal. Full-strength perky. Better than the tragic facemask she'd freaked him out with—but only marginally. Leo didn't like perky. And if he were being made to board Sunshine Smart's good ship *Lollipop* for this wedding *he* would be the one at the tiller.

'I thought we'd be emailing the invitations,' he said.

She gave him what could only be termed a pitying smile. 'Did you?'

That was all. She wasn't even going to bother arguing.

Um...no. That was not how it was going to work. 'It's the twenty-first century,' he said. 'And time is short. I've seen some brilliant cutting-edge online invitations.'

'Well, why don't you bring one of those examples to our meeting tomorrow on your tablet/device/notebook/ whatever you've got, and I'll bring some hard copy snail mail samples appropriate for a chic but traditional wedding celebration.'

'You're doing the soothe thing again.'

'Oh, dear, am I? I'll have to work on that,' she said.

It was obvious to Leo that she had no intention of doing anything of the sort. But he wasn't going to waste his breath pointing that out. He was tired enough from just *looking* at her.

'We'll talk tomorrow—*after* I've checked with Caleb,' he said shortly, and stood abruptly.

'Just one more thing, Leo, before you rush off.'

He looked down at her and she cleared her throat.

'What?' Leo asked, trying not to feel a sense of impending doom.

'Just...something that's going to have to start now, like right this second, if it's going to be ready in two months.'

'And are you going to share with me exactly what this all-important thing is?'

'Promise you won't get mad?'

'No.'

'It's important.'

'Waiting.'

'I wouldn't ask if it wasn't absolutely vital. It's just…' She stopped, ran her hand through her long hair, widened her eyes at him as though she were trying to impart something telepathically. Ran her hand through her hair again.

And he—

God! The eyes. Why hadn't he noticed her eyes before?

She huffed out a breath and pursed her lips. Exasperated because he hadn't read her chaotic mind, probably.

But all he could think about were her eyes.

'Hair,' she explained. 'It only grows one-point-two-five centimetres a month. One-point-three if you're lucky.'

'So?'

'You have to start growing your hair.'

He had no answer. Might well have been gaping like a hooked fish.

'Sorry—but if I didn't raise it now you might have shaved your head tonight and it would be a shame to lose those few millimetres.'

'I don't want to grow my hair,' Leo said. Ultra-reasonable. The way you talked to a person who was certifiably insane.

'But you will look so much better in the photos. And you have lovely hair.'

'And you know this…how?'

'I looked you up online and saw the photos from the launch of this place, when you had hair. Now, I'm not saying you're not very good-looking even *with* the shaved head. Tall, but not in a carnival freaky way. Lean—which is amazing, for a chef, if you ask me. Wonderful sharp cheekbones, brilliant smile— All right, I'm guessing the smile bit, since I haven't actually seen it, but I'm a good guesser. And really lovely eyes—amber is such an unusual colour, you know? Tigerish. But if you look quite delectable now, you will be absolutely, irresistibly *gorgeous* with hair.'

Leo stood there, gobsmacked. 'I've got to get to work,' he said when he could trust himself to speak.

'But you'll think about the hair, won't you?' she asked anxiously. 'And while you're thinking, maybe keep the razor off your scalp…just in case you *do* decide to look absolutely, irresistibly *gorgeous* at your brother's wedding.'

He looked at her. Noted her eyes again. Really stunning eyes. *She* would look absolutely, irresistibly gorgeous herself if she—

Aha.

Leo could have crowed, he was so pleased with himself. 'Let's make a deal—you go into the bathroom and wash off that eye-goop right now, and I will not shave my head…unless I see that crap all over your eyes again. The minute I see it, I'm reaching for the razor.'

And, yes! He'd stumped her. She was the gaping fish now.

He watched as she processed what he'd said. She lifted her bag off the floor and rummaged inside, pulled out a compact. Flipped it open, looked in the mirror. Widened her eyes, then squinted. Turned her head to peer sideways, then switched sides and did it again. 'You know that I have strange eyes, right?' she asked.

'Beautiful eyes.'

'Evil eyes.'

'Yeah, maybe lay off the sci-fi.'

'Oh, it's a real condition. It's called heterochromia iridum, and there are various theories about how you get it. Genetics, melanin levels, trauma, chimerism—which is kind of creepy because it means another foetus has merged with you in the womb, which in my case would mean there were initially three of us, because— Well, anyway, I don't like the idea of absorbing a sibling in the womb—hello, Dr Frankenstein!' Pause for breath. 'All that aside, I'm pretty sure they used to burn people like me at the stake as witches back in the day.'

'Nobody is going to burn you at the stake in modern-day Australia for having one blue and one green eye.'

'I've tried contact lenses, but there is nothing that makes you panic quite like a contact lens that's slipped up under your eyelid and you think it's going to be there for eternity unless you race off to the emergency room and have someone stick some implement in there against your poor squishy eyeball. Talk about bloodshot!' She pursed her lips. 'But I guess I could try them again—maybe some amber ones.' She looked into his eyes, considering. 'Because your eyes really are lovely, and I think I'd look kind of interesting with amber eyes.'

'You do that and I'm shaving my head.'

Sunshine took another look in the mirror, then snapped the compact shut. 'All right. Deal. I may need a little make-up on the actual day of the reception, just so I don't look Plain Janerama, but no camouflage paint in the meantime. I'm keeping the lipstick, though—I can't go completely naked. So! Where's the bathroom?'

Plain Janerama? Leo, speechless, pointed.

Sunshine got to her feet. 'No need to wait,' she told him.

'Oh, I'm waiting.'

She squared her shoulders. 'This is going to be *weird*,' she said, and tap-tapped away.

Leo checked that everything was in order in the kitchen, then returned to the table. He went through the checklist again. Swore under his breath. He suspected Sunshine Smart usually got her way in all things. Which meant she was in for a surprise, because just on principle he wasn't going to let that happen. He hadn't got where he was today by doing what people told him. His survival instinct told him always to go his *own* way, to *get* his own way.

He started jotting down menu ideas—appropriate for a dinner for twenty-five people—but hadn't got far when he heard the tap-tap of Sunshine's returning high heels.

She plonked herself into the chair opposite and did an over-the-top eyelash-bat at him.

Leo stared at her. He couldn't help it. Without the exaggerated eye make-up she looked fresh and clean and sweet as suckable candy. Her dark chocolate hair against the ultra-white skin of her face seemed more dramatic. With the edge of her heavy fringe now damp and misplaced, he could see how fine and dark her eyebrows were, and that they arched intriguingly towards the outer edge. Her eyelashes were thick and black enough to form a fine line around her eyes. And her eyes were simply spectacular. Heavy-lidded, slightly tilted, the colour difference so dramatic without the dark shadow and over-clumped lashes that he couldn't seem to stop looking at them.

'Well?' she asked, batting away.

'Better,' Leo said, with impressive understatement. He got to his feet. 'I'll see you tomorrow, then—an hour earlier, if you can make it. But you'll have to come to Mainefare—it's in the Pig and Poke pub. Do you know it?'

'Yes, I know it—and, yes, that's fine. But before you go can I ask just one more favour?'

Leo eyed her suspiciously.

'I'm staying for dinner,' she explained. 'Don't worry—I have a booking. It's just that my date—Gary, his name is—is a massive foodie, and he'd really love to meet you. Perhaps you could just pop out and say hello…?'

'Oh, sure,' Leo agreed easily. He'd been expecting something worse—maybe that he have a shot of Botox!—

and, anyway, speaking to his customers was part of his routine.

'And do you think I could have this exact table? It has a lovely view over the park. If it's reserved I'll understand, but—'

He caught his impatient sigh before it could erupt. 'You can have the table, Sunshine.'

'And could I have a Campari and soda while I wait for Gary?'

'Fine,' Leo said, irritated that it made him curious about her—because he would have pegged her for a Cosmopolitan girl. And who the hell *cared* what she liked to drink? 'I'll get one sent over.'

'And—'

'Good God, what else?'

'Just that it's Gary's birthday…so if there's a special dessert or something…?'

'Yes. I. Will. Send. Out. A. Special. Dessert. Now, are you all right for socks and undies, or do you need me to get you some of those too?'

'Actually, I never wear socks.' Sunshine smiled serenely. 'And I'm not wearing undies tonight—not under *this* dress!'

Leo could feel his eyes bug out of his head. 'Thanks for that mental picture, Sunshine. Anything else you'd care to share?'

'Well…'

'Yeah, hold that thought,' he said, and made a bolt for the kitchen. Where he leant against the wall and burst out laughing.

His sous chef looked at him as if he'd grown a gigantic unicorn horn.

Clearly it had been a long time since he'd laughed.

Yum.

That was the word that had been popping into Sunshine's head with monotonous regularity from the moment Leo had sent out a bowl of polenta chips with a gorgonzola dipping sauce to snack on while she drank her Campari.

Q Brasserie had an open kitchen, so she could not only smell but also see the magic being wrought on an array of seafood and meat—and, okay, vegetables too, although they were a lot less interesting if you asked her.

She rubbernecked as a steady stream of mouthwatering dishes was whisked past her en route to other diners, agonised over the menu choices and wished she could eat everything.

Sunshine basically Hoovered up her entrée of six plump, perfectly sautéed scallops, served with a Japanese-style dressing of cucumber, rice vinegar, mirin, and ginger. And it took great willpower *not* to beg a taste of Gary's mushrooms with truffle custard. She wouldn't normally covet a vegetarian dish but, come on, truffle custard? *Yum!*

The main meals were sublime. She ate every bite of her Angus beef brisket, served with smoked bone marrow and potato confit, and, giving in to her inner piglet on the date-taste issue, was in the process of polishing off one of Gary's divine king prawns—chargrilled with coriander and lime, *yum, yum, yum*—when up bowled Leo.

He'd changed from his jeans, T-shirt and way cool brown leather lace-ups into a spotlessly clean, double-breasted chef's jacket, finely checked pants and classy black slip-ons, and he looked sigh-worthy.

Leo looked at her well-cleaned plate. At Gary's. At the tiny piece of prawn on the end of her fork. His eyebrows shot up.

Sunshine knew she was presenting as a glutton—but so what? She liked food! Sue her! She calmly finished the last bite of prawn and laid her fork on her plate.

She made the introductions, then retreated as Leo engaged Gary in a conversation about food.

Gary looked a little starstruck. Which was kind of sweet. *He* was kind of sweet. Not that their relationship was going anywhere. This was their third date and from her perspective he'd settled into purely platonic material. She hadn't had even one lascivious thought about him.

The conversation moved on from food and Gary was explaining a little about his job. He was an investment banker—which was more interesting than it sounded. Truly!

'Nice talking to you Gary,' Leo said eventually. 'Dessert is on the house. Happy birthday, and enjoy the rest of your evening.

Leo had been aware of Sunshine beaming her approval all through his talk with Gary. It was irritating, like a tiny pebble stuck in your shoe, to have her there—just there… just…*there*. Like a hyped-up Miss Congeniality.

In fact the whole evening had been irritating, because that damned table he'd pinched from one of his regulars was in his line of sight from the kitchen, so he'd been in Peeping Tom mode all night. Watching as she ate. And ate and ate. As she made Gary laugh. And laugh and laugh.

Gary was clearly besotted with her. Poor guy. He was handsome—a nice man—but not in Sunshine's league. Not that Leo knew what Sunshine's league *was*, only that Gary wasn't in it. Which had been underscored by the expression on Sunshine's face when the Persian nougat glacé had arrived at the table. The way her glowing eyes had closed as she took the first bite, then opened as the taste hit her. How her mouth had oozed over the spoon…

And why hadn't he noticed the shape of her mouth before? Too much coloured gunk, he supposed. But once the lipstick had worn off she hadn't bothered reapplying it. Which was odd, wasn't it? He'd never known a girl *not* to race off and reapply her lipstick *ad nauseam* during dinner.

Not that Sunshine's lipstick habits were any of his business.

Except that now he couldn't miss her too-heavy top lip, glistening as she darted her tongue over it. The wide and chewable bottom lip. She had a little gap between her two front teeth that was kooky-meets-adorable. And she moved her mouth over her spoon as if she were having a food-induced orgasm.

He wondered if he was thinking in orgasm terms because she was going commando tonight. *Not* that he was going there. No way! *And please, God, get the thought out of my head!*

Whatever, she'd clearly appreciated the 2002 Cristal her boyfriend had ordered to go with dessert.

Leo preferred the 1996 vintage.

Talk about splitting hairs. What the hell was wrong with him?

He sighed. Stretched. It had been a long night, that was all. He just needed to get to bed. Right after he emailed Caleb. He was going to get the dinner party back under control at their meeting tomorrow. Put Sunshine the Bulldozer back in the shed.

Sunshine. *Groan!* She was like a six-inch electric blue thorn in his side.

So it didn't make sense that he would be humming as he thought about that manifesto-sized checklist of hers.

And damn if it wasn't that cheesy Natalie Clarke number about love biting you in the ass.

The most diabolically awful song of the century.

Clearly, he needed a drink.

God, he hated Barry White.

CHAPTER TWO

TO: Caleb Quartermaine
FROM: Leo Quartermaine
SUBJECT: Seriously?
Caleb, mate

What's the deal? Where's your invitation list? Are we really talking 150 guests? I thought it was an intimate dinner.

Sunshine is descending on me tomorrow to kick off the invitation process, so it would be nice to know who's got what expectations. So I don't end up looking like a completely clueless moron.
LQ

TO: Jonathan Jones
FROM: Sunshine Smart
SUBJECT: Wedding of the century
Hello, darling

Had dinner at Q Brasserie tonight—fabulous. We're meeting again at one of Leo's other places, Mainefare, tomorrow. Can't wait!

I've worked out that Mainefare is a play on words. Mayfair as in London (it's in a British-style pub) but with Maine as in Quartermaine and fare as in food. Leo is so clever!

Invitation samples attached: (1) ultra-modern, cream and charcoal; (2) dreamy romantic in mauve and violet;

(3) Art Deco—blue and teal with yellow, brown, and grey accents.

PLEASE like the Art Deco one, which I know sounds ghastly, but open it and you'll see!

All else is on track. Party of the year, I'm telling you! Sunny xxx

PS—and, no, in answer to your repeat question—I have not done it yet. You're getting as bad as Mum and Dad.

TAP-TAP-TAP. Same sound effect, just on floorboards.

Leo saw her scan the room. Mainefare wasn't as open as Q Brasserie and it was harder to spot people—so he stood, waved.

His eyes went automatically to Sunshine's feet. Coral suede. Maybe four inches high—he figured the missing inches equalled casual for her. Oddly, no polish on her toenails; now that he thought of it, he hadn't seen colour on her toenails at their previous two meetings. Fingernails either.

Hello, Mr Estee Lauder—since when do you start noticing nail polish?

He *didn't*. Of course he didn't. But she just looked like the kind of girl who wouldn't be seen dead with unpainted nails.

Then again, she didn't look like the kind of girl who would eat like Henry VIII either.

Sunshine gave him her usual beaming smile as she reached him. She was wearing a pair of skintight pants in dark green, with a 1960s-style tunic. The tunic was cream, with a psychedelic red and black swirl on the front that should have looked like crap but didn't. She had on the same sun/moon necklace, but no other jewellery. And that was kind of strange too, wasn't it? Where was the bling?

She kissed him on the cheek, same as yesterday, before he could step out of reach, and sat as though exhausted, thumping an oversized tote—rust-coloured canvas—on the floor beside her chair.

'Whew,' she said. 'I've got lots of samples with me, so that bag is heavy.'

Leo couldn't work out how she could wear colours that didn't match—her shoes, her outfits, her bags always seemed to be different shades and tones—and yet everything looked *I'm-not-even-trying* perfect. He'd been out with models and fashion PR types who didn't make it look that easy.

'Did you sort out the guest list with Caleb?' she asked, and had the nerve to twinkle at him.

'Yes,' Leo said unenthusiastically.

'So! A hundred and fifty, right?'

Gritted teeth. 'Yes, a hundred and fifty. But you can still forget every one of the venues you listed as options.' He sounded grumpy, and that made him grumpier—because there was really nothing to be grumpy *about*. It wasn't *his* damned wedding. But it was just...*galling*!

Sunshine observed him, head tilted to one side in her curious bird guise. 'Does that mean you have somewhere fantastic in mind to fit one hundred and fifty people? Somewhere that will be available with only two months' notice?'

'As a matter of fact I do,' Leo said. 'I have a new place opening next month. But it's not in Sydney. It's an hour and a half's drive south. Actually, it's *called* South.'

He was a bit ashamed of himself for sounding so smug about it—what was he? Fifteen years old?—but his smugness went sailing right by Sunshine, who simply clapped her hands, delighted.

Which made him feel like a *complete* churl.

Sunshine Smart was not good for his mental health.

'Oh, I've read about it!' she exclaimed. 'Perched on

the edge of the escarpment, sweeping views of the ocean. Right?'

'Yep.'

Another enthusiastic hand-clap. 'Perfectamundo. When can we go and see it?'

Perfectamundo? Good Lord! 'Not necessary,' he said repressively. 'I've personally handpicked the staff for South, and they know what they're doing. We can just give them instructions and leave them to it. But I can send you photos of the space.'

Sunshine was staring at him as though he'd taken leave of his senses. 'Of course it's necessary. Your staff may be excellent, but Jon is trusting me to make sure everything is perfect. I know exactly what he likes, you see, and I can't let him down.'

Leo sighed inwardly.

'We have to think about how the tables are going to be arranged,' she went on. 'The best place for speeches, where we'll do welcoming cocktails—I mean, is there an outdoor area for that?' Her hands came up, clasped her head at the temples as if she were about to have a meltdown. 'A *thousand* things.'

Leo felt a throb at the base of his skull. 'Let me think about it,' he said, just to staunch the flow of words. He wasn't *really* going to think about taking her to see the damned restaurant.

'Thank you, Leo!' She was back to twinkling, clearly nowhere *near* a meltdown.

Two months! Two *months* of this manipulative, mendacious wretch.

'So!' she said. 'Let's talk invitations. I have three designs to show you—and I won't tell you which is my favourite because I don't want to influence your opinion.'

'You won't.'

'Well, I wonder if, subliminally, knowing what I like

best might sway you.' Little knowing smile. 'Maybe to deliberately pick something that is *not* my favourite! And that would never do.'

He caught his half-laugh before it could surface. Laughing would only encourage her.

'And since we haven't discounted the email, I've got something to show you too,' he put in smoothly, because he'd be damned if his version was going to be dead in the water without a demo at least. 'It's something we did for the Q Brasserie launch.'

Half an hour later Leo was amazed to find that he'd agreed to a printed Art Deco-style invitation in blue and teal, with yellow, brown, and grey accents.

But he'd had a win too! Sunshine was so impressed with his electronic idea she'd insisted they send something like it as a save-the-date notice, linking to some artsy teaser footage of South's surroundings.

'But we'll keep the venue secret,' she added conspiratorially, 'because it will be fun to have everyone guessing, and they'll be so excited to find out it's South when the printed invitations arrive.'

He hoped—he *really* hoped—he hadn't just been soothed.

Sunshine took on the responsibility for getting the invitations printed and addressed, with names handwritten by a calligrapher she'd dated in the past. She would show Leo—who actually didn't give a damn—the final design before it went to print, along with handwriting samples. Leo was in charge of getting the save-the-date done for Sunshine's approval—and she most certainly *did* give a damn.

He was on the verge of disappearing to the kitchen when Sunshine circled back to South and her need to see it.

'It's not going to happen,' Leo said. 'You can't go on site without me. And the only time I have free is…is…daytime Monday.' *Ha!* 'Shop hours for you, right?'

Sunshine pulled out a clunky-looking diary.

He did a double-take. 'You're on Facebook but you use a paper diary?'

'My mother made it for me so I have to—and, anyway, I like it,' she said. 'Hemp and handmade paper. Jon and Caleb have them too. Play your cards right and you'll get one next year. And, yes! I can do Monday. Yay!'

Again with the *yay*. And the twinkle.

And that throb at the base of his skull.

Sunshine put her diary away. 'My hours are super-flexible. I mostly work from home, and usually at night, when I seem to be more creative—not during the day, and never in the shop unless I'm doing a particular display. Because I have a superb manager who would *not* take kindly to my interfering.'

'I like the sound of your manager.'

'Oh, I can introduce— Ah, I see, sarcasm.' She regarded him with a hint of amused exasperation. 'You know, I'm not generally regarded as an interfering person.'

He couldn't keep the snort in.

'Sarcasm and a *snort*! Better not debate that, then. So! Shall I drive us down?'

'I'm going to take my bike.'

Her face went blank. 'Bike?'

'As in motor,' he clarified.

'You have a car as well, though?'

'No, I don't.'

'Because we could get so much done if we drove down the coast together.'

'Except that I don't have a car.'

'But I have a car. You can come with me.'

'Sunshine, I'd better put this out there right now: you are not going to control me. I don't have a car. I have a bike. I am going to ride down the coast, because that is what I want to do. Why don't you just ride down with me?'

Mental slap of his own head! Why the *hell* had he suggested that? Sunshine Smart plastered against his back for an hour and a half? No, thank you!

Although at least she wouldn't be able to talk to him.

Still, she would annoy him just by *being* there. In her skintight pants...full breasts pressed into his back...breathing against the back of his neck...arms around him...hands sliding up under his leather jacket...

What? No. *No!* Why the hell would her hands need to be sliding up there?

'Thanks, but, no,' she said—and it took Leo a moment to realise she was talking about riding on the bike as opposed to sliding her hands under his jacket. *Thanks, but, no.* Sharp and cool—and not open for discussion, apparently.

And it...*stung!* Dammit.

'Why not?' he asked.

'Because I don't like motorbikes.'

Don't like motorbikes! Well, good. Fine. Who cared if Sunshine Smart didn't like motorbikes? Every other woman he dated couldn't *wait* to hop on the back of his Ducati!

Not that he was dating Sunshine Smart. *Argh.* Horrible, horrible thought.

Just let it go. Let it go, Leo.

'Why? Because you can't wear ten-inch heels on one?' That was letting it go, was it?

'I don't wear ten-inch heels anywhere—I'm not a stilt-walker. It's not about shoes. Or clothes. Or even what those helmets do to your hair.' She tossed said hair. 'It's just...' She shrugged one shoulder, looking suddenly uncomfortable. 'Just an antiquated little notion I have about staying alive.'

'Fine,' he snapped. 'You drive, I'll ride, and we'll meet there.'

And then she sort of slumped…without actually slumping. He had an absurd desire to reach over and touch her damned hair, and tell her…what? Tell her *what*?

That he would drive down the coast with her? Hell, no! Not happening. And he was *not* touching her hair. He didn't touch anyone's hair. Ever.

Leo all but leapt to his feet. 'I'd better get into the kitchen.'

'Right now? But—' Sunshine checked her watch. 'Oh. That took longer than I thought.'

She gave her head a tiny shake. Shaking off the non-slumping slump, he guessed, because the perk zoomed back, full-strength.

'I have other samples in my bag—you know, pictures of floral arrangements and cakes. And I was going to talk to you about shoes. I'm arranging some custom-made shoes for you for the big day.'

'Flowers can't be that urgent. I have a superb baker on staff, so don't get carried away on the cake. And I don't need shoes.'

'The shoes are a gift. From me. I'm doing them for Caleb and Jon too. And I promise it will not be an identical shoe gig—nothing like those ancient wedding parties with six groomsmen all wearing pale blue tuxes with dark blue lapel trim!' Dramatic shudder. 'Oh, please say yes, Leo.'

Leo looked down at his feet, at his well-worn brown leather shoes. Scuffed, but as comfortable as wearing a tub of softened butter. And he had other shoes. Good shoes. *Italian* shoes. He didn't need more. He didn't want her goddamned shoes.

But her hypnotically beautiful mismatched eyes were wide and pleading as he looked back up, and he found himself saying instead, 'I'll think about it.'

She smiled. '*Thank* you. There's a ton of stuff still to talk about, but I understand you're on a tight leash tonight, so you get going. And before we meet on Monday I'll do some legwork on the flowers front. And music… No, I won't do any legwork on that, because I know you used to go out with that gorgeous singer Natalie Clarke, and she would be perfect. I hope—' She stopped, bit her lip. 'Oh, dear, enough about the music. I'm sensing a teensy bit of animosity—that little tic next to your mouth gives it away, you know. But we still have clothes to talk about. Yours and mine, since we're the closest thing they'll have to an official wedding party. We don't want to look too matchy-matchy, but there's so much we *can* do to look part of the overall theme.'

Leo stared. He was doing a lot of that. 'You mean there's a *theme*?'

'I'm not talking about those horrifying Elvis or Medieval or Viking themes. Or Halloween—it's been done! I've seen pictures—with pumpkins! I mean just a touch of complementary colour, a certain style…things like that.'

'You're scaring me.'

'I promise you'll love—'

'*Really* scaring me. Later, okay? *Much* later.'

Sunshine wrinkled up her nose—and Leo had now twigged that this meant she was about to put a new argument, so he held up a 'stop' hand.

'I'll see you Monday, Sunshine. And in the meantime try and remember that the marriage will have already happened. This is just a celebratory dinner.'

'But—'

'Monday.'

She made a muted explosive sound, redolent of frustration. 'All right! Monday! But I'm staying here for dinner— not running away like a good little girl.' She tossed her hair again. Flick. Over her shoulder. 'I have a date.'

Leo kind of liked that huffy hair-flick—it made him feel as if *she* were the one off kilter for a change.

'Then I'll send over a Campari for you while you wait.' Calm. Reasonable. Charming, even.

'Lovely, thank you,' she responded. Calm, reasonable, charming.

'I won't be able to come out and speak to Gary tonight, though.'

'That's okay—Gary's not coming.'

Frown. 'But I thought you said…?'

'Oh, I see.' Little laugh. *Annoying* little laugh. 'No, to-night I'm having dinner with Ben.'

'Another investment banker?'

'No. Ben's an embalmer.'

Leo did the stare thing again. 'You're joking, right?'

'No.' Puzzled. Actually, seriously puzzled. 'Why would that be a joke?'

'An *embalmer*? How did you even get to *meet* an em-balmer? Are you making shoes for corpses?'

'Not that I *wouldn't* make shoes for corpses, but no.' Pause. He saw the tiny swallow. 'It—it was a subject I needed to—to research. Two years ago. For my…sister.'

'I didn't know you had a sister.' He thought back… something about her eyes? In the womb… Triplets…?

Twins!

Oh. Embalmer. Sister. Her twin sister was dead. And he was such a freaking idiot!

Because—oh, God. *no*—the face-morph. It was hap-pening again. Emptiness. Ashy skin. Trembling lips. What the hell *was* that?

'Sunshine…?'

No response.

'Sunshine!'

Alarmed.

She shook her head and the look was gone. But her eyes were filling and she was blinking, blinking, blinking, try-ing to stop the tears falling.

Crap! He reached over to the next table, snagged a napkin, held it out to her with a gruff, 'Here.'

She took the napkin but just stared at it. Another blink.

He watched, holding his breath... Just one tear, one drop, and he would have to...to... No, he couldn't... could he? Hovering, hovering... His heart was starting to pound...

And then she took a long, slow breath and the tears receded.

Leo took his own long, slow breath, feeling as though disaster had just been averted, and slid into the chair beside her.

'Sorry,' Sunshine said. 'My sister died two years ago. The anniversary is coming up so I'm feeling kind of... emotional about it. I should be over it by now, but every now and then...' That tiny head-shake, then she looked at Leo and smiled. 'Anyway, let's get back to—'

'What was her name? Your sister?' Leo asked, because he was not getting back to *anything* quite that easily.

Sunshine paused, but only for a few seconds—and her smile didn't waver at all. 'Are you ready for this, Leo? It's not for the fainthearted.'

Leo didn't know if he was ready, not ready, or why he had to *be* ready.

In fact he didn't know squat.

He didn't know why he hadn't let her change the subject as she'd clearly wanted to do. Why her unwavering smile was bothering him. Why he wanted to take her by the shoulders and shake her until she let those jammed-up tears fall.

He didn't know a damned thing—*least* of all why he should be interested in Sunshine Smart's dead sister.

But he said, 'Worse than Sunshine?'

'Ouch! But, yes—at least Moonbeam thought so.'

'Moonbeam?' He winced. 'Seriously? I mean...*seriously*?'

Little gurgle of laughter. 'Yep.'

'Good God. Moonbeam. And Sunshine.'

She was playing with the hem on the napkin he'd given her, picking at it with her fingernails.

'So what happened?' Leo asked.

She looked down at the napkin. Pick, pick. 'Hippie parents.'

'No, I mean what hap—?'

'Oh, dear, I've snagged the hem,' Sunshine said, and put the napkin on the table. 'Sorry, Leo.'

'I don't care about the napkin, Sunshine.'

'Actually, table napkins have an interesting history. Did you know that they started out as lumps of dough, rolled and kneaded at the table? Which led, in turn, to using sliced bread to wipe your hands.'

What the hell? 'Er—no, I didn't know that.' Thrown. Completely thrown.

Extra-bright smile. 'But you were asking about Moonbeam. Actually, it's because of her that I'm sitting here with you. She and Jonathan dated as teenagers.'

He was staring again—couldn't help it. 'No way!'

'Yes way! But Moon realised pretty quickly that she'd need to swap an X for a Y chromosome if their relationship was going to get to the next level, even though Jon adored her. So—long story short—she encouraged Jon to leap out of the closet, with me hooked in for moral support, and the three of us became super-close—like a *ménage à trois* minus the sex. And *voilà*—here I am, planning Jon's wedding to your brother.' Her brilliant smile slipped. 'One of the reasons I miss Jon so much is because he's a link to my sister.'

Jon dating a girl. *Ménage à trois* minus the sex. Bread as *table napkins*? Leo didn't know what to say.

'Anyway,' she went on, 'I don't have to explain that to you. I know you miss your brother too.'

'It can't compare.'

'Yeah, I guess…I guess you can jump on a plane if you need to see Caleb.'

'That's more likely to happen in reverse.'

'You mean him jumping on a plane? Oh, no, I see— *him* needing to see *you*.' She looked him over. 'I get that. You're the dominant one, you're the one doling out the goods, and you don't *need* to see anyone.'

The perceptiveness startled him.

'So no emotional combustions! It's a good way to be,' she went on. 'In fact my approach to relationships is based on achieving a similar core of aloofness, of control. Of mastery over my emotions.'

He was a little awed. 'Your approach to relationships?'

'Yes. Separating sex from love, for example—you know, like that *ménage à trois* with me, Jon, and Moon. You have to agree that it makes life easier.'

'Easier, maybe. Not better.'

'Of course it's *easiest* to leave the love out altogether. That's what I do now.'

'What? Why?'

She tapped her chest lightly, over her heart. 'No room in here.'

'You're not that type of person.'

'Well, I *do* have to work hard at it,' she conceded.

'What? Why?' God, he was repeating himself!

'Because my natural inclination is to care too much about people. I have to take precautions to guard against that.'

'What? Why?' Nope—he was *not* doing another repeat! 'I mean, what are you scared of?'

'Pain,' she said simply. 'Because it hurts. To care deeply. It hurts.'

Leo wanted to tell her the whole argument was ridiculous, but the words wouldn't come. What did he know? He

was living proof that sex was usually loveless, no matter
how much you wished otherwise.

At least Sunshine could actually touch a person without having a panic attack, so she was way ahead of him.
For sure Gary and Ben wouldn't have let Sunshine have
those mini-meltdowns and sat there like blockheads, hand-
ing her restaurant napkins. How was he supposed to find
what Caleb had when he couldn't put his arms around a
tearful woman? Did he even deserve to, stunted as he was?

'But we were talking about embalming,' Sunshine said,
and she was twinkling again. 'Which is much more interesting. A very technical and responsible job. And it does
make you think, doesn't it?'

Leo, reeling from the various changes in conversation
he'd been subjected to for the past few minutes—shoes,
pumpkins, napkins, sex, love, embalming, *napkins*—could
only repeat stupidly, 'Think…?'

'Well, cremation or burial? It's something we all need
to plan for. If you're interested—as you should be, if you
ride a motorbike—I'm sure Ben would be happy to—'

'Er, no—that's fine, thanks.' Leo got to his feet with
alacrity. 'I'll send over that drink.'

Halfway through the night, Leo poked his head out of the
kitchen. Ostensibly to gauge how the place was humming
along, but really—he was honest enough to admit it—to
check out Sunshine's date.

And Ben the embalmer was handsome enough to give
Alexander Skarsgard a run for his money. Like a freaking Viking!

They'd ordered the roast leg of lamb—a sharing dish
that came with crispy roast potatoes, crusty bread rolls
and assorted side dishes and condiments. Enough food
to feed the entire cast of *The Hobbit*, including the trolls.

Twice more Leo peered out at them. Both times Ben

was laughing and Sunshine was about to shove a laden
fork in her mouth. Leo was starting to think Sunshine
could single-handedly have eating classified as a cham-
pionship sport.

Since he thought dining with a woman who actually ate
would make a nice change, he didn't know why the sight of
Sunshine chomping up a storm with Ben was so annoying.

But it was. Very, *very* annoying.

Another laugh floated through the restaurant and into
his straining ears.

Right! He ripped off his apron. He was going to find
out what the hell was so funny.

He washed his hands, changed into a clean chef's jacket
and headed out.

Sunshine looked up, startled. 'Leo! This is a surprise.'

She quickly performed introductions as one of the waiting staff rushed to find a spare chair for Leo, who was ex-
amining the almost demolished lamb leg.

Leo raised his eyebrows. 'Didn't like it, huh?' he said,
settling into the quickly produced chair.

Sunshine groaned. 'Not funny. I'll have to start dieting tomorrow.'

'That will be a one-day wonder,' Ben said, and winked
at Sunshine.

Winked! Who the hell *winked* at people?

Sunshine laughed. 'Or you could kiss me instead, Ben,
because—interestingly—kissing burns six and half calories per minute. As long as it's passionate.' She pursed
her lips. 'I guess passion supersizes the metabolic effect.'

Ben, in the process of sipping his wine, choked. 'Where
do you get all these facts?'

'The internet.'

Ben grinned. 'Better brush up on your arithmetic,
Sunny, because if I kiss you for, say, fifteen minutes—
and any longer is just *asking* for chapped lips—it's going

to net you a hundred calories max. Basically, we'll burn off two thirds of a bread roll.'

'Are you talking yourself out of a kiss?' Sunshine asked.

She was doing the eyelash-bat thing, and Leo decided it made her look like a vacuous twit. He only just stopped himself from telling her so.

Ben smiled at Sunshine. A very *intimate* smile, by Leo's reckoning. 'You know I'm up for it,' he said. 'But we're going to have to make it a marathon and buy a truckload of lip balm if you keep that up.' He nodded at her fingers, which were hovering over the food.

Sunshine snatched up a small piece of crispy potato and popped it into her mouth. 'It's a vegetable,' she said. 'Doesn't count.'

'Oh, that's a *vegetable*!' Ben laughed. 'And you're a *nut*, Sunshine.'

Sunshine smiled serenely. 'If that's the analogy we're going with, you're a piece of meat.'

Ben gave her a *faux* mournful look. 'Oh, I know I'm just a piece of meat to you. We all are.'

A phone trilled.

'Mine,' Ben said, reaching into his shirt pocket. He checked the caller ID. 'Sorry, I have to take this.'

'All?' Leo asked as Ben left the table.

Sunshine laughed. 'Just a "poor me" thing with my exes. They get a bit club-like.'

'What? There's like a *legion* of them?'

Another laugh. 'Not quite.'

Leo leant forward, fixed her with a steady gaze. 'Are you sleeping with both of them? Gary *and* Ben?'

She stopped laughing. 'And you're interested be-cause…?'

'Just wondering where everyone fits in relation to that guff about sex and love you were spouting earlier and the whole pieces of meat thing.'

'It's not guff.'

'*Total* guff.'

She considered him for a moment. 'Well—I've never been in love, but I *have* had sex. And I'll bet you've had enough sex to write *Fifty Shades of Leo*—but no wife. No steady girlfriend, even, right? No…love…perhaps?'

He felt his jaw clamp. God, he'd love to show her fifty shades of Leo. She wouldn't be looking at him in that curious bird way at the end. 'That's not the point,' he ground out.

'That's exactly the point. What's wrong, Leo? Not enough room in there?' She leant over and tapped her fingers on his chest, right over his heart. *Into* his heart, it felt like. 'I don't think you should be lecturing me just because I have sex without love the same as you do.'

'You're supposed to want them both.'

She tossed her head. 'Well, I don't. I won't. Ever. And glowering at me isn't going to change that.'

'I'm not glowering. I don't glower.'

'Oh, you *so* do. It's kind of cute.'

'I'm not cute.'

'Sure you are—in that I'm-a-typical-male-hypocrite kind of way.'

'I'm not a hypocrite either.'

'Go and get yourself nicely monogamised and I'll believe you.'

'Monogamised isn't a real word.'

That twitch at the side of her mouth.

Leo felt his temper surge. 'And I *am* monogamous.'

'Yeah—but one-after-the-other monogamy doesn't count if there's a hundred in the pipeline.'

He wanted to haul her out of her chair and… And what? And *nothing*, that was what. Nothing.

'Ben's coming back so I'll leave you to it,' he said. 'I've got some dessert coming out for you.'

She bit her bottom lip. 'Oh, dear—I really will need to start a diet tomorrow.'

Leo got to his feet. 'Just get Ben to kiss you twice.'

Sunshine grabbed his hand to keep him where he was.

His fingers curled around hers before he could stop them—and then his fingers stiffened. He pulled his hand free, flexed his fingers.

Sunshine's eyes flickered from his hand to his face. There was doubt in her eyes. And concern. And a tenderness that enraged him. He didn't need it. Didn't need Sunshine-bloody-Smart messing with his head or his goddamned hand.

'Why are you upset with me, Leo?' she asked softly.

He was unbearably conscious of the scent of her. Jonquils. A woman who'd just stuffed herself silly with meat shouldn't smell like flowers, so why did she?

'I'm not upset with you,' he said flatly. *Liar*. 'I'll email you a map for Monday.'

He strode back to the kitchen, furious with himself because he *was* upset with her.

But that was the 'what' of the equation. What he couldn't work out was the 'why'.

What? Why?

Oh, for God's sake!

CHAPTER THREE

TO: Jonathan Jones
FROM: Sunshine Smart
SUBJECT: Wedding of the century
Quick update, darling…

Invitations are underway—wording attached. We're going with smart/cocktail as the dress code, although obviously I will be wearing a long dress as befits my bridesmaid status.

Off to check the venue in the morning. It shows every indication of being divine.

Next we'll be working on the menu, but having now eaten at two of Leo's establishments I have no doubt it will be magnificent.

I wish I could meet a chef. Well, obviously I HAVE met one now, but I mean one with jumpable bones!
Sunny xxx

PS—Leo rides a motorbike! And, no, I still haven't done it, but soon.

TO: Caleb Quartermaine
FROM: Leo Quartermaine
SUBJECT: Coming along
Sunshine has the invitations under control and I'm attaching the save-the-date we've decided on. If I don't hear

from you in the next day or so I'll go ahead and get this out as per the War and Peace-sized invitation list.

Meeting Sunshine at South in the morning. And if she raises any concerns you'll have to arrange bail for me because I'll kill her.

I'm growing my hair—hope you're happy. And I am apparently having a pair of shoes custom-made for me. Was that your idea? Because I WILL get you back.
LQ

'Wow,' SUNSHINE SAID out loud.

South had to have the best position of any restaurant in the whole world.

Well, all right, she hadn't been everywhere in the whole world, and she was sure there must be oodles of well-situated restaurants all over the planet—in fact she would look up 'most scenic restaurants in the world'—but it was spectacular.

The restaurant was perched on the edge of the cliff. But in some mind-blowing engineering feat the entrance to it was positioned actually *over* the cliff and doubled as a small viewing platform. The floor was transparent, so looking down you could see a landscape of trees curving steeply to the beach. Looking directly forward, you could see the deep blue of the ocean; looking to the side and backwards gave you a view into the restaurant. No tables and chairs in there yet, but the space was sharp and clean, with a seemingly endless use of glass to take advantage of the view.

She breathed in the ultra-fresh air. It was windy, and her hair was flying everywhere, but she didn't care. This venue was perfectly...*perfect* for a wedding celebration.

Perfectly perfect. That had been Leo's description of the private room at Q Brasserie. He'd been annoyed with himself over the way he'd described it, which had made her want to hug him, because it was just *not* something to be annoyed about.

Not that he was the cuddly teddy-bear type you could pat and jolly out of the sullens. He was impatient and stand-offish and most of the time just plain monosyllabic cranky. There was no reason at all to feel that he needed to be hugged more often.

And yet…she wanted to put her arms around him right now.

Wanted to be close to him, held by him. Comforting. Comforted.

Dangerous, debilitating thought.

It had to be the proximity of the ocean messing with her head. For which she should have prepared herself before her arrival. Instead here she was, not knowing when or how hard the jolt would hit her—only knowing that it would.

So she would force it—get it done, dealt with, before she saw Leo. She didn't want to slip up in front of him again.

She took a breath in. Out. Looked out and down, focus-ing her thoughts… And even though she was expecting it to hit, the pain tore her heart. The memory of Moonbeam was so vivid she gasped.

Moonbeam had believed she belonged to the ocean—and Sunshine had always felt invaded, overrun, by the truth of that when she was near the coast, even when she was far above the water, like now.

One of her most poignant memories was of their last time at the beach. Darkness, rain, and Moonbeam exulting as she raced naked into the waves. *'This is where I'm me!'* Moon had yelled, and Sunshine, laughing but alarmed as she tried to coax her out of the freezing, dangerous, roiling surf, had called her a crazy Poseidon-worshipping hippie.

Three days later Moonbeam was dead.

Sunshine touched her sun and moon charms. She longed so keenly for her sister just then she couldn't move, could barely breathe. The loneliness, the hunger to be so close to someone that you were like two sides of the same coin, was like a knife wound. But not a sharp wound; it was a *festering* wound that wouldn't close, wouldn't heal.

'Sunshine?'

She took a moment, forcing the depression to the back of her consciousness with a shake of her head as she'd trained herself to do in public. Defences securely in place, she turned, smiling, to face Leo, who was standing at the doors leading into the restaurant.

'Hi, Leo,' she said.

Leo pushed the heavy doors further open, inviting her to enter. She started to lean up to kiss him as she crossed the threshold, but he jerked away before she could connect and she stumbled. He grabbed her elbow. Released it the nanosecond she regained her balance.

Ah, okay! She got it. He didn't want her to kiss him.

In fact...thinking back over their few meetings...she would go so far as to say he didn't want her to touch him in any way, ever.

And she'd just been daydreaming about putting her arms around him. Way to give the man a heart attack!

Was it just her, or did he have a problem touching all women? And if it was a problem with women generally, how did the man manage to have sex with a human?

Maybe he didn't. Maybe he had a blow-up doll.

Maybe it wasn't just women.

Maybe he had a problem touching men *and* women. Maybe he had a problem touching pets. *And* blow-up dolls.

Maybe he had an obsessive-compulsive disorder, hand-washing thing going on.

Hmm. She'd read something that might help in that case—about systematic desensitisation...or was it exposure therapy...?

In Leo's case it would mean touching him often, to get

him to see that nothing diabolical would happen to him just because of a bit of skin contact.

She could do that.

It would be a public service, almost.

A favour to a man who was going to be family—well, kind of family.

What was more, it would be *fun*.

'Oh, dear. I'm sorry, Leo. I took you by surprise, didn't I?' She bit her lip. 'I should have learned by now not to launch myself at people when they aren't ready! I once ended up in an embarrassing half-kiss, half-handshake, nose-bumping, chokehold situation. Has that ever happened to you?'

'No.'

'Well, just to make sure it never does I'll give you an indicator before I kiss you in future—say…puckering up my lips like a trout, so you'll know it's coming.' She stopped and thought about that. 'Actually, I wonder why they call it a trout pout when women overdo the lip-filler? Trout don't seem to have excessively large lips to me.'

He was looking at her lips now.

'Not that my own lips are artificially inflated, if that's what you're wondering,' she assured him, moving further into the restaurant. 'They're just naturally troutish. If trout really *do* have thick lips, that is. I definitely need to have another look at a photo of a trout.'

Leo's gaze had moved on to her hair. In fact he was looking at it with a moroseness that bordered on the psychotic.

What the *hell* was going on in his head?

'Is something wrong with my hair?' she asked, and flicked a hand at it. 'Do I look like I stuck my finger in an electrical socket? Because it's windy out there.' She reached into her bag—an orange leather tote—and pulled out an elastic band. Bundling the tousled mess of it into a bunch at the back of her head, she tucked the ends under and roughly contained it. 'There—fixed,' she said. 'I need a haircut, but I'm not sure how to style it for the wedding so it has to wait. I have a great hairdresser—actually, I used to date him.'

'*Another* one?'

'Another…? Oh, you mean someone else I used to date? Well, yes. Anyway, Iain—that's my hairdresser—says he needs to see the dress first. Some people might say that's a little neurotic, but he's a genius so I'm not arguing. And, of course, if I did argue it would be a pot-kettle-black thing, because I'm just as neurotic. I can't design your shoes, for example, until I know what you're wearing.'

He looked a heartbeat away from one of those glowers he supposedly didn't do. It was his only response.

'That was a hint, by the way, to let me know what you're wearing.'

'Yep, I got that.'

Silence.

'So!' she said. 'What do you think? About my hair? Should I keep the fringe? It won't grow out completely in two months, but it should be long enough to style differently—say, like…' She pushed the fringe to one side, smoothing it across her temple.

'I like the fringe,' Leo said.

Words! Yay! But he was *still* frowning.

And now he was looking at her dress.

Okay, so it was a little tight—hello! After two nights in a row at his restaurants, never mind yesterday's two-minute noodles, sugar donuts, and family block of chocolate, what did he expect? But nothing *that* remarkable. Kind of conservative. Just a nude-coloured woollen sheath. V-neck, knee-length, three-quarter sleeves, no fussy trim.

His eyes kept going, down her legs to her shoes. Five-inch-high nude pumps.

'Problem?' she asked, when his eyes started travelling back up, and she must have sounded exasperated because that stopped him.

At last he looked in her eyes. 'You look good—as usual.'

Oh. 'Thank you,' she said, and actually felt like preening.

'But I don't want you to break your neck wriggling around in that dress and tottering on those heels. The building is finished but there's still some debris around that you could trip over.'

And we're back!

This was going to be a long day. A long, *fun* day. He was just so irresistibly grumpy!

She stepped towards the windows. 'This is just brilliant!' Turned to shoot him a broad smile. 'Are you going to give me a tour, Leo?'

He nodded—and looked so uninviting that Sunshine almost laughed. Well, there was no time like the present to commence his therapy and start touch, touch, touching!

Brace yourself, Leo darling.

'Yes, but be careful,' Leo was saying, oblivious. 'And leave your bag—it looks heavy.'

Sunshine dropped the bag on the spot. 'Tell you what,' she said, walking back to him, 'I'm just going to hold on to you so you don't have to worry about the state of my fragile limbs.' She took his arm before he could back away. His arm felt hard and unyielding, like a piece of marble. Or petrified wood. Petrified! Perfect. She beamed up at him. 'Lead on, Leo.'

His jaw was shut so tightly she thought he might crack a tooth.

Oh, dear...oh, deary me! This was going to be *good*.

This was *bad*, Leo realised.

Actually, he'd realised it the moment he saw her standing on the viewing platform outside, looking glamorous and yet earthy. And wistful. And...sad.

So she was sad—so what? She recovered like lightning, didn't she? Like the other times. There was no reason for him to want to... Well, no reason for anything.

And her hair was annoying! Out on the platform the wind had been blowing it every which way and she hadn't given a thought to the tangle it was creating, and then she'd shoved the mess of it into a band as though it didn't matter. She *should* care about her damned hair the way every other woman he'd ever dated cared.

Not that he was dating her.

It was destabilising, that was all, to have his perceptions mucked around with.

As was the way she'd cast that expensive-looking orange leather carry-all thing onto the floor—as though it were no more valuable than a paper shopping bag.

And the fact that she never wore nail polish.

The way she could make her eyes twinkle at will.

And that fresh flower smell of hers.

The jolt when she took his arm and looked up at him with mischief printed all over her face like a tattoo.

He didn't want to feel gauche when he pulled away from her touch and nearly caused her to face-plant—and then embarrassed because she laughed it off and blamed herself when he *knew* that *she* knew the fault was his. Because Sunshine, he was coming to realise, was no dummy.

And he certainly didn't want to feel disapproving, like a damned priest, just because she was dating two men simultaneously and didn't love either of them. Because she was right about one thing: who was he to lecture her?

Leo flexed his arm under her hand, which felt disturbingly light and warm and...whatever. It was nothing. Meant nothing. It was just her keeping her balance. The same as holding on to a railing.

He took a slow, silent breath. 'Let's start with the kitchen,' he said, and led her though swinging doors into a large room of gleaming white tiles and spotless stainless steel surfaces. 'Everything in here is state of the art, from the appliances to the ventilation system.'

Sunshine let go of his arm—relief!—and turned a slow circle. 'It's kind of daunting. Although I think that about every kitchen.'

'You don't like to cook?'

'I just do *not* cook. I can't. I did once boil an egg, although it ended up hard like the inside of a golf ball.' That stopped her for a moment. Distracted her. 'Have you ever peeled off the outer layer of a golf ball?' she asked. 'It's amazing inside—like an endless rubber band wrapped round and round.'

Not exactly a riveting fact, but she did seem to have an interest in the oddest subjects. 'You boiled it too long,' he said. *Yeah, I kind of think she figured that out herself, genius.*

'I ate it, but I haven't boiled an egg since. And, really, why boil an egg when you can pop out to a café and have one perfectly poached with some sourdough toast?'

'And that's the only thing you've cooked? The egg?'

'I've made two-minute noodles—as recently as yesterday.'

'Didn't you help out at home when you were a kid?'

'That was the problem.' She ran a finger along the pristine edge of one of the cooker tops. 'My hippie parents are vegetarian. It was all bean sprouts, brown rice and tofu—which I actively detest—when I was growing up.' She gave one of those exaggerated shudders that she seemed to luxuriate in. 'Tofu casserole! Who wants to cook *that*?'

She opened an oven, peeked inside.

'You're clearly a *lapsed* vegetarian.'

She turned to face him. 'Capital L, lapsed! From the

moment I bit into a piece of sirloin at the age of fifteen—on a Wednesday, at seven-thirty-eight p.m.—I was a goner. I embraced my inner carnivore with a vengeance. Meat and livestock shares skyrocketed! And two days later I tried coconut ice and life was never the same again. Hello, processed sugar! I don't have *a* sweet tooth—I have a shark's mouth full of them!'

'Shark's mouth?'

'Specifically, a white pointer. Did you know they have something like three hundred and fifty teeth? Fifty teeth in the front row and seven rows of teeth behind, ready to step up to the plate if one drops out.'

This was more interesting than the make-up of a golf ball, but not quite as intriguing as the calorific benefit of a passionate kiss.

And he wished he hadn't remembered that kiss thing—because it came with a vision of her kissing the Viking embalmer.

Sharks. Think about sharks. 'The only thing I know about sharks' teeth is that they can kill you,' he said.

'Hmm, yes, although the chance is remote. Like one in two hundred and fifty million or something. You've got more chance of being killed by bees, or lightning, or even fireworks! But that was just an illustrative example. So! I'm a processed-sugar-craving carnivore, to my parents' chagrin.' She stopped. Took a breath. 'Seriously, I must have the metabolism of a hummingbird, because otherwise I'd be in sumo wrestler territory. You know, hummingbirds can eat three times their own weight every day!' She ran a hand down her side and across her belly. 'Not that I can do *that*, of course,' she said sadly.

'No,' Leo agreed. 'You're not exactly skinny.'

A surprised laugh erupted from her. 'Thank you, Leo. Music to every girl's ears!'

'That wasn't an insult. I'm a chef—I like to see people eating.'

'In that case, stick with me and you'll be in a permanent state of ecstasy.'

And there it was—*wham!*—in his head. The image of her licking the glaceé off her spoon. Ecstasy.

He swallowed—hard. 'You could take a cooking class.'

'I think the cooking gene was bored out of me by the time I left the commune.'

'The commune? So not only are your parents hippies but you lived on a *commune*?'

'And it was *not* cool, if that's what you're thinking. Less of the free love, dope-smoking and contemplating our navels, and more of the sharing of space and chores and vehicles. Scream-inducing. If you have any desire for even a modicum of privacy do *not* join a commune.' She did the twinkle thing. 'And, really, *way* too much hemp clothing. Not that I have anything against hemp—I mean, did you know the hemp industry is about ten thousand years old? Well, probably you didn't know and don't care. But you have to admit that's remarkable.' Stop. Breathe. 'However, let's just say that I don't want to wear it every day.'

Oddly enough, Leo could see her wearing hemp. On weekends, down at the edge of the surf, with her hair blowing all over her face and her polish-free toes in the water.

It must have been the mention of the commune, because that was not a good-time girl Sunshine Smart image.

Enough already! 'Let's move on,' Leo said.

'What about plates, cutlery, glasses, serving dishes? You're sure everything will be here in time?'

'Yes, it will all be here. And it is all brand-new, top-quality, custom-designed.'

'Not that I have any intention of telling you how to stock your restaurant…' She bit her lip. 'But can you send me photos?'

Leo sighed heavily. 'Yes, I can send you photos.'

'Excellent. And can I see the bathrooms?'

She took his arm again, and he didn't quite control a flinch. Thankfully Sunshine seemed oblivious, although he was starting to believe she was oblivious to approximately nothing.

Escorting her into the men's and women's restrooms as though they were out for an arm-in-arm stroll along the Champs-Elysées felt surreal, but Leo knew better than to argue. He wouldn't put it past her to start imparting strange-but-true facts about the toilet habits of some ancient African tribe if he did, and his nerves couldn't take it.

At least she looked suitably dazzled by what she found. Ocean-view glass walls on the escarpment side, with the other walls painted in shifting shades of dreamy blue. Floors that were works of art: murals made of tiny mosaic tiles, depicting waves along the coast. And everything else stark white.

'I could live in here—it's so beautiful!' Sunshine marvelled.

'And I will, of course, send you a photo of the toilet paper we're using,' Leo deadpanned as they walked back to the dining area.

Sunshine looked at him, struck, lips pursing. Leo could almost see the cogs turning.

'You know,' she said slowly, 'I read something somewhere about a pop star who has *red* toilet paper provided when she's on tour, so do you think—?'

'No, I do not,' he interrupted. 'Forget the red toilet paper.'

The nose was wrinkling. 'Well obviously not *red*. I was going to suggest a beautiful ocean-blue. Or sea-green.'

'No blue. Or green. You'll have to content yourself with your victory over my growing hair.'

Sunshine laughed, giving up. 'It's coming along very nicely.'

She ran her hand over the stubble on his head and his whole body went rigid.

Leo stepped away from her, forcing that hand to drop and simultaneously dislodging her other hand from his arm. 'And so are your eyes,' he said, just for something to say—and didn't *that* sound bloody fatuous? How could eyes *come along*? They were just there—from birth!

Although...hmm...something about them wasn't right. Her pupils were a little bigger than they should be, given all the light streaming into the room.

Why were they standing so close that he could see her damned pupils anyway? It wasn't a crowded nightclub. They were the only two people in a big, furniture-free space. There was nothing to bump into. No reason for them to occupy the same square foot of floor. He took another step back from her.

She was considering him with a blinking, slightly dazed look that worried him on a level he didn't want to acknowledge.

And there went that tic beside his mouth.

'I saw my parents yesterday,' she said, and her voice sounded kind of...breathy. 'They like the new natural look—as you could imagine. Mum talked about sending you a thank-you card, so brace yourself for some home-made paper and a haiku poem. Apologies in advance for the haiku!' Stop. Little laugh. 'But strangers are doing a double-take when they look at my eyes now, which makes me feel a bit naked.'

'Don't knock naked. I've had some of my best moments naked,' Leo said, and wondered what the hell was happening to his brain. Disordered. That was what it was. You didn't go from talking about hair to eyes to nakedness. At least *he* didn't.

In fact there was altogether too much talk of underwear, orgasms and sex between them as it was, without tossing *naked* around.

He took yet another step back. Tried to think of something to say about homemade paper instead, because he sure knew nothing about haiku poetry. But Sunshine was giving him that dazed, blinking look, and he couldn't seem to form a word.

'Yeah, me too,' she said.

Leo had a sudden vision of Sunshine naked, lying on his bed. The almost translucent white skin, the long chocolate hair. Voluptuous. Luscious. Steamy hot. Smiling at him, sea-eyes sparkling.

He shook his head, trying to get the image out of his head.

And then Sunshine shook *her* head. 'So! Tables!' she said, and took hold of his arm again—and this time it seemed to hit him straight in the groin.

Leo, looking everywhere *except* at Sunshine, had never enthused so happily about inanimate objects in his life. The choice of wood for the chairs; the elegant curved backs; the crisp white tablecloths and napkins; the bar's marble top and designer stools. And still his bloody erection would not go down!

Go down. Sunshine Smart going down. On him.

Bad.

This was bad, bad, bad.

Walking a little stiffly, he showed her the outdoor terrace. Talked about welcome cocktails. Described the way the decking had been stained to match the wooden floor inside. Back in. Suggested positions for the official table. Indicated places for dancing—except that Caleb had told him that dancing was likely to be off the agenda, so why he was pointing that out was a mystery. Just filling the space with words. *Any* words. Waiting for that erection to subside.

And at the end, when she looked at him with those

twinkling blue and green eyes of hers, he still had a hard-on and he could still—*dammit!*—imagine her naked. On his bed. Kneeling in front of him. Walking towards him. Away from him.

Help!

'Can you email me the layout so I can refresh my memory when I need to?' Sunshine asked. 'Oh—and tomorrow I'll have the invitation design to sign off. Are you happy for me to do it, or would you like to see it?'

'I'd like to see it,' he said, and couldn't believe he'd actually said that. Because He. Did. Not. Care.

'I could email it.'

'No. Not email.'

Sunshine pursed her lips. Her 'thinking' look—not that he knew how he knew that.

'I really do have to be in the store tomorrow,' she said. 'Some new stock is coming in and I have a very specific idea for the display. And you're working tomorrow night, right?'

'No—night off,' he said, and was amazed again. He *never* took a night off.

She brightened. 'Great. Where shall we meet?'

'I'll cook.' Okay. He had lost his mind. He was *not* going to cook for Sunshine Smart. He never cooked for girlfriends. And she wasn't even that. Not even *close* to that. Even if he did want to have sex with her.

Damn, damn, damn. Goddamn.

Sunshine's eyes had lit up like a Christmas tree. 'Really?'

Could he back out? Could he? 'Um. Yes.'

'At my place?'

No—not at her place. Not anywhere. 'Um. Yes.' So he had a vocabulary problem today. Brain-dead. He was brain-dead.

'Just one teensy problem. Most of my kitchen appliances have never been used.'

'I love virgin appliances.' *Arrrgggghhh*. Again with the sexual innuendo. He was clearly on the verge of a nervous breakdown.

'In that case you will have an orgasm when you walk in my kitchen.'

Orgasms. Oh. My. *God*.

Sunshine checked her watch. 'And, speaking of orgasms, I'd better go.'

Huh? What the hell*?*

'I'm being taken to that new Laotian restaurant the Peppercorn Tree tonight,' she said, as though that explained anything. 'I checked the menu online. *Very* excited!'

Okay, he got it. *Whew.* It was the thought of *food* making her orgasmic.

And then her words registered. 'Being taken'. As in date.

'Gary or Ben?' He just couldn't seem to stop himself from asking.

'Neither of them. Tonight it's Marco.'

Marco. *Marco? Three* men on a string now? Not to mention the calligrapher. And the hairdresser. And there was probably a butcher, a baker, and a candlestick-maker in there somewhere.

'You sure there was no free love on that commune?' he asked, and thanked heaven and hell that he sounded his normal curt self.

'Love's never free, is it?' Sunshine asked cryptically. And then she smiled. 'That's why I'm only interested in sex.'

Before Leo could think of a response she tap-tapped her way out of the restaurant, clearly with no idea he was having a conniption and might need either medical or psychiatric intervention.

CHAPTER FOUR

TO: Sunshine Smart
FROM: Leo Quartermaine
SUBJECT: Photos
Attached are the images we discussed yesterday, plus the restaurant layout with a sketchy floor plan.

I've also included a photo of the toilet paper. White.

I'll be making pasta tonight, and bringing some home-made gelato.

LQ

TO: Jonathan Jones
FROM: Sunshine Smart
SUBJECT: All going swimmingly—and shoes!
Darling!

Checked out the venue yesterday—scrumptious. Caleb has photos.

Your shoe design is attached. As requested, not too over the top! Black patent with a gorgeous charcoal toe-cap. The shoes will work brilliantly with the dark grey suit and red tie.

I'm sending Caleb's design to him directly—he says you don't get to see his outfit before the big day! And you have the contact number for Bazz in Brooklyn to get the shoes made, so make an appointment, and quickly because he's super-busy.

Leo's are next. And, speaking of Leo...drumroll...
tonight he's cooking me dinner!

We'll get onto the wedding menu tonight too. I'm thinking we should lean towards seafood, but with a chicken
alternative for those who are allergic, and, of course, a
vegetarian (dullsville) option.

Sunny xxx

PS: Was Marco Valetta always such a douche? Had
dinner with him last night and he spent the whole meal
talking about his inheritance—scared his father is going
to gobble it up on overseas travel. Seriously, let the man
spend his own money any way he wants! Marco thought
he was going to get lucky, but after banging on all night
about money and then suddenly switching to the subject of lap dances??????? As if!!!! He is SO off my Christmas card list. I'll bet Leo Quartermaine would never be
such a loser.

PPS: I saw a statistic recently that said about twenty-
five million dollars is spent on lap dances each year in
Vegas alone. Amazing!!!!

TO: Leo Quartermaine
FROM: Caleb Quartermaine
SUBJECT: Loving the Sunshine...

...and I don't mean the New York weather, which is icky-
sticky right now.

Just warning you, bro, that my custom-designed shoes
are eye-poppers. I love them—but I'm the flamboyant
type. Better prepare yourself!

Love the invitations, love the save-the-date, love the
fact that you sent Sunshine a photo of the restaurant toilet rolls (yep, she told me). Think I love Sunshine too if she
can get you to do that. Jon tells me half the male population of Sydney is in love with her—gay and straight—so
I'm in good company.

Also glad about your hair—go, Sunshine! And glad about South.

Can't wait to marry Jon. Seriously, I don't care where or how we do it, as long as we do it. The party is just the icing on an already delicious cake.

Your turn now. Hope you're out there hunting instead of spending every spare minute slaving over assorted hot stoves.

And please tell me the bunny-boiler Natalie is under control. If she turns up at the reception I am getting out the power tools and going for her.

CQ

SUNSHINE LIVED IN an apartment in Surry Hills. The perfect place for people who didn't cook, because wherever you looked there were restaurants. Every price range, every style, and practically every ethnicity.

Leo had sent a ton of supplies and equipment ahead of him, because he had a shrewd understanding of what he could expect to find in Sunshine's cupboards—i.e., nothing much—and the thought of overbalancing the bike while lugging a set of knives was a little too Russian roulette for his liking.

He'd been cursing himself all day about offering to cook for her. Cursing some more that he'd offered to do it at her apartment—his own, with a designer kitchen and every appliance known to man, would have been so much easier. But then, of course, he wouldn't get to see what her place was like. And, all right, he admitted it: he was curious about that. He imagined boldly coloured walls, exotic furniture, vibrant rugs, maybe some kick-ass paintings or a centrepiece sculpture.

He buzzed the apartment and she answered quickly.

'Leo!'

He could hear the excitement in her voice. How did she

do that? Could she really, truly, be that enthusiastic about everything?

'Yep.'

'Fourth floor,' she said, and clicked open the door to the lobby.

She was waiting for him, apartment door wide open, when he got out of the lift.

Her hair was piled on top of her head—kind of messy, but very sexy. She was wearing an ankle-length red kaftan in some silky material that managed to both cling and flow. It had a deep V neckline and was gathered at the base of her sternum behind a fist-sized disc of matching beads. Voluminous sleeves were caught tightly at the wrists. She looked like a cross between a demented crystal healer and a Cossack dancer—but somehow bloody amazing.

His eyes, inevitably, dropped to her feet. She was barefoot. *Good God! Stop the presses.*

'I am *so* looking forward to this,' Sunshine confided, and puckered her lips.

Leo steeled himself, and after the tiniest hesitation she went right ahead and laid the kiss on him.

'That pucker was enough warning, right?' she asked with a cheeky smile. And then she rolled right on before he could answer. 'And I was right—trout do *not* have especially thick lips. So! This way,' she threw over her shoulder, and walked to the kitchen.

She gestured to three boxes on the counter. 'Your stuff arrived about ten minutes ago.'

'Good. I'll unpack everything,' he said, but he was more interested in the uninterrupted view into her apartment afforded by the open-plan kitchen.

And it was…disappointing.

White walls. No paintings. A serviceable four-seater dining suite in one section of a combined living/dining room in a nondescript, pale wood—pine, maybe. The couch was basic, taupe-coloured. A low coffee table in front of the couch matched the dining suite. There was a television atop a cabinet that matched the other furniture. Carpet a similar shade to the couch. Absolutely nothing wrong with any of it, but…no. Just *no*!

He nodded towards the living room. 'What's with the porridge-meets-oatmeal thing out there?' he asked, shrugging out of his leather jacket, and tossing it onto one of the stools on the other side of the kitchen counter.

'Oh, I thought you'd like it.'

Leo was speechless for a moment. Seriously? *That* was how she saw him?

When she came to his apartment she would see just how wrong she was!

Not that she *would* be coming to his apartment. But if she *did*…

Nope, he had to address this now or he wouldn't be able to cook. 'You've seen my restaurants—do they look like they've been furnished from a Design for Dummies catalogue?'

'I guess I didn't imagine you did that part personally. But there's nothing intrinsically wrong with a neutral colour palette, you know! And… Well…' She waved a hand at the living area. 'This part wasn't me, or it would be very different.'

'So who was it?'

'Moonbeam—and she just went for quick, basic, affordable. Out here and in her own room.'

'But aren't twins supposed to…you know…have the same taste?'

'Negativo.'

'So that's a no, is it?' Leo asked dryly.

'A big no way, José.'

Eye-roll. 'So, no?'

'Okay! No.' Matching eye-roll. And then she smiled softly. 'Unlike me, Moon didn't care about *stuff*.'

'What did she care about?'

'Life, the earth, the universe…et cetera.'

'So it stands to reason she wouldn't expect you to make a shrine out of a few pieces of pine, right? Why don't you change it?'

'I can't.'

'Why not?'

'I just…can't.' She looked at the boring furniture as though it were some Elysian landscape. 'Don't you ever want to freeze a moment? Just…*freeze* it? Hang on to it?'

'No, Sunshine, never,' he said. 'I want to move on. And on and on.'

She turned to him. 'You're lucky to be able to see things that way.'

'Actually, it's the *absence* of luck that made me see things that way. The desire to *change* my luck. To have more—a better life. To get…everything.'

Their eyes caught…held.

And then Sunshine gave that tiny shake of the head. 'Anyway,' she said, 'there's quite enough me in this apartment. I just keep it behind closed doors because it's scary for the uninitiated.'

Was she talking about her bedroom? 'Closed doors?'

She pointed at a closed door at one end of the living area. 'My office.' Pointed at another closed door behind her. 'Bedroom.'

Leo's mouth had gone dry. Over a freaking *room*? No—over just the *thought* of a room! But he couldn't help it. 'Show me,' he said.

She twinkled at him. 'You're not ready for that, Leo. But think a cross between Regency England and the Mad Hatter's tea party in the office, and Scheherazade meets Marie Antoinette in the bedroom…'

He looked at the bedroom door hard enough to disgust himself. What did he think was going to happen? An 'Open Sesame' reveal? Why did he care anyway?

'So! Leo! How do we start this gastronomic enterprise?'

Leo dragged his Superman-worthy gaze away from the bedroom door and refocused on Sunshine—the vivid, unique, laughing eyes; the luxuriant hair; her free-spirited yet glamorous dress; her naked feet.

'You're not wearing any shoes,' he said. *Duh! Of course she knows she isn't wearing shoes! They're her feet, aren't they?*

'I'm generally barefoot when I'm at home. But I do have a lovely pair of black beaded high heels that I wear with this dress if I'm going out.'

He could picture her, tap-tapping her way into South with sparkles on her feet, the red silk billowing. He knew he was staring at her feet, but they were very sexy feet.

And then his eyes travelled up. Up, up, up... To find her watching him, her eyes dazed and wide, lips slightly parted.

She licked her lips.

'Sunshine...' he said.

'Yes?' It was more a breath than a word.

'Um...' What? What was he doing? *What?* 'Feet.' *Doh!* 'I mean shoes!' he said desperately. 'I mean mine.'

She looked down at his feet. 'I like them. Blue nubuk. Rounded, desert boot-style toe. White sole.' Her eyes were travelling up now, as his had done. 'Perfect with...'

Holy freaking hell. He hoped she couldn't see his erection as she got to—

Argh. He saw the swallow, the blink, the blush. She'd seen it.

'Jeans,' she finished faintly.

Disaster. This was a freaking disaster. *Say something,*

say something, say something. 'I meant for…for the…the wedding,' Leo said.

And, really, it was a valid subject. Because he was starting to get curious about what she would design for him. Although it would probably end up being the shoe equivalent of a Design for Dummies pine bookshelf: plain black leather lace-ups.

'Oh!' She took a breath, smoothed the front of her dress. 'Well! I need to see what you're wearing first, remember?' She blinked, smiled a little uncertainly. 'So! Pasta? I even bought an apron!'

Food. Good. Excellent. Something he could talk about without sounding stupid or crotchety or boring or…or crazed with inappropriate lust.

Because he could *not* be in lust with Sunshine Smart. They were polar opposites in every single possible, conceivable way. Like light and dark. Bright and gloomy. Joyful and… *Oh, for God's sake, get over yourself!*

'You've got pots and pans, right?' he asked.

'Yes. And most of them are even unpacked.'

'*Most* of them? How long have you lived here?'

'Two and a half years.'

Leo ran his hand over his head. If he'd had hair he would have yanked it. Two and a half years was long enough to unpack *all* the pots and pans. 'I need a medium saucepan and a large frying pan. And what about bowls? Plates? Cutlery?'

'Oh, plates and stuff I have.'

'You get all that out while I unpack the food.'

She started humming. Off-key.

Leo peeked as she opened cupboards and slid out drawers. Just the bare minimum.

He opened the fridge to stow the wine he'd brought—empty except for butter, milk, soda water, and a wedge of Camembert.

Freezer: a bottle of vodka and half a loaf of bread.

The kitchen had one of those slide-out pantry contraptions, which he opened with trepidation. A jar of peanut butter. A packet of lemon tea. A box of sugary kids' cereal. A tin of baked beans that looked a thousand years old. And—sigh—three packets of two-minute noodles.

'Right,' she said proudly, and pointed to the pot, pan, bowls, and forks she had lined up on the counter. She reminded him of a hyperactive kitten being given a ball of wool to play with after being cooped up with nothing all day.

'How old are you?' he asked suddenly.

'Twenty-five—why?'

'You look younger. You act younger.'

'So I'm fat *and* immature?'

'You're not fat.'

She laughed. 'But I *am* immature? Just because I can't cook pasta? How unfair. I'm not asking you to design a boot, am I?'

'Yeah, yeah. Just go and put on your apron,' he said, and then wondered what he thought he was doing as she hurried towards a tiny alcove off the kitchen. What *she* thought she was doing! She wasn't going to be in the kitchen with him! She didn't cook! She had scoffed at the idea of cooking classes. So she didn't need a goddamned apron.

But when she came back she was beaming, and he couldn't find the will to tell her to go and watch TV while he made dinner.

He took one look at the slogan on the front of her apron—*Classy, Sassy, and a Bit Smart-Assy*—and had to bite the inside of his cheek to stop the smile. He was *not* going to be charmed. Like Gary and Ben—and probably Marco. Iain. And the tinker, the tailor, the soldier, and the spy.

'Come on, it's cute—admit it!' she said, possibly wondering about the strangled look on his face. 'You know, I used to be called Sunshine Smart-Ass in school, so seeing this in the shop today was like an omen. Not a creepy Damien omen. I mean like a sign that I am going to nail this pasta thing.'

'Smart-Ass. Why am I not surprised?' Leo asked through his slightly twisted mouth. Damn, he wanted to laugh.

She'd messed up her hair, getting the apron on. He could see part of her temple, where her fringe had been pushed aside. He realised he was holding his breath. Because... because he wanted to kiss her there.

Half the male population of Sydney is in love with her, he reminded himself. *And you are not—repeat not—going to become a piece of meat in the boyfriend brigade.*

Leo unpacked his knives and chopping boards, liberated extra plates and dishes from the cupboard, unearthed additional gadgets from his magic boxes.

'Come here so you can see properly,' he said as he started arranging ingredients on the counter.

Sunshine moved enthusiastically to stand beside him. The wave of heat emanating from him was very alluring. She edged a little closer. Breathed in the scent of him, which was just...well, just *him.* Just super-clean Leo. Could she manage to get just a bit closer, so that she was just—*nearly*—touching him, without him panicking and hitting her with a cooking implement?

His arm, naked below the short sleeve of his T-shirt, brushed hers—*that* was how close she was, because there was no way he would have done that on purpose—and she felt like swooning. Wished, quite passionately, that she hadn't worn sleeves so she could feel him skin to skin.

And it had absolutely *nothing* to do with exposure therapy either.

It was, plain and simple, about sexual attraction. *Mu-*

tual sexual attraction—at least she hoped the impressive bulge in his jeans that had taken her by surprise earlier was Sunshine-induced and not some erectile dysfunction... like that condition called priapism she'd read about on the internet...

Not that she was going to ask him that, of course, because men could be sensitive.

But with or without erectile dysfunction, she wanted to have sex with Leo Quartermaine!

Was it because he was cooking for her? There was definitely something off-the-chain seductive about a man—a *chef* man—making her dinner.

But...no. It was more than that.

Something that had been sneaking up on her.

Something to do with the way he jumped a foot inside his skin when she kissed him on the cheek. The little tic at the corner of his mouth that came and went, depending on his level of agitation. The slightly fascinated way he looked at her, as though he couldn't believe his eyes. And listened to her as though he couldn't believe his ears. The way he gave in a lot, but not always. And how, even when he let her have her way, the *way* he did it told her he might not always be so inclined, so she was not to take it for granted.

How bizarre was that? She liked that he gave in—and also that maybe he wouldn't!

She even kind of liked the fact that he tried so hard never to smile or laugh—as though that would be too frivolous for the likes of him. It was a challenge, that. Something to change. Because everyone needed to laugh. The average person laughed thirteen times a day. She would bet her brand-new forest-green leaf-cut stilettoes that Leo Quartermaine didn't get to thirteen even in a whole year! Not good enough.

Now that she'd acknowledged the attraction it felt moth-to-a-flame mesmeric, standing beside him. No, not a moth—that was too fluttery. More like the bat that had flown smack into the power line a block from her apartment. She'd seen it this morning, fried into rigidity, felled by a jolt of electricity.

Poor bat. Just going along, thinking it had everything under control, contemplating its regular upside-down hang for the night, then hitting a force that was greater than it and—*frzzzzz*. All over, red rover.

Poor bat—and poor her if she let herself get too close to Leo. Because she had a feeling he could fry her to a crisp if she let him.

Not that she would let him. She *never* got too close. That was the whole point of her 'four goes and goodbye' rule. Protecting her core.

Leo had managed to move a little away from her—which she rectified.

'This is a simple fettuccine with zucchini, feta, and prosciutto,' he said, clueless.

He moved once more, just a smidgeon. And Sunshine readjusted her position so she was just as close as before. *Poor Leo—you really should just give up!*

He managed another little edge away. 'We're going to fry some garlic, grated zucchini, and lemon zest, and then toss that through the pasta with some parsley, mint, and butter. Finally we'll throw in some feta and prosciutto—again tossed through—with a little lemon juice, salt, and pepper.'

He was—gamely, Sunshine thought—ignoring the fact that she was practically breathing down his neck.

He cleared his throat. Twice. 'This—' he was showing her a container '—is fresh pasta from Q Brasserie. I thought about making it here, but that might have been too much for a two-minute noodler to cope with.' He shot her a teeny-tiny smile—more of a glint than a smile, but *wowee*! *Be still my heart, or what?*

Sunshine watched as Leo started grating the zucchini

with easy, practised efficiency. There was a long scar on his left thumb, and what looked like a healed burn mark close to his right wristbone. Assorted other war wounds. These were not wimpy hands.

And, God, she wanted his sure, capable, scarred hands on her. All over her. It was almost suffocating how much she wanted that.

She kept watching, a little entranced, as Leo set the zucchini to one side, then grated the lemon rind. Next he grabbed some herbs and started tearing with his beautiful strong fingers as he talked…

His voice was deep and kind of gravelly. '…into strips,' Leo said.

Hmm… She had no idea what the start of that sentence had been.

He unwrapped a flat parcel—inside were paper-thin slices of prosciutto—and put it in front of her. 'Okay?' he asked.

'Sure,' she said, figuring out that she was supposed to chop it, and grabbed a knife.

'No,' Leo said, and took the knife away.

Lordy, Lordy. He'd actually touched her.

Sunshine felt every one of the hairs on her arm prickle. She was staring at him. She knew she was.

He was staring back.

And then he stepped back, cleared his throat again. 'Tear—like this,' he said, and demonstrated. Another clear of the throat. 'You do that and I'll…I'll…find the …cheese.'

She was humming again as she massacred the prosciutto.

And blow him down if it wasn't a woeful attempt at Natalie's signature song—the truly hideous *'Je t'aime-ich liebe-ti amor You Darling'.*

He started crushing garlic with the flat of his knife as though his life depended on it.

She was still tearing. And humming. *Please* tell him she didn't have the same insane cheesy love song obsession as Natalie. Who was *not* going to be performing at his brother's wedding! Once when he'd been mid-thrust, and Natalie had sung a line of that awful song, he'd choked so hard on a laugh he'd given himself a nosebleed; that evening had *not* ended well.

'Done,' Sunshine said, and looked proudly at the ripped meat in front of her.

Leo winced.

'What do you want me to do next?' she asked, with that damned glow that seemed to emanate from her pores.

'Salad,' he said, sounding as if he'd just announced a massacre.

Which it was likely to be—of the vegetable kind.

'We'll keep it simple,' he said. 'Give these lettuce leaves a wash.'

Sunshine took the lettuce leaves and ran them under the tap, her glow dimming.

'What's wrong?' he asked as he took them from her.

'Salad. It's so…vegetarian.'

She looked so disgruntled Leo found himself wanting to laugh again. He swallowed it. 'It's just a side dish. And there's meat in the pasta, remember?'

She wrinkled her nose. *Oh-oh.* Convoluted argument coming.

'I'll do it with a twist,' he offered quickly. 'I'll put some salmon in it, and do a really awesome dressing that doesn't taste remotely healthy. All right?'

Her nose unwrinkled. 'Okay, *if* you go a little heavy on the salmon and a little light on the lettuce.'

He choked. 'Am I designing that boot for you? No? Then

just shut up and see if you can cut these grape tomatoes into quarters. They're small, so be careful.'

She mumbled something derogatory about tomatoes, but made a swipe with the knife.

'Quarter—not slice,' Leo put in.

She nodded, wielded the knife again.

'And not mash, for God's sake,' he begged.

Sunshine made an exasperated sound and tried again.

Leo turned his back—it was either that or wrench the knife from her—and concentrated on the salmon he'd packed as a failsafe, coating it in herbs, then laying it in a pan to fry.

Sunshine was onto the song about love biting you in the ass, throwing in the occasional excruciating lyric—and he wanted so badly to laugh it was almost painful.

Mid-song, however, *she* laughed. 'Oops—that song is just too, too, *too* much, Hideous,' she said.

Damn if he didn't want to snatch her up and kiss her.

Instead he gave her some terse instructions on trimming the crunchy green beans to go into the salad, which she did abominably.

He put water on for the pasta, then turned back to the bench.

'Next, we'll—' He stopped, hurriedly averting his eyes as Sunshine arranged the salad ingredients in a bowl. 'We'll just slide the salmon on top—' shock stop as his eyes collided with the mangled contents '—and now I'll get you to mix the dressing.'

He lined up a lemon, honey, seeded mustard, sugar, black pepper, and extra virgin olive oil.

Sunshine considered the ingredients with the utmost concentration. 'So, I need to juice the lemon, right?'

'Yes. You only need a tablespoon.'

'How much is a tablespoon?'

Repressing the telltale tic, he opened the cutlery drawer and took out a tablespoon. 'This is a tablespoon.'

'Oh. How much of everything else?'

Limit reached. 'Move out of the way. I'll do it. I put a bottle of wine in the fridge. I think—no, I *know*—I need a nice big glass of it, if you can manage to pour that. Then go around to the other side of the counter, sit on that stool and watch. You've already thrown my kitchen rhythm off so things are woefully out of order.'

'It seems very ordered to me.'

'Well, it's not.'

Sunshine shrugged, unconcerned. 'You know, I feel like one of those contestants on your show.'

A thought too ghastly to contemplate!

Sunshine slid past him on her way to the fridge, brushing against his arm. *God!* God, God, *God*! Her brand of casual friendliness, with the kisses and the random touches, was something he was not used to. At all.

He didn't like it.

Except that he kind of did.

Dinner resembled a physical battle: Sunshine leaning in; Leo leaning *way* out.

A less optimistic woman would have been daunted.

But Sunshine was almost always optimistic.

As they ate the pasta and salad they argued over assorted wedding details, from the choice of MC—*'What are you thinking to suggest anyone but yourself, Leo?'*—to the need for speeches—Sunshine: yes; Leo: no!—to whether to use social media for sharing photos and videos of the function—over Leo's dead body, apparently.

By the time the pannacotta gelato was on the table Sunshine was in 'what the hell?' mode. Seven weeks to go— they had to move things along.

'So!' she said. 'Music!'

He went deer-in-the-headlights still. 'Music.'

'Yes. Music. I hear there's no dancing, so we can scrap the DJ option.'

'Correct.'

She pursed her lips. 'So! I've located a heavy metal band. I also know a great piano accordionist—surprisingly soulful. And I've heard about an Irish trio. What about one of those options? Or maybe a big band—but did you know that a big band has fourteen instruments? And where would we put fourteen musicians? I mean, I know the restaurant is spacious, but—'

'I know what you're doing, Sunshine.'

She blinked at him, the picture of innocence—she knew because she'd practised in the mirror. 'What do you mean, Leo?'

'Suggesting horrific acts and thinking that by the time you get around to naming the option you really want I'll be so relieved I'll agree instantly.'

'But that's not true. Well...not *strictly* true. Because I *have* named what I really want. Natalie Clarke.'

'No.'

'Why not?'

'Because.'

'Because why?'

'Caleb doesn't want her there.'

'Is that the only reason? Because I can talk to Caleb.'

'It's the only reason you're going to get.'

Sunshine gave him a bemused look. 'Is this because you used to date her? You know, I'm good friends with *all* my exes.'

'I, however, am not.'

'Why not?'

Leo scooped up a spoonful of gelato. Ate it. 'I just don't do that.'

'Why not?'

'They're just not that...that kind.'

'Kind?'

'Kind of person. People. Not the kind of people I'm friends with.'

She nodded wisely. 'You're choosing wrong.'

He took another mouthful of gelato. Said nothing.

'Because you don't want someone, really,' she said. 'You're like me.' Sunshine tapped her heart. 'No room in here.'

Leo's spoon clattered into his bowl. 'I've got room. Plenty. But I want...' He stopped, looking confused.

'You want...?'

'Someone...special.'

'Special as in...?'

'As in someone to throw myself off the cliff for, leap into the abyss with,' he said, sounding goaded. 'There! Are you happy?'

'My happiness is not the issue here.'

He dragged a hand over his head. Gave a short, surprised laugh. 'I want all or nothing.'

'And Natalie didn't?'

'She wanted...the illusion. She wanted the illusion of it without the depth.'

'Oh.'

'Yes—*oh*.'

'Not that I think there's anything wrong with not wanting the depth.'

'Of *course* there's something wrong with it,' he said with asperity. 'You're wrong about the whole no-room, sex-not-love thing.'

'Each to his or her own,' Sunshine said. 'And I still don't see why Natalie can't perform at the reception. You wouldn't even have to talk to her. I could do the negotiations.'

He snorted.

'Why the snort?'

'Forget it.'

'I am *not* going to forget it.

'Look—' He stopped, shot a hand across his scalp again. 'No, I don't want to go there.'

'Well, I do!'

'Oh, for God's sake!' Leo looked at her, exasperated. 'Natalie is a bunny-boiler, okay? She would not settle for negotiating with you—she'd be aiming for me. Always, *always* me. Got it?'

Sunshine sat back in her seat. Stared. *'No!'*

'Yes!'

'But…why?'

'How the hell do I know why? I only know the what— like eating at one of my restaurants every week. Driving my staff nuts with questions about me. Sending me stuff. So just leave it, Sunshine. I know another singer. Her name's Kate. I'll give you some CDs to listen to.'

'Is she an ex?'

'No. She's just a good singer with no agenda.'

Sunshine sighed inwardly but admitted defeat. 'Fair enough.' She stretched her arms over her head and arched her back. *'Mmm.* Next time maybe you should teach me how to make paella. I love paella.'

'One problem with that plan,' Leo said. 'I am never entering a kitchen with you again.'

'Oh, that's mean.'

'Think of the poor tomatoes.'

'What was wrong with the tomatoes?'

'Other than the fact that they looked like blood-spatter from a crime scene?'

Sunshine bit her lip against a gurgle of laughter. 'What about the prosciutto? I managed to tear that the way you showed me.'

'Flayed flesh.'

'Ouch,' Sunshine said, but she was laughing. 'What about how I scooped the gelato?'

'Please! Like ooze from a wound.'

'It's a good thing I don't have any coffee, or we'd be up to poison.'

'Since I didn't see an espresso machine in that shell of a kitchen, poison sounds about right.'

Rolling her eyes, Sunshine pushed her chair back from the table. 'Well, then, I will make you some tea—something all well-bred hippies *can* do. Unless you have some words to throw at me about scalded skin. The invitation is on the coffee table, waiting for your approval, so why don't you check it out while I clear up? Something *else* I can do.'

She watched from the corner of her eye as Leo moved to the couch, sat, reached for the invitation.

He was smiling—full-on!—as he slid the pad of his thumb so gently across the card, as though it were something precious. Oh, he did look good when he smiled. It was kind of crooked, with the left side lifting up further than the right. A little rusty. And it just got her—*bang!*—right in the chest.

Fried bat, anyone?

Tearing her eyes away, Sunshine finished making the tea.

'So! Is it okay?' she asked, sliding two mugs onto the coffee table and sitting beside Leo.

He turned to her, smiled again. *Heaven!*

'It's great. The calligraphy too.'

'I guess the next step is to discuss the menu.'

Leo picked up his mug. 'I'm going with a seafood bias, given the location.'

'Uncanny! Exactly what I was thinking.'

'Canapés to start. Local oysters, freshly shucked clams

served ceviche-style, poached prawns with aioli, and hand-milked Yarra Valley caviar with *crème fraîche*.'

'*Ohhhhh...*'

'Buffalo mozzarella and semi-dried tomato on croutons, honey-roasted vegetable tartlets, and mini lamb and feta kofta'

'*Mmm...*'

'Just champagne, beer, and sparkling water—we don't need to get too fancy with the drinks to start. But any special requirements we can accommodate on request.'

'Good, because Jon's mother will insist on single malt whisky—and through *every* course. *Nothing* we say ever dissuades her.'

'Well, it's better than a line of coke with every course.'

She gaped at him. 'Line of...?'

'Natalie,' he said shortly. 'Another reason she will not be performing at the wedding. Just to be absolutely clear.'

'That's...' She waved a hand, lost.

'Anyway, moving on. The first course will be calamari, very lightly battered and deep fried, served with a trio of dipping sauces—lime and coriander, smoked jalapeno mayonnaise, and a sweet plum sauce.'

'Oh, Leo, could you teach me how to make that at least?'

'No. The main meal will be lobster, served with a lemon butter sauce and a variety of salads that I wouldn't dare describe to you.'

'Lobster! Oh.' She took a sip of tea. 'You know, Leo, I saw the most intriguing thing about lobsters on the internet.'

'Yes?' He sounded wary.

'They are actually immortal! They stay alive until they get eaten.'

'That can't be true.'

'Which means coming back as a lobster in the next life wouldn't be such a bad thing. Except...' Nose-wrinkle.

'Well, I'm not sure that when they're caught they're always killed humanely. So you might be lucky enough to live for ever—or you might get thrown into a pot of boiling water and be absolutely screaming, without even having the ability to make a sound, because some sadistic cook couldn't be bothered to kill you first.'

Leo gave a sigh brimming with long suffering. 'Okay—barramundi it is,' he said. 'Coated with lemon and caper butter and wrapped in pancetta, served with in-season asparagus.'

'That sounds divine. And so much more humane.'

'I am *not* a lobster sadist,' Leo said, sounding as if he were gritting his teeth.

'Well, of course not.'

There was the tic. 'And they are not immortal.'

'Well, they might be—who would know? And they can, a hundred per cent, live to about one hundred and forty years. Which is *almost* immortal.'

He regarded her through narrowed eyes. 'How is it you've made it to twenty-five without being murdered?'

'You're definitely watching too many crime shows.'

'Dessert,' he said firmly. 'I'm thinking about figs.'

'Figs. Oh.' Sip of tea.

'"Figs oh" *what*? Is this the fruit version of your vegetarian hang-up? Because there *will* be sugar, you know.'

'It's not th— Actually, it *is* partly that. But, more to the point, I think fig pollination is kind of disgusting.'

He had that fascinated look going on.

'Wasps,' she said.

'Wasps?'

'They burrow into the fig and lay their eggs in the fruit, then die in there. *Ergh*. And it's quite brutal, because on the way in the poor wasp can lose her wings and her antennae—it's a tight fit, I guess. Come on—you have to agree that's a bit repulsive. And sad too.'

Leo had closed his eyes. Tic, tic, tic.

A moment passed. Another. He opened his eyes and looked at her. 'So, we'll serve a variation on the glacé I made for you at Q Brasserie—perhaps with a rose syrup base. And, because it's a wedding, some Persian confetti.'

Sunshine beamed at him. 'That's just perfect.'

'And remember I know your modus operandi, Sunshine Smart-Ass.'

'But I don't have one of those!'

Leo simply put up the 'stop' hand. 'For the non-seafood-lovers there will be ricotta tortellini with burnt-sage butter sauce as an alternative first course, and either chargrilled lime and mint chicken or a Moroccan-style chickpea tagine for your fellow commune dwellers for the main course.'

'Oh, even the chickpea thing sounds good. Because chickpeas are sort of like the meat of vegetables, don't you think?'

'No, I don't.'

'What about the cake?'

'Four options: traditional fruit cake, salted caramel—which we can do with either a chocolate or butterscotch base—or coconut.'

'Oh! *Oh!* Could we do one of those cake-tasting things? You know, where you sit around and try before you buy? I would *so* love to do a cake-tasting.'

'For the love of God, can't we just ask the guys what they want?'

'What would be the fun in that?' Sunshine asked, mystified.

Leo ran that hand over his head. 'I'll talk to Anton—he's my *pâtissier.*'

'And I have the most amazing idea for the decoration. Kind of Art Deco—my current favourite thing. Square tiers, decorated with hand-cut architectural detailing, in white and shades of grey, with painted silver accents. Wait a moment—I've got a photo.'

Sunshine leapt off the couch and raced into her office, grabbed the photo and raced back out. 'What do you think?' she asked, thrusting it at him.

But Leo was looking past her into the office.

She'd forgotten to close the door.

'Oh,' she said, seeing through his eyes the green-striped wallpaper, the reproduction antique furniture painted in vivid blues, reds, and yellows, the framed prints of lusciously coloured shoes through the ages hung on the walls.

The urn with Moonbeam's ashes. In his direct line of sight. *Oh, no!* Sunshine raced back to close the door.

'So!' she said, her heart beating hard as she came back to sit beside him. 'So! The cake.'

'I'll talk to Anton,' Leo said absently, still looking at the closed door.

Sunshine decided drastic action was needed—just to make sure he didn't ask to actually go in there.

Going with gut feeling—and, all right, secret desire— she hugged him.

He seemed to freeze for a moment, and then his arms came around her. He gathered her in for one moment. She heard, felt him inhale slowly.

Wow! He was actually touching her! Voluntarily! Except that this wasn't exactly touching—it was more. Better! Absorbing! He was absorbing her! Talk about exclamation mark overload!

His arms were so hard. So was his chest. It should have felt like being pulled against a brick wall…and yet there was something yielding about him. His hand came up, touched the back of her head, fingers sliding into her hair.

Good. But Sunshine wanted more. Much more.

She pulled out of his arms, sat back, looked at him. 'I don't know how you're going to take this, Leo,' she said, 'but I want to have sex with you.'

CHAPTER FIVE

LEO STARED. COULDN'T so much as blink.

A minute ticked by.

She was waiting for him to speak, her head tilted—the curious bird look.

Had he heard correctly?

Had Sunshine Smart just told him, taking matter-of-factness to the level of an art form, that she wanted to have *sex* with him? And that she didn't know how he'd *take* that confession?

'What did you just say?' he asked at last, and his voice sounded as though he hadn't used it for a month.

'Just that I want to have sex with you.' Sunshine pursed her lips, considering him. 'Are you shocked? Horrified? Appalled? Because you don't look interested.'

'Gary. Ben. Marco.' He listed them without elaborating.

'Gary, Ben and Marco?' she said, as though she had no idea what he was getting at.

'How many lovers do you need?'

She gave him an *Aha!* kind of look, then said simply, 'Okay, I'll tell you. I'm not sleeping with any of them. I'm not sleeping with anyone. I *hoped* there would be a spark with Gary, but it never developed. Ben? Twice. But that's ancient history, and we won't talk about his addiction to cheesy love songs in the bedroom.'

Momentary distraction. '*Ben* and cheesy love songs? What *is* it with people and cheesy love songs?'

'I know—it's crazy! So, of course, it was never going to go anywhere. Marco—well, that would be a cold day in hell.' She looked at him. 'But there's no need to talk it to death. If you're not interested let's just move on. We have a tough seven weeks ahead, and there's just not enough time for us to go through an awkward phase.'

'How the hell am I supposed to *move on*?' Leo asked, incredulous.

'I said I wanted to have sex with you—not that I wanted to marry you. And only up to four times, which is my limit.' She looked at him thoughtfully. 'You don't suffer from priapism by any chance, do you?'

'From *what*?'

'Guess not. Well, then—are you, perhaps, a virgin who's signed some sort of pledge?'

'No, of course I'm not a *virgin*.'

'Well, I don't know why you say *"of course"* like that. There are more virgins out there than you realise. In fact I read on the internet that—'

'And what do you mean, only up to four times?' he asked, jumping in before she could give him virgin facts. Because he did *not* want virgin facts.

'Any more than four times and things get messy. You know—emotional. If you don't want to develop a relationship it's best to set a limit. And I don't. Want to develop a relationship. I mean; I *do* want to set a limit. Hmm, you're giving me that look.'

'What look?'

'That *she's insane* look.'

'That's because you are. Insane.'

'I'm just sensible, Leo. Men do this stuff all the time. Pick up a girl in a seedy bar—not that we're in a seedy bar, of course, but you get the picture—then race her off to the bedroom, then do the I'll-call-you routine when they have no *intention* of calling. So why can't I? Well, not the I'll-call-you thing—I would never say I'd call someone and then not do it. And there really is no *reason* not to call. Regardless of whether you want to have sex with them again. Because you had to like them in *some* way to get into bed with them in the first place, so you should want to see where the friendship goes, shouldn't you? The sex part is kind of incidental—because sex is just…well, *sex*.'

Pause.

Thank God. Because his head was spinning.

'I guess what I'm saying,' she continued, unabashed, 'is that it's better to be up-front about what you want— just sex, just friendship, sex and then friendship. What-ever! But no tragic *I love you* just to wring an orgasm out of someone.'

'What if you *do* fall in love?'

'I won't. I never have. And I never will. I told you be-fore: I won't let myself care that much.'

'So you're saying Jonathan and Caleb should give up the idea of marriage and just have sex?'

Her face softened. 'No, I'm happy for them. And I know the love thing works for lots of people—my parents are a prime example. It just doesn't work for me.'

'How do you know if you've never been there?'

'Haven't we already had this discussion?'

'Not thoroughly enough, Sunshine.'

Another pause. 'All right, then. The fact is I'm too… intense. I feel things too intensely.'

'Not thoroughly *enough*,' he repeated.

She bit her lower lip, worried it between her teeth. And then, haltingly, she said, 'I didn't recover—not properly— from my sister's death.' The tears were there, being blinked furiously away. 'I can't describe it. The agony. The… *agony*.'

'That's a different kind of love,' he said, but gently.

'A different *kind*, yes. But the *depth*... I just think it's safer, for me, to splash in the shallows—not to swim out of my depth.' She laughed, but there was no humour in it. 'Huh. A line of coke and I'd be Natalie.'

'You're nothing like Natalie. And you already have strong, deep ties—to Jon, to your parents...'

'Yes. I love Jon, and I love my parents. But it was too late to do anything about them; they were already here.' Small tap over the heart. 'I'm just limiting further damage.' She tried to smile. 'And, anyway, the in-love kind of love would be the *most* damaging. Because I know how I'd be in love. Kill for him, die for him...'

'The kind I want.'

'The kind you *say* you want, anyway. Into the abyss, off the cliff. But you'll see, when you've fallen into the abyss, that there's anguish there—in the fear of losing the one you love, or even just losing the love. And I can't—won't—go through that. Because next time I just don't know how I—' She stopped. Blew out a breath. 'Let's not go there. Let's just keep the focus on sex.'

Leo could hear muted noises from outside floating up from the street. Traffic. A laugh. A shout. But inside it was quiet. 'So you've restricted your lovers to a four-night term ever since Moonbeam died? And none of them ever wanted to take things further?'

'They knew it was never going to happen. And I've managed to stay good friends with all of them despite that—which is more than you can say. Well, all of them bar one.'

'And what went wrong with him?'

'He just doesn't like women dictating the terms, so we didn't even make it to the first...what would you call it?... assignation? Yes, assignation.' She did the curious bird thing. 'I'm guessing you're in his camp.'

Leo had no idea, at that point, *what* he thought. But he didn't like Sunshine telling him which camp he was in, thank you very much! 'No, I'm not in that camp.'

Sunshine smiled. 'So! Are you saying you *would* consider it, Leo? Sex, I mean?'

'No, I'm not saying that either.'

Another smile. 'Shall we try a little experiment, then?'

Long silence. And then, 'What kind of experiment?'

'I'll kiss you and you can see how that makes you feel.'

He opened his mouth to say no.

But Sunshine didn't let him get that far.

She simply moved so she was straddling him. She undulated, once, against him, and he thought he would explode on the spot. *Holy hell.* Then she settled, cocooning him between her forearms as she gripped the back of the sofa, one hand on each side of his head. Jonquils. Red silk. Heat and buzz and glow. She dipped her head, nipped his lower lip.

'No, that wasn't the kiss—that was me signalling my intention, as I promised to do.' She smiled. 'So! Ready?'

Any thought of denying her went straight out of his head like a shot of suddenly liberated steam. Leo gripped her hips, ground her against him, wanting her to feel his raging erection—although he didn't know why, unless her form of insanity was contagious—and took over, devouring her mouth with a hard, savaging kiss.

Her mouth was amazing. Open, luscious, drawing him in. His tongue, hot and agile, swept the roof of her mouth, the insides of her cheeks, under her super-sexy top lip. The tart sweetness of the lemony tea was delicious when it was licked from inside her. He could feel that slight gap between her front teeth. He moved his hands, cupped her face to keep her there, just *there*, so he could taste more deeply.

He could feel his heart thundering. Became aware that her hands were now fisted in his shirt as she rocked against him, forced her mouth and his wider still. She was whimpering, alternately jamming her tongue into his mouth and then licking his lips. And rocking, rocking, *rocking* against him until he thought he'd go mad with wanting.

Then her hands were moving between them, fingers plucking at the button of his jeans, which opened in a 'thank God' moment, then sliding his zipper down, freeing him.

'Ah...' he gasped, pulling his mouth away so he could breathe, try to think. But it was no use. He had to kiss her again.

She reeled him back in, pulled him closer, angled him so that when she lay back, flattened on the couch, he was on top of her.

Then his hands were there, pulling up the red silk. Up, up, up. So he could touch her skin, which was like satin. No, not satin—warmer than satin. Velvet...like velvet. His fingers slid higher, closer. He didn't want to wait—couldn't wait—*had* to feel her, to be in her the fastest way he could get there.

Without disengaging his mouth from hers, he plunged his fingers into her. Again. She arched into the touch.

She didn't speak, but breathed out words. His name. *'Leo. Yes, yes. Leo...'*

And then it wasn't his fingers but him needing to be there, buried in her as deep as he could go, panting, straining, wanting this, wanting *her*, silently demanding that she come for him. For *him*.

He felt her body tightening, straining, heard his name explode from her lips as the orgasm gripped her. He pushed hard into her, and kissed her drugging mouth again as he followed her into a life-draining release.

They lay there, connected, in a tangle of clothes, spent.

After a long moment Sunshine gave a shaky laugh. 'That was some kiss,' she said.

But Leo didn't feel like laughing. He felt like diving into her again…and also, contrarily, like getting the hell away from her. From her rules. Her determination to fix him in the place where she wanted him. Just where she wanted him. No further.

Awkwardly, he disengaged himself from her body.

Sunshine sat up, pushing at her hair with one unsteady hand and at her dress with the other. She looked like the cat that had got the cream.

Infuriating.

Mechanically, Leo adjusted his clothing. He was appalled to realise he hadn't even *seen* her during that mad sexual scramble. Did that make him some kind of depraved, desperate sex fiend, that he'd treated her body like a receptacle? But then, he hadn't really *needed* to see her to know very well that it was her driving him wild—so wild he hadn't been able to think past the need to be inside her.

'Are you sorry?' Sunshine asked softly.

She was watching him with wary concern.

'No. Yes. I don't know.'

Tiny laugh. 'Multiple *choice*? How…comprehensive.'

He stood abruptly, shoved his hands in his pockets, not trusting where he'd put them otherwise.

'Leo, don't go. We have to talk about this.'

He shook his head.

She got to her feet, took his hand. 'You will get all angsty if you leave now, because it happened so fast and we weren't expecting it to go like that. We can't have angst; we have too much to do. Come on, sit with me—let's make sure we can get back to normal before you go.'

How did you talk yourself back to *normal* after that?

How did a kiss turn into rip-your-heart-out sex in one blinding flash of a moment? And that complete loss of control… It had never happened to him before. No condom. Not even a *thought* of one! He was shaken. Badly.

And—God!—she was still holding his hand, and he was rubbing his thumb over her knuckles, and he hadn't even noticed he was doing it. He didn't *do* that touchy-feely stuff.

He dropped her hand and stepped back. 'You're dangerous, Sunshine,' he said.

She looked startled. 'It's not like I'm a black widow spider or a praying mantis.'

'What the—? All right, I think I get the black widow spider. But what's so dangerous about a praying mantis?'

Her eyes lit. 'Oh, it's really interesting! Praying mantises can only have sex once the female rips off the male's head. Imagine! At least you still have your head.'

Leo felt his lips twitch. But he was *not* going to laugh. It was not a funny situation. It was an *angsty* one. Angsty? God.

'On that note, I'm going,' he said.

'But we have to talk.'

'Not now. Meet me… I don't know… Tomorrow. At the Rump & Chop Grill. Five o'clock. It's only a few blocks from here. I'll send someone for my kitchen gear in the morning.'

'All right, tomorrow,' she agreed, and walked with him to the door, where she stopped him. 'Leo, just so you can think about it before then…I want to have sex with you again. We have up to three more opportunities, and there doesn't seem to be a reason not to use them. We just need to schedule them so we don't get distracted from the wedding preparations.'

He was staring again. Couldn't help it.

'Far be it from me to distract you, Sunshine,' he said.

So!

Yowzer!

As Sunshine wallowed in her bubble bath, lathering

herself with her favourite jonquil-scented soap, she pondered what had happened.

It sure hadn't been a cheesy-love-song experience. More like heavy metal—hard and loud and banging. But maybe with a clash of cymbal thrown in. She smiled, stretched, almost purred.

She knew she would be reliving the sex for an hour or so—that was par for the course. The sexual post-mortem...a normal female ritual. Remembering exactly what had happened, what had been murmured, who'd put what where.

But at four o'clock in the morning she was still trying to piece it together and parcel it off. She wondered if the difficulty was that she didn't have a precise anatomical memory of the experience. She couldn't recall everything that had been said, every touch, every kiss. She just had an... *awareness*. That it had been so gloriously *right*, somehow.

Which was strange. Because technically it shouldn't have been that memorable. They hadn't taken off their clothes; Leo hadn't touched her breasts—which she'd always counted as her best assets—and he hadn't even bothered to look at the goods before plunging in—which was a waste of her painfully acquired Brazilian!

But none of that seemed to matter because the *can't wait* roughness of it had been more seductive than an hour of foreplay. She hadn't needed foreplay. Hadn't wanted finesse. Hadn't thought about condoms. Hadn't thought about anything. She'd been so hot, so ready for him.

She wondered—if that rough-and-ready first time was any indication—just how magnificent the next time would be.

Because there *would* be a next time. She was going to make sure of it.

TO: Jonathan Jones
FROM: Sunshine Smart
SUBJECT: Party news

Isn't the menu great? Leo=food genius.

Just the wedding cake to go. I'd tell you the options, but if you chose one I wouldn't get my cake-tasting, which you know I've always wanted to do.

Leo cooked the most amazing meal last night. He is so different from the men I usually meet. More mature, steadier. Kind of conservative—I like that.

His hair is coming along too.

Sunny xxx

TO: Sunshine Smart
FROM: Jonathan Jones
SUBJECT: Do not sleep with Leo Quartermaine
DO NOT!!!!! That would be all kinds of hideous.
Jon

TO: Jonathan Jones
FROM: Sunshine Smart
SUBJECT: Re: Do not sleep with Leo Quartermaine
Oops! Too late!

But how did you know? And why hideous?
Sunny

TO: Sunshine Smart
FROM: Jonathan Jones
SUBJECT: Re:Re: Do not sleep with Leo Quartermaine
OH, MY FREAKING GOD, SUNNY!!!!!!!!

How do I know? For starters because every second word you're writing is 'Leo'!

He's not the type to enjoy the ride then buddy up at the end. You know his parents were drug addicts, right? You know he basically dragged Caleb through that hell and into a proper life?

He's a tough hombre, not a poncy investment banker,

soulful embalmer or saucy hairdresser. This is not a man for you to play with.

Let's talk tonight—10 p.m. your time. With video. No arguments.

Jon

Sunshine got to the Rump & Chop Grill fifteen minutes early. Although it was part of a pub, it had a separate entrance on a side road—which was locked.

She decided against knocking and inveigling her way inside to wait. That would have been her usual approach. But Leo already had one bunny-boiler on his tail, as well as being in a state about last night, so it was probably best not to look *too* enthusiastic.

Fortunately there was a café across the road, where she could wait and watch for him. Which would give her time to think.

Because Jon's email had thrown her.

The thing with Leo was a simple sexual arrangement. No need for concern on *anyone's* part.

So he'd had drug addict parents? And, no, of course she hadn't known that! How could she have, unless someone had told her? And why did it make a difference anyway? Unless Leo was a drug addict himself—and given his obvious disgust over his ex-girlfriend's coke habit that seemed unlikely.

Did Jon think the fact that Leo and Caleb had navigated a hellish childhood would put her off him? It clearly hadn't put Jon off Caleb, so why the double standard? And Caleb had come through unscathed. He was a terrific guy—very different from his brother, of course—at least from what she'd seen during their internet chats. Funny and charming and *out there*. Not that Leo wasn't also terrific, but he certainly didn't have Caleb's lightness of spirit.

But it was to Leo's credit, wasn't it, if he was the one

who'd dragged them both out of the gutter? She admired him *more*, not less, because of it. Liked him more.

Okay—*that* could be a problem. She didn't actually *want* to admire or like him more, because admiration and liking could lead to other things. And what she wanted was to keep things just as they were.

Hot man, in her bed, up to three more times. Finish.

As she would tell Jon, very firmly, tonight.

So! For now she would stop thinking about Leo's horrible childhood and concentrate on the wedding reception. *Not* that Jon deserved to have her fussing over it after that email, but...well, she loved Jon. And she was going to make the bastard's wedding reception perfect if it killed her.

While she sat in the café, disgruntled, sipping a coffee she didn't even want, she scanned the checklist. Having the function at South was brilliant, but it did add an extra task: finding accommodation for people who wouldn't want to drive back to Sydney. She figured they would need two options—cheap and cheerful, and sumptuous luxury. If she could get it sorted quickly, hotel booking details could be sent out with the invitations. She was sure Leo wouldn't want to traipse through hotels with her, so she would shoot down the coast herself and just keep him in the loop via email.

Right. The next urgent thing on the list was what Leo was wearing.

At least it was urgent from *her* perspective, because his shoe design hinged on it. And so did her outfit.

She was dying to wear her new 1930s-style dress in platinum charmeuse. It looked almost molten. Hugging her curves—all right, a little dieting might be required—in an elegantly simple torso wrap before tumbling in an understated swirl to the ground. It even had a divine little train. And she could wear her adorable gunmetal satin peep-toes with the retro crystal buckles.

But there was no good glamming to the hilt if Leo was going to play it down. And so far, aside from his pristine chef's whites, she hadn't seen an inclination for dressing up. Just jeans, T-shirts, sweaters. Good shoes, but well-worn and casual.

She heard a roar, and a second later a motorbike—it had to be his—pulled up outside the restaurant. One economical swing of his leg and he was off, reefing his helmet from his head.

Her heart jumped into her throat and her stomach whooshed.

Nope.

This was not going to work.

She couldn't think about clothes or shoes or hotels when he was still riding that damned bike. She was going to have talk to him about it. *Again*. And again and again. Until he got rid of it.

She straightened her spine and set her jaw. She was *not* to going to spend the next seven weeks dreading his death on the road! She stashed the wedding folder into her briefcase, threw some money on the table and exited the café.

Leo saw Sunshine the moment she stepped onto the footpath, his eyes snap-locking on to her from across the road. She looked good, as usual, wearing a winter green skirt suit that fitted her as snugly as the skin on a peach, and high-heeled chocolate-brown pumps.

'Leo, I have to talk to you,' she said.

He waited for that smacking kiss to land on his cheek.

But his cheek remained unsullied. She was clearly agitated—too agitated to bother with the kiss.

Well, good, he thought savagely. She *should* be agitated after last night. *He* certainly was.

'Yep, that was the plan,' Leo said, and unlocked the door.

Sunshine was practically humming with impatience as he relocked the door and escorted her to a table in the middle of the restaurant.

'I'll just check the kitchen and I'll be back,' he said, and almost smiled at the way her face pinched. *Yeah, cool your jets, Sunshine Smart-Ass, because you are not in control here.*

Not that that he was necessarily in control himself, but she didn't have to know that he hadn't been able to think straight since last night—let alone make a decision on her offer of three more pulse-ricocheting bouts of sex.

He was a man—ergo, it was an attractive proposition. But sex just for the sake of sex? Well, not to be arrogant, but he had his pick of scores of women if that was all he wanted. All right, the sex last night had been fairly spectacular, although hardly his most selfless performance, but it was still a commodity in abundant supply.

So, did he want more than sex from Sunshine?

Even as the question darted into his head he rejected it with a big *hell no*.

He didn't like perky and he didn't like breezy. Perky and breezy—AKA Sunshine Smart—were synonyms for negligent in his book. Choosing the shallows over the depths, wallowing in the past instead of confronting life head-on, the whole sex-only mantra. That kind of devil-may-care irresponsibility described his deadbeat parents, who'd not only offered up their bodies and any scrap of dignity for a quick score, but had been so hopeless they'd dropped dead of overdoses within days of each other, orphaning two sons.

Okay, the 'poor little orphans' bit was overcooked, because he and Caleb had stopped relying on them years before their deaths—but the principle remained.

So, no—he did *not* want more than sex from Sunshine.

And he didn't need *just* sex from her either.

All he needed from cheery, perky, breezy, ditzy Sunshine Smart was a hassle-free seven weeks of wedding preparations, after which he would set his compass and sail on.

Pretty clear, then.

Decision made.

Sex was off the table.

And the couch. And the bed. And wherever else she'd been planning on frying his gonads.

And he would enjoy telling her. Quickly—because he'd made this decision several times throughout the day, then gone back to re-mulling the options, and enough was enough.

But when he sat down across from Sunshine, all primed to give her the news, she forestalled him by saying urgently, 'Leo, you need to get rid of that motorbike. It's too dangerous.'

He took a moment to switch gears because he hadn't been expecting that. Sex, yes. Clothes, yes. Shoes, fine. But not the motorbike again.

'Yes, well, as it's my body on it, you can safely leave the decision about my transportation to me.'

'There's no "safely" about it.'

He looked at her closely, saw that there was nothing cheery-perky-breezy-ditzy in her face.

'Whoa,' he said. 'Let's take a step back. What's really behind this?'

'I want you to be alive for the wedding—that's all.'

'That's not all, Sunshine. Tell me, or this discussion is over.'

She dashed a hand across her fringe, pushing it aside impatiently. Looked at him, hard and bright and on edge, and then, 'My sister,' exploded from her mouth.

Leo waited. His hands had clenched into fists. Because

he wanted to touch her again. He felt a little trickle of something suspiciously like fear shiver down his spine.

'You may think it's none of my business—and it's not, strictly speaking,' she said. 'But it's not my way to stand aside and *not* say or do something when death is staring someone in the face. How could I live with myself if I didn't interfere and then something happened to you?'

'And you go around giving this lecture to everyone on a motorbike?'

'No, of course not—only to people I…' She faltered there. 'People I…know,' she finished lamely, putting up her chin.

Leo considered her for a long moment. *Not buying it.* 'Your sister. I want the whole story. I assumed…an illness. Wrong, obviously. I should have asked.'

'I didn't want you to ask. I didn't *let* you ask. Because to talk about that…to you, with your bike…it would have been a link. And I couldn't… But now…' Pause…deep breath while she gathered herself together. 'Sorry. I'm not making sense. I'll be clearer. Moonbeam had a motorbike. She crashed and she died. I was on the back and I survived. We were the cliché identical twins—inseparable. And then suddenly, just like…like…' She clicked her fingers. 'I was…'

The words just petered out. He saw her swallow, as if she had a sharp rock in her throat.

'Alone?' he finished for her.

'Yes. Alone.'

He waited a heartbeat. Two. Three.

She kept her eyes on his face, but apparently she wasn't intending to add anything.

'Sunshine,' he said softly, 'death is *not* staring me in the face. I'm not a teenage hothead burning up the road. I'm thirty. And I'm careful.'

'What if someone not so careful knocks you off?'

'Is that what happened? Did someone run your sister down?'

She shook her head, looking as if she would burst from frustration. 'No. She was going too fast. Missed the corner.'

Leo ran a hand over his head. Tried to find something to say. He was scared to open his mouth in case he promised her that, yes, he would give up the one carefree thing he allowed himself. They'd known each other for one week: she couldn't really care—had said she *wouldn't* care. And he would *not* be seduced into sacrificing his bike by the thought that she did.

'Look,' he started, and then stopped, ran a hand over his head again. 'It's not your job, Sunshine, to worry about me.'

'But I *do* worry about you. *Please*, Leo.'

There was a loud crashing sound from the kitchen. 'I have to check that.' Leo got to his feet, but then he paused, looking down at her. 'I shouldn't have started this. Not here, where there are too many distractions. Go home, and we'll pick it up another time.'

'I'm eating here tonight,' Sunshine said. 'And, no, I am *not* turning into a stalker. I have a date. Iain.'

His eyes narrowed. 'The hairdresser? The ex, who's now just a friend?'

'That's right.'

'As long as it *is* ex. Because while you and I are sleeping together—even if it is only four times—there isn't going to be anyone else in the picture. Got it? I'm not into sharing.' He heard the words come out of his mouth but couldn't quite believe they had. *Okay*, so he'd changed his mind and sex was back on, apparently.

'Well, of course!' Sunshine said. 'Actually, the main reason I asked him to come tonight was to check your head.'

'Check my head?' Leo repeated, not getting it.

'To make sure it's going to be long enough—not your head, because obviously that's not growing any more, but your hair.'

'He is *not* checking my head, Sunshine.'

That damned nose-wrinkle. 'But I think—'

'No,' Leo said, and strode into the kitchen.

Where he burst out laughing and stopped half the staff in their tracks.

'What?' he asked.

But nobody was brave enough to answer.

Sunshine did not enjoy dinner.

Not that the food wasn't great—because who couldn't love a Wagyu beef burger with Stilton, and chilli salt fries on the side?

And Iain had brought sketches of the most fabulous hairstyle for the wedding. Finger waves pinned at the base of the neck and secured with a gorgeous hairclip. Her fringe would be swept aside—*please* let it be long enough—and similarly clipped above her ear.

But neither the food nor the sketches was enough to take her mind off that damned motorbike, and the fact that Leo, who was so sensible, didn't seem to understand that it had to go.

So she fumed. And, because she'd always supposed she didn't carry the fuming gene, the unwelcome evidence that she could get as wound up as a garden variety maniac bothered her.

They'd had sex. That didn't mean she had a hold over him, of course, but it made him...well...someone more important than a casual acquaintance.

She became aware that Iain was sing-songing her name softly from across the table and snapped her attention back to where it should have been all night.

'That's better,' he said.

'Sorry, Iain. I haven't been good company tonight.'

'You're always good company, Sunny.'

She smiled at him. 'You're too nice.'

'Nice?' He gave a short, almost bitter laugh. 'Was that the limiter?'

'What? No!' She looked at him, dismayed. 'The problem was—is always—that I just don't want…that.'

'Someone's going to change your mind, Sunny—and all of us who have been forced to accept the limit are going to be mighty annoyed.'

All of us? Good Lord! 'You make it sound like there's a zombie camp of men out there, slavishly doing my bidding! And nobody is going to get annoyed—because I'm *not* changing my mind, ever. *And* I also happen to know you're dating Louise, so— Oh!'

She stopped abruptly. Stared past Iain.

Because Natalie Clarke, accompanied by a pretty guy vaguely familiar as a model—Rob-something—was being seated at the next table.

Natalie was stunning. Gold skin, glorious copper hair, perfect rosebud mouth, pale grey eyes. She was superslender, wearing a tight black leather skirt and a cropped black jacket. Black suede boots that made Sunshine green with envy.

Natalie shrugged out of her jacket to reveal a teensy white top; a black demi-bra was clearly visible underneath.

Iain's eyes went straight to the mother lode!

Sunshine, swallowing a laugh, kicked Iain under the table. *Bolt-ons*, she mouthed at him.

So? He mouthed back, and the laugh erupted after all.

Natalie, venom in her grey eyes, looked sharply, suspiciously, over at Sunshine and Iain.

Oh. That was just *nasty*. Imagine if Natalie ever got wind of what she'd done with Leo last night! Crime scene for sure—blood spatter, flayed flesh, ooze, *and* poison, and possibly a meat cleaver in there as well!

Then Sunshine noticed the tattooed butterflies flitting down Natalie's arms, and laughed again before she could stop herself.

Oops. *Extra* venom. And not much of a sense of humour, obviously.

Sunshine shifted her attention back to Iain and made a valiant effort to ignore Natalie—but it was impossible not to hear the overly loud one-way conversation from Natalie to Rob-the-model. All about Leo!

Blah-blah…so boring that Leo never, ever cooked for people outside his restaurants. *Ha! Prosciutto fettuccine, anyone?* Blah-blah…swank parties with Leo. Blah-blah…celebrities she and Leo had met. Blah-blah…she and Leo, part of the scene. *And who said 'the scene' with a straight face?* Blah-blah, blah-*blah*!

Natalie was pushing food around her plate as she talked; Rob was at least eating, but he was also smirking. *Smirking*—was that the most infuriating facial expression in the world?

The two of them would intermittently disappear to the bathroom, then come back talking too fast and too loud. When they disappeared for the fourth time Iain mimed coke-sniffing and Sunshine grimaced.

Natalie and Rob returned to the table and within moments were back on topic: Leo. And then, clear as a bell, 'I'll take Leo back when I'm ready—because, no matter what, he's good in bed.'

Tittering laugh from Rob.

People at about six different tables were staring at Natalie, entranced.

Sunshine felt her blood pressure shoot up. If she wasn't a pacifist she would want to slap Natalie for doing this to Leo—and in his own restaurant, dammit! Sunshine's heart was racing, her brain fizzing. She felt light-headed. She was going to have to do something to stop this.

'Really, *really* good,' Natalie continued, taking in her audience, 'which is kind of psycho, because he can't even touch you unless he's fu—'

Sunshine let out a loud, long peal of exaggerated laughter, drawing all eyes. She felt like a prize idiot, and Iain was obviously uncomfortable, but it was the only option she could immediately think of to shut Natalie up.

Sunshine was racking her brain for a way to proceed when Rob solved the dilemma by jumping to his feet and clutching at his neck.

Natalie stared ineffectually at her choking date.

Someone called out for a doctor.

The manager was racing to the kitchen.

Two diffident waiters approached the table, probably hoping someone would get there before them.

The diners—apparently not a doctor amongst them—seemed frozen. No movement. Just watching.

Sunshine got to her feet with a sinking heart. On the bright side, this dramatic development had shut Natalie up. On the not so bright side, Sunshine suspected she was about to star in the next scene. She hovered for a few seconds. *Please someone else help...please.* But—nope! Sunshine sighed. So be it.

Focusing her mind, Sunshine strode to the table. 'Out of the way,' she said, pushing past a still gaping Natalie.

Sunshine thumped Rob on the back. *Nothing.* Again. Once more.

Nope. Whatever was lodged in his throat wasn't going to be beaten out of him. Rob wasn't coughing, wasn't making a sound; he was just turning blue. His eyes stared, entreating. His hands tugged at his shirt collar.

Okay, here goes. Quickly, calmly, Sunshine moved behind him, wrapped her arms around him and placed a fist between his ribcage and where she guessed his navel was. Then she covered the fist with her other hand and gave one sharp tug upwards and inwards.

A piece of meat came flying out of Rob's mouth and he staggered, grabbing at his chair, dragging in breaths.

The restaurant broke into spontaneous applause and Sunshine felt her face heat.

Thank God the waiters were now taking control.

She started to return to her table and saw Leo standing just outside the kitchen. He was staring at her as though he'd just witnessed the Second Coming.

Sunshine couldn't remember ever being so embarrassed.

She was almost relieved when Natalie's squeal snagged his attention.

His eyes widened, then narrowed as they returned to Sunshine. Not happy!

Sunshine would have laughed if she hadn't felt so shaken. What on earth did he believe had just happened? That she and Natalie had been having a friendly chat while Rob stood there choking? Maybe that Sunshine was persuading Natalie, mid-Heimlich manoeuvre, to sing at the wedding reception against Leo's express wishes?

At this point Sunshine would prefer to hire *herself* to warble a few off-key songs!

She was almost glad when Natalie, squealing again, rushed towards Leo and threw herself into his arms. Leo, looking frazzled, backed into the kitchen, pulling Natalie with him.

Frazzle away, you idiot, Sunshine said in her head, and quickly returned to Iain.

'You're amazing,' he said, standing to pull out her chair.

'Anyone could have done it,' she said dismissively. 'I'm just glad I didn't break any of his ribs—that's the main danger. And I don't want to sit, Iain. I want to go home. I have another high drama to get through tonight: a video call with Jon.'

'Why high drama?'

Sunshine sighed. 'You're not the only one worried about the zombies.'

'Jon, you're wrong.'

Those were the first words Sunshine had managed to edge into the conversation since her initial 'Hello' three minutes earlier.

Not that 'conversation' described the incendiary soliloquy Jon had been delivering, which covered her unsatisfactory outlook on life, her ill-preparedness to deal with a man of Leo's darkness, a disjointed reminder to ensure she was taking precautions—which caused her a momentary pang of guilt about the unprecedented lack of a condom last night, although she *was* on the pill and that had to count for something—and the general benefits of not actively courting disaster.

'No, Sunshine, I'm not wrong,' Jon said, and seemed ready to relaunch.

Sunshine headed him off by jamming her fingers in her ears. She raised her eyebrows, waiting. And at last he smiled.

She removed her fingers from her ears. 'This is not worth so much anxiety, Jonathan.'

'I'm worried about you, Sunny. About the way you've been living—no, only half living—since...'

She held her breath. Watched as Jonathan hesitated...

'Ever since Moon, Sunny,' he continued, but more gently. 'This four-times-only thing. The blocking yourself off from anything more. It's not *you*!'

'Yes, it is.'

'It's not.' Sigh. 'I know I'm wasting my breath.' Another sigh. 'Well, you will not be able to dictate terms to Leo

Quartermaine. Look, Leo is going to be my brother-in-law, and you're like a sister to me. I need you two to like each other. Calmly, rationally, *like* each other.'

'I'm always friends with the men I've slept with.'

'He is not like the others.'

She rolled her eyes. The zombie camp! 'There aren't that many of them, you know!'

'I know Sunshine—you talk a good game, but you don't fool me. You never have. Sleeping with a guy is the exception, not the rule. But, whether it's two or ten or a hundred guys, Leo is not like them and he will not be your friend at the end. There are other men in Sydney, and a ridiculous number of them seem happy to have you lead them around by their sex organs. Why did you have to pick Leo?'

'It kind of— He kind of— Look, the situation picked itself. That's all.'

'You mean you had no control over it? Neither of you?'

Sunshine thought back to last night. The way 'no-touch' Leo had gathered her in when she'd given him that one hug. How she'd melted just from the feel of his fingers in her hair. The way the kiss had spiralled...

'Apparently not, Jonathan.'

'This is bad, Sunny.'

'I promise not to let it interfere with the wedding.'

'You can't promise that. There are two of you.'

'I'm not going to start asking your permission before sleeping with someone,' she said, exasperated.

Pause. Silence. Jon looked morose.

'Jon?'

More silence.

'Jon—where does that leave us?'

'It leaves us, very unsatisfactorily, at loggerheads,' he said. 'And while we're there I'm going to raise the other subject you hate. Where are Moonbeam's ashes, Sunshine?'

Sunshine stiffened. 'They are in the urn, here in my office, where they've always been. Want to see them?'

'Don't be flippant. Not about this. She'd hate it, Sunny. You know she would. When are you going to do it?'

Sunshine managed a, 'Soon.' But it wasn't easy getting the word out of a suddenly clogged throat.

'You've been saying that for two years.'

'Soon,' she repeated. 'But now I have to go. I have to finish the new handbag designs.'

'I'll keep asking.'

'I will do it. Just…not yet.'

'I love you, Sunny,' Jon said, looking so sad it tore at Sunshine's heart. 'But this isn't fair. Not on Moon. Not on your parents. Not on you. You've got to let yourself get over her death.'

'I…can't. I can't, Jon.'

'You have to.' Another sigh. 'We'll speak soon.'

Sunshine signed off.

Work. She would work for a while.

But half an hour later she was still sitting there, staring at the urn that held Moonbeam's ashes. The urn was centred very precisely on top of the bureau Sunshine had painted in her sister's favourite colour—'cobalt dazzle', Moon had called it.

Sunny tapped at the computer, found her list of Moonbeam's favourite beaches. The options she'd chosen for scattering the ashes.

But not one of the options felt right. Not one!

She put her head on the desk and cried.

When Leo left the restaurant, a little after midnight, he intended to ride home, throw down a large brandy, think about life, and go to sleep.

What a night. Sunshine. Natalie. And the Heimlich manoeuvre.

The bloody Heimlich manoeuvre.

Just when he needed so badly to think of Sunshine as frippery and irresponsible she had to go and save someone's life—and then look surprised when people applauded her for it. The difference between Sunshine's calm, embarrassed heroism and Natalie's ineffectual hysterics had been an eye-opener of epic proportions.

And it had come after the Moonbeam story, which had already had his heart lurching around in his chest like a drunk.

So he needed home. Brandy. Thinking time. Bed.

He wasn't sure, then, why he left his motorbike where it was and walked to Sunshine's apartment block.

She would be asleep, he told himself as he reached the glass doors of the entrance. But his finger was on the apartment's intercom anyway.

'Hello?'

Her voice was not sleepy. And he remembered, then, that she worked mostly at night.

'It's Leo.'

Pause. Then buzz, click, open.

She was waiting at her door. Barefoot. In a kimono. Seriously, did this woman not own a pair of jeans or some track pants? Who slummed around alone in their own home after midnight looking like an advertisement for *Vogue* magazine in a purple kimono complete with a bloody *obi*?

Her hair was loose, her face pale, her eyes strained.

He was going to thank her for saving Rob's life.

He was going to ask her why she knew how to do the Heimlich manoeuvre.

He was going to tell her that he'd found out exactly what had happened and that he was an idiot for thinking, when he'd seen her near Natalie, that—

She cleared her throat. 'I didn't talk to Natalie except to tell her to move out of the way.'

'I don't care about Natalie,' he said—and realised that he really, *really* didn't.

'Then why are you here?'

'I'm claiming assignation number two,' he said, and kissed her.

CHAPTER SIX

SUNSHINE DREW HIM backwards into the apartment. Kiss unbroken.

Leo slammed the door with his heel. Kiss unbroken.

Sex—just sex, Sunshine said to herself.

Leo pulled back as though she'd voiced the thought, looking at her with eyes smouldering like a hungry lion's.

Sunshine grabbed his hand and dragged him to the bedroom. Kissed him again as she flipped the light switch and the fairy's lair lights she'd had embedded in the ceiling winked to life.

He angled her so he could kiss her harder, *harder*. He started to shake—she could feel it—and he broke the kiss, his breathing ragged. He rested his cheek on the top of her head as he held her in his arms, his freight train heartbeat beneath her ear.

She heard him laugh softly and pulled back, watching as he took in the room.

It was pink. Every shade of pink from pale petal, to vibrant sari, to raspberry. The walls were the colour of cherry blossoms, stencilled in white in a riot of floral shapes and curlicues—like an extended henna tattoo. There was a chaise-longue, footstools, a window seat curtained off with diaphanous drapes. At one end of the room was a half-wall that divided the bedroom from the dressing room, with its orderly arrangement of garments, shoes, and bags, which in turn led through to her bathroom.

A scene was painted on the dividing wall: a woman donning a flowing deep rose robe. Sunshine had made it a 3D work of art, building an actual Louis XIV gilded dressing table and mirror into the scene.

There was *a lot* to look at.

Leo moved towards the bed, which was king-sized, shrouded by fuchsia hangings and piled high with cushions in macaroon pastels. He touched the gauzy curtains.

'Seriously, Sunshine?' he asked, a smile in his voice.

Sunshine arched an eyebrow. 'If you want to get laid tonight, I suggest you keep a civil tongue in your head.'

'That's not where my tongue wants to be.'

Those words made her toes curl.

'Come here, let me undress you, and we'll find some place to put it,' Leo said softly.

Sunshine walked over to him, her heart jumping.

His hands reached for the *obi*.

'Wait,' she said. 'I need to warn you—I'm...scarred.'

He waited, hands at her waist.

'The accident. I have a...a scar. Two, actually. Not... small.' She hunched a shoulder, suddenly self-conscious. 'I don't want you to be shocked.'

His response was to slowly, slowly unwrap the *obi* from around her waist, then the under-sash. The kimono fell open and Leo sucked in an audible breath.

'My God,' he said, in a voice just above a raspy whisper.

'I know—they're awful.'

Leo's fingers reached, traced along the incision marks. He shook his head. 'The *My God* wasn't about the scars, Sunshine.'

Sunshine was having trouble catching a thought, her breath. 'Then...what?'

'*My God*, you are so beautiful. And *my God*, I am itching to put my hands all over you.'

'Then do it,' she whispered. 'I have no intention of stopping you.'

His fingers tensed against her flesh. And then, with both hands, he reached for her shoulders, sliding his hands under the kimono, pushing it back until the heavy fabric dropped with a quiet whoosh to the floor. He stood gazing at her.

Sunshine kept absolutely still, watching him as his nostrils flared, his hands fisted at his sides. It was both torture and delight to stand motionless as lust shimmered between them. Leo was still fully clothed, and that somehow made her feel more wanton, sexier. Her nipples were hardened points; she could feel them throbbing. Could feel a swelling between her legs as his gaze moved over her. Down, up, down. The suspense was almost unbearable. And yet she wanted the delay. Wanted to draw things out. Slow everything down so that she could wallow in this overwhelming need caused by nothing more than his eyes on her.

Then both his hands moved. With the tips of his trembling fingers he touched the centre of her forehead. Slowly his fingers moved to the bridge of her nose, across her eyebrows, down her cheeks to her mouth, her jaw, neck, collarbones. When he got to her breasts he paused at her nipples to circle and pinch. Her knees almost buckled. But inexorably his hands moved again, fingers sliding across the long, straight scar that ran over her ribs, down to her hips, across her belly, then to the juncture of her thighs.

He stopped there. Looked intently at her bare mound, licked his lips. 'Very, very pretty,' he said.

Both hands slid between her legs, fingers playing there while her breathing quickened.

'I think we've found a place for my tongue,' he said,

suddenly finding that one excruciatingly sensitive nub, focusing there.

'Are you going to take off your clothes?' Sunshine asked breathily as his fingers continued to tease her.

'Yes. But first...'

His fingers shifted, exploring her, dipping and sliding and slipping, but always returning to that one tiny place. Sunshine gasped again. Her legs were trembling as he continued to work her, pinching, stroking, rolling, lunging into her.

'Ah, Leo— God!' Sunshine cried out, and came suddenly, with a long groan.

Her head dropped back as his fingers continued to caress her, soothing now, and then one hand cupped her possessively, stilled.

Easing away from her, he started removing his clothes with short, efficient movements. The leather jacket was shrugged off and dropped to the floor. Sweater and then T-shirt were ripped over his head. Boots were yanked off. Jeans shoved down, kicked aside.

Good Lord. He was...divine. Not a steroid-pumped muscle in his whole body. Just perfectly defined, hard, lean lines of strength. Broad shoulders. Beautifully crafted biceps. Smooth, hairless, sculpted torso with that wonderful V leading to his groin. Narrow hips. Long legs. And the jut of him, big and hard, rising from that gorgeous dark blond nest, was mouth-watering. She wanted her mouth there. And her hands. And the inside of her.

'Come here,' he said. 'I want to feel you all over me.'

Sunshine thought she might swoon, just hearing the words—except that she was desperate to take him up on that offer. She *wanted* to be all over him.

She walked into his open arms and they closed around her. The top of her head didn't even reach his chin, and the feeling of being cocooned, surrounded by him, was glorious.

'You feel good there.'

'I feel *very* good,' she said throatily, and he laughed. 'And so do you,' she added as his erection nudged her belly. 'We can get that part of you a little closer, I think.'

'No rush tonight,' he said. 'If we only have three assignations left I'm going to make them count. So...now I'd like to see you spread out on that Taj Mahal bed.'

He edged her backwards, reaching out to push the hangings aside, following her down onto the bed, kissing her as he lay on top of her.

For one fraught moment he slid between her thighs, held still, teasing both of them with the promise of the length of him as it pulsed there against her wet opening. He buried his face against her neck and sucked in a breath, another, one more.

'God, it's hard to wait,' he groaned against her hair.

'Then don't,' Sunshine said, shifting to try and get him to slip inside.

He withdrew. 'I want to play with you for a while first. And this time we won't forget the condom.'

With great concentration he arranged Sunshine on the bed against the cushions, raising her arms above her head so that her breasts were tightened and jutting, the chain she always wore caught between them.

He kissed her eyelids closed and then put his mouth at the corner of hers, his tongue flicking out to taste. She gasped, and his tongue slid smoothly inside her mouth, swirled once, then retreated to lick at the corner again. He kissed down her chin, her throat, then...nothing.

She opened her eyes to find him sitting back on his heels, looking at her. 'What's wrong?' she asked.

'Nothing,' he said. 'I just like looking at you. I don't think I've ever seen skin as pale as yours. And these...' His hands reached out, hovered over her breasts. 'I'm almost scared to touch in case I come in three seconds.'

'I want you to come.'

'No—don't move your arms,' Leo ordered, and his hands settled on her breasts, squeezed gently, massaged. 'God. God, God, God...' he said, and it really did sound like a prayer.

He lowered his head and closed his lips over one nipple, sucked it sharply so that she moaned.

He stopped instantly. 'Sorry—but you're driving me crazy. Did I hurt you?'

'No,' she said, her legs moving restlessly. 'I just want you so much. *So much,*' she wailed as his mouth sucked hard again.

He commenced a steady rhythm, tugging, tonguing, pulling back to lick.

When he shifted to the other breast she couldn't help herself—her arms came down to circle him, to pull him closer, closer.

'Come inside me,' she whispered. 'Please, Leo.'

He shook his head and started moving lower. He stopped again as his mouth touched the scar. He pulled back to see it, then touched it gently with his fingers, running them over the length of it, then across the dissecting scar that ran perpendicular to it, across her ribs towards her back.

Sunshine held her breath, waiting for...what? She didn't know. Didn't want to believe that it mattered, what he thought of her imperfections. All that mattered—all that *could* matter—was the promise of the orgasm flickering low in her belly.

And yet she didn't release her breath until he moved again, kissing his way to her mound. He stopped again. Shuddered out a breath against her. Then he was kissing her there, over and over again.

'Beautiful. Delicious,' he murmured in between licking kisses, his tongue dipping just low enough to make her squirm. 'Open wider for me.'

She shifted her legs, hips rising off the bed, soundlessly urging him to shift, to slide that clever mouth right between her spread legs. When, finally, he did, using the very tip of his tongue to separate the lips of her sex, breathing deeply as he slid the flat of his tongue along the seam, she screamed his name and climaxed almost violently.

He kept his mouth there, his tongue on that fizzing knot of nerves, until the waves receded.

And then, with a groan, he slid back up her body and thrust inside her. 'Ah, thank you, God,' he groaned, and any semblance of control snapped.

He pounded into her, teeth gritted, gripping her hips as though his life depended on leveraging himself off them so he could go harder, deeper.

Sunshine could feel his orgasm building and tightened her inner muscles, holding, wanting… 'Come, come,' she said, and then the explosion ripped through him.

Long moments later he rolled onto his back, bringing Sunshine with him so that she was lying on top, her thighs falling either side of him. 'Forgot the condom again,' he said.

Sunshine frowned. 'I've never forgotten before.'

'Do we need to talk about it?'

'Only if you have a disease.'

'Then we don't need to talk.' He secured her more tightly against his chest. One hand was in her hair, smoothing through the strands.

Silence. Minutes dragged on.

Then, 'The Heimlich thing… Why?' he asked.

She shrugged, self-conscious. 'I saw a story on the internet about a woman who choked to death. If someone had known what to do she wouldn't have died. So I…I learned.

Just in case. Typical that the first time I had to use it was on Natalie's boyfriend!'

'He's not her boyfriend. He's her bitch.'

'Ouch.'

'I wish I could say that was me being malicious, but it's just the truth.'

'I certainly don't understand what you saw in her.'

'Me neither. I guess we get what we deserve.'

She looked up at him, perplexed. 'Why would you think you deserved her? Deserved...*that*?'

Leo shook his head, shrugged, clearly uncomfortable. 'Just history. Perpetuating the crappiness of my life. Because she wasn't my first mistake—just the most persistent.'

Mistake. Something about the word made Sunshine shiver. Mistake...

'You're cold,' Leo said. 'And I have a brilliant idea—let's actually get *in* the bed.'

Sunshine latched onto being cold as a viable excuse for the sudden chill prickling along her skin. She slid under the covers, busied herself positioning cushions so that she was propped up against the bedhead, half turned to him.

She toyed with her chain, rubbing the sun and moon charms between her fingers.

'Sun and moon,' Leo said, watching her. 'For Sunshine and Moonbeam?'

'Yes. The business is called Sun & Moon too. Not sure what we were going to do when we changed our names.'

'You were going to change your names? Don't tell me: Sue and Jenny?'

'Do I look like a Sue?'

'Actually, you look like a Sunshine.'

'Harsh! Well, Moonbeam was definitely *not* a Jenny! She was going to be Amaya—it means Night Rain. She figured it was a close enough association with the night, if not with the moon specifically.'

'Nice. And yours?'

'Allyn. Do I look like an Allyn?'

'I told you—you look like a Sunshine.'

'Oh, dear. Daunting. Well, Moon said Allyn meant Bright and Shining One. Close enough to sunshine, in her opinion. And she said it suited me.' She frowned, thinking. 'I've thought a lot over the past two years about making the change. Wondered if doing the thing we planned to do together on my own would help me accept...move on. My parents aren't so sure.'

'Tell me about them,' Leo said.

'My parents? Oh, they're very zen! Quite mad. And completely wonderful. Always there. Supportive, but never smothering. They let Moon and me leave the commune when we were fifteen, so we could see a different way and make informed decisions about how we wanted to live. They made sure we had a safe place to stay, a good school to go to, money for whatever we needed, while we worked it out. And they seemed to understand even before we did that Moon was the true hippie and I was... well, something in between a hippie and an urbanite. Moon would have raced straight back to the commune if not for me being anchored in the city.' She smiled, remembering. 'We started our business with money our father inherited but didn't need. It was given to us simply, with love, on our eighteenth birthday.'

'Lucky.'

'Yes. But it's not all sparkles and roses, you know. There's the haiku to deal with!'

'Ah, the haiku. What is it?'

'You'll find out—that poem is coming.'

'Can't wait.'

'You have no idea!'

'But…they were okay with you girls changing your names?'

'They weren't insulted, if that's what you mean. They were fine with it if we wanted to do it.' She bit her lip. 'But Dad had a sidebar conversation with me because he thought Moonbeam was browbeating me.'

'And was she?'

'Not browbeating—nothing that brutish. She was… *persuading*!' Sunshine said, and smiled, remembering. 'But I was happy enough to be persuaded if she wanted it that badly. And I owed her, for staying.'

Sunshine closed her eyes, picturing her sister.

'Tell me more about Moonbeam,' Leo said.

Opening her eyes on a sigh, Sunshine adjusted her position in the bed. 'Well, you know what she looked like—me! But slimmer. And with the most beautiful green eyes— both of them. Other than looks, though, we were completely different. I was the carnivore; she was vegetarian. I was…well, as you see me. Friendly, touchy-feely, chirpy.'

'And…?'

Sunshine fiddled with her necklace. 'Moon was… intriguing. I was *Mary Poppins*; she was *Crouching Tiger, Hidden Dragon*. When the kids made fun of my devil eyes I would laugh it off, but she would go all superhero.' She laughed suddenly. '*Is* there a hippie superhero? What a wonderful idea. I'm going to do a web search on that.'

'So she was your protector?'

'Oh, yes. And my cheer squad. And my…everything. She was smart, and had an amazing flair for numbers, so although the business was my idea she was the CEO. And she didn't even want to be in the city!'

Sunshine adjusted the quilt. Fussed with a cushion.

'She said that left me to concentrate on the creative stuff because she was not into fashion like I was. She would wear a suit for business if I chose it for her; otherwise she would drag on whatever clothes and shoes came to hand. I, on the other hand, was obsessed with colour and shape and style.' She shrugged, a little sheepish. 'And I really love shoes!'

'Funny, I hadn't noticed that.'

She hit him with the cushion. 'Don't make me take you behind that wall and show you my shoe collection. I haven't known a man yet who could cope with the sight.'

'Are you *really* going there? Talking about the men you've had in here? I'll go there if you want, Sunshine, but I don't think you'll like it.'

She opened her eyes at him. 'Oh, that sounds very alpha male.'

He didn't smile. 'You'll see alpha, beta, gamma, *and* zeta male if you go near another man, Sunshine.'

'Oh, alpha, beta, *and* zeta?'

'Alpha-beta-*gamma*-zeta. And don't roll your eyes.'

'Sorry.'

'I said don't roll your eyes.'

'All *right*!' Sunshine said, laughing.

'So, I think,' Leo said quietly, after a long moment, 'we're up to the bike, aren't we?'

Sunshine nodded, sat a little straighter. 'The bike,' she said. She pulled a different cushion onto her lap and started playing with the fringe. 'She bought it because she liked the wind in her face and the freedom of riding. It was too big for her, but she wouldn't be told.'

She stopped there.

'And...?' he prompted.

Sunshine reached for the charms. 'We were at a party. Her boyfriend *du jour*—Jeff—mixed us up and tried to kiss me. Moonbeam went into melodrama mode and stormed off, dragging me with her.'

'Was she angry with you?'

'God, no! She knew I would never poach. And truthfully…? She wasn't even angry with Jeff. She was just restless. Bored with being in the city. And tired of Jeff. So what he did gave her an excuse to dump him. She thought…she thought he'd done it accidentally-on-purpose because he actually preferred me. We were dressed so differently, you see, it couldn't have been a mix-up.'

'Did that happen often? A boyfriend switching sides?'

'No. Never before.'

'And so…?'

'And so we clambered onto the bike.' She shivered. 'She was wild that night, riding too fast. She took a turn badly, and…well. Moonbeam died instantly. Her neck snapped at the base of the helmet.' She swallowed. 'I got carted off to hospital, where I went through twenty-eight pints of blood.' She moved restlessly. 'Internal bleeding. They had to take my spleen—which apparently you don't really need, so go figure! And they took half my liver, which was haemorrhaging. Actually, did you know that the liver regenerates? Which means the chunk of my liver they cut out has probably grown back. Amazing!'

'I'm sorry, Sunshine,' Leo said.

She rearranged herself in the bed again—flustery, unnecessary activity. 'Which brings us to the important part of this discussion. Getting rid of your motorbike.'

Leo said nothing.

'Leo? You understand, don't you?'

He nodded slowly. 'I understand why you hate motorbikes—because you blame yourself for the accident. You feel guilty because you couldn't talk your sister out of that bike. Because she stayed in the city only for you, where she was an unhappy fish out of water. Because of what her boyfriend did. The way all those things led to both of you being on the bike at that precise moment at that speed. Because she died and you didn't. And you're here and she's not.'

Sunshine brushed away a tear. 'That's about the sum of it. I just miss her so much. And I'd do anything to have her back.' She looked at him. 'But you can't bring someone back from the dead. So *please* get rid of it, Leo. Please?'

'You don't understand what that bike means to me.' He grimaced. 'My parents...they were druggies, and they didn't give a damn. Your parents made sure you had support. I was my own support—and Caleb's. Your parents made sure you had money, but when I was still a child I had to steal it, beg it, or make it—and I did all three! There was never food on the table unless I put it there. So I haunted restaurants around the city, pleading for leftovers. Eventually one of the chefs took pity on me and I got a job in a kitchen, and...' Shrug. 'Here I am.'

Sunshine touched his hand.

He looked at where her hand was, on his, with an odd expression on his face. And then he drew his hand away.

'I'm not telling you all that to get sympathy, just to explain,' he said. 'And it could have been a lot worse. We weren't sexually abused. Or beaten—well, not Caleb. And me not often, or more than I could take. Mainly we were just not important. Like a giant mistake that you can't fix so you try to forget it. I grew up fast and hard—I had to. The upshot is that I don't do frivolity. I'm not sociable unless there's something in it for me. I don't stop to smell the roses and hug the trees. I just push on, without indulging myself. Except for my bike.'

'I see,' Sunshine said. And she did. It was so very simple. Leo had his bike the way she had Moon's ashes. Something that connected you to what you'd lost—what you couldn't have: in her case her sister; in his a carefree youth.

She swallowed around a sudden lump. 'We're not going to find common ground on this, are we? Because you deserve one piece of youthful folly and I can't bear what that piece happens to be.'

She got out of bed, grabbed her kimono off the floor, quickly pulled it on, and turned to face him. 'This means, of course, that we'll have to call it quits at two.'

'At two…what? O'clock?'

'Two *times*—as in not *four*. As in assignations.'

'Why?'

Why? She had a sudden memory of that electri-fried bat. 'Because the thought of you on that bike already upsets me too much. That's going to get harder, not easier, to cope with if we keep doing…*this*.'

'This?'

'Sex,' she said impatiently. 'It's my fault for starting it, and I'll cop to that. I threw myself at you when you didn't want to go there. The blame is squarely here, with me.'

'If we're talking blame, I threw myself at you tonight.'

Sunshine dragged the edges of the kimono closed and started looking around for her sash. 'Well, let's *un*throw ourselves.'

'Come back to bed, Sunshine, and we'll talk about it.'

'Bed is the wrong place to talk.'

'Four assignations was what we agreed on,' Leo said.

'*Up to!* They're the salient words. *Up to* four. I've never got to four before. I've never got past two! And you can see why. It gets too emotional.'

Leo shoved the quilt aside, got out of bed. 'I'll do you a deal on the motorbike,' he offered, and started tugging on his clothes.

'What kind of deal?'

Wary. *Very* wary.

'I'll get rid of the bike the day after our fourth assignation. Or when you change your name to Allyn. Whichever comes first.'

She licked her lips nervously. 'That's an odd deal.'

'Is it? I'm offering to give up a piece of a past I never really had—the bike. In return, you give up something you can't accept is past its use-by date—your sister's two-year hold over you.'

'She doesn't have a hold over me.'

'If she didn't have a hold over you the four times thing wouldn't exist. So—my bike for going where no man has gone before and risking the magic number four.'

'No.'

'Then take the alternative option and change your name. You said it might be a way of moving on, so do it. Move on, Sunshine, one way or the other.'

'I...I don't know,' she said, agonised.

'Take some time and think about it,' he said. 'But not too long. Because—in case you haven't quite figured me out yet—I don't wait for what I want. I just go out and get it. Even if I have to steal it.'

'You don't really want me.'

'I'm like an immortal lobster—who really knows? Let's get to number four and see.'

'Well, you can't *steal me*.'

'Don't bet on it, sweetheart. I've spent my life getting my own way. And I can take things from you that you never knew you had.'

She located her *obi* and whipped it up off the floor. 'That's not even worth a response.'

Leo just smiled and started pulling on his boots.

She tried, twice, to tie the sash, but her fingers were clumsy.

And Leo's hands were suddenly there—capable, efficient, tying it easily.

'Thank you,' she said stiffly when he had finished, and flicked her hair over her shoulders. 'I'll see you out.'

She walked Leo to the apartment door. 'So!' she said. 'I'll email you about...about the clothes for the wedding and a few other things. And then... Well...'

'And then...well...?' Leo repeated, looking a little too

wolfish and a lot too jaunty for a man who was waiting for an answer about sex that could, should—no, *would*!— go against him. And then he leant down and kissed her quickly on the mouth.

She jumped back as though he'd scalded her.

'It's just a *stolen* kiss, Sunshine,' he murmured. 'Think of the calories.'

Sunshine stared into the darkness long after returning to bed.

Leo would give up his motorbike.

Into her head popped an image of Moonbeam— laughing as they left the party that night. Giving a wild shout as she started the bike. Zooming off with Sunshine on the back, gripping her tightly.

And then darkness. And that feeling. Waking up in hospital and knowing, without needing to be told, that Moonbeam was gone. She never wanted to experience that desolating ache again.

Leo didn't understand what it would do to her if something happened to him. And that said it all, didn't it? She'd only known him for one week, and already she was terrified that something would happen to him.

What a conundrum. She could get him to give up his bike if she slept with him twice more. But if she slept with him twice more she would be getting dangerously close to him. And she couldn't risk that.

Or...

She could get him to give up his bike if she changed her name. And she just wasn't sure what that would mean. Maybe it would help her accept Moon's death. But maybe it would be a betrayal—taking a twins' decision and making it a solo decision. Moving on when Moon couldn't.

And did anything matter more than keeping Leo safe?

Sunshine threw off the covers—what a restless night

this was turning out to be!—and yanked on her kimono, leaving it fluttering as she raced from the room and into her office.

There, on the high-gloss blue bureau, was her sister. Her sister, who had wanted her ashes to be scattered at a beach under a full moon.

Instead here she was. Beautifully housed in a stunning antique cloisonné urn featuring all the colours of the rainbow.

But an urn—no matter how beautiful—wasn't the ocean.

And the ocean was where Moonbeam belonged.

Leo stared into the darkness, thinking about the simple pleasure of touch.

It didn't take a psychologist to work out what his issue was—the fact that his parents had never touched him the way other parents touched their children. Because there had been more important things to do than give their son the affection he craved. Like shoot up. Suck in the crack. Snort up the meth.

It had been different for Caleb, because Leo had made it so. Leo had looked after Caleb, put his needs first, fought his battles, protected him. And so Caleb wasn't reserved, wary, driven, and damaged—like Leo. Caleb attracted affection and gentleness and love. Leo attracted people like Natalie, for whom his remoteness was a challenge and his celebrity something to use.

'You're choosing wrong,' Sunshine had said—but what if he was choosing *right* and he was getting exactly what he deserved?

It wasn't as if he could choose Sunshine Smart as an alternative. She didn't *want* to be chosen by anyone.

So why he was offering to give up his motorbike for her was a mystery.

So what if he never had sex with her again?

So what if she went on grieving for her sister for the rest of the life?

Leo punched his pillow. Forced his eyes closed.

And there she was, warning him about her scars. So beautiful. And damaged, like him. But wanting to *stay* damaged—*unlike* him.

His eyes popped open and he punched the pillow again.

God, but she irked him.

Her perkiness irked him. Partly because he wanted to think that it made her shallow…and yet she'd learned the Heimlich manoeuvre and wasn't afraid to use it.

The way she chucked crazy facts into her arguments—about the sexual habits of praying mantises, the questionable immortality of lobsters, regenerating livers, and so on and on and on—irked him. Because most of the time that stuff was fascinating. And even if it wasn't, it was fascinating to watch those unique eyes glow with the wonder of it.

Her boring living room irked him, because it shouldn't be like that. Not that her décor was any of his business. And the fact that he could be bothered to think of her apartment irking him irked him too.

Her pink bedroom irked him. All right, it didn't—because it was kind of amazing. But it *should* irk him, and the fact that it *didn't* irk him irked him.

Her propensity to kiss and touch and pet him irked him. And it had irked him even more when she hadn't kissed him hello at the restaurant.

Her four-times maximum irked him. And the fact that he'd refused to accept that they were stopping at two irked him.

Two times. *Two.* Not three, not four—two! Her terms. Everything on her terms, right from the moment she'd ambushed him on the couch.

Well, he'd picked her as a wily little dictator from Day One. But she was *not* going to dictate to Leo Quartermaine. He would have her as many damned times as he *wanted* to have her.

He punched his pillow again. Hard.

CHAPTER SEVEN

TO: Leo Quartermaine
FROM: Sunshine Smart
SUBJECT: Wedding update
Hi Leo

I'm attaching a photo of my dress. If you can send me one of your suit and tie—I'm assuming a tie?—I'll know if this is okay or if I have to go back to the drawing board. And I can get your shoe design finished too.

So, the shoes. You'll need three fittings—twenty mins each time—and you can schedule these to suit yourself as I won't be needed. I'm attaching Seb's business card— Seb is the shoemaker—and once you've approved my design all you need to do is call him.

And, trust me, once you've had custom-made shoes you'll never go back. Which might not be good, now I think of it, because they're hellishly expensive (not these particular shoes, of course, because it's a special deal for me, as well as being a present).

The other attachment is of some floral arrangements for the restaurant. I think the all-white ones, so as not to distract from the view. What do you think?

I'm going to scoot down the coast on Sunday to check out some hotel options for guests who want to stay overnight. I know you're super-busy so I can handle this and email all the info to you.

And then we need to confirm the music—Kate is amazing—when you have a minute.

Hope all is well.

Sunshine

OH, NO, SUNSHINE Smart-Ass, you are not going down the coast without me.

That was the first thought to leap to Leo's mind after he read the email.

The second was that she had a bloody nerve adding the 'Hope all is well', because she had to know all was *not* well. Not by a country *mile* was all 'well'. 'All' wouldn't be 'well' until he had her exactly where he wanted her.

A sudden image of her naked, in his arms, had him erect and almost groaning. Even though that was not what he'd meant. What he'd meant was on her knees and—

Argh. Another image.

Figuratively speaking on her knees, not physically.

But—nope, the image wouldn't budge.

He took a steadying breath and forced himself to open Sunshine's attachment, hoping it wouldn't be her *in* the damned dress—which, of course, it was. Looking very hot. And, of course, she had her foot stuck out so he could see her amazingly sexy shoes.

And, since he knew he had to see her in the flesh in that dress, he would up the ante on his suit so that he matched the formality—*and* send her the damned photo so he could get his shoe design.

And he would tell her that he would most definitely meet her at South on Sunday, when they would discuss flowers and confirm music and go and see the hotels *together*.

Ha!

Hope all is well.

Bloody, *bloody* nerve.

* * *

Sunshine, who had laboured long and hard over the wording of her email to Leo to give it just the right sense of moving-on friendliness, opened Leo's reply with some trepidation.

She wasn't sure what to expect—but the three terse lines certainly hadn't been laboured over.

Meet you at South at two p.m. Sunday. Will confirm everything then. Suit pic attached.

So! She guessed she'd better start working on getting rid of the horrible fluttery feeling in her stomach before Sunday. *Surely* she could be her normal carefree self in four days!

Cautiously she opened the attachment he'd sent.

And—oh—flutter, flutter, flutter. And he wasn't even *in* the photo!

The suit, photographed on a dummy so she got the full effect, was in a beautiful mid-grey. Three pieces, including a waistcoat, which she adored. The pants were narrow and cuffed. The two-button jacket was ultra-contemporary, but also sexily conservative. A white shirt, a tie in a fine black, silver and white check, and a purple and silver pocket square shoved insouciantly into the left breast pocket.

That suit, his physique, his dourly handsome face, his hair... He would have all the female guests drooling over him.

Maybe she shouldn't have made him grow his hair... *And where did* that *unworthy thought come from? If three centimetres of hair snares him a new bed partner—good!*

Well, every woman might be drooling, but only one woman could design his shoes. All right, that sounded incredibly lame. But so what?

She was going to do the design right now. And give it

to him on Sunday. And he was going to love—not like, but *love*—his shoes, dammit!

The motorbike was in pole position when Sunshine pulled up outside South. He couldn't have made it more visible if he'd had it on a dais under a spotlight.

She knew right then that he would be yanking her chain all day. *Stealing* her sanity!

Her stomach, which had finally started to settle into a relatively stable buzz, started rioting again. She sat in her car, taking some deep breaths and giving herself a stern talking-to: he was not a teenage hothead and he would *not* kill himself; she didn't care if he *did* kill himself; *she'd* kill him if he didn't get rid of the bike. And so on.

Not the most intelligent conversation she'd ever had with herself. And completely ineffectual, because her stomach was still going crazy.

If *only* she'd had the nous to call it quits with Leo after the first time she might still be a properly functioning adult.

Well, spilt milk and all that. She would just have to find a way back to normality before it affected the wedding preparations. Because the wedding was what was important. Not her, not Leo—the wedding!

She straightened her shoulders, flung open the door, and scrambled out of the car. She would have liked to have *disembarked* from the car, in case Leo was watching, but she was wearing her most complicated shoes and a too-tight dress! Compensating, she practically glided to the boot and, with what she considered great panache, swung her portfolio out. She left the briefcase behind, though—it was hard to look cucumber-cool when you were carrying a briefcase *and* a portfolio. Not that it usually bothered her, but... Well, *but*!

She took another deep breath as she entered the restaurant and saw Leo.

His hair was at Number Three buzz-cut stage. His jeans were black. He was wearing a fitted black superfine wool sweater. Sex on a stick. Even the black biker boots didn't have the power to dampen the desire that hit her like a punch.

He walked towards her—a purposeful kind of prowl that made her tongue want to loll. *Not* that there would be any tongue-lolling going on today.

She went to give him a reflex kiss on the cheek, but pulled back as it hit her that this was now fraught with difficulty.

His slow smile told her he'd registered her state of confusion. And then, to her shock, he leant down and kissed *her*. Sweet, slow, warm brush of lips against her cheek.

'Oh,' she said inanely.

He simply raised his eyebrows. And she knew what he was doing. He was playing the *Dare You* game! *Dare you to question that*. Well, she would *not* be dared.

He gestured to the dining area. 'As you can see, the tables and chairs are in,' he said. 'We're basically ready. I'm doing a trial dinner in two weeks, then we'll have a month to tweak. It will be a full moon on the trial night, so the view should be amazing. I'm inviting mostly locals, and some food and lifestyle media, but because it's a rehearsal for the wedding you'll have to come—obviously.'

Dare you! Dare you not to come.

Oh, how she wanted to say she couldn't make it. But that would be a mammoth case of cutting off her nose to spite her face, which he knew very well.

So, 'Of course,' she said.

He nodded at the portfolio in her hand. 'What's that?'

'Your shoe design.'

'Let's have a look,' Leo said.

Ordinarily, Sunshine would have gone a little theatrical, starting with a narrative and then positioning the designs on an easel. But today she merely pulled out the sheets and thrust them at Leo.

She watched, trying not to care, as he flicked through them.

She saw the shock come over his face and wished she could snatch the drawings out of his hands and rip them up.

Leo took them further into the restaurant and laid the pages on a window table, where light streamed brightly through.

He darted a looked up at her. 'Not what I was expecting,' he said.

'What *were* you expecting?'

Small pause. Quick smile. 'What's the shoe equivalent of a pine bookshelf?'

Huh? 'I guess…black leather lace-ups…?'

'Bingo.'

'Not that there's anything wrong with black leather lace-ups.'

'And yet…?'

Sunshine shrugged. 'And…yet.'

Okay. Leo admitted it. He wanted the damned shoes.

The design was sharp, lean, streamlined. No decorative stitching. Toes that were subtly rounded but also somehow pointed. No laces—monkstraps, fastened with sleek silver side buckles.

Plain and yet edgy.

And the colour was astounding. They looked black, but there was a suggestion…a sheen…of purple.

He cleared his throat. 'Thanks.'

'Do you…do you think you'll wear them?'

'Can you really get that colour? And those buckles?'

'I have the black-violet leather reserved. And I've already ordered the buckles—they're real silver.'

Black-violet. Perfect. 'Then, yes, I'll wear them, Sunshine.'

She smiled, her eyes glowing with joy, and he felt his heart start that heavy thump he'd hoped wouldn't happen. Not today—not when he wanted to be securely in the driver's seat for a change, keeping Sunshine a little off balance.

Of course his first sight of her, hauling herself out of that ancient, minuscule bright yellow car—Holy Mother of God, could a car *be* more perfect for her?—had almost derailed that plan on the spot, because *he* was the one who'd felt suddenly off balance.

It was the dress, he told himself. It was a monumental distraction, that dress. Petal-pink, too damned tight, too damned short.

And the black heels—too bloody high, with little black pearls studded in the leather and those crisscrossed ribbons around her ankles. How could a man *not* think about sucking her toes when he saw those shoes?

Thank God he'd got that first surge of heat under control enough to kiss her cheek instead of shoving his tongue halfway down her throat. Because that had been touch and go!

Now, however, the heart-thump suggested derailment was imminent again.

Well, he would just have to share the derailment around.

'So, then, let's go check out hotels,' he said.

'Are you—? Are you going to come with me? In the car?'

He thought about saying no—he'd realised that seeing him on the bike was going to be her breaking point and he wanted to get to that point fast. But in that tiny car of hers they would be very close to each other. So close she'd be able to feel him even without touching. He could use that. He was *sure* he could use that.

'Yes,' he said. 'The car.'

But when he squeezed himself into the passenger seat, and the scent of jonquils hit him like Thor's hammer, he thought perhaps he had made a tactical error. He just freaking *loved* that smell.

'Seat belt,' she said, and waited like a good little Girl Scout until he'd buckled up before starting the car.

He could see a faint blush on her cheeks. She'd get a shock if he touched her there. One finger along the rosy heat.

So he did, finding it shockingly easy to do.

But touchy-feely Sunshine swivelled as though he'd slapped her.

She stared at him.

He stared back.

And then he smiled. 'You know, Sunshine—your pupils are dilated. Got any internet facts to share about dilated pupils?'

Yes, Sunshine knew all about dilated pupils.

But she wasn't answering that.

Not with visions of straddling him right there in his seat popping into her head. He was so close that every time she changed gears her hand brushed his thigh. She had a sneaking suspicion he was deliberately putting his leg in the way. Another yank of her chain? She'd said hands-off, so he—the great un-toucher—had decided it was hands-*on*, just to needle her into a decision. And she'd thought he'd needed exposure therapy for his touching phobia!

It was just as well the first hotel was close to the restaurant. It was such a relief to be out of the car and in the open air.

Until Leo put his hand in the small of her back to guide

her across the car park to the hotel entrance—*enough with the touching, already!*—and she wanted to slap him.

She was a *pacifist*—she should *not* want to slap!

Sunshine stepped away from Leo the moment they were inside the hotel.

'I loved what I saw on the internet about this place,' she said, with an enthusiasm that actually managed to sound insincere even though she truly meant it.

That was what Leo was doing to her. Making her over-babble.

She looked around, taking in the use of dark wood, the pale stone floor. 'I think I'm going to book my own room here. Are you planning on staying overnight? I think you should. You know, you don't want to...to ride...after the party.'

Babbling. Shut up, shut up!

'I won't be riding home if I don't have a bike,' he pointed out calmly. Yanking her goddamned chain! 'But in any case I have a house here, and hopefully there'll be furniture by then.'

'A house? By then?'

Ugh. She'd turned into a parrot. A babbling parrot.

'The house was only built last year, and it's largely a furniture-free zone.'

'Are you going to live down here permanently?'

'Not permanently. I have too much on my plate in Sydney.'

Sunshine knew all about having too much on your plate. It kept you nicely occupied so you only had to think, not feel.

Think. Not feel.

That sounded good.

Think, not feel.

If she just remembered that everything would be all right.

And if she thought—ha—*thought!*—about Leo's full plate, it was clear that although he might talk about this mythical abyss-jumping woman of his dreams he was no different from her. He couldn't *fit* that kind of commitment into his life. Otherwise he would have it by now. He had enough women to choose from, for God's sake! She'd looked him up on the internet again yesterday, and seen the paparazzi photos. And, all right, that particular bit of searching had been a weak moment that she would not be repeating!

So! He didn't have it because he didn't want it.

And neither did she.

So she could stop the silly panicking.

Think, not feel.

'You could stay with me,' Leo said as one of the hotel staff approached them. 'The night of the reception.'

Okay, she couldn't stop panicking just yet, because her stomach was rioting again. 'I don't think that would be a good idea.'

'Don't have to think,' Leo said, and touched her cheek. 'You can just feel.'

How the *hell* did he lock on to her thoughts like that? 'You are freaking me out, Leo.'

'Am I?' He sounded delighted. 'All you have to do is agree to two more times and I'll stop!'

Sunshine turned gratefully to the hotel manager.

Introductions. Small talk. All good.

And then the manager asked, 'Shall we start the tour with the honeymoon suite?'

Sunshine choked on a laugh.

Which made Leo choke on a laugh.

So much unresolved between them—seething lust, and different takes on life, and twisted psyches—and here they were, being whisked off to the honeymoon suite like a couple of newlyweds.

'Wonderful,' Leo said, biting the inside of his cheek as Sunshine choked again.

She carefully kept her eyes off him when they reached the suite, looking around with a desperate kind of eagerness.

The suite had a touch of Bali about it, with a low bed of dark carved wood and a beautiful wood floor leading out to a private bamboo garden and plunge pool.

'Oh, so perfect! I might book it for myself,' Sunshine gushed.

Oh, no, you won't. 'Or for the actual honeymooners, perhaps?'

'Oops. Got carried away! Bamboo does that to me.'

'*Bamboo* does that?'

'Yes. Did you know it produces up to thirty-five per cent more oxygen than hardwood trees and absorbs four times as much carbon?'

'No, Sunshine, I did not. But I can see how that would make you want to honeymoon with it. There's something so sexy about carbon absorption.'

She giggled, then choked again as she tried to stop it. 'Well, I'm sure there are other wonderful rooms here that will suit me very well,' she said.

'I'm sure there are, but you'll like my place better,' Leo said, and almost laughed to see the flicker of panic race across her face.

Her face was flushed, her eyes wide, her lips parted so he could see that little gap between her teeth.

And, God, he wanted her. Wanted to run his hands up her legs and under her dress. To put his mouth on her, make her beg. Wanted to hear her sigh his name, feel her shudder. Wanted—

Ouch. To do something with his painful erection.

Okay—they were going to have to rush through this hotel tour.

Then rush through the next hotel.

Because it was three o'clock.

And by four o'clock he intended to have her at his house, preferably naked.

'So! Leo!' Sunshine said, pulling up at South at a quarter to four. 'Accommodation is sorted. I'll cover the card with the list of charities for donations in lieu of gifts and get that included with the invitation. Roger to no MC—just you welcoming the guests. No official speeches, just a repeat of their wedding vows. Clothes are done. Shoes underway. Kate is on board to sing. I think we can cover everything else via email.'

Leo hadn't made a move to get out of the car. He just sat there.

'Cake,' he said.

'The—the guys can just pick that, can't they? Like you originally suggested.'

'Sunshine, I brought down four miniature decorated cakes because you wanted a tasting, and if you think I'm taking them, untouched, back to Anton—who is monumentally temperamental and had to be talked into making them in the first place—you can think again.' *Forgive me, mild-mannered Anton...*

'Oh, then I guess... Or maybe I could cut a piece of each and—'

'And then there's the seating plan. I've got the night off.' *Go, Pinocchio.* 'I don't know when I'll get another, so we may as well get that sorted.'

'But I—I...I have a date.'

'Date?'

'Er...Tony. The calligrapher.'

'The calligrapher is an ex. Break the date.'

'How do you know he's an—? Oh, I told you, didn't I?'

'Yep. And in any case we haven't resolved the two versus four issue—you're mine until we do.'

Sunshine dragged in a breath. Held it.

'Breathe, Sunshine. It's just cake.' *Like hell.* 'And I also have a sample Anton made as a potential wedding favour to show you.'

She was looking torn. 'But we could do *that* via email.'

'And I have everything I need to make meat-lovers' pizza.'

Her mouth fell open. 'Oh, well, in that case.' She started getting out of the car.

'What are you doing?' Leo asked.

'Going into the restaurant.'

'No, we're going to my house.'

'I thought there wasn't any furniture.'

'It's not quite *that* basic. There's a completely fitted-out kitchen. With food. And a makeshift dining suite, although the table is on wheels. Some balcony furniture. Bathroom stuff. A mattress.'

Dare you! Dare you to come!

Her nose was wrinkling up; he could practically see the arguments bouncing around in her head.

'Think of the cake, Sunshine.'

'All right,' she said, with the air of a Christian martyr marching towards the lions' den.

'Good,' Leo said, and started getting out of the car.

'What are you doing?'

'I'll take the bike. You follow me. I'll grab my jacket and keys while you call Tony.'

'Tony?' she asked, blankly. And then, 'Oh, yes. Tony. I…'

'Forgot Tony? Poor Tony.'

For the first time ever Leo rode like a bat out of hell.

He didn't feel good about it, because he knew Sunshine

would be in a state—but he also knew it was the most effective way to smash through the wall she was trying to erect between them. The best way to *not* end up like Tony and all the others who had never got to the magical fourth assignation.

Well, Leo Quartermaine was not a piece of meat. He was getting to number four, and if it took the damned motorbike to get there so be it.

He was going so fast he had to pass the house and double back twice so Sunshine could keep sight of him. She was still lagging behind when he zoomed off the road and into the carport, but he was sure she'd been watching him closely and would find her way.

He wondered what she'd think of his place. The nondescript carport gave no hint that it was the gateway to a modern architectural masterpiece. Once they left the carport, however, and headed down a steep set of steps, it would be like entering a different world. The house was basically a long, horizontal strip of wood and glass cut into the side of a low cliff. A second set of steps led from the house to a beach so secluded it was like Leo's private patch of ocean.

The Fiat finally puttered in and Leo braced himself for her reaction, looking closely at her partly averted face as she got out of the car.

Very blank, very pale.

Without speaking to him she went to the boot, took out a cherry-red briefcase, fixed the strap over her shoulder. And then she turned towards him, and he saw that the weird face-morph thing had happened, that she was trembling.

And Leo knew he could never do that to her again.

She followed him to the top of the stairs, where he stopped. 'Are you all right?'

She merely looked at him, but he was relieved to see things settling back into place.

'Take off your shoes,' Leo said. 'It will be safer.'

'Don't talk to me about *safe*.'

'Then give me your briefcase.'

'No. Let's just see how you like thinking about my breaking body tumbling down those stairs, with my anklebones smashed in these heels and my briefcase cracking my skull open.'

'All right. I'm sorry I rode like that.'

She was speechless for a moment, and then she drew back her arm and punched him in the shoulder. At least it looked like a punch; it felt more like a slap with a cushion. 'You told me you weren't a teenage hothead,' she said shakily.

'I'm not. I'm sorry.'

'Shut up, Leo. I'm too angry with you to hear an apology. And there had better be six kinds of meat on that pizza after putting me through that! And *buffalo* mozzarella!'

Buffalo mozzarella—what a zinger.

He only barely managed not to laugh. 'Just give me the damned briefcase,' he said, biting the inside of his cheek.

She punched him again. Same shoulder. She clearly wasn't a candidate for cage fighting if that was the best she could do. 'You are *not* carrying my briefcase, Mr Alpha-Beta-Zeta,' Sunshine said.

'Don't forget the Gamma.'

She tossed her hair over her shoulder and waved him imperiously on: start the descent.

Leo took the first step, and the next, and the next, navigating slowly, staying just a half-step ahead. If Sunshine stumbled, if she even gasped, he would turn and catch her and toss her over his shoulder and carry her even if she kicked and screamed all the way.

But Sunshine—the epitome of high-heeled confidence—didn't put a foot wrong, and they arrived at the entrance to the house without incident. He opened the door and gestured her in ahead of him.

The use of glass was similar to what he'd done at South, except that where South had windows the house had full-length glass doors, opening onto a long veranda. The view was just as stunning. But because the house was so much lower, and perched within a cove, it had a more intimate connection with the beach.

Sunshine was walking slowly, uncertainly, to the glass doors.

'Go out,' Leo urged, stripping off his jacket and tossing it onto one of the few chairs.

She put down her briefcase and slid one of the doors open. Stepped onto the wooden deck, walked over to the edge.

He followed her out, wondering what was going through her head as she looked out.

'My sister would have loved this,' she said.

Moonbeam. *Quelle surprise.* 'And you?'

She half turned, looked into his eyes. He could see the tears swimming.

Because of Moonbeam? Or him and his bone-headed motorbike stunt?

Whatever! Leo simply reeled her in, held her close.

So mind-bogglingly easy to touch her now he'd set his course. So easy…

Her head was on his shoulder, and then she turned her face to kiss the shoulder she had punched earlier.

'I'm sorry for punching you,' she said. 'I've never punched anyone before.'

'I don't know how to break it to you, but those punches didn't hurt.'

'Then I hope it hurts washing my Beige Amour lipstick out of your woollen top. And I won't be sorry if it *doesn't* come out.'

'You can draw a map on the back in Beige Amour, okay? I deserve it.'

He could feel her breath, her spiky lashes against his neck.

'You made me so mad,' she said.

'I know. I'm sorry.'

'And you're supposed to have haphephobia. We shouldn't be standing like this.'

'I'm supposed to have *what*?'

'Fear of touch.'

He swallowed the laugh. This was *not* the time to make fun of her. 'But, Sunshine, we *are* standing like this. Maybe that means I'm making progress on my phobia. So...how's *your* phobia tracking?'

He heard her breath hitch, felt it catch in her chest. She pulled out of his arms and turned back to the view for a long moment. He thought she wasn't going to answer, but then she turned back.

'If you mean my reluctance to get emotionally close to people, that's not a phobia—it's an active choice.'

'The wrong choice.'

'The right choice for me.' And then she gave a shuddery kind of sound that was like a cross between a sigh and a laugh. 'Okay, you've yanked my chain. I've punched you. Let's move on before I start boring myself. We have things to do, so onwards and upwards: let them eat cake! Did you know that Marie Antoinette never actually said that?'

Sunshine took herself off to explore the house while Leo prepared the cakes.

The house was designed to give most rooms a view. There was a generous living/dining area, a cosy library, which had shelves but no books, and two private wings—the main bedroom/bathroom wing, with an atrium that reminded her of the honeymoon suite at the hotel, except that it was plant-free, and the other with three bedrooms, each with an en suite bathroom.

Leo had thrown a roll of paper towels at her when she'd poked her head in the kitchen, so she wasn't sure what that looked like, but she was in love with the rest of the house.

It just needed interior designing. Because the only decorative item in it so far was a massive ornate mirror on the wall in the living room. Some kind of feng shui thing—reflecting the water view for peace and prosperity? She would have to look that up.

Leo was looking inscrutable as he wheeled the dining table over to her, which made her suspicious—because what was there about cakes, plates, cutlery, napkins, and glasses to warrant inscrutability?

Well, she was not going to be inscrutabilised—and she didn't *care* if that wasn't a real word! She was simply going to eat the cake, and later the pizza, like a rational woman who did not care about anything but the state of her stomach, and then drive home.

She examined the four perfectly decorated cakes. Oh, dear, she was on the cusp of a ten-kilo weight-gain.

Then she noted that Leo was pouring champagne.

'Careful—I'm fat *and* I'm driving,' she said.

'You're not fat. And driving...? We'll see.'

'Just cut the cake, Leo,' she said, not about to get into an argument so soon after she'd punched him. He couldn't *force* the champagne down her throat anyway.

Leo cut and served slices of the first cake. 'Traditional fruit cake, fondant icing.'

Sunshine took a bite. It was moist, rich, and utterly delicious. 'This one, for sure!' she said, and scooped up another forkful.

'Pace yourself. Don't vote too soon,' Leo said.

She didn't bother responding—her mouth was too full.

'You *can* have another piece, you know,' Leo offered as she scraped up a last smear of icing.

'I have to lose weight or I won't fit into my dress,' Sunshine said repressively—and then she realised the absurdity of that, given the state of her plate, and burst out laughing.

'Hey, eat as much as you want! I was just trying to protect the plate—it looked like you were trying to dig a trench in it.'

'Leo!'

He held up *I surrender* hands.

'Oh, just cut the next one,' she said, gurgling.

'Salted caramel Mark One. Pastry base covered with a film of sticky salted caramel, topped with chocolate cake layers interspersed with caramel and cream filling.'

Sunshine took a bite. Closed her eyes as flavour flooded her. She took another forkful from her plate. Sipped champagne. 'It is *so* rich and delicious.'

Leo waited while she took one more bite. Another. One more. A sip. One more. 'Finished?' he asked at last, deadpan.

Mournfully, she examined her empty plate. 'I told you I had an unhealthy interest in desserts.'

'"A shark's mouth full of sweet teeth" was how you put it.'

'It may be worse than that. It could be more like a hadrosaur's teeth. They have nine hundred and sixty—*and* they're self-sharpening!'

'What the hell is a hadrosaur?'

'A type of dinosaur.' She sighed, dispirited. 'So! I am a dinosaur—and not even a meat-eating one!'

Leo laughed so suddenly it came out as a snort.

Which made Sunshine laugh. 'Let's get onto salted caramel Mark Two before I lapse into a state of abject depression.'

'You? Abject depression while eating *cake*? That would be something to see!'

'And you will see it, I promise you, if you don't look after my hadrosauric teeth and cut me a piece of cake.'

He cut a slice and handed it over. 'Your wish, my command! Similar to Mark One, but with butterscotch cake layers.'

Sunshine ate, interspersing mouthfuls with an occasional moan of ecstasy. 'Do you have a favourite?' she asked, forking up the last mouthful. 'Because I have to tell you this is harder than I thought and I don't think I'm going to be able to choose.'

'As it turns out, I do have a favourite—but I'm not telling,' he said. 'Subliminally, knowing what I like best might sway you—maybe to deliberately pick something that is *not* my favourite—and that would never do.'

'Oh! I see what you did there! Bouncing my own words about the invitation design back at me.'

'For my next trick I will spout random facts about the mating habits of the tsetse fly.'

Sunshine laughed. 'I'm going to look that up, and next time I see you—'

'I beg you—no!' He slapped another piece of cake on her plate. 'Coconut vanilla bean cake, layered with coconut meringue butter cream.'

Sunshine stared at it, not sure if she could actually fit in another bite. But it looked so good. She picked up her fork. Ate. Sipped more champagne, then looked at her glass. 'Hey—you refilled that.'

'It was empty,' Leo explained.

Sunshine huffed, but her concentration was already moving back to her plate. One more forkful. Another. Again. Empty plate. She licked her lips, looking at the rest of the cake longingly.

'See? You didn't need to know my favourite,' Leo said. 'You decided on your own. The coconut.'

'Yes. Coconut. It would almost be *worth* getting married just to have that cake. Do you think I could have another tiny piece?'

'You can eat the whole damned cake as far as I'm concerned.'

'Dieting from tomorrow, then,' she said, holding out her plate.

Leo cut another slice. 'Don't diet, Sunshine. I like the feel of you just as you are.'

The words, the tone of his voice, made the hairs on the back of her neck stand up. 'That's…that's…immaterial. But, anyway, wh-what's your favourite?'

He smiled. A narrow-eyed smile. She didn't trust that smile.

'The fruit cake,' he said. 'But I have an idea for how we can both get our way. Compromise is my new speciality.'

Was that supposed to be meaningful? 'Both get our way with what?' she asked cautiously.

'With the cake,' Leo said, all innocence, and put the extra slice on Sunshine's plate.

He looked at her for a long moment and Sunshine saw that little tic jump to life near his mouth. She was so nervous she almost couldn't sit still. She stuck her fork into her cake, raised it to her mouth.

'And with our assignations,' Leo said smoothly.

Sunshine jerked, and the piece of cake hit her just at the corner of her bottom lip and fell.

'Two, four…there's a three in the middle,' he said, in that same dangerously soft voice.

And then, before she could string a lucid thought together, he leant in and licked the corner of her mouth.

'Just thought I'd…steal…that little drop of cream,' Leo said softly.

Dare you.

Tic-tic-tic, beside his mouth.

'I'll tell you what,' he said silkily. 'I'm going into the kitchen to organise the first compromise I was talking about. You sit here, finish your cake, look at the view, and think about the second. Think about why it is that a woman like you, who believes sex is just sex—you did say that, right?—is so freaked out by the idea that a man actually does want to have just sex with her.'

With a last piercing look at her, and a short laugh, he left the room.

And, oh, how hard it was to have her words come back to bite her. Because she had said that. Sex was just...sex.

Except that it seemed in this particular case it wasn't.

Because she was thinking about Leo too much, and caring too much, and worrying too much. The motorbike. The damned motorbike. Maybe without the motorbike they would be entwined right now on assignation three and she would be blithely uninterested in anything except his moving body parts.

So do the deal, Sunshine, and he'll get rid of the bike.

Sex twice more. Or change her name.

She touched the corner of her mouth, where he'd licked the cream, and her skin seemed to tingle.

Restless, she got to her feet, walked out onto the veranda.

'Look at the view,' he'd said.

But even that wasn't simple.

He had no idea what the view did to her. And here the beach was so disturbingly close...

She hadn't been on a beach in two years.

Leo was right: Moonbeam did have a hold over her. A hold she seemed unable to break. A hold she was too... scared...to break. Well, she would go down to the beach now and yank her *own* chain and see what happened. And

then she would tell Leo. She would tell him—she would...
God, she didn't know what she would say. Or do.

But one drama at a time.

Deep breath.

Beach.

Heart hammering, she bent to remove her shoes. Took the first step before she could think again, kept going until the sand was beneath her feet.

It felt strange. And good. Comforting, almost, to have her feet sink into the sand. The scratch of salt on her face, the roar and rush of surf sounding in her ears.

Sunshine felt her sister in the wild, careless, regal, lovely essence of the place. Pulling at her, drawing her closer and closer, until she was at the water's edge and the waves were slapping at her ankles.

She let out the breath she hadn't realised she was holding on a long sigh.

This tiny private beach was it.

What she'd been looking for. Waiting to find.

Leo's beach was her sister's final resting place.

She felt tears start, and swiped a shaking hand over her eyes.

And then she felt Leo behind her.

CHAPTER EIGHT

'I'M NOT VAIN enough to think you're crying over me, Sunshine—so why don't you tell me what the big deal is about the beach?' Leo asked.

Heartbeat. Two. Three. 'Moonbeam.'

'I thought we'd get around to Moonbeam. Everything always circles back to her.'

She turned sharply towards him. 'What's wrong with that?'

'Just the fact that she's *dead*.'

She covered her ears, gave an anguished cry, and the next thing she knew she was in his arms.

'I'm sorry. *Sorry*,' he said, and kissed her temple. 'But, Sunshine, your sister doesn't sound like the kind of person who would have wanted you to freeze, to mark time just because she wasn't there.'

'She—she wasn't. But I can't help it, Leo.'

Long moment. And then Leo said, 'So let me help you. Tell me—talk. About Moonbeam and the beach.'

She waited, shivering in his steady hold, until the urge to weep had passed, and then she pulled out of his arms and stood beside him, looking out at the horizon.

'Sunshine?'

'She told me that when she died she wanted her ashes scattered at the beach—to mix with the ocean.' She turned to look up at him. 'Why would she say that when she was so young? Do you think she knew what was going to happen?'

'I don't know, Sunshine.'

'I didn't do what she wanted. I couldn't. Can't.'

'So…where is she?'

'In an urn in my office. You were looking straight at her—that night you cooked me dinner. I was scared you'd guessed. But it was just my guilty conscience getting the better of me. Because why would you ever guess?'

'There's no need to feel guilty, Sunshine.'

'I've got my sister in an urn in my office—the exact opposite of what she wanted. What does that say about me?'

'That you're grieving.' He smoothed a windblown lock of her hair. 'You'll find a way to do what she asked. But even if you never do it won't matter to Moonbeam. It's not really Moonbeam in that urn. She's in your heart and your head. Not in the urn, Sunshine.'

She turned back to the ocean, gazing out. 'A full moon. A quiet beach. She said it would be up to me to do it on my own—no friends, no family. Just me and her.' The tears were shimmering and she desperately blinked them back. 'I think she knew how hard it would be for me. I think she knew I would take a long time. I think she didn't want to pressure me into doing anything before I was ready. I want to do it, Leo. I *do*. But…'

'Well, we have a beach,' Leo said slowly. 'And a full moon coming up. You'll be here…'

He let the words hang.

She was still. So still. And then she turned to him again. 'You wouldn't mind?' Haltingly. 'You'd let me do that?'

'Yes, I would let you. And, no, I wouldn't mind.'

'I'll…I'll think about it. I'm not sure… Not yet…'

'That's fine. The beach will always be here, and there are plenty of full moons to choose from.'

She shivered.

'You're cold,' he said. 'Come back to the house.'

She could feel him behind her as she walked across the sand and up the steps. Like a tingle inside her nerve-endings. She could feel him watching as she brushed the sand from her feet, slipped on her shoes, retied the ankle laces.

And then, 'What next?' she asked, breathless. Wanting, wanting… *What?*

But Leo merely gestured for her to go into the house.

He'd cleared the table and positioned in the middle of it a small white cardboard box with Art Deco patterning. 'Open it,' he said.

Sunshine lifted the lid to find a one-portion replica of one of the wedding cake choices. Except that on top was a decorative three-dimensional love knot formed from two men's ties.

'Compromise number one,' Leo said. 'Fruit cake—for the wedding favours. It lasts longer than the other cakes, so can be made in advance. The ties will be identical to what Caleb and Jonathan are wearing on the day.'

'Anton is a genius.' She turned to him, felt her heart stutter at the hungry look on his face. 'So! We nail the seating plan now and we're done, right?'

Leo stepped closer to her. 'That makes you happy, Sunshine, doesn't it?'

'Of—of course.'

'The fact that we've done all the planning? Or that you don't have to see me again?'

'But I *do* have to see you,' she said faintly. 'At the trial dinner.'

'You're scared of me.'

'That's…insane.'

'Prove it.'

'There's nothing to prove. And how could I prove it anyway?'

'Kiss me.'

She goggled at him. 'Excuse me?'

'You used to. Every time you saw me. Before we had sex, at least. I thought things didn't change for you just because you had sex with someone.'

'They...they don't.'

'Then kiss me hello. Or you can make it goodbye, if you want. But do it. The way you used to. Just a kiss on the cheek.'

She shook her head.

He smiled. 'Ah. So *you're* the one who won't touch now, Sunshine.'

'I—I do. I mean, I can. But it's not... I just...'

He reached out, grabbed her elbow, and she jumped back.

'See?' he said. 'What's the problem? You've stayed friends with all your exes. Why not me?'

'You're not an ex.' Her eyes widened as she realised what she'd said. 'I mean, you *are*.' Stop. Breathe. Swallow. Hair toss. 'Of course we're friends.'

'So kiss me.'

She gave an exaggerated, exasperated sigh. 'All right,' she said. She leant forward and kissed his cheek. 'There! Satisfied?'

'No. Do it again. Slower. And touch me this time. Your hand, somewhere on me.'

'Ridiculous,' she muttered.

'Just do it.'

She touched his wrist, the burn mark. 'What happened there?'

'Hot pan, don't change the subject—and that's not touching.'

'Okay—where do you want me to touch you?' she asked, rolling her eyes with great theatricality.

His eyebrows shot up. He blinked. Slowly. Again.

Seriously? He was thinking about *there*?

But, 'Improvise…' was what he said.

With the air of a person suffering a fool, and *not* gladly, she ran her fingers up his forearm. 'There.'

'Now do that and kiss me at the same time.'

'This is stupid.'

'Do it.'

Huffing out an agitated breath, Sunshine leant up and gave him a fleeting kiss on the cheek while her hand gripped his forearm.

'There! Satisfied?' she said again. Hmm. That had come out a little too breathy.

'Not good enough—you're not usually that tentative. Try again.'

She stood there, chewing her lip for a moment, and then, as though going into battle, she grabbed him by both arms and kissed him lingeringly on the cheek.

She felt the sizzle, the almost convulsive need to press into him. Jerked back. Stared. 'So!' she said, a little unsteadily.

'It's not going to work, Sunshine,' he said.

'I did it. It worked.'

'You know what I mean.'

'If you're talking about sex, I—I told you. Two times. Over. Done with. Moving on.'

He stepped closer. 'I didn't agree to two. You're not moving on—not in any sense. And I still want you.'

He looked into her eyes. She could feel the lust pulsing out of him. She could smell it. Almost taste the musky promise of it.

'You want me too,' he said. 'I can *see* it. Your eyes… You know, the size of a person's pupils is the result of a balancing act between the autonomic nervous system, which controls the fight-or-flight response, and the parasympathetic system, known for its rest and digest functions—I read that online. Another fact to add to your collection.'

He stepped closer still.

'But I prefer a simpler explanation—sexual interest in what you're looking at makes your pupils dilate. And yours, Sunshine, are looking mighty dilated.'

He pulled her into his arms, kissed her hard.

'Compromise number two, Sunshine. And assignation number three. You're not leaving here until it's done.'

CHAPTER NINE

WITHOUT WAITING FOR a response he reached for the zipper at the back of her dress and slid it down. He peeled the dress over her shoulders, down to her hips.

The dress fell to the floor and she stood there in her underwear. He'd never seen her underwear before, but wasn't surprised to find it was the sexiest in the world. Petal-pink, the same colour as her dress—and he had a sudden insight that Sunshine's underwear would always match her clothes. He'd never been a lingerie man. Until today, when he was confronted by Sunshine's wispy, lacy bra, with its tiny ribbon bows, and the matching French knickers that reminded him of a frothy strawberry dessert.

His heart was hammering wildly in his chest. He touched the bra, the knickers. 'These are staying on,' he said, and turned her to face the mirror, where they could both watch as his hands covered her breasts, caressed her through the lace, slid down her body.

When his fingers dived beneath the elastic of those gorgeous knickers he could see her eyes close, her mouth gasp open. That gap between her teeth looked so damned *hot*!

Then she threw her head back against his shoulder, opened herself to him, and he couldn't think about anything except his desperate need to have her.

'Touch me—touch me, please,' she whimpered, and his

hand slid down, between her legs, where the heat and the wetness of her almost made him come on the spot.

She orgasmed quietly—a single, sighing groan easing through her parted lips; she went so boneless she would have melted to the floor if he hadn't been holding her.

But Leo wasn't done. He kissed her ear. 'Watch,' he said, and she opened her eyes, watching in the mirror again.

He lifted her right leg slightly up and outwards, so she could see the movement of his fingers as they slid beneath the silk of her knickers.

'I love these,' he said, tugging the crotch aside a little, then dragging the waist down so she was just a little exposed, open to him.

Behind her, he smoothly, quietly, undid his jeans. Her eyes were heavy-lidded, glittering, fixed on his as he sheathed himself inside her. It was almost gentle, the way he moved—and it was a test of his control, because he was wild for her. But this time, this coupling, was all about acceptance. And so he moved slowly, stayed still inside her for long moments…and when he did move it was by infinitesimal degrees, never withdrawing from her, always there. Hands running across her skin, along the scars. Until that groaning release of hers again, when he gripped her hips and followed her, groaning her name, holding her, as the waves washed over them, unhurried, sweet, delicious.

At last she stepped away from him, bent to retrieve her dress, slid it on. She turned her back for him to zip her into it.

The he turned her to face him. Put his hands on her shoulders. 'Sunshine?' His voice had that gravelly postcoital timbre to it.

No smile. Just a haunted look unlike any he'd ever seen on her face.

'I—I'm going to go now.'

'The champagne. It's too soon to drive. You should wait.'

'I didn't want all that champagne.'

'We'll do the seating plan. Over pizza, remember?'

'The *seating* plan?' She sounded incredulous.

'I— Yes. No. Whatever you want.'

'Leo, I can't do this. I don't want to.'

'The seating plan?'

'No, not the damned seating plan. The sex. The chat. The post-coital friend routine.'

'You said you were always friends afterwards.'

'It's different. I…I care about you. And it's not kind or—or…fair to do this to me.'

'Do what?'

'Try and put me in a position where I will end up caring *more*—because that's what will happen. I don't know why you'd bother, unless it's some twisted game. Or a challenge just because I set the rules.'

'I don't play by the rules, Sunshine.'

'And I don't want to be a challenge.' She pushed tiredly at her fringe. Then squared her shoulders. 'So! I'll tell you what. You win. You come and claim your fourth time. Let's just do it. The sooner the better. And then the deal is done. Because I am not going past that.'

She could see the triumph flare in his eyes.

'Deal,' he said. 'But before we get to that I'm going to make you pizza. Then we're going to dot every *i* and cross every *t* of this wedding and get it the hell out of our relationship. And then I'm going to take you to bed and make love to you, and draw a line under assignation number three.'

She could feel her breathing quicken, her pulse start skittering, the throbbing rush between her legs.

And then Leo, smiling, added, 'But first I'm going to

read you the haiku poem your mother sent me—which I have to say I kind of liked.'

No.

No, no, no, *no*!

But it didn't seem to matter how many times she said no in her head.

Because it was there, hurting her chest, stretching her heart.

Shimmering brightly, beautifully. Overwhelming and terrifying.

She was in love with Leo Quartermaine.

It was hardly surprising that she'd fallen in love with him, Sunshine thought on her drive back to Sydney the next morning.

The best sex of her life—possibly of *anyone's* life…in the *whole history of mankind*. Meat-lovers' pizza. Tiramisu. The offer to scatter her sister's ashes a stone's throw from his house. But, really, the absolutely unfair kicker—an appreciation of her mother's haiku poetry: evidence that he was probably seriously nuts.

The eyes are sublime
Glowing without the blackness
Liberated now

What had her mother been *thinking*?

And who the hell could actually *like* that?

And how could you *not* fall in love with a guy who did?

The signs were there already that this gobsmacking love was going to be an absolute misery. She'd asked Leo to text her so that she'd know he'd got home safely—and instead of telling her not to be a lunatic Leo had smiled and said, 'Sure.'

He'd smiled! *Smiled*!

What was going to come next—checking him for cuts and scalds after a shift in the kitchen?

Er...*no*! Thank you very much.

Well, it was a new thing. Maybe it wouldn't last. Maybe they would have their fourth assignation and then, once they'd gone their separate ways, it would fade.

Except...she was already feeling a little distraught at the idea of going their separate ways.

So, no. No time to waste.

She had to take action immediately.

Their relationship had to be reversed. They had to return to the way they'd been before she'd hugged him on the couch and started this killer snowball rolling down the mountain.

They had to be friends. Just friends. Without the depth. The way they should have been all along.

Which meant no fourth assignation.

And if she didn't want to renege on their deal that meant...

Sigh.

One name-change, coming up.

To: Leo Quartermaine
From: Sunshine Smart
Subject: Loose ends
Hi Leo
Here is a copy of my name-change application. So no need for assignation number four.

The process apparently takes about four weeks. Please let me know when you've sold the bike. You will find cars are so much more convenient. Well, maybe not for parking. But think of getting around when it's raining.

I know we're all sorted for the wedding, which is great because I am up to the gills in handbags for the next week or so, but let's catch up before the trial dinner.
(Allyn) Sunshine Smart

PS: I'm assuming it's okay for me to invite a date to the trial dinner, because I owe Tony.

Leo read the note three times before it sank in.

Allyn.

She'd chosen the name-change option over more sex with him.

Well, what moron had offered her that *out?*

And then one fact pierced him like a nice, long, sharp lance between the eyes: he didn't want her to change her name for *any* reason. She was *Sunshine*. Sunshine *suited* her. Okay, he was perhaps a little unhinged, because Sunshine wasn't an appropriate name for any human being—only for dish-washing liquid—but it bloody well did suit *her*, dammit.

The second fact smacked him behind the head like one of those quintain things that swung on a pole when you hit it with your lance: maybe the sex wasn't as good for her as it was for him.

After one appalled moment he discounted that. He recognised melt-your-socks sex when he saw it, tasted it, touched it, did it.

So did she, obviously. And it scared the crap out of her.

But to go straight from his bed to the Registry of Births, Deaths and Marriages…?

Well, sorry, but that was just an insult!

He thought back to last night.

He'd read her the haiku and she had looked like some kind of wax mannequin…but then, she'd made it obvious she wasn't a haiku fan.

She'd rallied to argue with him over the remaining wedding preparations. Par for the course.

She'd eaten the pizza as though it were going to be her last earthly meal—no surprises there.

Dinnertime conversation had been as peculiar as usual,

with Sunshine imparting strange but true facts. Leonardo Da Vinci had invented scissors—*who knew?*—there was a maze in England shaped like a Dalek—*how cool was that?*—forest fires moved faster uphill than downhill, and the crack in a breaking glass moved faster than three thousand miles per hour.

Then they'd had more amazing sex, using tiramisu in ways that would make it his favourite dessert for eternity.

And this morning she'd kissed him goodbye. On the mouth. As though she did it every day. And he'd *liked* that.

She'd asked him to text her when he got home. And he'd *done* it—*happily*.

So...*what*? Now he was supposed to accept that it was all over?

And what was the deal with *let's catch up before the trial dinner*?

Was she freaking *kidding* him? He was not *catching up* with her. Unless it was to bang her brains out in assignation number four.

Did she think he didn't know when he was being friend-zoned?

He *wasn't* going to be friend-zoned by Sunshine Smart.

He was not Gary or Ben or Iain or Tony—relegated to coffee catch-ups, Facebook status updates, and being taken to dinner to check people's hair-length.

He was *not* her freaking friend.

His brain felt as if it were foaming with rage.

He would email her telling her he would *not* be catching up with her before the trial dinner. And when he saw her at the trial dinner he would drag her aside and force her to tell him that she—

His brain stuttered to a halt there.

Tell him that she...that she...

That she...

Into his head popped a picture of her kissing him good-bye that morning.

Asking him to text her when he got home.

That she…

That *he*…

Oh, my God.

All or nothing. Off the cliff. Into the abyss.

She was the one.

She would fight tooth and nail not to be, but that was what she was.

The one.

And Leo had no idea what to do about it.

It's hemp, Jim, but not as we know it.

Leo had done a double-take the moment he'd seen Sunshine.

Hemp was not sexy.

Everyone knew that.

So why did the sight of Sunshine Smart wearing it make him want to drool?

A simple loose ankle-length column of dark bronze—and, God, he'd love to see her underwear in *that* colour—with two tiny straps fastened at the shoulders in untie-me-please bows. She'd left off the lipstick as well as the eye-goop and looked fresh as a sea breeze. Her hair was loose. Towering heels in gold. Gold drop earrings, straight as arrows, pointing to those mind-game bows. She also had a thick gold cuff clasped around one arm, just above the elbow. But she never wore jewellery…

Well, obviously she does *sometimes, imbecile.*

Yep. A hundred and fifty guests to feed, and he was pondering Sunshine's jewellery-wearing habits. *Great.*

He strode over to her. 'Sunshine.'

'Allyn,' she corrected.

'Not yet, though, right? And—' he turned to the guy

who had popped up beside her like a cork in a pool '—you must be Tony. Let me show you to your table.'

Leo led them to their seats, introduced them to the others at their table.

And then... Well, her fringe was getting long. She'd brushed it aside—training it for the wedding, he figured—but one piece had sprung back over her forehead. He smoothed it back to where it was supposed to be.

Her gorgeous eyes widened. He heard her quick intake of breath, saw the daze in her eyes. It felt like a 'moment'—one of those bubble-like moments where everything was right with the world.

He sensed Tony watching him. Everyone else at the table too.

Good, he thought savagely. *I'm marking my territory, people, and she belongs to me.*

It had been two weeks since Sunshine had seen Leo—two weeks in which the only contact he'd made had come in the form of three niggardly emails: one rebuffing her suggestion that they catch up before tonight—which had hit her like a blow—the second a message about wines for the wedding, with the most *casual* mention that he'd sold his bike and bought a 'nice safe Volvo'—how dared he be casual about that?—and the third with details of tonight's trial dinner. She suspected it was the same email he'd sent to all guests, except that to hers he'd added, *Don't forget to bring your sister.*

With so little encouragement to pine for him, and fewer reasons to worry about him now that he was *sans* motorbike, Sunshine figured she should have managed to get her wayward emotions under control. But the bike sale hadn't seemed to lessen her anxiety over him. She thought, and thought, and thought about him. *All the goddamned time.* Exactly what she'd been trying to avoid.

And then that one touch of his, brushing her fringe aside, and her emotions had surged so suddenly she'd almost thrown herself at him.

Now just the sight of him walking to the middle of the restaurant and clapping his hands to get everyone's attention, looking so delicious in that crisp white jacket, started her stomach jumping like popping candy.

He made a welcome speech—explained what would happen, ran through the menu, asked people to make sure they passed on all feedback, good and bad—and all through it Sunshine stared at him as though he were a nice big bowl of tiramisu...

When he left for the kitchen the whole night suddenly felt flat—and it didn't reshape itself except when he made his occasional forays from the kitchen to take a momentarily empty seat and chat to guests.

But never at Sunshine's table. And she didn't know whether to be happy about that or not. On the one hand she wouldn't have had to strain every minuscule cilia in her ears, trying to hear what he was saying. But on the other he'd surely notice that she had become, in just two weeks, the equivalent of a fried bat.

And then he was at the table next to hers, and Sunshine caught his eyes on her for the first time since he'd shown her to her table.

The hairs on the back of her neck stood up. She couldn't breathe. Couldn't think. Couldn't even seem to swallow. He was nodding at something the woman next to him was saying but he was looking at Sunshine.

After ignoring her for two whole weeks he was daring to look at her as if he would drag her off to a corner, rip off her clothes and—

His head jerked to the side, towards the entrance, and Sunshine's eyes jerked reflexively. There was a disturbance going down, being played out in a series of split-seconds.

An escalating pitch of voice. A scuffling sound. A shift of bodies. And—

Natalie Clarke. *Uh-oh.*

Within seconds Leo was up and walking swiftly over to Natalie, taking her arm, murmuring to the restaurant manager who'd been trying to handle the situation, and escorting Natalie out onto the viewing platform.

Sunshine felt a little as she had that night at the Rump & Chop Grill. Light-headed with fury on Leo's behalf… desperate to protect him. She didn't even wait for her head to tell her heart it was none of her business. With a fixed smile and an incoherent murmur about a 'wedding issue', Sunshine took off after Leo.

CHAPTER TEN

SUNSHINE REACHED THE viewing platform just in time to see Natalie land a swinging slap against Leo's cheek.

The burst of rage that flared in her head made her shake. 'What the *hell's* going on?' she demanded, grabbing Natalie's hand as it drew back for a second go.

'Go back inside, Sunshine,' Leo said, and tried to shove her behind him.

'You!' Natalie said contemptuously. 'Choke-girl! *You're* the Sunshine person?' She looked Sunshine up and down. 'They say at Q Brasserie that he's besotted with you. But he doesn't know *how* to love someone. He's not capable. He can't even *touch* you.'

Sunshine didn't bother answering. She simply manoeuvred herself beside Leo—which required a sharp nudge with her elbow, since he seemed determined to keep her out of harm's way—and then took his hand in hers, brought it to her lips, kissed it, rubbed it against her cheek.

'Really?' she asked Natalie, with a raise of her eyebrows.

Surrendering, Leo drew Sunshine protectively against his side. 'Natalie,' he said, 'tonight is a private function. And there are journalists inside who are probably wondering what the hell's going on out here. Can we *not* play this out in a blaze of publicity? Go back to Sydney—or there's a hotel nearby if you don't feel up to driving back tonight.'

'Why don't I go and wait at your house, Leo?' Natalie purred the question, shrugging out of her coat. She shimmied a little, sinuous as a snake.

Sunshine, beset by another burst of rage, stiffened, and Leo squeezed her hand slightly. Telling her to let it go.

And she should. She knew she should...

But Natalie licked her lips and raised one eyebrow, and the rage consumed her.

Sunshine laughed—a brittle laugh that sounded nothing like her. 'I'd forgotten about the tattoos,' she said. 'Butterflies. They're the gang rapists of the insect world, you know.'

She heard Leo choke on a laugh and she squeezed *his* hand. Hard.

Natalie fluttered one arm out to look at her tattoos. 'Don't be ridiculous.'

'They are so desperate to mate they perch on a female pupa—that's the metamorphosis stage, you know, where they go from larva to—'

'This is disgusting.'

'I *know*!' Wide-eyed. 'Especially because they perch there in a pack and wait for the female to emerge. And she's still limp, and her wings haven't even opened, and the first male just kind of grabs her and...well, you get the picture. And then the others take their turn.'

'That's...' Words seemed to fail Natalie.

Sunshine was contemplating Natalie's arms sadly. 'Next time get an eagle; at least they mate for life.'

Natalie stood there, quivering with impotent rage, staring from Sunshine to Leo.

One fraught moment. Another. Three people on one small viewing platform. Nobody moving.

And then, with a last look of loathing at Sunshine, Natalie turned on her heel and stalked off the platform.

Sunshine dropped Leo's hand and stepped back. '*Now* I'll go back in,' she said.

'Why did you even come out?'

'I just…I just thought you might need some support.'

'It looked a little like a leap into the abyss to me.'

No. *No!* 'I just don't like violence. And she slapped you. It made me…mad.' She looked at his face, which was still reddened where Natalie's hand had connected.

Half-laugh as he ran his fingers over his cheek. 'Yeah, you'll have to lift some weights if you want to match her.'

Sunshine, conscience-stricken, felt the colour drain from her face. 'Oh, my God, you're right. I'm just like her.'

Leo took her hands in his, pulled her towards him. 'You're nothing like her.'

'But I punched you!'

'And then you kissed it better, remember?'

'I— Yes, I remember.'

She shivered.

'Are you cold?

Nod. 'I brought a coat, but it's in my car.'

'Then come here,' he said softly, and drew her in, folding his arms around her. 'And Moonbeam? Is she in the car too?'

She nodded again.

'So it's happening?' he asked gently.

Another nod. 'Yes, if you're sure you don't mind.' And then, just a whisper, 'Tomorrow is the anniversary of… of…'

'Ah, Sunshine.' He stroked his hand over her hair and they stayed like that for a long moment. 'We'll disappear as soon as dessert is cleared, okay?'

'Tony…'

'Yeah—I don't give a rat's ass about Tony, and neither do you.'

'I don't think rats' asses are an apt comparison.'

'A horse's ass, then.'

She giggled, and then buried her face against his chest to stifle it. Because it wasn't funny.

'Whatever he is, he can fend for himself,' Leo said. 'Because I know he didn't drive down with you. Aside from anything else, I know you wouldn't have him in the car with Moonbeam.'

'How do you know that?'

'Because I just do.' Slight pause. 'So that stuff about butterflies—was it true?'

'Well, it's true of *certain* species,' Sunshine said, drawing slowly out of his arms. 'I'm not sure about *all* species.'

He opened the door to the restaurant, laughing. 'Poor Natalie. Probably *not* arms full of rapists.'

'Do you think I should tell her?' Sunshine asked, feeling suddenly guilty.

'If I could find pupil dilation on the internet I'm sure Natalie can find rapist butterflies,' Leo said. 'I like the thing about the eagles, though. Mating for life.'

It was time.

Sunshine was standing on his veranda at the top of the stairs, barefoot, with the urn in her arms. She was wearing a long knitted garment over her hemp dress. It flowed down to her ankles. No fastenings. A little bit witchy, a little bit hippie—perfect for a ceremonial ash-tossing.

'Right,' she said, and stood there looking irresolute.

Leo simply waited.

'Right,' she said again, with a tiny nod this time. And then she shot a look at Leo over her shoulder. 'I have to do this myself.'

'I know. I'll come down to the beach, just in case you need me, but I'll stay at the base of the steps.'

'I won't need you.'

'In case.' Implacable.

She looked paler than usual. Tense. And oddly hopeful.

And then she straightened her shoulders and started down the steps.

Leo waited two minutes, then followed. By the time he reached the sand her toes were in the wash.

He knew he would never forget the image of Sunshine, alone, surrounded by moon, surf, sand, night, as she lifted the urn to her face, kissed it.

And then she took off the lid and threw it behind her, discarded.

As if on cue an offshore breeze stirred, and Sunshine threw her head back, hugging the urn to her chest for one brief moment. Then, in one sudden, decisive movement, she threw the ashes up and out towards the water. She repeated the move once more. Then she bent, filled the urn with the seawater rushing in, waited while the water receded, then raced in again...tipped the urn so its contents hit the sand just as the new wave broke. And the last of Moonbeam's ashes were carried out to the ocean.

The minutes ticked by.

The breeze died away.

The rhythmic whooshing of surf on sand continued.

Life goes on.

And then Sunshine tossed that beautiful urn aside as though it were nothing but a broken shard of shell and walked back up the beach towards him, silent, tears streaming.

He opened his arms and she walked right into them. He said nothing. Just held her as her tears gradually eased, then stopped.

Staying in the circle of his arms, she looked up. 'Thank you,' she said. 'You know, she would have loved you.'

And you? he wanted to ask. But instead he said, 'Come to bed, Sunshine.'

She looked at his face in the moonlight. Touched his cheek. Nodded. 'One last time.'

She woke wearing one of Leo's shirts, alone on the mattress.

The makeshift curtains were drawn, except for a crack through which a piercing sliver of light beamed.

She got out of bed to tug the curtains back—and there it was: Moonbeam's beach. Wild and beautiful and... peaceful. Perfect.

Leo wandered in, wearing unbuttoned jeans and a navy blue T-shirt.

And the feeling of peace evaporated as her stomach started its usual Leo-induced cha-cha.

Time for reality.

'I'm about to make you an omelette,' he said, smiling. 'It will only be a few minutes, if you want to come out on the veranda when you're ready. And don't worry—there will be chorizo in there.'

A dart of panic stabbed her. 'No. I don't want it.'

'Don't like chorizo?'

'It's not about the ingredients.'

The smile vanished. 'Then what is it about?'

'The fact that you never cook for people.'

'And yet I do it for you.'

Her breath hitched. 'But I—I don't want you to cook for me.'

'Why not?'

'Because it's not what you do. You shouldn't change for me. Because...'

'Because...?'

'Because I can't change for you.'

'I haven't asked you to.'

'Oh.' That took the wind out of her sails. 'That's...good. I was scared because...'

'Because?'

'Well, Natalie said last night the people at Q Brasserie…they think you're besotted with me. That wouldn't be good.'

'I'm not besotted,' he said. 'Does that reassure you?'

'Yes. No. I don't know.'

'Multiple *choice*, Sunshine? How…comprehensive.'

'No. I mean—yes, it reassures me,' she said. 'I just… want us to be on the same page.'

'What specific page are you talking about?'

'Page number four,' she said. 'Four assignations. All settled. And I'm glad we did it. I was feeling guilty because you gave up your bike, and I never got around to filing the papers to change my name—because it didn't feel right, somehow. And I still…owed you.'

'Is that what last night was about? Honouring the deal?'

Last night came rushing back at her—the gentleness and joy of it. The way he'd hovered over her, lavishing her with his touch. Hands so sure and wonderful. The layered feelings of his mouth sliding over her, sometimes gentle, sometimes demanding. Worshipping her body with his— that's what it had felt like. Whenever she'd made a sound he'd been there, kissing her, soothing her. And even when she'd made no sound he'd been just there—something of his, on her.

But now, the morning after, with the terror of love choking her, she wanted to throw herself at his feet and beg him never to go, never to die.

But he couldn't promise that.

'Yes,' she whispered. 'I owed you and now we're done.'

She snatched her dress off the floor and started walking away.

'Where are you going?' Leo asked

'To the bathroom. To change.'

Leo folded his arms over his chest. 'Not only have my

eyes been all over your body, but so have my hands and my mouth. And now you're running to the bathroom?'

She paused, undecided. And then, with a defiant shrug, she ripped off the shirt she was wearing, dragged her dress over her head.

Leo bent, scooped something off the floor. 'Forgetting these?' he asked.

She snatched the tiny bronze-coloured panties from him and struggled into them while trying to stay covered.

'There,' she said. 'Happy?'

He watched her, brooding, hooded. 'No.'

'Leo, what do you want from me?'

'I want to know where you think we go from here—one month out from the wedding.'

'Well, we're going to be family. Sort of...'

'I'm not your brother.'

'I meant more like...like surrogate family. Like friends.'

'I'm not your friend.'

'But we *could* be friends.'

'I told you way back when that I don't do that.'

'I know you don't, usually—but I'm not like your other exes.'

'And I'm not like yours. I won't be Facebook "friending" you, making it to a movie, popping out for a coffee, or catching up over a casual dinner where we give each other a kiss on the cheek goodnight.'

'But why not?'

'Because I want you.'

She stared helplessly at him as her heart thudded in her aching chest. 'You already said you *didn't* want me.'

'I didn't say that.'

'You said you weren't besotted.'

'That's different. I want you, all right...the same way you want me. And it's got nothing to do with friendship.'

She swallowed. God. God, God, *God*. 'I—I don't want to…to want you like that.'

He moved like lightning, grabbing her arms and hauling her up on her toes. 'But you do. Your pupils are telling me you do, Sunshine,' he said, and smiled. 'Nice and big—for me.' He nudged his pelvis against her. 'Like that—nice and big. For you.'

She swallowed convulsively. 'You know I can't let myself love you.' The words sounded torn from her throat.

'Who mentioned love? Not me—*you* did, Sunshine. You.' He kissed her, a hard, drugging, wrenching scorch of mouth and tongue that made her melt and steam and long for him.

She almost cried out a protest when he stopped.

'Call this thing between us anything you want—except friendship,' he said. 'Because I will *never* be your friend.'

He let her go suddenly, and she stumbled backwards.

'I'm giving you fair warning, Sunshine: I *will* have you again. Five, six, seven times. Or ten, twenty. Anything except four. I will have you again, and there will be nothing friendly about it.'

Frustrated and furious, Leo went down to the beach after Sunshine had left.

No—she hadn't 'left'; she had run away, as if all the demons of hell were after her.

He needed a swim to snap his tortured brain back to a modicum of intelligence. And he hoped the water was frigid. He hoped—

Oh.

Oh, God.

There, a metre from the water, skewed in the sand, was the urn Sunshine had tossed aside last night.

And it was more effective than a swim in frigid water ever could have been.

Because it brought back every heartbreaking moment of that scene on the beach as the woman he loved had finally found the courage to say goodbye to her sister. The way she had given herself to him so sweetly afterwards, with gentleness and acceptance and yearning, and a heated desire that had seemed insatiable.

The contrast to this morning was not pretty.

He ran his hands over his head. Today was the anniversary of Moonbeam's death. And what had he done? Pushed and pushed her, without even giving her a chance to think. All but demanding that she strip for him, forcing her to kiss him, telling her he would take whatever he wanted, when he wanted.

It had been his survival instinct—alive and kicking—telling him to go his own way, *get* his own way, no matter what *she* wanted.

But seeing the urn was a concrete reminder that his way was not hers.

She had taken two years to farewell the sister she adored. She wasn't ready to love anyone else. Was too scared of the pain of it and too guilt-stricken to reach for what her sister could never have.

And he didn't have the right to force the love from her.

Not the right, and not the power.

She didn't want him to have all of her, the way he craved.

And if she couldn't give him her all, he was going to have to find a way to settle for nothing.

CHAPTER ELEVEN

'I will have you again, and there will be nothing friendly about it.'

Those words had been going around and around in Sunshine's head incessantly for four long weeks, until she'd started to wonder if she'd be too scared to go to the wedding.

She hadn't even been able to pluck up the courage to go to the airport to meet Jon's flight, because she was so certain Leo would be there—ready either to pounce on her or ignore her, and she didn't know which would be worse.

Now she'd finally got to see Jonathan, he didn't waste time on small talk. She barely had time to slap a Campari into his hand as he took a seat on her couch before he fixed his eagle eye on her across the coffee table and asked, 'What's going on with Leo, Sunshine?'

'What do you mean?

'Only that you went from mentioning his name in your emails to the point where I wanted to vomit to complete radio silence a month ago. And he did the same to Caleb.'

'Oh.'

'Yes, *oh*. I did warn you it wouldn't be hands across the water singing "Kumbaya" at the end.'

'Strictly speaking, that's hands around the campfire.'

'I will build a campfire and throw you on it if you give

me internet facts in the middle of this discussion. What happened?'

'It was the four-times rule.'

Jon rolled his eyes. 'Yes?'

'I wanted to stop at two, because I was…liking him too much, I guess. And he didn't want to stop.'

'But you stopped anyway?'

'Well…no. I couldn't seem to resist.'

'And the problem is… ?'

'That I just… I can't stop. Wanting him, I mean.'

'So *have* him.'

'You know I can't do that.'

'What I know, Sunny, is that you tell yourself a lot of crap! How do you know it's too painful to love a man when you've never done it? And don't hide behind the four-times rule. It's easy for you to pretend you've always stopped at one or two or even none because you're scared of caring too much. But the truth is you stop because you don't care *enough*! Which brings me back to Leo and the fact that you obviously finally *do* care enough. *What* is the problem?'

'I'm scared.'

'Sunny—love *is* scary. Not just for you, for everyone.'

'He doesn't love me. He only *wants* me.'

'So make him love you.'

'You can't make someone love you.'

'The Sunshine Smart *I* know can—if she wants to.'

'Well, she *doesn't* want to.'

'Just think about it.'

'No.'

'Then I'm telling your mother you asked for a book of original haiku poems for Christmas.'

She sputtered out a laugh. 'You're a rat, Jonathan.'

'Pour me another Campari and get me the computer. I'm going to look up Sydney's hottest models and try to choose Leo's next girlfriend. And when he nails her I am going to hire a skywriter to scrawl "I TOLD YOU SO" over Bondi Beach.'

And then Jonathan left his seat, came over to her, lifted her onto his lap. 'Sunny, darling one, give yourself a break and grab him.'

'How can I when…when Moonbeam…?'

'Moonbeam! *Sunny.* God, Sunny! Is *that* what this is about? She can't have love so you won't? She never wanted you to throw yourself onto her funeral pyre. That is so *not* her. And reverse the situation—would you have wanted *her* to give up living?'

'No. Of course not! And I know she would have loved him…and that makes it easier. If only…'

'If only?'

'If only he would never die,' she said, and buried her face against his chest.

'Oh, Sunny.' Jon kissed the top of her head. 'Would it really hurt any less just because you're not together? Wouldn't that be worse?'

'It's so hard. *Too* hard.'

'Yeah, life's hard. So why make it harder?'

Sipping a gin and tonic, Caleb leant back in his chair and examined his brother, head on one side.

It reminded Leo of Sunshine's curious bird look. And he couldn't bear it. He surged to his feet and paced the room, trying to shed some of the nervous energy that had infiltrated his body as the countdown to the wedding—to when he would see Sunshine again—began.

'Now that it's just us, suppose you tell me what's going on with Sunshine?' Caleb suggested.

'Nothing.'

'What happened? Did she fall in love with you and you had to hurt her feelings?'

Silence as Leo slid into his seat, picked up his drink and took a long swallow.

'Well?' Caleb prompted. And then his gaze sharpened. 'Oh, boy.'

'"Oh, boy"—*what*?'

'It was the other way around. You fell in love with *her*, and she had to hurt *your* feelings.'

'Not exactly.'

'Blood from a stone, or what?'

Leo put down his drink, ran his hands through his three centimetres of hair. 'We had an agreement—sex only. Four times.'

Caleb nodded, understanding. 'The four-times rule.'

Leo shot a startled look at Caleb. 'You *know* about that?'

'Yep. And you obviously agreed to it. Idiot. So then what?'

'And then she wanted...less.'

'She wanted less. Why? You were no good in the sack? Because that's not what I've heard.'

'Because she didn't want to care about me. Not just me—about anyone.'

'That is the dumbest thing ever.'

'It's a long story that I'm not going to go into except to say that she's not looking for romantic attachments. She only wants to be friends. But I pushed it. I pushed and pushed until I got all four times. But it didn't work. '

Caleb choked on his drink. 'She didn't *friend*-zone you!'

'She tried. I refused.' Deep sigh. 'And I ended up with nothing.'

Caleb was staring at him, flabbergasted. 'You are one dumb bastard.'

'Thank you,' Leo said dryly, and jumped to his feet again, pacing.

'So what are you going to do?' Caleb asked.

'Get through the wedding. Try to accept it's over.'

'That's not the Leo Quartermaine I know.'

'She was up-front from day one and I should have accepted it. The thing with her sister—it was devastating for her. I should have understood and left her alone, but I...' Stop. Start again. 'Instead I pushed her and pushed her.' Stop. Start again. 'And what right do I have to push her into feeling something she's not ready for?'

'We're never ready—none of us—for love.'

'She didn't fall in love with me. She wouldn't let herself.'

'So change her mind.'

Leo came to a stop in front of Caleb. 'She won't do it. She says that she would be anguished in love—live for him, die for him. That's the only way for her to love.' He stared at his brother. 'And I don't think I...'

'You don't think you...?'

'Deserve it. Deserve *her*. All I could say to her the last time I saw her was that I would *not* be her friend, that I would have her again—and again, and again—and that she couldn't stop me.' He was shaking now. 'That's the kind of thing someone like Natalie would want to hear, not Sunshine. The Natalie Clarkes are for me, not the Sunshine Smarts.'

A hopeless, helpless shrug.

'And she ran for the door faster than you could blink. And then I went down to the beach and I saw the urn and it hit me—what she'd been through the night before, when all I'd wanted was to help her find peace. But that morning...the anniversary...I was pushing her because I wanted more.' He scrubbed his hands over his face. 'No wonder she ran away from me.'

Three paces away. Three back.

'As soon as I saw the urn, Caleb, I knew that she would never belong to someone who's clawed and scraped his way out of hell, who's learned to grab and take and steal. Well,

I won't steal from *her*. I mean, who am I to steal from her what she doesn't want to freely give? Why would I think I'm special enough to—?' Stop. Start again. 'Who am I to even *want* it?'

Caleb stood slowly. 'Who are *you*, Leo? Just the bravest, best, most wonderful—' He broke off, grabbed Leo in a fierce hug.

For long moments they clung together. And then Caleb drew back, tears in his eyes.

'Now, I don't pretend to know the significance of the urn. But I know this: you deserve *everything*. And I'm going to give you an argument that will appeal to the noble, valiant, chivalrous, gallant core of you that our pathetic parents did *not* manage to destroy, no matter what you think.'

He gripped Leo by the shirtfront, looking fiercely into his eyes.

'You know why you deserve her? Because you will look after her better than any other man on the planet. Because you will live for *her*, die for *her*. How will you forgive yourself if some substandard joker breaks down her defences—someone who *won't* live and die for her? Who won't throw himself into that freaking abyss you carp on and on about? Think about that, Leo. Think about *that*.'

Leo stared at his brother.

And then he smiled.

CHAPTER TWELVE

THE WEDDING DAY was perfection.

It was warm, the sun was shining, and the restaurant sparkled.

A romantic day. A glorious day.

A day for *not* throwing yourself at the drop-dead gorgeous man that you were head over ears in love with. Even if every hair on your body tingled the moment you saw him stepping onto the terrace in shoes *you'd* designed, as if he owned the world and knew exactly what to do with it.

Even if you wanted to run your fingers through his newly grown hair and slide your hands over the lapels of his sharp and sexy suit, to lean in and take the clean, soapy smell of him into your brain via your nasal cavity.

Sunshine had thought getting her first Leo sighting out of the way would take the pressure off her, but it seemed to have had the opposite effect. Every one of her senses had sprung to life and seemed to crave something that could be found only in his immediate orbit.

Despite her wildly thumping heart and her clammy hands she tried to look serene as she made her way around the terrace, greeting, smiling, chatting. Her parents were looking as deliriously happy as usual. They'd brought Leo a batch of carob and walnut cookies. And a homemade diary for next year. And a haiku poem, framed, as a thank-you for inviting them to the beach that morning to see Moonbeam's final resting place.

They'd told her that he'd loved everything, that he was wonderful. She'd thought for an insane moment they intended to adopt him!

Sunshine was wondering whether to apologise to him about the framed haiku—at least it would be a valid reason to approach him—when, amazingly, she saw him go over to her parents. The three of them looked like a secret club as they whispered together, and then Leo was enfolded in her mother's arms and hugged almost convulsively. And then her father hugged him. The three of them were laughing, looking so *right* together. And then Leo kissed her mother on the cheek, shook her father's hand in a two-handed grip, and moved away.

Oh, my God. How the hell was she supposed to fall out of love with a man who was like *that* with her parents?

He really, *really* must like haiku!

There was just one thing left on Leo's wedding to-do list: make Sunshine fall in love with him before the cake-cutting.

Caleb was sure he could do it. Jonathan had threatened him with violence if he didn't at least try. And even her parents had given him a few pointers.

But he knew she was going to be a tough nut to crack.

Watching her do the rounds in that glistening, shimmering, silver dress, practically floating in those amazing shoes, he had felt his heart both soar and ache.

She'd painted her nails silver, and was wearing glittery earrings and a matching ring in addition to the swinging sun and moon chain. Her hair was perfect—even the fringe was behaving itself. She was wearing a slick of eyeliner;

she'd told him she would way back, when they'd struck their deal, so it was allowed. And deep rose lipstick.

Gorgeous, gorgeous, *gorgeous*.

Five times he'd tried to approach her. Five times he'd lost his nerve.

The upshot was that by the time everyone was seated they hadn't spoken a word to each other. Not one word.

But he nevertheless felt as connected to her as a piano wire to its tuning pin—he was sure if they just got the tension right the music would soar. How poetic was that?

He was aware of every mouthful she ate during dinner, and every mouthful she didn't. He heard every laugh. Caught every quickly averted look from those miraculous eyes whenever he glanced in her direction.

And then Jon and Caleb were moving to the small podium. Standing there, holding hands. Leo started to panic.

Time was almost up.

Jonathan cleared his throat, tapped his glass, and Sunshine held her breath as all eyes turned to the newlyweds.

'It's *that* time of the evening,' Jonathan said. 'All of you here tonight are close to one of us—and hence to both of us. You've shared our journey. You know our story. We are so happy to be home, to be here, to be with you. So happy that we don't intend to bore you to death with speeches! All we want to do is share with you the vows we spoke to each other last week in New York.

'They're short vows—but the words are very important to us. So…here goes: *Caleb, you are the one. When I look in your eyes I see my yearning…and the truth. When you smile at me I know I can tell you anything and find everything. When we touch I feel it in every breath, every nerve, every heartbeat. When we kiss it is magic and delight. And home as well. When you laugh, when you cry, when you rage, and even when you sneer—because you*

*sure can sneer—I am with you. You are everything to me
and always will be. Caleb, my one, this is my vow to you.*'

Caleb blinked hard.

'Oh,' he said. 'That's the second time—and it gets me
just as much as it did the first time. My turn: *My Jonathan.
I have known love before. Friends, colleagues. Most im-
portantly brother—and off-script, because Jon won't mind,
Leo, by God, you know how important you are to me—
but never before this love. This love is wrenching. Lovely.
Scared. Careful. Proud. This love calms me. Excites me.
Reassures me. Delights me. This love is everything. This
love—my love—I will not and cannot be without. This love
I give back to you—you will never be without it. Jonathan,
this is my vow to you.*'

Sunshine, her breath caught somewhere in her chest,
felt an acrid sting at the back of her nose. Tears. She was
going to cry.

Because *she* wanted that kind of love. *Wanted* it. *So*
much.

Leo had told her a month ago that he would not be her
friend, that she would come to him. But she had been too
scared. And now it was too late. Because Leo hadn't even
spoken to her—had barely looked at her today. And she
was *still* too scared.

She walked quickly towards the entrance, smiling, eyes
full of tears. Four steps away. Three. Two. One—

Her arm was grabbed. She was spun around. And Leo
was there. Unsmiling.

'What is it, Sunshine?' he asked. 'Did it hit you? Finally? That it's what you want?'

'I can't, Leo.'

'Enough! I've had *enough*, Sunshine. You damned well
can. I'm lonely without you. I need you.'

Her heart ached, throbbed. But she shook her head.

He ignored the head-shake, took her hand, dragged her to the ladies' restroom.

'A restroom?' she asked. 'We're going to have this discussion in a restroom?'

'Oh, it's not just a restroom,' he said. 'It's a restroom with custom-made blue and green toilet paper.'

She stared at him. 'With...?' She whirled. Raced into one of the cubicles. Laughed.

He'd followed her in and she turned. 'Why?' she asked.

'Because I love you,' he said.

'What kind of juxtaposition is that? Toilet paper and love?' She could hear the breathiness in her voice. *Oh, God—oh, my God. Is this happening?*

'The toilet paper is a big deal, Sunshine. A *very* big deal. Because I said I'd never do it—and yet I did. People can do that, you know. Say they'll never do something and then do it. Like fall in love when they say they have no room in their hearts.'

'You s-said...you t-told me...you were not—*not*—besotted with me.'

'I'm *not* besotted with you. Besotted is for amateurs. I'm madly, crazily, violently in love with you. It's not the same thing. We're talking a massive abyss, no parachute.'

She swallowed. 'Leo, I—I...'

'Think about it,' he urged, stepping closer. 'You suck at making lists—I excel. Complementary.'

Impossible laughter. Choked off. 'Romantic,' she said.

'You do your best work at night, and so do I. So we're synchronised.'

'*Very* romantic.'

'You know stupid stuff and I want to hear it.'

She slapped a hand over her mouth, swallowing the giggle.

'You eat,' he said, starting to smile. 'I cook.'

'Hmm...'

'Getting closer, am I? Because I will cook for you morning, noon, and night—sending people all over Sydney into a state of shock! I will name a cut of meat after you. I will teach you to cook paella. I will invent a five-course degustation dessert menu just so I can watch you devour sugar.'

Half-laugh, half-tears. 'Oh, Leo.'

'I will play *"Je t'aime-ich liebe-ti amor You Darling"* in the bedroom.'

'You will not!' she said.

'That was a trick one. But you can *decorate* the bedroom. The bamboo is ordered, just in case you want a Balinese honeymoon suite, but you can do it any way you want. Perhaps go easy on the pink, though. And— Look, don't you *get* it? Do I really have to keep going?'

She was almost breathless. Staring. Hoping. Wanting this—him. 'What do I have to do in return?'

He grabbed her hand, flattened it against his heart. 'You get the easy bit. All you have to do is love me.'

She looked into his eyes. Knew that there still wasn't any room in her heart—because he'd taken up every bit of it.

'That's too easy. Because I already do love you.' Her eyes widened. 'Oh, my God, I said it. I love you. I've jumped. No parachute.'

He closed his eyes, took a deep breath. Opened them. So serious. 'I have a very particular kind of love in mind. I have to belong. To you. I have to *belong* to you, Sunshine.'

'I know,' she said. 'You want me to throw myself off the cliff. Sink into that damned abyss. Pour my soul into you and drown in you so that you are everything. Live for you, die for you. Too easy, I'm telling you!'

He let her hands go to pull her into his arms, kissed her mouth. 'And I want you to look at our beach and know that your sister is at peace, and that I am always with you to bear whatever grief you have.'

She was crying now, and he was wiping her tears with his thumbs.

'And children,' he said. 'I want a daughter named Amaya Moonbeam.'

More tears. 'Oh, Leo.'

'And a second daughter who can take on Allyn. And a son named whatever the hell you want. Only perhaps not Oaktree or Thunderbolt or Mountain.'

How could you laugh and cry at the same time? 'I can manage that.'

He kissed her again. 'And shoes. I want custom-made shoes. I'm not wearing any other kind from now on.'

'Well, that goes without saying.'

'And maybe a weekly haiku.'

'Um—no! We are *not* encouraging my mother in that.'

'Okay. But your parents get their own wing in the beach house, so they can be close to their daughters any time they want and teach me how to be the kind of parent who brings up wonderful kids.'

Crying hard. 'Leo!'

'And I still want you to change your name. But only your surname—to make you mine, Sunshine Quartermaine. With a ten-tier coconut vanilla bean wedding cake to seal the deal.'

Sunshine sighed and leant into him. Kissed him so hard his heart leapt. 'The medulla oblongata,' she said, rubbing her hand over his heart.

He felt the laugh building. 'The what?'

'The part of the brain that controls the heartbeat,' she said.

'God, I love you,' he said. 'So! Let's go and give the old medulla oblongata a real workout. Because what I really, really want right now, Sunshine, is assignation number five. And tomorrow morning we'll go for number six. And I— God, someone's coming in. What the *hell* are we doing in a restroom? Let's blow this joint.'

* * * * *

'Let's make sure everyone believes that we are on a date, OK? And try and look happy about it. A lot of women would pay to be in your shoes.'

'I'm not a lot of women.'

He'd gathered that. 'Then you'll have to fake it. Let's go.' Glancing at his watch, he gestured to her bag. 'Leave that. I'll get someone to take it out of here.'

'Give me five minutes. I need make-up. And shoes, for that matter.' She leant down to pull out a silver clutch bag and a pair of shoes. Long, elegant feet slipped into lime-green high-heeled wedge sandals and his pulse kicked up a notch.

Enough. Straightening up, she pivoted to face the mirror, leaving him with an alluring view of her bare back, the black dress tapering down in a V to the voluptuous curve of her bottom.

Adam forced himself to turn away.

'I'm ready.'

He swivelled round and a whoosh of air was expelled from his lungs as desire upped another notch. In a few minutes she'd been transformed from au naturel beauty to glamorous allure. Which meant she had him coming and going.

Her hazel eyes shimmered and her lips were outlined in glossy dark red. Lips he wanted to claim right here. Right now. *Oh, hell.* He was screwed; no way was his libido leaving this party.

Dear Reader

This book is incredibly special to me—partly because it is my Mills & Boon debut, but also because I am so excited that Olivia and Adam, who lived inside my head for a long time, have made it into the big wide world.

The first chapter of this book wrote itself—I knew that nothing would stop Olivia from getting to Adam once she had him in her sights. I also knew that Adam would put up the fight of his life to avoid being bagged.

But there the book stopped. Until one day not so long ago when Olivia and Adam demanded I get them out of the ladies' restroom and let them try and sort out what happened next…

So I did!

I hope you enjoy reading about the trials and tribulations that beset them on their sometimes rocky path to love.

Nina xx

HOW TO BAG
A BILLIONAIRE

BY
NINA MILNE

Published in Great Britain 2014
by Mills & Boon, an imprint of Harlequin (UK) Limited,
Eton House, 18-24 Paradise Road, Richmond, Surrey, TW9 1SR

© 2014 Nina Milne

ISBN: 978-0-263-24680-3

Harlequin (UK) Limited's policy is to use papers that are natural, renewable and recyclable products and made from wood grown in sustainable forests. The logging and manufacturing processes conform to the legal environmental regulations of the country of origin.

Printed and bound in Spain
by Blackprint CPI, Barcelona

Nina Milne has always dreamt of writing for Mills & Boon®—ever since as a child she discovered stacks of Mills & Boon® books 'hidden' in the airing cupboard. She graduated from playing libraries to reading the books, and has now realised her dream of writing them.

Along the way she found a happy-ever-after of her own, accumulating a superhero of a husband, three gorgeous children, a cat with character and a real library… Well, lots of bookshelves.

Before achieving her dream of working from home creating happy-ever-afters whilst studiously avoiding any form of actual housework, Nina put in time as both an accountant and a recruitment consultant. She figures the lack of romance in her previous jobs is now balancing out.

After a childhood spent in Peterlee (UK), Rye (USA), Winchester (UK) and Paris (France), Nina now lives in Brighton (UK), and has vowed never to move again!! Unless, of course, she runs out of bookshelves. Though there is always the airing cupboard…

**HOW TO BAG A BILLIONAIRE
is Nina Milne's debut for Modern Tempted™!**

**This title is also available in ebook format
from www.millsandboon.co.uk**

For my husband, Sandy, and our children,
Jack, Harmony and Harry.
Thank you for putting up with me whilst I wrote this book.
It probably wasn't easy.

PROLOGUE

August edition. Glossip *magazine*

Today's advice column is for all you gold-diggers out there.

How to bag a billionaire in six easy steps.

Looking for a lifestyle change?

Down on your luck?

Don't despair! How about you bag yourself a billionaire?

OK, ladies—here's how you do it:

1. Identify your target:

He needs to be loaded and he needs to be single—and wouldn't it be a bonus if he were drop-dead gorgeous, as well? Too much to hope for? Not today. Because we have done some digging and found a dream target for you. Drumroll, please... We give you Mr Adam Masterson, Founder and CEO of Masterson Hotels. Richer than rich and sexier than sin.

2. Discover what he likes in a woman:

We've done some research and it wasn't easy, folks. Adam Masterson is a bit of a dark horse. But the good news is that over the past years he has been seen about town with a variety of types. Blonde or dark. Small or tall... This field is open to all. Adam Masterson's only criteria is beauty: the man likes his ladies easy on the eye.

3. Adjust yourself accordingly:

Hubble, bubble, toil and trouble… Lotions, potions, get on with the motions! Start beautifying, ladies.

4. Work out your target's routine:

This is a tough one. Adam Masterson has no routine—Paris one day, London the next. But we have it on good authority that his swish flagship hotel might be the place to start.

5. Waylay target:

Time to find your inner minx and cook up some schemes.

6. Seduce target:

Over to you…

Adam Masterson is out there. He is worth billions and he is worth bagging. Who will bag him first?
Happy Hunting!

CHAPTER ONE

SHE COULD GET arrested for this.

The thought pounded her temples as Olivia Evans glanced around the dark and thankfully deserted London alleyway at the back of Masterson Mayfair, the flagship of Masterson Enterprises hotel portfolio.

Why had she thought gatecrashing one of London's most exclusive parties was a good idea?

A bead of perspiration prickled her forehead. Swiping it away with an impatient gesture, she pressed her lips together hard. This was a good idea because it was the only idea left. It was imperative that she see Adam Masterson before he gallivanted off on yet another business trip. She had tried every conventional method of contacting him, but the man was more closely guarded than the president of the United States. There was every possibility his PA doubled as Head of National Security.

Desperate times called for desperate measures; hence Operation Break and Enter.

Olivia hauled in a breath; with any luck that would push the panic down. One final glance around and, standing on her tote bag, she applied herself to the task of picking the window lock. Amazing how some childhood skills didn't desert you. Even those learnt from one of the more unsavoury of her mother's boyfriends. The thought of her mother had her shoving the hooked pick deeper into the lock until she felt it butt into the mechanism; she would not give up now.

Nerves knotted inside her before giving way to a buzz of exhilarated relief as the lock gave. Pocketing the pick, she pulled the window open, then jumped off the tote bag. She thrust the bag through the gap a minute later.

So far, so good. Her reconnaissance of the hotel had been spot-on; the room she had chosen as an access point was a small conference room which wouldn't be in use tonight as the hotel was being exclusively given over to a charity gala. Hosted by Adam Masterson. *Finally* she had him in her sights.

She scrambled up onto the window ledge and her nerves retied themselves right back up. What her recon *hadn't* bargained for was the size of the window gap.

Logic. Angles. Weight. Mass distribution. Those were the things to focus on—because, come hell or high water, Olivia *would* get inside. Never mind that it looked to be physically impossible.

So should she wriggle in forwards on her tummy or try to get in backwards? There were so many things that could go wrong: she could get stuck, she could fall into the arms of a waiting security guard... Maybe this wasn't such a brilliant idea.

But if she gave up now then she wouldn't get a chance to talk to Adam Masterson.

That was unacceptable.

Good thing she was flexible.

Adam Masterson perched on the edge of his security officer's desk and scowled at the CCTV footage of the woman balanced on the windowsill.

What the hell was she doing? Apart from an excellent impersonation of Catwoman. Dressed completely in black, with a beanie pulled low over her forehead, it was impossible even to know her hair colour.

More to the point, who the hell was she? Journalist? Photographer? Wishful thinking... He'd already arranged publicity for the event. Which meant here was yet *another* hopeful player in the new party game Bag a Billionaire. Bad enough that he knew the ballroom would soon be awash with legitimate guests scheming how to waylay him over the canapés. At least they'd paid for the privilege, with the money going to a more than worthy cause.

Tendrils of memory threatened and he cut them off before they could take hold. He'd had his daily surfeit of grim memories already today, following his earlier conversation with his ex-wife and the news that she was remarrying. He was happy for Charlotte, but the exchange had brought back recollections of a time in his life he was less than proud of. *Way* less.

Plus, it had highlighted the way their lives had gone in the eight years since their disastrous union. There was Charlotte, with the happy-ever-after she had always wanted; here was Adam, being pursued by a bunch of women mining for his gold.

Speaking of which, right now he had to contend with his gatecrasher. He bit back an exasperated groan; he didn't need this. The entire billionaire-bagging thing was getting old.

'Do you want us to apprehend her?' Nathan asked.

Adam pulled himself into the present and focused on the screen. The woman appeared to be engaged in some sort of internal Q and A session before she wriggled limbo-dancer-like through the gap in the window.

An arrow of desire shot straight through him.

He ran a hand over the top of his head. Talk about misplaced. A probable stalker, a definite intruder, was breaking into his hotel and his libido had decided to come to the party. The woman landed on the floor, glanced round the empty room and opened the bag she had pushed through earlier.

Adam opened his mouth to instruct his security chief to get a team down there.

And closed it again on a strangled gargle, unable to wrench his eyes from the screen as the woman pulled the black beanie from her head and shook out a mane of extraordinary hair. Strawberry blonde tresses, with the balance towards strawberry, fell past her shoulders.

Crossing her arms, she hoisted her black jumper over her head to reveal a white tunic top, and then with a little twist pushed her jeans down her hips.

Misplaced or not, desire pulled his libido's strings. Time to get a grip; better yet, maybe it was time to get a date. Clearly it had been too long—ever since that article had appeared and the baggers had emerged from the woodwork he'd put himself on a stint of enforced celibacy. Partly because the thought of being chased for his money brought a tang of distaste, and partly because he wanted any press attention to be focused on his charitable activities and not his bedroom ones.

Until now it hadn't been an issue.

'So what next?' Nathan asked.

It was a good question.

The woman was now fully clothed in an outfit that at a glance resembled the uniform worn by all hotel employees; she'd obviously done her research. White tunic top, black trousers—she'd even got a clipboard. The intent look on her face backed up the determined set of her jaw as she swept her magnificent hair into an efficient bun.

Picking up the bag, she opened the door and walked down the corridor. Her stride confident, she looked as though she knew exactly where she was going and why.

Of course there was no way he would allow her access to his guests; it was just fascinating to watch her at work. The first bagger to catch his interest and certainly the most resourceful.

But enough was enough. Time to mobilise the troops.

Before he could say anything Nathan's massive body tensed as she ducked into the ladies' restroom. 'Better hope she *is* a bagger. For all we know she could be building a bomb in there.'

Staring at the screen, Adam concentrated on unclenching his jaw. It was an outside chance, but it was still possible that the intruder was armed. And he had let a moment of inappropriate attraction blindside him. A pulse started to beat in his cheek and he closed his eyes, grounded himself, before pushing himself away from the desk in a single lithe movement.

'Close the ladies'. Be discreet. Say it's a plumbing problem and send your men down there in cleaners' uniforms.'

Nathan nodded. 'I'll go in and get her out,' he said.

Adam shook his head. 'I screwed up. I'll go in.'

'But…'

'No buts,' Adam said. 'We could've stopped her by now. That was my call and I didn't make it.' Too busy stewing over the past whilst lusting over a stranger. Who said men couldn't multitask?

'I still think…'

Adam shook his head. If he didn't sort this one out himself the strawberry blondee stranger would haunt his dreams for too long. Best to make her real. Expose her as the avaricious gold-digger she undoubtedly was whilst avoiding the baggers no doubt waiting to hunt him down in the ballroom.

He picked up his tux jacket and gave Nathan his best impression of an action hero. 'I'm going in.'

* * *

Olivia mentally ran through her entire and extensive repertoire of swear words. This was ridiculous! This was supposed to be the easy bit. The bit where she locked herself into a cubicle and transformed herself from faux hotel employee to fake ballroom guest. All she had to do was change into a party dress. Good grief! What sort of personal shopper couldn't get herself into a dress? A dress she'd tried on at home with no problem.

But now the stupid zip on the stupid little black blend-right-in dress was stuck. Worse, she couldn't get out of the skintight concoction to *un*stick it.

As she twisted she lost her balance and the back of her knee thunked the lip of the toilet seat. 'Ouch!' Biting her lip, she stilled. Please let there be no one out there. Though…surely there *should* be someone out there? Guests must have arrived in droves by now so it made sense that someone would want to freshen up in the ladies' restroom.

That was the essence of the last stage of her plan. Guests would only be allowed entry into the hotel on production of an invitation, embossed and coded and impossible to duplicate. This was a private party, an annual gala that raised hundreds of thousands of pounds for Support Myeloma, thanks to the auctioneering powers of Adam Masterson. But she was already in the building, and as the invitations were inspected at the foyer of the hotel Olivia figured she should be safe.

Particularly as the plan was to leave the ladies' with a group of other women who would serve as camouflage. Then she would find a large potted palm and lurk unnoticed until the moment arrived when she could snag Adam Masterson.

After all, she was good at lurking at parties.

Memories skittered through her brain as echoes of raucous laughter peppered with the pop of champagne corks reverberated in her eardrums. How she had hated the numerous shindigs her mother had hosted, even as she'd understood Jodie Evans's desperate need to extract fun out of every second of a life that had stacked the odds against her. Olivia hadn't begrudged her mother one of those seconds of fun; she had wished with all her heart for Jodie to be happy. The knowledge that she could never repay everything she owed her mum was always with her.

Closing her eyes, she sucked air into her lungs. For goodness' sake! This was not the time for a trip down memory lane. Any minute now someone was bound to come in here so she had better hurry up. How hard could this be? She was *flexible*, remember? She reached round for the zip.

'Need a hand?'

Olivia froze as an unmistakably male voice drawled out the question.

In slow motion she forced herself to look up at the man observing her over the top of the cubicle. He must be standing on the toilet in the next door cubicle, her brain told her dully, trying to operate past the volcano of panic about to erupt in her chest.

Dark hair, light brown eyes, square jaw, a nose that was ever so slightly off-shape... Recognition slammed her like a sucker punch. 'It's you,' she breathed.

His eyebrows pulled together in a deep frown as his lips tightened. 'In the flesh,' he said.

Olivia opened her mouth but the words evaporated under the heat of his gaze. Plus, she was damned if she knew the best way to explain her presence. Blurting out her reason for being there whilst standing half-dressed in a toilet cubicle had *not* been part of the Masterson Master Plan.

Still, she was going to have to work with what she had; this was an opportunity. 'Mr Masterson,' she began. 'I can expl—'

'I need to check your bag,' he broke in.

'My bag?'

'Yes, your bag,' he said, his impatience tingeing the air.

Olivia glanced down at the bag in confusion. Looking back up at the exasperation that lit the brown eyes, she realised his motivation was irrelevant. Right now it seemed clear he wouldn't listen to anything she said until she gave it to him. She ducked down awkwardly and picked up the bag.

'I'll come round,' he said.

She heard the thud as he presumably jumped down from the toilet; she pushed the door open and held out the bag. 'Look, is this really necessary?' she asked, a shudder of aversion shivering through her as he started to sift through the contents.

'Yes,' he stated. 'My security chief is worried that you are locked in here constructing a bomb.'

Fabulous! Her stomach plummeted into a free fall of panic; she was under suspicion of being a terrorist.

Come on, Olivia. Calm down. You've talked your way out of worse than this before.

Though she suspected that talking her way past this man would be akin to melting iron with an incense stick.

Still, she had to try. She took a step forward out of the cubicle and straightened her spine.

'I realise all this is a bit bizarre, but I'm not a terrorist and I'm not here with the intention of hurting anyone. If—'

Adam Masterson wasn't so much as looking at her, let alone listening. Instead he was on the phone.

'Nate,' he said. 'I've checked the bag. Our enterprising intruder locked herself in the toilet to get dressed, not to build a bomb.' He listened for a moment and then put the phone back into his pocket.

OK. At least the terrorist theory had been knocked on the head. Not that Adam Masterson looked relieved; if anything the set of his lips was even grimmer, the frown deeper. Time to try again.

'Look, I'm truly sorry,' she said. 'I never meant to cause so much hassle. I really, *really* just want to—'

A derisive snort interrupted her. 'I know what you really, *really* want to do, and I'm really, *really* not interested.'

Olivia frowned. 'You can't possibly know why I'm here.' She was having trouble enough believing it herself.

Adam pulled his phone out of his pocket.

'Hang on!' Olivia said. 'You've got to listen.'

He shook his head. 'Nope, I don't. I've got to get Security in here to remove you from the premises.'

The panic erupted in her chest; this was her chance and she'd blown it. Unless… Maybe now was the time to utilise her black belt in taekwondo.

Propelled by the sheer impossibility of failure, Olivia launched herself at him.

'What the—?'

Taking advantage of his millisecond of surprise, she knocked the phone from his hand.

To no avail.

In a fluid movement he'd caught the mobile and shock juddered Olivia's body as she collided with an immovable wall of chest. Strong arms locked behind her back in a hold way too powerful for her to break even as she leant back, shoving her palms flat against his chest.

Her breath escaped in short, sharp pants as she looked up at him. For a fleeting second his light brown eyes darkened and focused on her lips. Unable to help herself, she dropped her gaze to his mouth as a sudden shiver prickled her skin.

A shiver not of fear but of desire.

Which was ridiculous. Right now her instincts should have kicked in; she should be at least attempting to struggle free. Instead she couldn't stop staring at the mesmerising shape of those firm, capable lips. His heart pounded under her hand; her fingers curled into the silk of his white shirt.

As she pressed her own lips together to moisten them something primal flickered in his eyes. His arms tensed to pull her forward. Then abruptly he released her.

Her skin tingled where his arms had touched her and Olivia stepped backwards, until the cold marble of the counter pressed into the backs of her thighs. Her heart thumped painfully against her ribcage. Perspective—she desperately needed to locate some. Along with control. Her master plan was in tatters and somehow she had to salvage it. Before Adam Masterson called Security.

He stood there, those gorgeous lips set in a grim line. Anger darkened his face; his eyes were cold chips of mud. 'Lady, just how far are you prepared to go to bag me?'

'Excuse me?' What was he talking about? Perhaps his proximity had addled her brain cells completely. Somehow she had to pull herself together and try and turn this situation around. She had no idea what had happened in those charged seconds in his arms but she couldn't let it ruin everything. 'I don't understand.'

An exasperated sigh hit the air. 'Drop the act. I know you're here to "bag me",' he said, hooking his fingers in the air to indicate quotation marks.

'As in murder you and put you in a body bag? Tempting, but given your security levels I'll pass.'

For a second she thought she saw his lips give the tiniest of quirks. Was it possible the man possessed a sense of humour?

He swiped his hand over his mouth and shook his head. 'You haven't heard of Bag a Billionaire?' The narrowed eyes, the creased forehead were both clear indicators of patent disbelief; the gleam of humour had obviously been a mirage.

'Nope. Honest.'

His frown deepened. 'In a nutshell, some idiot magazine reporter wrote an article advising wannabe gold-diggers on how to bag themselves a billionaire and identified me as the target. Since then I've arrived home to find a naked woman in my bed with "Kiss me Quick, Kiss me Slow" tattooed on her stomach and an arrow pointing downward, my mail yesterday included some rather explicit photographs, I have had women break the heels of their shoes and collapse in a heap in front of me, and women's cars seem to miraculously break down wherever I go.' Pausing, he eyed her. 'I'm sure you get the picture.'

'That's terrible,' Olivia said. 'But…'

'Terrible?' he echoed, the mocking note jarring through the air. 'I agree. Though I must say no one has resorted to gatecrashing a party with quite such style as you have.'

It took a minute for the implications of his words to sink in before outrage smacked her mouth wide open. 'You think… You mean… You think I'm like one of those women?'

He leant back against the wall, arms folded. 'You've broken into my hotel and thrown yourself into my arms in a dress that is conveniently falling off you—what do you expect me to think?'

Anger started to bubble at his sheer arrogance, stirred frothier by the small part of her that conceded the devil had a point.

One hand slammed on her hip even as the other held the dress up. 'I admit I've broken into your hotel, but I did not *throw myself* at you. I promise you I haven't risked arrest for the supposed pleasure of "bagging" you.'

For a moment he studied her face and she met his gaze full-on, saw something flicker in the milk chocolate depths. She prayed he could hear the truth in her voice. Otherwise he would have her marched out of here any second now and she couldn't let that happen. There was way too much at stake here—and not just for herself.

'Please,' she said. 'I understand why you are suspicious but you don't need to be. I promise. Give me a chance to prove it to you. Hear me out. Please.'

'Fine,' he said. 'You've got ten seconds.'

CHAPTER TWO

HARD TO TELL who was more surprised—the strawberry
blonde stranger or himself. Irritation coursed through his
veins; he'd been blindsided by a beautiful face and a spectacular body. This woman was bad news, and no matter
what lies she was about to spin from that gorgeous mouth
the key point was that they *would* be lies—a calculated
strategy with the aim of locating his wallet.

The chances of her not being a billionaire-bagger were
minuscule, yet there had been a vibrancy to her voice, a
desperate glint in those hazel eyes that had clouded his
usually impeccable judgement.

Pushing the sleeve of his tux jacket up, he looked at his
watch. 'Five seconds left. Four...three...'

'My mother is pregnant,' she blurted out.

Her words echoed around the bathroom and bounced
off the mirrored tiles.

What on earth did she expect him to do? Maybe she
wasn't a billionaire-bagger. Maybe she was crazy. 'Offer
her my congratulations,' he said. 'And now I think it's
time for you to go.'

'I need to tell you who the father is.'

Adam gusted out a sigh. 'Lady, if you think you can
scam me into believing it's me that's *not* going to fly.'

For a start his unwanted intruder had to be in her mid-

twenties, and he hadn't dated an older woman in a very
long time. But even if that weren't the case Adam always
made 100 per cent sure that pregnancy was an impossibility. One thing was certain in his life: he was not father material. After all, he was a Masterson through and
through and he knew his own limitations. The less than
stellar circumstances of his marriage had showcased his
shortcomings all too brightly.

'I'm not trying to scam anyone.' Her hands twisted into
the folds of her black dress. 'The baby's father is *your* father. Zebediah Masterson. And I need to find him.'

Long practice at the poker table kept his face neutral
even as her words travelled towards him in slow motion,
each one slamming into him with the force of a sucker
punch.

Come on, Adam. Keep cool. This was nothing more
than an über-clever scam, a fantastic concoction woven
to get his attention.

'Rubbish,' he stated.

'It's not rubbish.' One slim hand rose to jab the air in
emphasis; her other hand still held the black dress up. 'Or
rocket science. It's simple biology. My mum is pregnant
and Zebediah is the father. So I need to find him.'

Moisture prickled his temple with foreboding before
common sense reasserted itself. No way would Zeb want
a replay of fatherhood. Plus, surely even Zeb would have
bothered to get in touch over something like this?

'I don't think so,' he said.

'And *I* don't think you get it. I need to find him because
I need to tell him about the baby. He doesn't know.'

For a treacherous second relief ran through his veins;
if this preposterous tale was true at least Zeb hadn't deliberately walked away from another unwanted baby. The
way he'd walked out on Adam. *Whoa.* This wasn't about

the past; it was about the here and now and this no doubt mythical baby.

'I see,' he said, allowing scepticism to load each syllable. 'How convenient for you.'

Hazel eyes narrowed. 'There is nothing convenient about this. Have you any idea how difficult it is to locate your father? I've spent weeks looking for him and finally I discovered *you*. So if you could just tell me how to contact him I'll be on my way.'

Was she serious? 'Not happening.'

Brows just a shade darker than her hair arched. 'Why not?'

'Because I don't want you harassing my father with some trumped-up paternity suit.'

'Trumped-up paternity suit?' Her free hand clenched into a fist and he braced himself. 'Why are you assuming it's trumped-up? For—'

The buzz of his phone cut off whatever else she had been about to say. He pressed it his ear and Nate's voice erupted.

'What's going on in there? Guests are arriving thick and fast and they are getting more and more curious.'

'The intruder isn't a threat.' Or at least not to the guests; she was having a less than happy effect on him. 'I'll be there in a minute.' Once he'd decided what to do about Little Miss Minx and her preposterous claim. In the meantime, with any luck, his guests' curiosity might divert them from the billionaire-bagging hunt.

Dropping the phone back into his pocket, he studied her. Hmm... He drummed his fingers on his thigh as he went through the options, a glimmer of a possibility sparking.

'You can't just go,' she said. 'I need to know where to find your dad.'

'No.' Adam considered his idea from all angles. 'Turn around.'

'What?' Bewilderment layered her voice

'Turn around. I'll zip the dress up for you.' He tipped his palms into the air. 'You're going to the ball.'

It was the perfect solution. She remained where he could see her until he could disprove her story. And, as the icing on the cake, if he turned up to the ball with a beautiful woman on his arm he'd have a shield against all the other billionaire-baggers. Win-win. Adam made no effort to conceal the smirk that touched his lips.

There was a moment's silence as her jaw dropped. 'Don't be ridiculous.'

'I'm not being ridiculous. You strike me as a loose cannon. So until I understand the situation you will stay glued to my side.'

The words triggered an unwanted reaction: the thought of how she had felt in his arms earlier made his fingers itch to pull her right back to him. Madness, and yet she was the epitome of allure. The expressive hazel eyes, the delicate elven features and luscious mouth combined to make her ludicrously kissable.

Throw in hair the colour of sunset and a body that showcased curves in all the right places and he was in trouble.

His fingers tingled. *Hell.* All of him tingled and any desire to smirk left him.

Great. His libido had decided to overlook the fact that this woman was an adversary, only here as a player in an elaborate scheme. Though unlike the other baggers it could be that her plan was to forgo the billionaire and aim straight for the money. Use Zeb to get to the cash. His expression hardened. No way was that happening—and she'd seriously underestimated him if she thought it was.

'I have no intention of being glued to your side.' Pushing herself off the sink, she glared at him. 'And I am not coming to the ball. It doesn't even make sense.'

'It makes perfect sense to me. You could go to the press.

You could disappear and resume your quest for Zeb. You know what? I have no idea what kooky scheme you may come up with.'

'I wouldn't go to the press! *Why* would I do that?'

'Publicity? Money? Fun? I don't know.' Raking a hand through his hair, he stepped forward. 'Why would you break into my hotel to gatecrash my party? It's hardly the mark of a sane woman.'

'It's the mark of a desperate woman.' Anger sparked the hazel of her eyes with green flecks. 'Funnily enough breaking and entering wasn't my number one choice. I tried to get hold of you by more conventional methods but your PA wouldn't let me near you and you ignored my letters,' she continued. 'Presumably I fell into the probable billionaire-bagger category.'

'Honey, you *still* fall into that category.' And he'd better not forget it. Glancing at his watch, he muttered a curse. 'We can discuss all this later. Right now you are coming with me.'

'Says who? You can't force me to go with you.'

'Want to bet?' Adam took another step forward. 'Here's your choice. You can put your shoes on and accept my kind invitation or I will call the police and have you charged with breaking and entering. Your call.'

Her whole body vibrated in sheer disbelief. 'That's blackmail!'

'Breaking and entering is a criminal offence,' he returned.

'I had a good reason.'

'So do I. So, prison or party? Your choice.'

Her lush lips pressed together as she stared at him before hitching slim shoulders. 'Fine. I'll come to the party. But you have to promise me that afterwards you will give me your father's contact details.'

Unease solidified in his gut; there was no hint of insin-

cerity in her voice. In fact if push came to shove he would
swear she didn't want to come to the party at all.

'After the party we talk,' he said. Given twenty minutes,
he had no doubt he could rip her story to shreds.

'Fine,' she agreed, and reached round to tug at the zip
on her dress once more.

'Let me do that.'

For a moment he thought she'd refuse, but instead she
gave another little shrug and spun around to place one
palm flat on the marble counter, strawberry head bowed
as though she didn't wish to see his or her reflection in
the mirror.

Probably a good thing. Because confronted with the
smooth expanse of her back his lungs constricted and heat
tingled on his cheekbones.

It's only a back, Adam.

Yet his fingers trembled as he reached out and inadvertently brushed the base of her spine as he tugged at the zip.

'It's stuck,' he said, the words straining past the breath
of disproportionate desire that had hitched in his throat.

'I know that.' The snap of her words was insufficient to
drown her audible gulp; the small shiver that caressed her
skin in goosebumps testified to the effect of his touch. 'I
told you that I wasn't deliberately falling out of it.'

With relief he freed the silken material and whooshed
the zip up, the noise vying with the pounding in his ears

'So how will you explain who I am?' she demanded as
she turned to face him.

'I've been thinking about that.'

'Oh, goodie,' she said. 'Care to share?'

His lips twisted with the irony of his idea. 'Congratulations! You've bagged a billionaire.'

Her body froze into utter immobility before she shook
her head. 'I am *not* coming as your billionaire-bagger date.'

Adam frowned; behind the anger in her eyes was a vulnerable gleam of genuine horror.

'No way am I walking in there with everyone believing I'm with you for your money. I'd *rather* go to prison.'

'Don't be melodramatic. Who cares what people think?' Adam lifted his shoulders in pure indifference.

'In this case, me,' she said, as her hands slammed on the curve of her hips.

Irritation coursed through his veins at the continued sheer sincerity of her tone and the fact that he couldn't work her out.

'Tough,' he said. 'You're coming to the ball—and what's more you're coming as my date. I'd rather people assume you've bagged me than work out why you are claiming to be here. I do *not* want any publicity about this.'

'What happened to not caring about what people think?'

'Honey, I don't care what people think about *you*. I *do* care what they think about my dad. And right now I don't need the publicity backlash.' Not when he was hosting the gala tonight and launching another charity event the next evening. 'The press are already having a field day with the bagger theme.' Amazing how many women were willing to bare their bodies and perjure their souls by lying to the tabloids.

Resolve hardened in him. No way was all the hard work and effort he had put into the Support Myeloma charity going to waste. Not one copper penny should be diverted from the cause he championed in his mother's memory. An image of his mother sprang to mind: pale and weak, but still with the beautiful smile that would stay with him for eternity. Those last words of love: 'You brought me joy, baby. Remember that. Be happy. I love you.'

Adam blinked away the memory as a small assessing frown creased the brow of his new date for the night. 'So no matter what happens the press are not getting their grubby paws on this trumped-up story of yours.'

His words were calculated to annoy her; a riled adversary was far more likely to slip up. 'It is *not* trumped-up,' she said, the words hissing through gritted teeth,

Adam shrugged. 'The papers won't care whether it is or not; they will still have a good old grub around. Your life and your mother's life will be taken apart with a fine toothcomb.'

Her skin paled and wariness entered her hazel eyes. 'I don't want publicity, either. I just want to find your father. That's all.'

'I get that. But right now I have a charity ball to host and a reporter out there who will be very interested in who you are. So you are coming as my date.'

She expelled a gusty sigh. 'Fine.'

Anyone would think he'd asked her to hook up with the devil himself. 'It won't kill you. You may even have fun.'

'Yeah, right. Somehow I doubt that.'

Affront touched his chest. *Grow up, Adam.* Why did he care that she seemed so anti the whole idea of being with him? 'Then you need to pretend. I want to make sure all the other billionaire-baggers out there believe I'm bagged for the night.'

Her mouth smacked open. 'This gets better and better. So this isn't just for the reporter, or to keep me in sight. You're going to use me as *protection*. Big, strong man like you?'

'Size and strength aren't much use against a pack of scavenging gold-diggers.' He shrugged. 'I'll use what it takes. Hey, I've got no issues with using a beautiful woman as a shield.'

Her dark eyebrows rose. 'And if I *wasn't* beautiful?' she asked, and he could almost see icicles form around each word.

'Then it wouldn't work,'

Disdain flashed from her hazel eyes and desire tugged in his groin. Standing there in the simple elegant black dress, she looked magnificent.

'The magazine article specified that only beautiful women should enter the arena,' he explained.

His words did nothing to mollify her. 'No doubt based on your past dating career?'

'Most of my dates *are* beautiful,' he agreed. 'I'm not going to apologise for that.' Yet his conscience gave a sudden inexplicable twang. 'So let's make sure everyone believes that we are on a date, OK? And try and look happy about it. A lot of women would pay to be in your shoes.'

'I'm not a lot of women.'

He'd gathered. 'Then you'll have to fake it. Let's go.' Glancing at his watch, he gestured to her bag. 'Leave that. I'll get someone to take it out of here.'

'Give me five minutes. I need make-up. And shoes, for that matter.' She leant down to pull out a silver clutch bag and a pair of shoes. Long, elegant feet slipped into lime-green high-heeled wedge sandals and his pulse kicked up a notch.

Enough.

Straightening up, she pivoted to face the mirror, leaving him with the alluring view of her bare back. The black dress tapered down in a V to the voluptuous curve of her bottom.

Adam forced himself to turn away and pulled his phone out of his pocket. Time to alert Nathan as to what was going on and make sure any evidence of this bathroom caper was hidden from the no doubt goggling eyes and flapping ears of guests and reporters alike.

'I'm ready.'

He swivelled round and a whoosh of air was expelled from his lungs as his desire upped another degree. In a few minutes she'd transformed from au naturel beauty to glamorous allure. Which meant she had him coming and going.

Her hazel eyes shimmered and her lips were outlined in glossy dark red. Lips he wanted to claim right here. Right now. He was screwed; no way was his libido leaving this party.

CHAPTER THREE

PANIC SHEENED THE BACK of Olivia's neck as they approached the imposing ballroom door. This *so* hadn't been the plan. The plan had been more of a sidle into the ballroom, not a grand entrance. The plan certainly hadn't included snagging the role of Adam's billionaire-bagger date.

A woman only interested in the balance of his bank account… Olivia bit her lip. Fantastic. Here she was, playing the role she had always abhorred. Judging a man by wallet size had been her mother's gig.

Olivia had hated it. Hated that her mother was the quintessential gold-digger even whilst she'd known Jodie was looking out for the two of them the best way she could. Thrown out by her family, pregnant at sixteen, Jodie had used what she had. Her looks and her limitless sex appeal. Both of which had garnered her a more than respectable income and a less than respectable lifestyle.

'Hey. You still with me?'

The deep voice tinged with concern rescued her from Memory Lane and snapped her to the here and now. To the opulent room with its fluted pillars and glittering glass chandeliers. To the noise of laughter, the pop of champagne corks and the clink of crystal, all indicating the guests were having a good time.

Enough. Shaking off the past, she relegated it to where

it belonged. The past couldn't be changed. But the present and the future…? They were firmly in her control.

So it was time to locate her backbone. All Olivia had to do was allow the world to believe her to be a billionaire-bagger in order to discover the whereabouts of Zeb Masterson. Then her unborn brother or sister would have a dad. A proper father. The kind of dad that Olivia had yearned for so desperately: a dad who acknowledged his child and wanted to be part of her life.

'I'm right here,' she said, with a clench of her nails into her palm to ground herself.

'Then do you think you could smile?'

'I'm not a smiley person.'

'Well, it may be time to cultivate the art. Reporter at six o'clock and heading our way.'

He slid an arm around her waist and Olivia bit back a gasp, trying to ignore the snap, crackle and pop of desire that ignited in her at his touch. Instead she focused her attention on the blonde woman headed towards them with curiosity written all over her face.

'We'd quite given up on you.' The reporter put a hand on Adam's arm. 'Plus, we've all been dying to know who your mystery guest is. So introduce me.'

There was a heartbeat of silence.

Oh, hell.

Adam didn't know her name.

The reporter raised perfectly threaded blonde eyebrows.

Olivia opened her mouth just as Adam's hand tightened round her waist, twisting her body slightly so that she instinctively looked up at him. Not even a glint of alarm flickered in the brown eyes; instead liquid copper warmth melted over her. Her throat felt parched; he was gazing at her as though he couldn't keep his hands off her, as if names were a mere bagatelle.

Then he smiled—the kind of smile that had her toes

curling around the edge of her lime-green sandals. 'Sweetheart, this is Helen Kendersen, columnist from *Frisson* magazine.' He turned his gaze to the reporter. 'And this, Helen, is my nomination for *Frisson*'s Most Beautiful Woman of the Year award.'

His arm pushed into the small of her back and she stepped forward, holding her hand out. 'Olivia Evans,' she managed.

'So, how do you feel about having bagged yourself a billionaire for the night?' The reporter's voice was light, almost jokey, but her blue eyes were alert as she waited for an answer.

Olivia knew she should answer in kind—should have found time in the unprecedented disaster of this evening to prepare a witty, sophisticated comeback. But her brain refused to co-operate. Instead humiliation flushed her cheeks.

She heard a low laugh coming from her left and knew the question had been overheard.

Memories crowded her brain. There she was in the playground, surrounded by the pigtail brigade with their shiny shoes and perfectly packed lunches. *My mum says your mum is a tramp and you'll be exactly the same.* Noses in the air, holier than holy. *So I'm not allowed to play with you.* The chant taken up as they circled her. *Tramp, tramp, tramp...*

Her hands balled into fists at her sides; if only the solution now was as easy as it had been all those years ago. Unfortunately punching Helen Kendersen on the nose wasn't an option. Even more regrettably, her mind still hadn't formulated a single witty rejoinder. The only words coming to mind and being transmitted to the tip of her tongue were wildly inappropriate.

She sensed Adam's head turn and looked up to see his brown eyes rest on her face with an expression she couldn't interpret. His arm moved from her waist to drape around her shoulders, the soft fabric of his tux brushing her suddenly sensitised skin. The gesture was totally, unexpectedly protective.

'Wrong call, Helen,' he said, his voice pleasant but with an impossible to miss steely undertone. 'Credit me with a bit more sense. Olivia is not a billionaire-bagger; she is a bona fide date.'

A sudden warmth touched Olivia's chest. Was Adam defending her? She wasn't sure. It could be that he simply thought the assertion would definitively shield him from the baggers in the room. Whatever his reasons, he'd given Helen Kendersen pause.

The blue eyes sharpened. 'Well, colour me surprised,' she said. 'Especially as I can't remember you ever bringing a *date*, bona fide or not, to this event. And here was me assuming you were a billionaire-bagger who'd gatecrashed and somehow persuaded Adam to bring you along. Unless there's something I'm missing?'

Adam had been right. Helen's reporter antennae were practically quivering under the glittering lights of the chandeliers. Alarm pumped her veins with adrenaline; it was time to gear up and play her allotted role.

'Nope, you're not missing anything,' Olivia said. 'Here I am.' Spreading her arms wide, she could only hope her tone wasn't as hollow as her tummy. 'The genuine article.'

Helen tilted her blonde head to one side, a small frown on her face. 'Well, in that case I shall watch with interest. Adam's dating technique will add a definite frisson to my article.'

Great! Just what she needed—more frissons. Heaven help her, because right now the thought of Adam's dating technique was causing her tummy to flutter with a stampede of butterflies.

There came the Adam Masterson smile again. 'Knock

yourself out, Helen. But don't forget to interview all the people who donated auction gifts and get plenty of photos of the guests.'

'Yada, yada. Don't worry. I could do this in my sleep. Consider it done, darling. Enjoy yourself, Olivia.' With a little finger-wave Helen disappeared into the crowd.

Hah! *Enjoy?* As if *that* could happen; she was already garnering avid glances laced with speculation or envy. 'What now? I think she's suspicious.'

'Maybe. But all we have to do is display a dazzling show of dating technique and all will be well.'

'Oh, super-duper. Is that meant to make me feel better?'

'It's all I've got.' He started to walk forward. 'There's no need to panic. Follow my lead, look adoringly at me and we'll be fine. All we need to do now is circulate.'

All?

That was easy for Adam to say, because he was obviously born to circulate. Olivia could only watch him in admiration as they trekked around, her heels sinking into the plush carpet, on an endless circuit of the magnificent room.

Adam made sure he spoke with each and every individual guest—a laugh here, a gesture there, serious or jokey as the occasion warranted. But he also subtly promoted the auction at every turn. No wonder he didn't bring a date to this event; his focus was on working the room as host, leaving Olivia with nothing to do except be decorative.

Which gave her way too much opportunity to watch him. To study the way his body filled out his tuxedo to perfection. To appreciate the breadth of his chest, the power of his thighs, the lithe stride. To admire the planes and angles of his face, lit and shadowed by the glittering shards of illumination.

Little surprise her hormones refused to stand down; fuelled by unfamiliar attraction, intoxicated by his nearness, by his tantalising woodsy scent, they didn't know whether they were somersaulting or cartwheeling.

The result was a strange heat in her tummy, a dizzying awareness of Adam that wouldn't go away.

His broad thigh pressed against hers during the lavish dinner, making it hard to balance her food on her fork let alone appreciate the melt-in-the-mouth four courses.

Focus, Olivia. On the beautifully decorated table with its intricately folded napkins and stunning centrepieces of cream flowers. On the sparkle of the floating candles. On anything other than Adam Masterson and the flame of desire that licked her insides every time his arm brushed hers.

Madness. This was sheer, unprecedented stupidity.

The evening took on a surrealism in which her entire being was caught up in Adam Masterson. She was mesmerised by his auctioneering power as he stood on the podium and used a mixture of charm and unquestionable sincerity to entice bids so high that Olivia felt she was on a gigantic Monopoly board.

Problem was, *she* was the Scottie dog. Practically panting over Adam Masterson. Self-disgust mingled with panic as she gulped down fizzy water in the hope of cooling herself down. This was nuts.

Wrenching her gaze away from the podium, she sighed. Adam Masterson embodied everything she disliked: rich, arrogant—he was way too reminiscent of her mum's boyfriends. To say nothing of the fact that Olivia Evans didn't pant over *any* man; she wouldn't give one the satisfaction of having that level of power over her.

'No one believes a word of all this, you know.'

Olivia looked up from her study of the snow-white tablecloth and beheld a well-known face and figure. *Oh, just freaking fabulous.* Here was a woman whose pictures Olivia had pored over in the fashion magazines—an ice-blonde supermodel who had partied with designers galore, a woman Olivia would normally have loved to speak to. But instead of discussing style this was going to be a grown-up version of the playground.

Candice's iconic lip twisted into a sneer as she slid her svelte body, clad in shimmering gold, onto a chair to the right of Olivia. 'Genuine article, my ass.'

'Excuse me?'

'You heard me.' The supermodel crossed her legs, presumably to reveal the thigh-high slit in her dress to best effect. 'You're just another cheap 'n easy bagger after Adam's money and a quick shag you can run to the tabloids with.'

The venom-tinged arrows hit their mark, but Olivia was damned if she'd show it. Gripping her hands round the edge of the table to hide their tremor, she pushed the memory of childhood taunts from her mind and met Candice's gaze. *Play it cool, Liv.*

'And you are…?' Olivia asked, sensing that the idea of not being recognised would lance the model's ego—or at least divert the attack.

A hiss showed she'd bullseyed the target, but before Candice could respond Olivia heard the chair to her left scrape back across the marbled floor.

'Candice, here, paid good money to be here tonight in the hope of bagging Adam herself.'

Olivia turned as another catwalk regular, Jessie T, vivid in an electric blue sheath dress, dropped gracefully into the seat. Olivia's stomach plummeted; this really was the resurrection of her childhood nightmare—only instead of being surrounded by pigtails she was surrounded by stylish coiffures. For a second she was tempted to push the table over and do a runner.

Until the newcomer gave her a ghost of a wink as she pressed one elegantly manicured turquoise fingernail to her cheek. 'In fact, let me see… My guess is that Candice sees herself as a "high-class" bagger, who is after one night of making sweet love before she gets herself a slot in *Frisson* or *Glossip*. Sound right, Candice?' Jessie grinned as Candice pushed her chair back and rose to her stillettoed feet. 'She's just annoyed that her plans have been foiled by you, darlin'.'

With a swing of her trademark raven bob Jessie turned her back on her rival, apparently impervious to her poison-tainted glare, until finally Candice sashayed away towards the podium.

'Hey, Olivia, I'm—'

'Jessie T. I know. And…um…thank you.'

'No worries. Adam asked me to keep an eye on you. He figured you might have to take some flak.'

Olivia blinked, feeling that insidious warmth resurging in her chest. Adam might be using her as a shield but he was doing his best to protect her, as well.

'Don't look so surprised. Adam's a good guy. Hell, darlin', if I wasn't a happily married woman I'd give you a run for your money.'

Before Olivia could come up with a response Jessie rose to her feet with feline grace.

'Have fun. But a word of warning—watch out for Candice; she can get her panties in a tight twist if things don't go her way.'

The dark-haired woman turned and high-fived Adam as he approached the table, before heading towards a group that contained her Hollywood producer husband.

Olivia looked at Adam and wished her pulse-rate would calm down. 'Thanks for asking Jessie to look out for me. And…' she nodded at the podium '…you did an amazing job up there.'

'No problem—and thank you.'

There was pride in his voice, pride and something else. Almost as if he had a personal stake in the charity. Which would explain his dedication all night, his attention to every detail, and the way he had interacted with those guests whose lives had been touched by the terrible pain of cancer.

'It's a great cause,' she said softly.

'Yes, it is.' Silence lingered in the air between them and he rubbed a hand over his face as if to clear unwelcome thoughts. 'Now it's time to dance.'

Dance? 'I'd rather not.' In fact she'd rather stick needles under her nails. Because instinct told her that until she got her errant body under control dancing with Adam was a disastrously bad idea.

'It wasn't a request.' There was that steely undertone again—the voice of someone used to getting his own way.

'And I don't take orders.' Irritation added to her jangled nerves as she glared at him. Clearly *his* hormones weren't tripping over themselves at the thought of a dance with her.

'Helen has requested photos of us dancing, so I suggest we provide them. She's not a fool. Plus, she can hardly have missed how jumpy you are.'

'Of course I'm jumpy. Posing as your date isn't easy on the nerves. Especially as I haven't been briefed. I don't know the first thing about you.'

Brown eyes crinkled in sudden amusement. 'Most of my dates don't; I wouldn't worry about it.' He held out a hand. 'Come on, Olivia. Will you dance with me? One dance. It might be fun.'

Now, that really wasn't playing fair.

He'd knocked the moral high ground from under her feet in one deft manoeuvre. As for his smile… A curl of heat spread through her midriff right down to her toes.

She tucked a tendril of hair behind her ear. 'I truly can't dance.'

'Just follow my lead.'

'I wish you'd stop saying that.'

'Come on,' he urged again. 'We need to lull Helen's suspicions.'

Unfortunately Adam was right. 'I'm not sure her watching me stumble round a dance floor will help anything,' Olivia said as she stood up. 'But, hey, what's a little public humiliation?'

'You can't be *that* bad.'

As though on his say-so she would suddenly develop balletic ability. Olivia huffed out a sigh. 'Yes, I can. I'm totally uncoordinated. Penguins dance better than me. Don't make me make an utter idiot of myself.'

'Hang on tight and you'll be fine.'

Yeah, right. Hang on tight to which bit, exactly? Hanging on tight to any part of Adam seemed a terminally bad idea.

What was the matter with her? Her body had never, ever reacted to a man like this. Sure, her relationships had entered the bedroom, but the va-va-voom hadn't really revved up until… Well, quite a long way into proceedings. If she were brutally honest her bedroom dealings had been mostly va rather than va-va, and voom had rarely been accomplished.

Whereas now they weren't even in the vicinity of a bedroom, they were *in public*, and they hadn't even kissed. Yet her body was accelerating forward, fuelled by high-octane desire, and she couldn't find the brake.

Now they were on the wretched dance floor and Adam enfolded her waist, his fingers burning through the silky thin material of her dress. The breadth of his palm imprinted on her like a brand as he pulled her closer. Heat scorched through her; he was so close…. Firm, hard muscle pressed against her. His breath tickled her newly sensitised earlobe.

'You need to relax.'

As if *that* was going to happen; a bucketload of Valium wouldn't relax her.

'Arrgle…' The noise was all she could achieve.

She could see Helen seated at a table on the edge of the dance floor, directing the photographer.

'You're doing fine,' he murmured. 'But help me out a bit more here. Maybe put your arms round my neck.'

She did as he suggested and came flush up against his wide chest. Her breath caught in her throat and she watched his brown eyes darken, his pulse throb at the base of his neck. Olivia tangled her fingers in his hair and her lungs went on strike.

Suddenly an inability to dance was no longer her prime source of concern. There were more pressing worries. Literally. Her brain issued commands at military speed. *Don't melt. Don't dribble. Don't stroke. Don't lean your head on his chest. Do not get too close.*

It was all too late. Her eyes closed. Her body moved tight up against his. Her hips circled. Searched. Needed. Found an unmistakable reaction.

Her eyes flew open as a shiver shot through his broad frame; exultation flamed that *she* had caused it.

Olivia had forgotten where she was. Who she was. What she was. All she knew was this. This was real. Bone-meltingly real.

The music came to a stop.

Mortification loomed as she remembered exactly where, who and what she was. She was plastered to him; they might as well have been having sex on the dance floor.

For a timeless moment she felt the accelerated thud of his heart against her palm, looked up into eyes that had deepened to molten copper. Then he blinked, his eyelids lifting to reveal nothing more than speculation in their brown depths.

'That should do it,' he said.

'Do what?'

'Lull any lingering doubt in Helen's mind. *And* free me from any unwanted attention from other women.'

Humiliation arrived and encased her with an icy dose of reality.

Adam had orchestrated the whole thing—staged a scene designed to convince the most sceptical of reporters. But it couldn't all have been an act. No way had he faked what had happened in his trousers. What was *still* happening in his trousers. Whilst she was *still* glued to him.

Stepping backwards, she looked up at him, wanting answers.

This was all too much. Never had she been so out of control.

'So,' he said, his voice light. 'Give me ten minutes and I'm all yours.'

Lucky her. She was out of her depth and she didn't even know how to swim. 'I don't need all of you.' *Really?*

'Then you can have whichever parts you want. How's that?'

He stepped forward and her breathing quickened in response as his woodsy scent re-assaulted her already battered senses.

'I...' She needed to time to think, to dunk her body into an ice bath and enable her brain to regain perspective.

Instead, acting of their own will, her feet propelled her towards him to bring her right up close and personal with the hard bulk of his chest and the hardness of his still very present erection. *Well, hello again.*

'Come on,' he growled, the rasp of his voice clenching her tummy muscles. 'We're leaving.'

From somewhere a small modicum of common sense asserted itself. 'But what about the guests?'

'There's a free bar and plenty of food. They'll manage.'

'But...'

'Shh.' Adam laid a finger against her lips, the rough skin tantalising the softness of her mouth.

Olivia swallowed and the final vestige of self-preservation will-o'-the-wisped away into the sparkling hum of the ballroom. Her hand reached out and slipped into his and, oblivious to the murmurs of the guests, she walked with him across the ballroom floor.

To her surprise he retained her hand in his as they half walked, half ran across the marble foyer towards the lifts. Somewhere in the recesses of her brain a voice was hollering for her attention. Screaming at her that what she was doing was downright stupid. But as she gazed down at their hands it seemed to her that, injudicious or not, it was inevitable.

From the moment she'd seen Adam a fuse had been lit; the demon of desire had sizzled and snaked its way into existence and was demanding its sinful needs be met.

The lift door swished open and he tugged her inside, barely waiting until privacy was ensured before pulling her towards him.

CHAPTER FOUR

ON SOME LEVEL Adam knew this was a bad idea. Olivia Evans was a mass of contradictions and a billionaire-bagger to boot. But he just didn't give a damn. That dance had oozed desire. Her whole being had breathed out pure raw need, promised imminent fulfilment. If he'd been capable of thought he would have sworn that all Olivia wanted was to share his bed.

And now here she was, all her professions of caring about what people thought cast to the winds.

The soft curves of her body fused against him, and her apple scent was a further intoxicant. Adam leant back against the steel wall of the lift and offered thanks to the heavens it was for his private use only. So there was no reason not to taste those lush lips right this minute, not to plunder the mouth that had taunted him the whole evening long.

Her hazel eyes met his gaze, brimming with passion. Lifting a hand, Adam swept the mass of strawberry blonde hair off her face and cupped the angle of her jaw, gently smoothing his thumb over the plump softness of her lower lip. She exhaled, a small shudder running through her.

'I've wanted to do this all evening,' he murmured. 'Touch you without anyone watching.'

'I thought it was for show.'

'It was. Didn't mean it wasn't driving me crazy.' He caressed the bare skin of her shoulder, felt the ripple of goose-bumps his fingers left in their wake. 'This is for real,' he said, dipping his head to butterfly kiss the light sheen of desire that glistened across her collarbone.

The tang of salt mingled with the sweet infusion of apple and the taste sent heat straight to his groin.

With a sigh she tilted her head and he followed the trail to the crook of her neck; her breathing quickened and he felt her body quiver in response.

'Adam?' The question was a whisper as her fingers gripped his shoulders. 'Kiss me.'

The hounds of hell couldn't have stopped him now.

The texture of her lips blew him away—soft, lush, a hint of coffee mingled with cinnamon. An exhalation of surrender escaped her as she wrapped her arms around his neck and massaged his nape, then thrust her fingers into his hair, sending shockwaves down his spine.

Her tongue touched his tentatively and primal need jolted him as he skimmed his fingers down her back and cupped the curve of her heart-shaped bottom. Olivia moaned into his mouth and rubbed against him with an urgency that rivalled his.

The lift pinged to a stop and Adam gave a growl of pure frustration before reaching out and hitting the door's close button.

Olivia didn't even seem to notice. 'Want more…' she murmured against his mouth.

Small fingers pushed at his tux jacket and, understanding her intention, he shrugged it off, the heavy material falling to the floor with a thud.

'Better?' he asked.

'Better,' she said, tugging at his shirt buttons greedily, deftly pulling the edges of Egyptian cotton apart. 'Much better.'

She gave a small grunt of pleasure as she slid her hand

underneath; her touch electrified him—set up a chain re-action headed due south.

'My turn,' he growled, and tore at the zip of her dress, glissading the silken material downward so it shimmied to the floor.

No bra. Sweet Lord. Olivia stood tall and straight and stepped over the pool of black silk. Naked except for flimsy lacy knickers and the lime-green sandals.

'Perfect,' Adam breathed. Her breasts were large, her waist slender, hips voluptuous. A body he had every intention of worshipping for hours. 'Olivia, you are so very beautiful.'

And he was so very hard that any second now the tux pants would have to give.

A small frown etched her wide brow; almost as if he'd said something wrong. He kissed the frown away and cupped the heavy weight of her breast, his thumb swirling over her erect nipple.

A guttural moan escaped her lips to rebound in the steel confines of the lift.

He couldn't wait. He needed her responsive body writhing under him, at his mercy. Desperation roiled in his gut, his hard-on painful.

Damn it.

'While I would love to take you up against that glass plate, we have no protection.' His chest pumped as he hauled in air. He wanted her so damn bad. 'I need to get you to bed, Olivia. *Now.*'

She nodded, her face flushed, eyes wide and shell-shocked as he stooped to pick up her dress, held the silken black folds for her to step into. Stopping only to grab his tux and her clutch bag, he jabbed at the lift button.

Crowded thoughts tried to surface but he pushed them away. Instead he enclosed Olivia's hand; somehow it seemed imperative to keep a connection between them.

Fumbling in his pocket for his keycard, he tugged her along the plushly carpeted corridor.

One-handed, he slid the rectangular plastic in and waited for the green light. 'Come on,' he muttered, and heard her small breathless laugh beside him.

Finally, *finally* the key mechanism clicked and he pushed the door open to reveal the immense vaulted corridor that led straight to his bedroom.

Next to him Olivia froze, and without further warning she dropped his hand in an abrupt, almost savage movement.

'Olivia?' His brain tried to compute her reaction, struggling to function when his whole body was on high alert.

Her gaze flickered rapidly, eyes wide. Crazy though it seemed, it looked as though she were conducting an indepth survey of her surroundings.

This was the benchmark suite for all his hotels. The height of luxury—all sleek lines and on modern trend. There were flashes of abstract colour on the cream walls, gleaming wooden floors chosen by one of London's most iconic designers.

Her strawberry blonde head turned to study the lounge, the decadent enclave visible through the clear glass sliding door. Long dark eyelashes swept down once, then twice, before she slammed her hand onto her forehead.

'What the hell am I doing?'

She took another step away from him, her expression dubbing him the equivalent of Genghis Khan.

'I thought *we* were about to fulfil all our fantasies.'

Olivia winced, and for an insane moment Adam wondered if he'd imagined the past twenty minutes. Yet the tint of desire still touched her skin and his erection still ridged his pants.

'I need to leave,' she said.

'Whoa.' Adam stretched over to lean a hand against the door. 'Not so fast.'

An expression flashed across her face so akin to fear that affront seethed in his chest.

'Olivia, I'm not planning on keeping you here against your will, or taking anything you aren't offering. But after what just happened you can't just leave. Not without some sort of explanation.' His libido was desperate for some sort of elucidation, ever hopeful of a reversal in fortune.

Hell, there was a part of him tempted to pull her back into his arms, confident that her body would overrule whatever misgivings she was so suddenly exhibiting. But he couldn't do that—not after that flare of trepidation.

'So, spill,' he continued.

The tightness of her shoulders slumped fractionally but her body was still braced for fight or flight. Neither of which he would permit.

'I made a mistake,' she conceded, her voice taut, her hands smoothing the silken folds of her dress. 'It's as if I was caught in some sort of fog. A dream.' She stared at him, her chin jutting out. 'Now I've woken up.'

Disproportionate disappointment contracted his gut as the marvellous fantasies he had woven dissipated into the perfectly controlled air of the corridor.

Adam hauled in breath and willed his body to stand down—preferably every bit of it. After all, he'd weathered a lot worse disillusionment than this in his life, and it could be that Olivia was doing him a favour. Had he *really* wanted to let himself be bagged by any woman, however beautiful?

Answer: yes, he had. But if it wasn't going to happen then it wasn't going to happen. Time to move on.

He dropped his hand from the door and shrugged. 'Your call, Olivia. But for what it's worth I think we'd have been pretty awesome together.' They'd have been more than that; every instinct told him their bodies would be the perfect fit.

Her eyes skittered away from him, focused once more on the interior of his hallway. Though what was so damn fascinating about it, who knew?

'Maybe… Maybe not,' she said, placing a hand on the doorknob. 'I'll go down to Reception and get myself a room, but we need to sort out a time that we can talk. About Zeb.'

Zeb. *Damn.* He'd lost the plot, the dialogue *and* his brain. The import of her words slam-dunked and he thumped the palm of his hand right back against the door.

'Excuse me?' he said.

'Remember?' she said. 'The *baby.*'

She had to be kidding. 'The mythical baby? I thought you'd abandoned the whole "my mother is pregnant" bagging route. You can't just pick it back up now you've decided not to spend the night in my bed.'

Olivia stared at him. For a moment sheer shock rendered her speechless and her jaw threatened to hit the floor. Adam still believed she was another of those awful gold-digging women.

Worse, she almost couldn't blame him. She'd behaved exactly the way Candice had described her—cheap and easy. After a public display on the dance floor she'd kissed him in the lift, dropped her dress and allowed him a quick grope. If she hadn't been stunned back to reality by the opulence of his penthouse suite she'd have dropped her knickers, as well.

'I am not here to *bag* you.' Her words were so hopelessly inadequate she cringed. 'If I were I would have slept with you.'

'Nope.' A shake of his dark head accompanied a blaze of contempt. 'I think you've got your eye on the greater prize, Olivia. You nearly let yourself get carried away, but one look round here and you remembered just in time that there's more money to be had from a pregnancy scandal scam than a few hours in my bed.'

Oh, hell. She could see how it all made a certain hideous sense to Adam. How to explain to him that seeing this opulent bachelor pad had brought back to her the fact that Adam was a billionaire, a moneyed man who wanted her because she was beautiful—nothing more.

Just as all those rich men who'd peopled her childhood had coveted Jodie for her looks. At least her mum had put a price on her acquiescence; Olivia had been willing to give it away.

Taut silence enveloped them as Olivia gazed down at her sandals. Lime-green, with a tangerine flower carved from wood. Chosen to add pizzazz to the black dress. When it came to clothes, she knew what she was talking about. When it came to what had happened in the past hour…? Not so much.

All she knew was that she had to make this right. Because the baby was all that mattered. Guilt twanged in her chest that she had allowed her hormones to overrule that fact.

'Everything I told you about the baby is true. I realise I've screwed up. I understand you're suspicious. But please just give me half an hour. It doesn't have to be in the morning. We could do it right now.'

Adam held her gaze for a long moment, his fingers drumming on one muscled thigh. Then he gave an exasperated grunt, ran a hand over his face and back up through his hair.

'Fine. Let's *talk*.'

Pivoting, he turned and led the way into the enormous lounge, buttoning up his shirt as he walked. Relief and determination whipped around her tummy, along with a frustration she didn't even want to acknowledge. *Just great.* Her brain might have clocked the sheer awfulness of her actions but her body hadn't even begun to come to terms with the deprivation of promised pleasure.

Well, tough.

Control. She would *not* let lust control her. *Her* body, *her* hormones, *her* control. Sex was power—she *knew* that. It was a glittering token that could be used for or against you, and the only way to make sure you were on the right side was to be the one in charge.

Olivia had not been in charge in that lift; she'd been a woman possessed.

'Drink?' Adam had reached a black lacquered drinks cabinet of a type that looked as though you needed a degree in physics to open it.

'Please.'

Neither of them had touched a drop of alcohol all evening and a drink sounded a mighty fine idea. Perhaps it would knock the lust demon out so she could concentrate on conversation. Perhaps she should just swig from the bottle.

'Whisky OK?'

'Perfect.'

Like the play of his large capable hands as they deftly unstoppered the decanter.

Olivia tore her gaze away and stared around the room; better to focus on her surroundings than on the hands that had so recently touched her bare skin with such devastating effect.

'Wow!' She'd been so mesmerised that she'd actually missed the stunning effect of the floor-to-ceiling window that spanned an entire wall. Walking over, she gazed out at the lit-up panorama of London. 'The view is mind-blowing.'

'It never gets old,' he agreed as he moved next to her

and handed her a thick cut-crystal tumbler containing a generous slosh of amber liquid.

'Thank you.' With an effort she kept her voice steady despite the brush of his fingers activating that all too familiar shockwave through her.

'But I'm sure you don't want to waste your half an hour on the view,' he added. 'So take a seat and say whatever you have to say.'

With one last glance at the purple-black night sky, looking for a handy shooting star, Olivia turned away from the window and headed for the sofa.

Adam followed suit, dropping onto a cream-coloured couch.

He sprawled opposite her, crystal tumbler held loosely in one large hand, mussed dark hair glinting with copper in the muted overhead lighting. Olivia gulped down a slug of whisky in the hope that the fiery trickle would deaden his infernal impact on her senses.

She reached out for her evening bag, opened it and pulled out an envelope. Leaning forward, careful not to touch him, she handed it over and watched as he lifted the flap and pulled the photograph out.

'That's your father, isn't it?' Olivia said eventually. Not that she needed to ask: from the moment she'd seen Adam Masterson's image on the Masterson Hotels website she'd known. The likeness between the two men was too obvious for them not to be related. Enough that she hadn't even bothered researching him further. 'The woman in the picture is my mum. Jodie Evans.'

'That's Zeb,' he acknowledged. 'But this hardly proves he is the father of Jodie's baby.'

'It puts them both together at the right date, and, well, they look…' Olivia moistened her lips. 'Pretty relaxed together.'

And that was as far as she was prepared to go. She already had way too much knowledge of her mother's sex life—had spent too many nights of her childhood with her pillow over her head.

Adam didn't look as though contemplating the finer details of Jodie and Zeb's relationship was causing *him* any joy, either. His features scrunched into a scowl as his fingers drummed a tattoo on the leather arm of the sofa.

He nodded at the photo. 'When was this taken?' he asked.

'Four months ago. In Hawaii. Mum went there for a couple of weeks with friends.'

'Where she just happened to hook up with the father of a billionaire?' Disbelief dripped from his tone. 'Or did she target him in the hope of a pay-off?'

'What are you? A fully paid-up member of Cynics R Us? Mum didn't do anything of the sort. She doesn't need money.' Pride and determination pulled her spine straight. Neither Jodie nor Olivia Evans would ever rely on a man again, because now Olivia earned enough for both of them. Exactly as she had always vowed she would

'Everyone needs money, honey.'

'Not us. And you'd better believe it!' Hauling in a breath, she tried to see it from Adam's viewpoint. 'I get that you are sceptical, but this would be so much easier if you could just acknowledge I *might* be telling the truth.'

He raked a hand through his already rumpled hair and exhaled heavily into the cloud of silence. 'OK,' he said finally. 'I'll meet with your mother, see if her story checks out.'

'*No!*' The yelp escaped her lips too sharply and her panicked vehemence caused a hike of Adam's dark brows. 'You can't do that.'

'Because?'

Olivia clenched her hands into fists, thoroughly annoyed with herself for not anticipating his request. '*Because* Mum doesn't know I'm here.' Her conscience stabbed her with pins galore and had her squirming on the plush seat. 'If you must know she doesn't want Zeb to know about the baby.'

His face was immobile; each feature might as well have been hewn from granite. 'Why not?'

'She says it was a holiday fling and she won't burden a man with a child she knows he doesn't want.'

Adam's jaw tightened, his movements a little jerky as he picked up his glass. 'But you disagree with her?'

'I feel like a complete heel for going behind her back— but, yes, I do.'

'Why?'

The shadow in his eyes told her the question was genuine and that if she had any hope of convincing him she was going to have to answer. Not ideal. But if revealing her personal history would swing Adam's support then there was no choice.

Swallowing in an attempt to dislodge the pebble of discomfort that clogged her throat, she met his gaze. 'Because I grew up without a father and I want this baby to have a chance to have one. It's as simple as that, Adam. I promise.'

CHAPTER FIVE

ADAM DRUMMED HIS FINGERS on the arm of the sofa, the rapid tattoo making his knuckles ache.

Olivia's words had vibrated with sincerity, plucking an unwilling chord of memory within him.

Remembered frustration churned his guts. Desperate to know something about his father, his childhood self had pored over the single photograph he'd possessed. He'd plagued his mother for details until he had realised that Zeb Masterson wasn't exactly one of her favourite people. However much she'd tried to hide it.

In all conscience he couldn't doom another child to that experience.

An experience Olivia had shared.

The idea tugged at his chest, creating an unwanted connection between them. If, of course, she was telling the truth. About anything.

'What happened to your father?' he asked.

Shimmering eyelids swept down and up again as she surveyed him, her small frown indicating that she was pondering her answer or maybe even whether to answer at all.

'You brought the subject up,' he pointed out.

'I never knew him. My mother was very young when she fell pregnant—I'm lucky she kept me at all.'

She said the words with great care, as if she were stepping cautiously across the stepping stones of truth and missing out a fair few on the way.

Suspicion tingled Adam's nerves as he looked back down at the photograph. 'Jodie must have been *very* young.' The woman in the photograph couldn't be much over forty now.

'She was.'

'So it was a teenage romance that went too far?'

'Does it matter?' After a careful scrutiny of his face she huffed out a sigh and slammed her glass on the table. 'You think I'm making it up, don't you?'

'It's a possibility I'm considering, yes.'

'Fine. If you must know my father paid my mother to keep his identity secret. They struck a deal. He handed over a lump sum, she swore never to reveal who he is. Even to me.' She shifted on the sofa, clasped her hands together on her lap in a pose of defiance. 'Satisfied?'

Not really. Because he could sense her pain, knew she was telling the truth. Which moved him way into schmuck territory for forcing her confidence.

'Then *he* missed out,' he said. 'Not you. A man who would do that isn't worth knowing.'

Olivia blinked and a smile curved her lips for a fleeting second. 'Thank you. That's a way better response than saying how sorry you are.'

'You're welcome.'

The atmosphere tautened around them. His eyes snagged on her mouth and a memory of the taste of her kicked his pulse-rate up.

Her eyes shuttered again. 'It's also good to know that you *can* actually be nice. So, Mr Nice Guy...' The wedge heel of her sandal tapped on the wood of the floor. 'Will you help me?'

Adam locked on to those determined hazel eyes, half pleading, half insistent.

He tore his gaze away and rose to his feet; he had to break this spell Olivia was weaving. Instinct told him that she was telling the truth; further instinct told him that in this case his instincts were less than reliable—fuzzed and blurred by inordinate desire and a strange, tenuous bond that he would love to deny but couldn't.

Walking to the window, he stared out, forced his brain at least to make an attempt at logic. Olivia Evans could be a con artist extraordinaire. Or she could be telling the truth. In either case, logically he couldn't risk letting her go. If she were at his side she would either slip up and he would expose her web of deceit or he would remain in control of the situation.

There. Thinking was so much easier staring out at the cosmopolitan glitter of London by night. Even if the net result was dubious.

He turned to face her. 'OK,' he said. 'I'll contact Zeb.'

'Really?' A huge sigh escaped her lips as her shoulders dropped—the expelled tension was almost visible. Rising to her feet, she moved towards him, her hips swaying with an unconscious femininity. 'Thank you.'

She rested a hand on his forearm. Her touch was warm and yet it shivered his skin.

'If you could give me his phone number, I'll—'

'Not so fast. *I'll* contact him, Olivia. I'll talk with him and then we'll take things from there.'

She stepped away from him. 'No, no, no. That doesn't work for me, Adam. I want to be the one to tell him; I need to *see* his reaction. I don't know how all this is going to play out, and I don't know what your father will say or do. But I do know I need to be there when he says or does it.'

'No.' It was time to make a stand, to stop being sucked in by her beauty and do what he knew to be right. 'This is not negotiable, Olivia. Take it or leave it.'

She opened her mouth then closed it again, her protest

swallowed down even though anger flecked the hazel eyes with green. 'What happened to Mr Nice Guy?'

'This *is* Mr Nice Guy. You want to see Mr Not So Nice? Because *he* would've had you booted out of here long ago. Which is still a possibility. So, take it or leave it.'

A pause during which her eyes narrowed before, 'I'll take it. For now. But only because I'm beat. I'll head to Reception and sort out a room.'

'I've got a better idea.'

'What?'

'Stay here.'

'Say *what*?' Tiredness fled the room and Olivia wasn't sure which emotion to run with in the seething mass left in its wake. Anger vied with a certifiable urge to comply and won. Just. 'Are you *nuts*? I told you already what happened earlier was a mistake. An aberration. A...' However many more words for *mistake* there were in the thesaurus.

'Calm down.' The authoritative tone shut her up. 'The majority of my guests, including Helen Kendersen, are staying here tonight. It's included in the ticket price. Given they all believe that you're my date, it's probably better if you stay here. In the *spare room*.'

'Oh.' Now she felt like a gigantic idiot. Worse, she had the horrible idea that she sounded disappointed.

He raised his eyebrows. 'Unless, of course, you've changed your mind and you want to take up where we left off earlier?'

The words, faintly mocking, reminded her that Adam still didn't fully credit her story. Regardless of that, sleeping with Adam would mean the loss of any respect he had for her. To say nothing of the blow to her own self-respect.

'No. But thanks for the offer. And the offer of the spare room. I agree it would be more sensible if I stay here tonight.'

'That's sorted, then. Nate has had your bag sent up here anyway. Is there anything else you need?'

Your body. The answer popped into her mind, proving to her that she might as well found Idiots R Us.

'A spare toothbrush would be good.' Nothing sexual about a toothbrush. So focus on that. Bristles, plastic handle, toothpaste, flossing… Nothing attractive about that. 'If you've got one?'

'This is a hotel, Olivia. We provide multiple toothbrushes.'

Toothbrushes. He was talking about multiple toothbrushes; she was thinking about orgasms. 'There's one in the spare room already.'

'Fabulous. Super. Take me to it. The toothbrush, I mean.'

Five hours later Olivia opened bleary eyes and gave up. Sleep with Adam a mere couple of walls away wasn't possible. Not even in a bed that had literally taken her breath away. She had no idea how much a stay in a penthouse suite would cost but the decadent round bed alone would be worth it. Sumptuously comfortable and made for sin… it was no wonder her body had spent the night craving someone to sin with.

No. Not someone. *Adam.*

Olivia huffed out yet another sigh.

Coffee. She needed coffee. No—what she really needed was a hormone transplant. But she'd have to settle for coffee.

A glance in the mirror sent a shudder of sheer horror through her. Her hair had not coped well with the tossing and turning of her fevered body; if she went outside birds would be attracted to its nestlike properties. As for the bags under her eyes—they were fit for a luggage carousel.

OK. Ten minutes to make herself at least a little bit presentable. For her own sake, of course. Nothing to do with the chance that Adam might be an early riser.

Olivia pushed the door open and padded down the corridor to the kitchen. She filled the kettle up and pulled open a cupboard in the hope of finding coffee.

There had to be coffee. All hotels provided little sachets of instant granules. Surely a hotel of this ilk would have a jar of a luxury blend?

A fruitless search found some very posh tea bags that smelt woefully caffeine-free and way more like pot-pourri than tea—and then she saw it.

Whoa.

It was the mother of all coffee machines, the type that you would need ten hours' solid sleep and two degrees in *advanced* physics to use.

Next to it was a jar of coffee beans.

Might be quicker to eat a few.

Even as she contemplated the idea a knock on the main door of the suite distracted her and caused hope to surface. Maybe it was Room Service. Maybe Adam had ordered a full English breakfast and a steaming pot of coffee and maybe they were just outside the door.

Glory be!

Olivia scuttled down the corridor.

'Don't open it!'

The peremptory command reached her ears a fraction of a second too late; she'd already tugged the door towards her.

The pop of flashlights triggered a swirl of stars in front of her eyes. Unfortunately not bright enough to obscure the hideous sight of a scavenging pack of reporters on the threshold. Thank goodness she'd brushed her hair and pulled on jeans.

Various shouts permeated her eardrums.

'How does it feel to filch a man from a woman like Candice?'

'Where is the love rat?'

Then Adam was at her side, positioning himself so that his body shielded hers from view.

'No comment,' he said evenly, and with that he closed the door with a decisive bang and a succinct swear word.

Rubbing the back of his neck, he looked down at her. 'You OK?'

'No. Of course I'm not OK. I was expecting toast and scrambled eggs and sausages and coffee and I got a microphone shoved in my face. How did they even get up here?'

'That's exactly what Nathan is finding out. And heaven preserve the staff member who gave those reporters the keycode to the lift.'

A horrible thought filtered into her coffee- and sleep-deprived brain. 'They haven't found out about the baby, have they?' she whispered.

'No,' Adam said. He gestured down the hallway. 'I'll make coffee and explain.'

'Hold the explanations until the coffee kicks in.' Olivia watched Adam, reading the message sent by the grim set of his lips and the tightness of his jaw. Adam Masterson wasn't a happy man and she was pretty sure someone was going to pay the price.

'So what's this all this about?' she asked, coffee cup in hand. 'They mentioned Candice.'

'Yup. Candice has decided to score some publicity,' Adam said. 'According to her, she and I were an item and I specifically asked her to last night's event, where she thought I was going to ask her to move the relationship to a higher plane.' Adam broke off and snorted. 'This is utter drivel. Anyway instead I turned up with you, so according to Candice I'm a love rat and you're…'

'The other woman?' Horror clogged her throat and Olivia nearly choked. 'Who stole you away from Candice.'

This was the stuff of nightmares. Her friends, her clients, her mum would open the papers and she would be revealed as *the other woman*. The other woman who had slept with a man for his money.

'You've got to do something.'

'Damn right we're going to do something about it.'

Olivia frowned. 'You really care. And I'm guessing it's not my rep that you're worried about.'

'No, it's not,' he said. 'What I care about is the fact that Candice is planning to sabotage a charity event I'm co-hosting. I've sponsored the launch of a charity fashion show. Now Candice is threatening to boycott the show, along with the rest of the modelling community, and make a call for all the other women whose hearts I've broken to picket the show.'

Indignation heated her veins. 'She wouldn't really do that. Surely that's negative publicity for her?

'I assume she thinks it's worth it to paint me as London's premier love rat.' His stride increased, covering the travertine kitchen floor in a few easy lopes. 'Particularly at a charity function that means a lot to me. I will *not* let this event be disrupted.'

'Why don't you grovel to Candice?' Olivia paused, her imagination balking at the idea of Adam kowtowing to anyone. 'Apologise for the misunderstanding, explain that we're just friends. I'll back you up on that. We'll say that I'm a friend who agreed to pose as your date to protect you from the baggers. That you hadn't realised Candice was interested in you. That you are incredibly flattered and would love to go out with her. Then she'll walk the catwalk for you and everything will be fine.'

'No.' Adam stared at her as though she were mad. 'Just

no. But accept my congratulations on your excellent imagination and ability to fabricate a story.'

'At least I'm trying. Why don't *you* think of something?'

Adam came to a halt in front of the breakfast bar and Olivia gulped. Colour her shallow, but the man was flipping all her switches.

He'd pulled a shirt on over jeans but obviously not had the time to button it up, and the black edges gaped to reveal a tantalising glimpse of sculpted chest, a light smattering of hair that arrowed down over ripped abs.

'OK,' he said slowly. 'I've thought of something.'

Apprehension lifted the hairs on her arms as she waved a hand in the air. 'What?'

'It's a two-pronged plan. First I'll get Candice to back down.'

'How?'

'I'm going to offer her three dates with Noah Braithwaite.'

'*The* Noah Braithwaite?' Olivia said. 'Hollywood heart-throb?' The penny dropped. 'Also known as Noah 'Two Date' Braithwaite.'

'Yup. Noah and I are poker buddies—I'll persuade him. Candice will jump at the chance to be the woman who got a third date out of Noah Braithwaite.'

'OK. That should work,' Olivia said. 'Could you also see your way to getting her to rescind her allegations of me being a man thief?'

'That's prong two of the plan,' Adam said, and his lips curved up in a satisfied smile. 'Candice backs down, which leaves you and I still together. So, to prove that I am not a love rat who has abandoned you, *you* are coming to the fashion show as my date. You'll be icing on the cake of my respectability.'

'No way.' The response was instinctive, wrenched from her at gut level.

The previous night had been bad enough, being paraded as a possible gold-digger or at best a trophy girlfriend chosen for her looks. Olivia had looked up that article in the sleepless pre-dawn hours and knew now what she had already suspected. All Adam cared about were a woman's looks.

'Fine. I'll sweeten the pot. You play the part of my girlfriend at the fashion show and I'll take you to Zeb. *You* can tell him about the baby.'

CHAPTER SIX

ADAM KNEW HE'D made her an offer she couldn't refuse—he just wasn't sure why he'd made it. Doubtless he could have found a different way to persuade her to continue in her role.

'You mean it?' Those hazel eyes narrowed in suspicion, her thoughts presumably mirroring his.

'Yes.' And he did.

He'd tracked Zeb down in the sleepless small hours but he hadn't rung him. The image of Olivia's face had been too vivid, her voice still echoing in his ears. Her own father had rejected her very existence, denied her an understanding of her own genetic identity and roots. No wonder she had a need to see Zeb face to face to garner his reactions, good or bad, and Adam had no idea which it would be. And so he'd dropped his phone back on the bedside cabinet and left Zeb in ignorance.

'I mean it,' he said.

'This charity event is really important to you, isn't it?'

'Yes.' He hesitated. 'My mother died from myeloma.'

Her brow pinched in empathy. 'Oh, Adam. I'm so sorry.'

He clamped his lips into a grim line; it was too late to prevent the words. 'Don't worry about it. Point is I want this event to be a success. If it goes well it could become an annual event. I'll do what I need to make it work. So are you in?'

'I'm in.' Her bare foot tapped a nervous rhythm on the underfloor heated kitchen tiles. 'What next?'

'I'll sort out Candice and then we'll let the press in. Set the record straight.'

He'd expected her to demur, but instead she nodded as she glanced round and bit her lip thoughtfully. 'I'll set the scene. The secret of a good fabrication is in the detail.'

A pang of suspicion struck; was this an oblique way of telling him that *she* was lying? But now wasn't the time to wonder—best to file the doubt away for later.

'Fine. I'll call Noah.' He pulled his phone from his pocket. 'Noah? It's Adam. Remember that yacht you lost at our last game? Here's your chance to get it back. But there's a price.'

'Isn't there always?'

Adam swivelled at Olivia's muttered words but she was on her way out of the kitchen. His gaze lingered on the alluring sway of her hips, the curve of the heart-shaped bottom that had fitted so snugly in his hands.

'Adam?' Noah's transatlantic drawl in his ear pulled his mind out of the gutter.

'Yeah. Listen up…'

Half an hour later Adam went in search of his partner in crime to report. A glance into the spare room yielded nothing; the room looked completely unused. Not so much as a strawberry blonde strand of hair on the pillow.

He pulled the door closed and headed for his bedroom— and stopped on the threshold with a gargled snort. Olivia lay on his king-size mattress. Correction: Olivia was rolling around on his king-size mattress. If he'd wanted his libido to get any more excited he'd have said she was writhing.

'Olivia?'

Her body stilled, and then with careful, deliberate movements she swung her legs over the side of the bed and stood up.

'I was just…' She leant over, probably in an attempt to hide the pink-tinted angles of her cheekbones, but inadvertently giving him a glorious flash of cleavage. She tugged the duvet up to leave a glimpse of the sinfully rumpled black sheets. 'The bed needs to look like we both…*used* it.'

Her breath hitched audibly as she straightened, and hazel eyes flickered away from his as she swept her arm around the room.

'What do you think?'

Wrenching his gaze away from her, and his mind out of fantasy land, he followed the arc of her hand. Olivia's bag was on the floor by the corner of the bed. Her dress was slung over the back of a chair and…and *oh, hell*. Moisture sheened his temple as he spotted the wisp of lace peeping out from under the bed.

'Hopefully this looks as though I spent the night in here.' Chewing her bottom lip, she gave a small nod. 'I'll hang my clothes up in your wardrobe, too. As an added touch. After all, if we're saying we are serious then it may be best to at least imply I've stayed here before and I'm staking a claim.'

Doubt assailed him again, battering his mind.

'What is it?' she asked.

'Are you?' he asked. 'Staking a claim? Seems to me you're pretty practised in the art of fabrication, of making a mirage of the truth.'

Her head whipped round at neck-cracking speed. 'Say *what*? I'm doing my very best to help you out here, bolster your reputation, and you're doing what? Still accusing me of scamming you?'

'I'm simply observing that you are a self-confessed expert liar and you've certainly got a whole lot further than any other woman has thus far.' Hell, he was about to announce at a press conference that she was his serious girlfriend. No one had ever got this far. Except Charlotte.

Adam blocked off the thought. His ex-wife was not a topic he wanted or needed to consider right now.

Hands slammed on those curvy hips as she shook her head in patent disbelief. 'Believe what you like, Adam. I thought I was doing a good thing here. Candice is the one whose lies are threatening to derail your charitable event, and…' She hesitated. 'She is also sullying your reputation. That's wrong. Our lie… Well, it's not harming anyone and it's repairing the damage she's done. I don't have an issue with that. Do you?'

'Not a one,' he said. 'I'm questioning your expertise. That's all.'

Back went the teeth over the plumpness of her lower lip. Adam's gut contracted in a sudden desire to take over the action. To stop talking and start feeling.

Then she shrugged. 'I've had some experience in the art of dissembling. That's all. There were times when I was growing up when life was a bit hand-to-mouth and Mum and I needed to fabricate a believable story.'

'Who for?'

'Landlords, debt collectors, teachers… Things were a bit complicated sometimes and it was important to put on a bit of a show. No harm done, and when we were flush I always paid off any debts.'

Adam felt that insidious pull at his chest again. That sense of connection, of the shared experience of a childhood made less than stable by the antics of parents. Different experiences with different outcomes—clearly Olivia and Jodie had a bond that went a whole load deeper than any link he and Zeb had. Olivia and Jodie's had been forged in love.

Her level gaze didn't falter. 'But I'm not after anything from you, Adam. Except access to Zeb.'

'OK.' He stepped forward until they were mere centimetres apart, close enough for him to clock that her chest rose and fell in definite response to his nearness. 'Got it.'

'Good,' she said, and then the silence tautened as tension wove a web around them.

It would be so easy to tumble her backwards onto the bed and turn one aspect of their shared lie to truth.

Stop. Not possible. If he accepted Olivia's story as true then he accepted Jodie to be pregnant with Zeb's baby. So it didn't matter that he'd never laid eyes on Olivia until yesterday—didn't matter they met nowhere on the family tree: the unborn baby would link them together for ever. That would be plenty complicated enough without throwing sex into the mix.

So…

Drawing from his reserves of will power, he stepped backwards. 'You've done a great job in here. I've persuaded Candice to withdraw her story and Noah has agreed to play his part. The press will be here in about half an hour.'

'Right.' Olivia blinked and then, taking his cue, she nodded. 'I need to change. So can I borrow one of your shirts? That denotes seriousness, doesn't it? Wearing someone else's clothes—it's pretty intimate. Plus I slept in my shirt last night, so that's a bit grim, and I don't think the all-black outfit is right. It's too funereal-cum-cat burglar.'

Adam shrugged. 'Fine with me.' He gestured at the wardrobe. 'Take your pick.'

She glided over to the wardrobe and slid the huge mirrored door to one side. There was a long minute as she stared inside. 'Wow! That's a lot of clothes.' She turned. 'How long are you staying here?'

He frowned. 'I keep all my stuff here.'

'So you live here? It's your home?' Her face was creased with confusion, as though the concept was incomprehensible.

'I spend most of my time on the road, in one or another of the Masterson hotels. But I spend about a week or so a month here. So I guess it's a base.'

Olivia turned to survey the bedroom as if she were soaking in the surroundings anew. 'It's very…nice,' she said.

Nice? This was the height of luxury.

Adam followed her gaze to the enormous handcrafted wooden bed, the mirrored wardrobe, the glass desk and the flat-screen television. She'd already seen the lounge, with its enormous cream leather sofas heaped with textured cushions, the glass dining table surrounded by white leather dining chairs.

'Glad you approve,' he muttered, sarcasm dripping from his tone.

A flush bloomed in her cheeks. 'I'm sorry,' she said. 'That was rude of me. This is amazing. Honestly. Really impressive.'

'But…?' He wasn't at all sure why but he wanted to know what she thought. Curiosity, maybe, at her bizarre reaction? Other women oohed and aahed. Olivia Evans was struggling to find a suitable compliment.

Elegant shoulders lifted as she waved a hand around. 'It's just not very homey, that's all.'

Give him strength. *'Homey?'*

'Lived in. Personal. I mean, did you choose anything at all in here? Or out there? Where's the clutter?'

'I approved the design.' Irritation surfaced at the defensiveness that caused him to fold his arms across his chest. 'And I don't do clutter.'

His childhood home, where he had spent the first eight years of his life with his mother, had overflowed at the seams with knick-knacks and clutter. Maria Jonson had collected souvenirs of all her life's experiences: snow globes, vases, paperweights, statues, garden gnomes. They had all ended up in their small terraced house. Maybe because his mum had had some sixth sense that her life was doomed to end way too early.

Sadness weighed heavy in his heart, along with remembered grief at leaving that home, seeing the house and all those precious possessions sold or donated to charity by Zeb.

'Possessions clutter up life,' his newly discovered father had told him. He'd placed a light hand on Adam's shoulders. *'I know it's a hard concept, but you'll work it out. You've got a new life now, Adam. A life of adventure.'*

Words that had aroused such a conflict of emotion—sadness, excitement, guilt and fear—and set him inexorably on the path to becoming the man he was today.

Rubbing a hand over his face, Adam frowned. The past wasn't relevant right now. Neither were his interior decorating preferences. Or his attitude to clutter. *'Anyway,'* he said. 'Go ahead. Pick a shirt.'

She turned her attention back to the wardrobe and tilted her head to one side.

'Interesting,' she said. 'For a man who doesn't like clutter you sure do like clothes. What do you do? Find something you like and order it in every colour? You've got three styles in there. Long sleeves, short-sleeved shirts and T-shirts. Five colours each.'

Impressive. All the clothes were in a jumbled mass, and yet she'd analysed his wardrobe at a glance. Now she was looking at him with a disconcertingly assessing slant to her hazel eyes. To his own annoyance Adam realised he was rocking on the balls of his feet. As if he was uncomfortable.

'I asked the buyer in the boutique downstairs to stock my wardrobe. He came up, took my measurements and filled the wardrobe.'

'So an interior decorator bought your furniture, a boutique owner stocks your wardrobe, and you have nothing
personal. That's so...'

Adam rolled his eyes. 'Convenient?' he suggested.

She shook her head violently. '*No*. You don't get it.' She
huffed out a sigh. 'I know what I'm talking about. I'm a
personal shopper.'

It figured. No wonder she looked so damn good, and
no wonder she had taken such care with each and every
transformation. Burglar, hotel employee, ball guest, girlfriend... Olivia knew how to dress for every role.

'I run a company called Working Wardrobes.' Pride
rang in her voice and illuminated the elven features. 'But
the whole point is that I'm a *personal* shopper.' Her hands
gesticulated animatedly as she spoke. 'I don't look at someone and think six foot three, dark hair, chocolate-brown
eyes, ripped body, so I'll buy him two pairs of designer
jeans and four urban sweatshirts—' She broke off as his
eyebrows rose. 'For example...' she added hurriedly. 'Taking a completely random example.'

Her face creased into a fluster of dismay and he couldn't
help himself: a snort of laughter erupted.

After staring at him for a perplexed second she curved
her lips into a smile and then she was giggling. A full-on
giggle that bubbled forth and made him laugh. A proper
belly laugh. How long was it since he had laughed like
that?

Too long.

Almost as though she was thinking the same thing
about herself she stopped, lifted a hand to cover her lips
and stared at him.

Her eyes sparkled and she looked so gorgeous all he
wanted was to step forward and plunder the lushness of
her lips.

Every which way he went, that was where he ended up.

Leaning forward, she snatched a shirt from its hanger. 'I'll go and transform myself,' she muttered, and scurried towards his bathroom.

CHAPTER SEVEN

OLIVIA GULPED. THE SHEER surrealism of the situation boggled her mind.

Any second now Adam was going to walk through the swish lounge, open the door and let the press into the suite—aka Adam's home, or base, or whatever he called it—and she was going to pretend to be his girlfriend. How had this happened? *How?*

Olivia felt a small familiar roll of nerves in her tummy. This *was* like her years growing up—years when she had had to play roles varying from 'beautiful young girl throwing herself on landlord's mercy' to 'beautiful girl surprising rowdy revellers with a well placed kick'. But any second now adrenaline would kick in and she'd pull this off. Just as she always had.

She could do this. She flicked a glance across at Adam. *They* could do this. Because this time they were in it together; if she went down she'd be taking him with her.

'We've got this,' Adam said, coming up behind her. The warmth and strength of his body gave her reassurance whilst it also made her strum her with desire.

Minutes later Adam ushered in Helen Kendersen and the photographer from the previous night. 'Good morning, you two. And thank you for this exclusive. *Frisson* is honoured.'

With a newfound awareness Olivia knew that Helen and the photographer had some sort of a relationship. Could see it in their body language. Helen looked…content—sleek and sated. The photographer had a smile on his face that said all was right with his world.

An unexpected tingle of envy twanged her nerves. If only she'd pulled Adam down onto the sinfully rumpled black sheets of his sumptuous bed. Earned the right to wear his shirt.

Focus, Olivia.

'Would you like to have a look round?' she offered. 'And Adam can sort out coffee for everyone.'

An hour later Olivia allowed herself a cautious exhalation of relief. Putting aside the fact that she'd had to pose on the bed with Adam, with a sappy smile on her face, the whole interview had gone amazingly well. In fact she was impressed with herself. Clearly her acting skills hadn't deserted her any more than her lock-picking ones.

'There is one more thing I'd like to request,' Adam said. 'I'd like you to ask the billionaire-baggers to back off.'

Time to chime in. 'Adam and I would really appreciate that,' she said. 'We need time together, time to explore these new feelings, and it would be so marvellous if we could do that in peace. Without tripping over gold-diggers every way we turn.'

'Wow.' Helen's blue eyes glittered as they rested first on Adam's face then switched in speculation to Olivia. 'All this… It sounds like serious stuff.'

Olivia leant forward and primed her vocal chords for girlish excitement. 'Well, it's early days yet. But, yes, I'm hoping that Adam will find me pretty addictive.'

She looked up at Adam adoringly, just in time to see his jaw tense slightly.

Given the smile on Helen's face Olivia wasn't surprised;

it was the face of someone swooping in for the kill. She braced herself as the blonde woman leaned forward.

'It's interesting timing.' A small pause, and then, 'Tell me, Adam, could your sudden new desire for a relationship have anything to do with the impending marriage of your ex?'

With teeth-clenching effort Olivia prevented her jaw from hitting her knees. *Always stay in character.* She tried to look as though the existence of an ex wasn't headline-grabbing news in itself. An ex what? Girlfriend? Wife?

A sideways glance showed that Adam looked unfazed, and a sliver of suspicion wormed its way into her psyche. Had the whole Candice and charity event thing been a ruse? This might have been his intention all along—to use their supposed relationship to get at his ex-whatever. *Fabulous.* Now she was a pawn in a classic tit-for-tat game.

Adam's shook his head. 'Nope. No connection there, Helen. Charlotte and I have been divorced for years and I wish her nothing but happiness.' He nodded at Helen's notebook. 'I have an agreement with her that I won't bring publicity to her door and I try to abide by my word. So, in the interests of *Frisson* covering the Dress to Support Myeloma event later today, I'd appreciate it if you left her out of the article.'

There was that you-don't-want-to-mess-with-me voice again, and to Olivia's annoyance it made her shiver.

She stared at Adam, frustration seething at her inability to read his expression. Not that it mattered—the bottom line was that he didn't give a stuff about branding Olivia anything he liked whilst dragging her into the public domain. But when it came to *Charlotte* it was clearly very different.

And how catty did *that* sound? Olivia stiffened. Surely she wasn't jealous of Charlotte? Because that would be ludicrous. Yet, however hard she tried to deny it, a tiny part of her soul was tinged green. Which didn't make sense. Olivia Evans did not *do* jealousy. Men were notoriously unfaithful and only a fool would put herself in a position to be hurt. So it shouldn't, *couldn't* matter to her if Adam did still care enough for his ex to be scheming to win her back.

Adam gripped the back of the cream sofa and wondered how long it would be before Olivia erupted. She'd held it together for the remainder of the interview, but he'd sensed the vibrations of her inner fury.

Now that Helen and the photographer had left she paced the lounge, each angry stride thumping down harder on the gleaming wooden floor, one irate kick sweeping aside the thickly patterned rug that impeded her progress.

Five…four…three…two…one… And she screeched to a stop in front of the sofa.

'Didn't it occur to you to mention you have an ex-wife?'

'No.' It was no more than the truth; the topic of his marriage didn't rate anywhere on his conversation list.

'Well, it should have. Because then I wouldn't have looked like a first-class idiot because my so-called partner didn't bother to mention he has an ex-wife stashed away. You should have *told* me.' She stopped, presumably because she must urgently need to replenish her lungs.

He hesitated. Beneath the bravado he could sense a thread of vulnerability. 'Look, I'm sorry if you felt stupid—it truly didn't occur to me that Helen would link our relationship and Charlotte's remarriage.'

Olivia frowned, as if assessing exactly how many of his words were true and how many were lies. The sceptical rise of her dark brow indicated her verdict. 'Really?'

'Of course, really. Neither Charlotte nor her fiancé are in the public eye. I didn't expect Helen to even know about their engagement.'

'So it's not true?'

'Is *what* not true?'

A roll of her eyes indicated her frustration, but Adam had no idea what she was getting at.

'Helen's link. Are you using me to get to Charlotte? To make her jealous?'

'No.' His reaction came straight from his gut. Using Olivia as a barrier against the flow of gold-diggers with her knowledge was one thing. Garnering her help to salvage his reputation and the charity event—he had no problem with that. But no way did he want her to feel that he had exploited her; the thought turned his insides over with distaste. 'Everything I said to Helen was true. I *am* happy for Charlotte—she has found a great guy and I wish them both a very happy future.'

And all Adam's research had indicated that Ian Mainwaring should provide Charlotte with exactly that. Ian was worth a hundred of him—would look after Charlotte, give her love, a family... Everything Adam had promised her and failed to provide.

Memory echoed in his ears: her tears, her pleading. Her voice. *'You've broken my heart, Adam. I trusted you and now you've broken my heart.'*

Aware of Olivia's direct glance, Adam commanded his expression to be neutral. 'Bottom line is I am not trying to make Charlotte jealous. That's the truth.' The words sounded too serious; her gaze caused him a thread of discomfort at the sensitive subject at hand. 'Scout's honour,' he added, turning his lips up in a smile as he glanced at his watch. 'And now that's settled we'd better get a shake on. We need to be at Somerset House at five o'clock for the show.'

As anticipated, the information deflected her from any further questions. 'Five o'clock? But I haven't got a proper dress or...'

'Just buy whatever you need. The hotel has a boutique, or if you want to hit the shops I can get someone to go with

you.' For an insane moment he nearly offered himself up
on the shopping altar. Almost. He didn't shop. Full stop.
He had no intention of starting now.

'I'm a personal shopper. I'm quite capable of shopping
by myself.'

'Nope. You'll take one of Nate's men with you.'

Hurt lanced her eyes, along with a healthy dollop of
anger. 'What do you think I'm going to do? A runner?'

'No. I'm worried a reporter will make you uncomfortable, and I'm worried Candice may try and get to you.
That's why I want someone with you.'

'Oh.' Her lips curved up into a wide smile. 'That told
me. In that case, bring him on.'

Olivia surveyed her reflection. It didn't matter what she
looked like. *It didn't.* Because she wasn't bothered by what
Adam thought. She definitely did *not* want a repeat of that
hot, predatory gaze that turned her insides squishy and
sent heat shooting south. Definitely not.

There was some other explanation for the ripple of anticipation in her stomach. Perhaps it was horror that the
purchase of the stunningly gorgeous, shimmering creation
she wore had been chalked up to Adam.

But there was nothing else she could have done; she'd
been standing at the till of an exclusive London boutique that she'd always wanted to visit and Jonny, aka her
minder, had handed over a rectangle of plastic: the Masterson Hotels company credit card.

Outrage had clenched her rigid even as mortification
had coloured her face. Olivia had tried to protest. But all
her objections had fallen on deaf ears and stony ground.
Jonny had been obdurate; he'd been given an order direct
from Adam and as far as he was concerned it was more
than his job was worth not to follow it to the letter.

So Olivia had capitulated, salving her conscience with

the determination to repay Adam at the earliest given opportunity.

An almost savage swipe of glossy pink lipstick and she was done. And she still couldn't help but imagine Adam's face when he saw her.

Stupid. Stupid. Stupid.

She'd chosen the dress for its suitability and nothing else. Her reflection stared back at her—the perfect trophy girlfriend that any respectable businessman could be proud of. The spitting image of her mother, chosen for her looks. Adam himself had admitted it, and the article had been clear. Only the beautiful should apply.

And she qualified.

The dress screamed elegance and discreetly whispered class. The simple column cut skimmed her curves and the shimmering silver fabric swooped to just touch the floor, allowing her red-painted toenails to be glimpsed in the folds. The lacy top of the dress scooped around her neck and the short sleeves showed off the toned slenderness of her arms. Her hair was held back at the neck, leaving a side fringe to fall across her forehead, and she'd opted for the fresh-faced look with her make-up.

It was perfect, and worth every one of Adam's pennies.

Yet her soul felt tainted, further polluted by the fact that she actually wanted Adam's approval—wanted those brown eyes to darken and smoulder when he looked at her.

Olivia clenched her nails into her palms. This was plain *wrong*—for a variety of reasons that all bunched together around her chest, squeezing her tight with panic.

The knock on the door set her heart pounding. She had to get a grip. Had to gain control and squash all these feelings pancake-flat.

'Coming,' she called, and walked to the door, pulling it open. Her throat dried as she drank in Adam's appearance; if he'd looked gorgeous the night before, he looked positively sinful now. The dark suit was simple and fitted perfectly around the breadth of his shoulders. White shirt and silver tie, and that woodsy scent that made her dizzy.

Adam looked as shell-shocked as she did. His arms rose as if to touch her and then dropped to his sides. A slow smile touched his lips. 'You look superb, Ms Evans. You will outshine the entire catwalk and I will be the envy of every man there.'

His words were the equivalent of an iceberg's worth of cold water, cementing what she had already known. Confirmation that Adam wanted her on display to ensure his image hadn't been too tarnished by the exploits of billionaire-baggers and supermodels. As far as he was concerned that was what his credit card had bought and that was what he was entitled to expect.

A frown slashed his brows together. 'What's wrong?'

'Nothing. I'm glad I've come up to expectations.'

'What does that mean? I've told you—you look sensational. What's the problem?'

'There is no problem and don't worry. I won't disgrace you. I know the drill.' She'd grown up watching it, after all. How to dazzle with a smile, how to make the man you were with think he was the bee's knees, wings and stripes.

'Then let's go.'

Adam held his hand out and Olivia stared at it.

'Save it for the cameras,' she said, and saw the flash of something that looked perilously like hurt cross his features. Steeling herself to ignore it, she swept past him and headed for the front door and the waiting limo.

Once inside the car Olivia slid into the furthermost corner and listened as Adam pulled out his phone. His conversations all concerned the forthcoming event and amply demonstrated just how involved Adam had been in the organisational details.

Dropping the phone onto the leather seat, he reached into his inner pocket and pulled out a sheaf of paper.

'Is that your speech?' she asked.

'Yup.' He looked down, his lips moving as he ran his eyes down the sprawling handwriting.

Olivia leant her forehead against the cool of the window and silently castigated herself as shame wormed a warm trail through her body. Adam cared about this event because it raised money for a charity that tried to combat the disease that had taken his mother from him. And she was sitting here cavilling over the fact that through no fault of his own he needed a girlfriend on his arm to demonstrate his respectability.

Yuck. She was so busy worrying about what people would think of her, so caught up in her own emotional baggage, that she'd shoved her head straight up her own backside.

The limo glided to a stop and Adam placed the papers next to him and hauled in a breath.

'Adam?'

He turned to her and her tummy dipped.

'This event is going to be great,' she said. 'You'll wow them.'

Without letting herself think she slid across the seat, her dress skimming the smoothness of the leather, until they were thigh to thigh. Twisting her upper body, she smiled at him before cupping his jaw in the chalice of her palms. She leant forward and brushed her lips against his cheek. Her heart gave a pang at the realisation he must have shaved specially. Not a trace of the stubble that had grazed her face the previous day remained.

'Your mum would be proud of you. I know it.'

Before he could react, before she could throw caution to the winds and kiss him properly, she rubbed his cheek to get rid of the light gloss of pink she'd left behind, then shimmied back along towards the limo door, which Jonny had pulled open.

Olivia stretched out her hand to Adam. 'Let's go,' she said.

They emerged from the sleek black car into the swarm of fashionistas who thronged the environs of Somerset House, home to London's Fashion Week. The crowd of assorted styles and bursts of colour had Olivia swivelling and turning, feeling ideas sparking from the incredible array of combinations and patterns.

But through it all—down the red carpet that led to the enormous domed marquee, even as she smiled the smile and walked the walk for the camera—the thought of Adam filled her mind. His ripple of nerves as he'd practised his speech had moved her, shifted something deep within her.

As they left the crisp cold of the February evening to enter the marquee Olivia caught her breath. 'It's spectacular,' she murmured.

The canvas walls were lit by the bounce and eddy of multi-coloured lights in all different shades of blue that created a magical aquamarine display reminiscent of a fairyland. Garlands looped the ceiling and the ticket-holding guests were being shown to seats that held a complimentary goody bag.

'I'd better go and make sure everything is going to plan behind the scenes,' Adam said.

Olivia nodded. 'I'll stay here. I don't want to cause Candice to have a last-minute meltdown.'

'You sure?'

'I'm sure. Truly, Adam. Please don't worry about me.' She smoothed her hands down the soft lapels of his jacket, allowed her hands to linger on the muscular wall of his chest. 'You've got this.'

'Thank you, Olivia. I appreciate it. Truly.'

For a breathless heartbeat she thought he'd kiss her. Instead he squeezed her hands before releasing her. Turning, he headed backstage.

Heart still thumping, mind whirling, Olivia headed for her seat, picked up the goody bag and looked inside. An ornate card gave her a free stay in any Masterson Hotel, inclusive of travel, complimentary spa time, meals and drinks. A mini bottle of champagne stood alongside an expensive designer body spray.

And there in the corner nestled a tissue-wrapped package with her name scrawled on it—surely in Adam's handwriting? Olivia unwrapped the light blue folds and pulled out a delicate silver charm bracelet. A surreptitious glance around showed that no one else sported anything similar on their wrist.

Surprise and appreciation lodged deep in her chest as she saw the shape of the charm dangling from the chain. It was a wardrobe: an exact copy of her company's logo. A miniature wardrobe, complete with arms and legs.

Who knew how he'd got one made so fast? She'd only told him about Working Wardrobes that morning.

She clasped the silver chain around her wrist as the lights changed to illuminate the stand at the head of the catwalk. Conversation slowly cascaded away into an expectant silence as Adam and his co-host, Fenella Jowinski, a famous model of yesteryear, emerged from the shadows into the spotlight.

Following a short, pithy speech from Fenella, Adam stepped up to the microphone and Olivia clenched her hands together as she willed him good luck vibes. Not that it would be possible for anyone to guess he was nervous, the slight whitening of his knuckles as they clasped the edge of the podium the only clue. Otherwise his body was relaxed, his voice even and melodious without a hitch or a hint of edge.

'Ladies and gentlemen, and everyone else in the audience, I'd like to thank you all for being here today to support a cause that is very dear to me.'

Here Adam paused, his eyes scanning the crowded chairs and resting for a moment on Olivia.

'I had a speech all prepared—a speech full of statistics and stories and leaps in medical advances. It was a great speech, and I spent a very long time writing it. However, thanks to some words said to me just moments before my arrival here I've changed my mind. Someone said to me that my mother would be proud of me. I hope with all my heart that that is true. So, before we get down to the business of fashion and let loose the wonderful, dedicated women who will model some amazing creations, I would like to tell you about my mother—the wonderful woman who shaped my life for eight years.'

Olivia stilled. Only eight years? That meant Adam would have been just a child when his mother died.

Pressing her lips together to hold back a gasp of empathetic pain, she leant forward, wanting to hear every word.

'Maria Jonson was truly beautiful, inside and out. She had the capability of bringing joy and light to a room with the power of her smile. A single mother who gifted me a carefree childhood, she loved life and lived every precious second of hers to the full. She didn't have a glamorous job—she worked in an accounts department—but she had an imagination that soared.'

Olivia's heart twisted with pain as Adam painted a picture of a brave, wonderful, ordinary woman. A woman who'd sung and danced and read him stories. One who'd loved movies and spending time curled up under a duvet with her son and a bowl of popcorn. A woman who had collected so many knick-knacks and souvenirs of her life that their small house had overflowed.

A woman who had suddenly contracted myeloma and three months later passed away.

'I watched her get weaker, I watched her suffer, but right to the very end she gave me love. And that is why I am standing here today—because I want this disease to be stopped. So that it no longer can claim any more wonderful, ordinary, beautiful women like Maria Jonson. My mother. A woman who deserves to be remembered. I hope wherever she is now she is proud of me, as I am still proud of her.'

You could have heard the proverbial pin drop as Adam stepped down, and Olivia marvelled at what he had done. He had brought his mother's memory to life and he'd done so without being maudlin or displaying an ounce of self-pity.

Compassion and grief cloaked her at the thought of an eight-year-old Adam whose whole life had been wrenched topsy-turvy, desolated by the loss of the person who had meant everything to him. And for it to have happened so fast… He must have been terrified, alone, hurt and angry at fate.

Questions swirled around her mind—where had Zeb been? Not once in his speech had Adam even mentioned his father.

'Well, hell. I never knew *any* of that.'

Olivia jumped at the deep American drawl coming at her from her left. The large, craggy-featured blond man who must have seated himself whilst she had been deep in reverie gave her a warm smile, his dark blue eyes creasing.

There was no mistaking who it was: Noah Braithwaite—star of a string of box office hits. Amazing that she hadn't even noticed his arrival—the man was all about charisma—but her focus, her entire body and mind, had been tuned to Adam.

'You must be Olivia.'

'Yes.' Olivia forced herself to smile and shoved her feet firmly down on the smooth canvas floor of the marquee.

Racing across the catwalk towards Adam was not an option, however hard her body ached to hold him. He wouldn't thank her for it. The last thing he needed was for her to make some sort of public display when he had refrained from anything of the sort.

'I'm Noah. The man your enterprising boyfriend has sacrificed to Candice.'

'You got your yacht back,' Olivia pointed out a touch tartly.

'True. But never fear. Adam'll skin me of it again next poker night.' As if seeing her bristle, Noah grinned. 'Relax, Olivia. I'm teasing you. Adam knows damn well I'd have done it for nothing but the sake of friendship. I'm just hoping Candice isn't as big a diva as she's made out to be.' He winked. 'Speaking of whom, I'd better go to my allocated seat, where I can best see my three-date woman, or she'll throw a hissy fit.'

Olivia watched the show in a daze as models shimmied, sashayed and glided down the catwalk. Silks and satins and tweeds all interweaved in a dazzling display of talent and outrageous ingenuity. But even as she exclaimed in appreciation of the outlandish and the exquisite her gaze kept flickering back to Adam, pulled by a magnetic need to make sure he was all right.

It was a yearning that she had to hold in check until the end of the show when finally, *finally*, she wended her way through the crowd towards him.

CHAPTER EIGHT

'THANK GOODNESS THAT'S OVER.' Adam slid into the glossy limousine after Olivia and expelled a huge sigh. Unaccustomed weariness rolled over him and he flexed his shoulders before leaning back against the padded leather and tugging his tie off.

Two hours of mingling, of accepting condolences and congratulations, and he felt raw. Exposed, even. He'd managed to field the more personal questions, had tried to speak simply of his mother and the woman he remembered her to have been. Or maybe didn't remember enough.

'Do you regret your speech?'

He turned to look at Olivia, her profile silhouetted in the muted light of the car, shadows playing on her beautiful features.

Unease threaded him as he realised how good it had felt to have her by his side. His disquiet was almost enhanced by his feeling of gratitude when he remembered how she had shielded him where she could, her touch on his arm a balm.

And here he was, waxing lyrical.

The emotional impact of the whole event had quite simply temporarily knocked his perspective off course.

'No,' he said. 'I don't regret it because I do want her to be remembered.'

'It can't have been easy,' Olivia said, her voice low, warming him. 'But you did well, Adam. Really well. Maria *would* have been proud of you. She sounds like an amazing woman and an amazing mum.' She hesitated, twirling a stray tendril of hair round her finger. 'It must have been devastating for you when you lost her.'

He could shut her off, could simply say that he didn't want to talk about it. But to his own surprise he didn't mind. Olivia had stood by him all evening and helped him deflect exactly the same comments from strangers.

'I *was* devastated, and I had no idea how to deal with it. You could say I handled it badly.'

She shifted across the seat, turned so her upper body faced his, the silver of her dress shimmering in the dusky light. 'I think that's understandable,' she said.

'I was angry,' he said. So angry he could still feel the heat of it scorch him across the years. He'd been helpless and scared and he'd hated it. 'Angry with fate, with life. I was even angry with her for dying. For not somehow fighting it. Guess I took it personally.'

'I don't think there's any other way of taking it,' Olivia said.

He glanced at her. 'Is that how you took your dad's behaviour?'

'Yes.' Elegant shoulders hitched. 'My head tells me that he would have rejected any child. But my heart and soul knows he rejected *me*. Difference is my father had a choice. Your mother didn't.'

Adam nodded. 'I know that. I guess I feel bad that back then I was more caught up with what was going to happen to me than caring about everything she'd lost.' A guilt that had been enhanced further by Zeb's arrival. It had taken his mother's death to bring him what he'd wished for so fervently. The knowledge still soured his gut.

Next to him, Olivia shook her head. 'Don't even think about beating yourself up.'

A slender hand touched his arm, a tendril of hair wisped over his cheek and her smell enveloped him.

Close—she was so close—and, damn it, he didn't want to talk any more.

Or think any more.

He just wanted to feel.

Her hazel eyes met his, their green flecks glowing in the dimness of the car's interior as she scanned his expression.

There was no hesitation. In one lithe movement she moved closer to him. Elegant fingers reached up and cupped his jaw. Her fingers were so slight and gentle and yet they branded him. Her touch glided over his stubble and around to the nape of his neck; the caress jolted desire through his system.

He released the clip that held her hair back and dug his fingers in the glorious silken tresses, angled her face towards him.

Olivia parted her lips and his name escaped into the air—part groan, part entreaty. Shifting closer to her, he lowered his lips to hers. Her scent swirled round him and he was lost. Caught in a spirally vortex of desire. He could taste the fizz of champagne that lingered on her lips, and when his tongue stroked hers she moaned softly into his mouth, her fingers curling into his shirt.

Closer... He needed her closer. Adam spanned her slender waist with his hands and hoisted her onto his lap, cursing at the constraint caused by the long silver folds of her dress.

With a murmur of frustration Olivia hitched the shimmering material up around her waist and straddled him, her long, smooth thighs pressing against his. Adam's now almost painful erection strained at his zipper, pushing against her hot core.

Fingers splayed, he smoothed up the soft bare skin of her thighs and she shivered in response. Her breathing quickened as he tiptoed his fingers farther up and reached the wispy lace of her knickers.

She was so wet, so responsive. His hips jerked upward and she writhed against him; their movements bordered on being frantic.

Breaking the kiss, she straightened. Magnificent. More beautiful than anything he'd ever seen before. Hair tumbled in wild disarray around her flushed face. Hazel eyes dark with a primal desire.

'Adam, please…' she murmured, her voice ragged.

He slid his finger under the lacy edge of her knickers, desperate to watch her shatter for him.

'I'm right here.'

And her expression changed. The glow of desire receded and her face leeched of all colour as she stared down at him with a look of sheer horror.

In one awkward movement she twisted from his lap and desperate, jerky hands pulled the shimmering folds of her dress down her thighs.

She leant back against the seat and lifted her hands to her face. A muffled curse escaped her fingers.

Adam forced his breathing to a regular pattern and tried to calm both his veering heart and his hard-on.

'Olivia—' he began.

She shook her head. 'Please don't say anything. I'm sorry. And I'm mortified. And I really want to somehow pretend this didn't happen.'

'Again?' He couldn't help himself; frustration and confusion roiled inside him. 'No can do, Olivia. It happened. *Again*.'

'I'm sorry, Adam. I'm behaving like an idiot.' She dropped her hands from her face and shifted even farther away from him. 'Clearly my body is having some sort of hormonal meltdown. But I will not give in to it. I *hate* this. This attraction. I just want to turn it off.'

Despite himself, he smiled. 'Attraction doesn't work like that. You can't just turn it off.'

'I can. I have to.' Her voice vibrated with desperate conviction. 'Attraction is nothing more than a chemical reaction.'

'Exactly. And you can't change chemical reactions.'

'No, but you can make sure that you don't drop the potassium into the water.'

'Or you can enjoy the explosion,' he said.

'And pick up the pieces later? Not my style.'

It wasn't his, either. The important thing for him in any relationship was mutual short-term enjoyment, after which both parties went their separate ways in—and this was key—one piece. He'd created enough mess to last him a lifetime. A memory of Charlotte's tearstained face accosted him and it was all the reminder he needed.

So what the hell was he doing now? Enjoyment did *not* include sharing his feelings about his mother's death. Talking about Maria to keep her memory alive was one thing; spilling his guts to Olivia was a whole different situation.

And, whilst he had no doubt there would have been plenty of instant and mutual gratification going on if she hadn't pulled back, that wasn't the point. Shock rendered him mute. He hadn't so much as considered any of his usual rules and regulations—hadn't even bothered to find out Olivia's views on relationships.

Way to go, Adam.

So an explosion was a sucky idea, however hard his hard-on was. Olivia Evans had issues. She was emotional dynamite and it was time to get out of the laboratory. There would be other women, other attractions. *But not like this.* No, not like this—and a damn good thing, too.

'Not my style, either.'

'Then we're agreed,' she stated. She plunged her hands into the shimmering folds of her dress as she turned to face him. 'So let's move on. I've done my part of the deal. Now it's your turn. You need to take me to Zeb.'

'Ah. Yes. That.'

'Yes. That.' Her eyes narrowed in sudden suspicion. 'Don't you *dare* renege on our deal.'

'I'm not. It's just a little bit more complicated than I mentioned.'

'Complicated how?'

'Zeb's in Thailand.'

There was a pause as Olivia's lips, still swollen from his kisses, opened and closed.

'*Thailand?* He's thousands of miles away and you didn't think to mention it?'

Adam felt her outrage and welcomed it; at least it dissipated the sexual tension that still whispered in the air. Plus, anger was as good an outlet for frustration as any, and he knew that Olivia must be feeling plenty frustrated. She'd pulled herself from the brink of orgasm. Come to that, he wasn't feeling any too relaxed himself.

Served him right for being so quick off the mark and for letting this whole situation get out of control.

'I didn't see the need,' he said. 'I'll honour my side of the deal. I'll take you to Thailand.'

'Just like that?'

'Sure. It's a few hours away by plane. We pack. We go.'

'I can't just up sticks and fly to Thailand. When's Zeb coming back?'

Ah. 'He's not.'

'What do you mean? He *lives* in Thailand?'

'Zeb doesn't live anywhere.'

Olivia frowned. 'So he's like you? Does he live in a hotel?'

The innocent question scraped Adam's nerves; if only

Olivia knew how like his father he was. 'Zeb's a modern-day nomad.'

Dismay etched Olivia's beautiful features; her hazel eyes drenched with disbelief. 'But he must have a…a base? Somewhere? Give me something here, Adam.'

'He doesn't have anything,' Adam said flatly. 'No address at all. Zeb believes that bricks and mortar are an unnecessary responsibility. He very rarely stays in the same place for more than a few weeks and he goes wherever the whim carries him.'

'But where does she leave his things? His possessions?'

'He carries them with him.'

'You're kidding me?' She bit her lip. 'It's not exactly what I was hoping for.'

No doubt she'd been hoping for the full package: a man who would be happy to have a child, would settle down and play happy families complete with white picket fence.

He pushed down the surge of sympathy; it was better for Olivia to know it as it was. 'Zeb is a wanderer. He won't change that for anyone.' He rubbed a hand over his face. 'It's a Masterson trait, Olivia,' he said, trying to keep the bitterness from his voice. 'We don't do settling down.'

Zeb hadn't, and Adam certainly hadn't. He'd tried—hell, he'd tried. He'd married Charlotte with high hopes of that white picket fence for himself. Hopes he'd dashed to the earth a mere two years into the soulless purgatory that settling down had turned out to be. For him. Not for Charlotte. Charlotte had been in her element, nest-building, whilst the chintz-patterned wallpaper had been closing in on Adam.

'It's not possible. But that isn't the point. Nomad or not, he still needs to be told about the baby. So we'd better get ourselves to Thailand.' Sort this fiasco out, then life could return to normal.

'It's not that easy.'

'Sure it is. Leave it to me,' Adam said as the limo glided to a stop outside the imposing front of his Mayfair hotel.

The deep throb of the aeroplane's engines reverberated in Olivia's ears. Just twenty-four hours later and she was on her way to Thailand. Ko Lanta, to be precise. Excitement surfaced as she looked down at her tablet, where a glorious picture of a white sandy beach evoked relaxation. According to the blurb, the island was a veritable paradise—a scenic miasma of forest, hill, and coral-rimmed beaches.

Unfortunately Olivia wasn't going to Ko Lanta to admire the verdant beauty of the island or to absorb the sun's brilliant rays. Her remit was to meet with Zeb. Yet the anticipation refused to recede completely, still fizzed defiantly in her tummy. Worst of all, she had the feeling that the reason for its existence wasn't the hotness of her destination—it was more to do with the hotness of her travelling companion.

She eyed Adam across the aisle of the private jet and felt heat seep into her skin; embarrassment still fresh over the whole crazy hot-and-heavy interlude in his limo. The only saving grace was that she'd stopped it. On the verge of what had promised to be the mother of all orgasms.

Yay. Nice timing, Liv.

Served her right. Shame twisted her tummy at the memory of herself straddling him in the back of a car, Adam's hand up her skirt, the plea in her voice as she'd begged him for release.

Double yay!

This whole overwhelming attraction was so confusing. All she'd wanted to offer Adam was solace—not a quickie in the back of his car. Mind you, looking at him now, she had no idea how she had dared even to offer him comfort, let alone anything else. The past few hours Adam had been utterly unapproachable, a veritable machine of efficiency while she'd run around sorting out cover for her work for a week. But the man who had confided in her, the man who had kissed her senseless and nearly robbed her of every last vestige of control had vanished.

Which was a *good* thing.

The sigh she emitted was way too loud; Adam looked up from his laptop.

'Is there something you need?'

'Nope. I'm fine.'

'Good.'

His attention was diverted straight back to the screen and a thoroughly irrational annoyance sparked inside her. If he'd deigned to tell her more about Zeb a little bit earlier instead of clinging to his stupid belief that she was a billionaire-bagger, maybe she might have had more time to prepare for this trip. Plus, how come he got to sit there all cool and collected whilst she sat here reliving the scene in the limo?

She sighed again, even louder, and tapped her nails against the table in a deliberate beat.

'Olivia. If there is a problem please feel free to share. What is it?'

'I was just wondering why you insisted I take a week off.' An outright fib, but she didn't care. It might be childish but she wanted him distract him.

'Because it makes sense. Zeb comes and goes as he pleases. He only got to Ko Lanta a couple of days ago, so he should still be there. But if he's moved on we'll need to track him. It's not worth the risk of losing him again.'

Her sigh was genuine this time; Zeb wasn't exactly turning out to be the kind of man she had envisaged when she'd embarked on this search.

Though, come to think of it, Adam still hadn't told her much about Zeb at all, really. A sideways glance confirmed that he had returned his attention to his laptop and clearly figured their conversation to be closed. His expression was shuttered, his forehead creased in a frown of concentration.

Olivia hauled in breath. Well, tough. They would be in Thailand soon, and she'd be meeting Zeb shortly after. Surely she was entitled to some information about the man?

'Adam?' she said.

'Yes?'

Impatience tinged the air as he looked up and Olivia stiffened her spine.

'Could you tell me something more about Zeb?'

'More?' Dark eyebrows rose, for all the world as if he'd already given her a three-tome biography of Zeb. 'There isn't any more to tell.'

'Sure there is. So far all I've got is a man who wanders the world and has no wish to settle down.'

'What else do you need to know?'

Olivia shrugged. 'Well, what sort of father was he?' She hesitated. 'I noticed you didn't mention him in your speech, and…' And, man, she was an idiot. The penny plummeted down. 'That's why your mother brought you up on your own. Zeb didn't stick around.'

Adam's lips set in a grim line before he let out a whoosh of air and leant back, pushing his laptop back. 'No, he didn't,' he said.

Compassion, confusion and anger threaded through her. 'And you didn't think to mention this earlier?'

'No, I didn't.'

Keep calm, Liv. 'Care to expand on your reasoning?'

'Sure. Zeb walked away when my mum told him she was pregnant. Thirty years ago. Doesn't mean he'd do the same now. Plus, when Mum found out how ill she was she hired a PI to track him down. Zeb turned up a few weeks after the funeral and took me with him on his travels.'

His tone was way too bland. Olivia knew right down to her tippy-toes that there was a lot more to the story. The set of his lips also informed her that that was all she was going to get.

'And? What sort of dad was he then?'

Adam shrugged. 'He was exciting, unpredictable, fun. He taught me how to play poker and how to look out for myself.'

A shadow crossed his eyes on those last words, and Olivia would swear the air had become tinted with a wisp of bitterness.

As if he realised it Adam tipped his hands in the air and smiled. 'He made me into the man I am today. I'm pretty happy with that.' The plane started its descent and Adam snapped his laptop shut. 'And on that note, it looks like we're here.'

Olivia gazed out the window and for a minute wished that she was here on a holiday, visiting a country she had only dreamed of.

A sigh of sheer appreciation escaped her lips as they disembarked into the incredible warmth of the Thai sun. She shrugged off her light cardigan and tipped her face up to the sun's rays. Deep warmth suffused her as the sun soaked into her skin.

'Incredible,' she murmured as she followed Adam across the tarmac to a waiting taxi. 'So, two hours and we'll be on Ko Lanta?' she asked.

'Less. I've got a taxi booked, and then a speedboat. I've got seasickness tablets if you need them.'

'I should be fine. I haven't been on many boats, but I've never thrown up, either.'

'It's a bit bumpy, and you may get a bit wet, but it's the quickest way to get there.'

The remainder of their trip was achieved in silence, and anticipation built in Olivia with each bump of the car over the long, dusty road. Hope looped the loop in her tummy as she inhaled the salty sea spray and the speedboat skimmed

the glittering turquoise waves. The journey was bringing
them inexorably closer and closer to Zeb.

A man walked towards them as they stepped off the
deck of the speedboat onto the pier at Ko Lanta.

'Adam. It is good to see you.'

'Gan. Good to see you, too.' Adam turned to Olivia.
'Olivia, this is Gan. He taught me how to snorkel many,
many moons ago.'

The small, compact man's wrinkled face creased further as he smiled. 'Welcome to Ko Lanta, Olivia.'

'Thank you, Gan.'

'Can you take us straight to Zeb?' Adam asked.

The smile dropped from the elderly man's lips and he
shook his head. 'Sorry, Adam. Your father is no longer
here.'

Leaden disappointment weighted Olivia's tummy, but
Gan went on hurriedly.

'He will be back. He has gone on a trip. In five maybe
six days he said he will be back. But he has taken a boat
and I have no way of contacting him. I am sorry, Adam.
I could not stop him.'

'That's OK, Gan. It's not your fault. And it could be a
lot worse. At least we know he's coming back. All we have
to do is stay put until he gets here.'

All? Olivia bit her lip and tried to suppress the rising
swell of panic. More waiting. More time with Adam. On
a gloriously beautiful sun-drenched island where there
would be no handy distractions. No reporters or charity
events or work. Just Olivia and Adam, stranded on an isle.

Adam looked down at her and a rueful smile tugged
his lips, as though his mind was travelling the same path
as hers. 'Right now,' he said, 'I could do with a drink.'

'I'm with you on that.' Drowning her sorrows seemed
like an excellent short-term solution. Maybe she and Adam

could work out a way to follow Zeb, contact Zeb...*something*.

Gan nodded at their bags, then at the Jeep parked on the side of the road. 'Where are you staying, Adam? I can take your bags to the hotel and drop you off if you like?'

'Gan. You're the man,' Adam said, with a smile of genuine affection on his face.

Clearly there was a bond between the two men, which meant Ko Lanta must be a place Adam visited frequently. A pang struck her. Maybe this was his holiday destination of choice. How many other women had he brought here?

Not that the answer mattered to Olivia. In the slightest.

Fifteen minutes later she jumped out of the Jeep, waved to Gan and followed Adam to a bamboo shack beach bar. Wooden benches and tables dotted the golden sand that shimmered in the rays of evening sunshine. The beat of reggae music blended with the lapping of the waves to create an atmosphere so laid-back she could feel her frayed nerves being soothed.

Adam indicated a table and she slid along the sun-warmed teak with a sigh as a bare-chested waiter with a small drum strapped around his waist sauntered across the sand, placed a tray with two frosted glasses of beer on the table and high-fived Adam.

'Adam. Gan said you'd be here.'

'Saru. How are you doing? Where's your dad?'

The young man beamed. 'He's semi-retired now. He's away. On a cruise, would you believe? How long you here for?'

'A week or so.' Adam gestured to Olivia. 'This is Olivia.'

Saru shook her hand with a wide smile and then moseyed along to greet an arriving family, his hands beating a jaunty tune as he walked.

'Saru's a mean drummer,' Adam said. 'He and I used to busk in the old town together.'

An image of a bare-chested Adam with a drum around his muscular waist, busking on the dusky streets, sun glinting in his hair, filled her mind. So real, so vivid she felt she could reach out and touch him.

'You can play reggae? You busked?'

Adam grinned. 'I'm hot stuff.'

Didn't she know it? Olivia picked up her glass, welcoming the cold against her heated flesh. She drank, the strong taste puckering her lips even as the temperature refreshed her.

'It's beautiful here,' she said as she absorbed the sight of the sea, watched the mesh of different blues blend into an endless aquamarine expanse. 'I can see why you come here so often.' And, heaven help her, in this moment she wished she was here as one of his women.

'It's a great place to relax,' Adam continued. 'So relax, Olivia.'

'I *am* relaxed.'

A smile tugged his lips and her tummy back-flipped as her toes crunched into the warm sand.

'No, you aren't. Your leg is jigging up and down, your hand is clenched around your glass way too hard, and you have a perma-frown creasing your forehead.'

Well, no way was she about to explain that her lack of relaxation was to do with her escalating panic as to how she could spend a week in his company without losing her already tenuous grip on control.

She glared at him. 'OK. So I'm not relaxed. I was psyched up to meet Zeb and now he's not here—won't be here for days.'

Adam stretched his long legs out. 'Exactly.'

Desire and irritation jangled her nerves at his sheer carefree attitude and she took another gulp of beer. 'Exactly what?'

'There is nothing we can do except wait, so why not make the best of it? When's the last time you had a holiday?'

Olivia opened her mouth and closed it again. Surely she must have had a holiday at some point? There'd been that weekend away with her best friend, Suzi, but she didn't think that was what Adam meant. Even that had been a year ago.

She shrugged. 'Time goes so fast,' she said finally. 'And I suppose I don't want to waste money. I've got a mortgage and bills, and my mum's—' Olivia broke off.

'And your mum's what?'

Why shouldn't she tell him? It was nothing to be ashamed of. 'Allowance. I give my mum an allowance. She went through a lot to support me as a child—now it's my turn to look after her.'

Adam raised his eyebrows. 'So your mum holidays in Hawaii and you stay at home?'

'I'm happy with it that way.'

For a moment she thought he'd say more but then he shook his head. 'The point is you can't remember the last time you had a holiday. So here you are. In Thailand. Perfect weather. No work. So let go. Relax. Have a holiday.'

'A holiday?' she echoed. 'I'm here to find Zeb. Not loll about on a beach.'

'But Zeb isn't here and there's nothing you can do about it.'

'There must be something. Can't we radio him?'

'Gan tried that. No response.'

Broad shoulders hitched, his blue T stretched over the breadth of his chest and Olivia gulped.

'Accept it, Olivia. I know it's tough, but we're stuck on this beautiful island.'

'Yes, well, that's the problem, isn't it?' Olivia tried to gulp the words down but it was too late; she'd been so busy gawping at his display of muscle she'd spoken without thought.

'What is?'

'The "we" bit of it. You. Me. I'm sure that if I was stuck on this island by myself relaxation wouldn't be an issue. But you…you make me edgy.'

'No need. We're both agreed that we aren't going to act on our attraction, so surely we can get past it and enjoy some chill-out time? Have some fun? You can do that, right?'

The look he cast her was so full of challenge tempered by a glint of mischief that she was torn between the desire to slap him or sample him.

'Of course I can,' she said through clenched teeth.

'I don't believe you. I reckon you've forgotten how to wind down, Olivia. If you ever knew.'

'That is ridiculous. I am an expert at taking it easy.' She took another defiant gulp of beer. The taste was welcome, smooth, and cold as it slipped down her throat.

Adam followed suit and her hungry eyes watched, mesmerised by the sturdy column of his throat. *Enough*. They were supposed to be past the attraction—and, hell, if Adam could get past it so could she.

'I've *bulldozed* past that ridiculous attraction thing.' She waved her hand in the air. 'And I'm the Queen of Chill.'

His smile widened into what could definitely be classed as a positive grin. A wolfish grin. 'Good. That's sorted, then.' He lifted his glass. 'To our holiday.'

'I'll drink to that,' she said, and drained the glass.

Caution tried to rear its head and was instantly decapitated by the Queen of Chill. True, her head was spinning a little. True, she'd had no sleep and little food. But both those things could be remedied. Soon. After maybe one more drink.

As if reading her mind, Adam rose. 'I'll get you a refill. And some water and some food.'

'Fabulous.'

Picking up their empty glasses, he strode towards the

bamboo enclosure. He was so tall, so broad, so damn imposing and oh, so very delicious. His every stride was adding to her head-spin. Hell, by the end of a week with Mr Hotter Than the Core of the Universe she'd be eligible for a starring role in a horror movie.

Nope. Nope. Nope.

Get with it, Liv.

The attraction had been annihilated and they were on holiday. Chillaxing.

May all the gods help her!

CHAPTER NINE

AFTER CONFERRING WITH Saru on the question of food Adam exited the dim interior of the bar and paused in the doorway to absorb the dusky beauty of the evening sky.

His thoughts raced. A holiday with Olivia, brought about by Zeb's all too predictable runner. Adam had asked Gan not to mention Adam's arrival, but even so Zeb would have suspected something was up. After all it was Zeb who had taught Adam his poker table skills; he had uncanny instincts and an ability to read body language the way other people read magazines. A spooked Zeb would have seen an impromptu sailing trip as the perfect solution— would hope that by the time he came back the trouble he'd scented would be long gone.

Well, he was in for a surprise, because Adam was going nowhere.

Instead he and Olivia were going to stay here and have a holiday.

He must be nuts. *Stellar idea, Adam. Give the man a medal. For sheer foolishness.* But Olivia was in evident need of a break and the words had somehow fallen from his lips without permission from his brain. *Enjoy some chill-out time. Have some fun. Past the attraction.* Amazing he hadn't been struck by lightning for such an enormous fib.

But the point was this attraction *was* under control. *His*

control, not his libido's. At the end of the day Olivia was
a beautiful woman, but one who was off-limits. He was a
grown-up, and he was perfectly capable of spending a relaxed few days with Olivia.

Adam glanced out to the sea, where the sun was just
beginning to dip down. The sky was an electric, vivid orange speckled with tinted tangerine clouds. It was the perfect way to start any holiday.

He flicked his gaze to her, wanting to see her reaction.

'For Pete's sake,' he muttered, and strode across the
sand.

Olivia looked up from the napkin on which she was
industriously scribbling notes from the illuminated tablet
on the tabletop.

'Tha—' she began as he placed the tray down.

Adam walked around and placed his hands on her already sun-kissed shoulders. The warmth of her skin tingled his palms as he gently turned her upper body to face
the horizon.

'Oh…' She sucked in a breath of sheer wonder and his
whole body stood to attention; the sound that fell from
her lips held the same resonance as yesterday in the limo.
For a second the sunset dimmed—a mere backdrop to the
memory of her astride him, flushed and needy.

Olivia gave a small wriggle of her shoulders and he
kneaded his fingers into the tight knots of her shoulders.
Relaxed? This woman had a long way to go before she
was anywhere near. And *he* didn't have far to go until the
silken texture of her skin, her small huff of pleasure as he
dug deeper, pushed him to the brink of discomfort.

Come on, Adam. Past the attraction, remember? Yeah,
well, he was only human. Perhaps a friendly massage
wasn't the best way forward.

Releasing her shoulders, he stepped backwards and

walked round to his seat, the distance between them a welcome one. He gestured to her list. 'So what's that?'

'It's a list of things to do this week,' she said. 'I was researching Ko Lanta.'

'I thought the Queen of Chill would be more into lazing around on the beach soaking up some rays.' Preferably in a skimpy bikini; even better if Olivia was in need of a handy sun-cream applier. Sure, his libido might not be in control, but it deserved something; he might not be able to bed her, but there was nothing wrong with a bit of healthy appreciation.

A resolute shake of her head indicated disagreement. 'I may never get to visit Thailand again—I've got to make sure I see everything.' She picked up her glass and took a gulp, then transferred her attention to the serviette. 'There's this tour where you trek through the jungle, climb up a dried-up waterfall and get to a limestone cave. It sounds awesome.'

'I know the one,' he said. 'One of my favourite places.'

'Perfect. We'll definitely go there, then. And there's a national park with a lighthouse, and loads of other stuff. First thing tomorrow I'll need to get some proper shoes and suitable clothes, though. I didn't really pack for a holiday.'

'What *did* you pack for?'

'Meeting Zeb.'

'I'm not entirely sure I'm with you.' Presumably beach clothes were beach clothes.

'Well, take this for example.' Olivia waved a hand at her outfit. 'I put a lot of thought into it. Grey trousers and a light grey tunic top. Muted colours, but not funereal. Non-threatening, non-judgemental. I was aiming for soothing and neutral.'

'Is that how you think all the time?'

'What do you mean?'

Adam glanced down. 'I look at my clothes and I think

blue T-shirt and beige chinos. You use your clothes to play a part.'

'No, I don't.'

'Then what's *your* style? Enquiring minds want to know.' His theory was that Olivia used clothes to define her, wore them as armour.

'It's all my style. I'd never wear anything I didn't like.'

'I get that. But it seems like all your clothes have a purpose—to set you up in a certain role. You're always projecting an image.'

For a second a look of confusion entered her hazel eyes. As if he'd flummoxed or at the very least flustered her.

She took another hefty swig from her glass, almost draining it. 'That's all so much psychobabble,' she declared as she put her glass down with exaggerated care. 'Anyway, you're a fine one to talk with your co-ordinated-by-some-one-else wardrobe.' She rested her elbows on the table so she could prop her chin in her hands and surveyed him a touch owlishly. 'I think you should let me dress you.' Tilting her head to one side, she gave a slightly fuzzy smile. 'Oops. That may have come out wrong.'

'Nah. It would have come out wrong if you'd asked if you could *undress* me.'

The giggle she gave was infectious, 'Seriously, though, let's go shopping. It could be fun.'

Fun? What the hell...? But maybe it would be—and it was her holiday, after all. Perhaps he could persuade her into buying that skimpy bikini or a tiny little pair of shorts that would barely cover her heart-shaped derrière. Hell, yes.

'OK. I'm in. You choose me some clothes and I'll choose you some clothes. I don't want to spend a week with you dressed in your "soothe Zeb" outfits. I want to be seen with—'

'Oh, here we go!' Olivia shook her head and her lush lips actually curled.

'Here we go, where?'

'To the part where you want to display me on your arm as some sort of trophy.'

'Olivia. What the hell are you talking about?' He poured her a glass of water and pushed it across the table.

She eyed it belligerently before picking it up. 'It doesn't matter.' She waved the glass and water droplets fell onto the tabletop. 'Let's have another drink. My round.'

'Uh-uh.' Adam shook his head. 'No more beer until you explain.'

Olivia chewed her bottom lip for a moment and then shrugged. 'You drive a hard bargain, Masterson. Fine. You want to know? I'll tell you. It's *complicated*, being beautiful.'

'Are you for real? Women would kill to look like you and you're complaining?'

She shook her head. 'It means men only want you for your looks.'

'Not only. There's more to it than that.'

'Hornswoggle.' Olivia looked impressed with the word, her lips formulating the syllables again. 'Take us, for example. You and me. Not that there is a you and me any more. But when there was. You with me?'

'Faint but pursuing. Keep going.'

'Well, *you*—' she pointed at him '—were attracted to me because of my looks. If I didn't have this face, if I'd arrived in your hotel with greasy hair dressed in a bin bag, I wouldn't have had any effect on you at all.'

'Not true.'

'Totally true.' She waved a finger at him. 'I looked up that billionaire-bagging article, Adam. Your only criteria is beauty. *"Blonde or dark. Small or tall... This field is open to all. Adam Masterson's only criteria is beauty: the man likes his ladies easy on the eye."* Not a mention of personality. So—*ha*! I rest my case and I'll go get us a beer.'

'Not so fast.' Adam snorted. 'You're quoting a rubbishy magazine article. It's hardly gospel.'

Olivia wrinkled her nose before pouring herself another glass of water. 'OK, Mr Holier Than Thou. List the last five women you slept with. Then tell me—were they beautiful or were they not?'

Adam could feel metaphorical ropes digging into his back; a sudden urge to loosen his collar overcame him and he wasn't even wearing a shirt. Those five women ranged back over a three-year period but, yes, they were all beautiful. Mind you, until this moment, with Olivia's accusatory eyes boring it into him, he'd never seen it as a problem.

'I *like* beautiful women,' he said. 'Does it count in my favour that they were all a different type of beautiful?'

'Nope, it doesn't,' she said. 'All it shows is that you like variety.' She nodded sagely. 'And what were all those women wearing when you met them? How did they look? Were they dressed to attract? Made up to show themselves at their best?'

How he wished he could claim that at least one of those five women had been met at a farm, in wellington boots, up to her knees in pig muck. But honesty, along with the knowledge that those hazel eyes would see straight through him, compelled him to admit, 'Yes.'

'Double *ha*!' Another shrug and a small smirk tugged those lush lips. 'There you have it. I win. Just admit it, Adam. Looks matter and clothes matter. Especially to men like *you*.' She jabbed her finger at his chest.

He raised his eyebrows. 'Men like me? What does that mean?' And why did he know he wouldn't like the answer?

'Men with the money to buy whatever and whomever they choose.'

'Ouch. Are you suggesting I *buy* my women?' Good thing his ego was fairly robust.

'Not exactly,' she admitted as she tilted her head to one side and studied him, a small critical frown creasing her forehead. 'You're good-looking, you're charming—*maybe* your women would date you regardless of your wallet.'

'Well, gee. Thanks for the vote of confidence.'

'My point is that your money eases your path. It means that even when you're old and wrinkly beautiful women will always be available to you and you know that. So you'll keep sampling the variety and so it will go on—for ever and ever, amen.' She tipped her hands up. 'A bit like a conveyor belt.'

A conveyor belt? 'That implies each woman is the same,' he countered. 'Every woman I date is different and I've liked every single one.' Well, he hadn't *dis*liked any of them, at any rate, and that counted for something, right? 'And—' he allowed a reminiscent smile to play about his lips, wanting her to remember he had a lot more to offer a woman than the contents of his wallet '—I'm pretty sure they all have very fond memories of me.'

Her face tinted pink, as if she were reliving the memory of their recent activities in lift and limo. But then she rallied and pressed her lips together in a line of disapproval. 'Hmmph. No doubt they do. And I'm sure you give them an expensive souvenir of their time spent gracing your bed.'

'Sure I give them presents.' Actually, he didn't even do that. He just sent them off to shop in the boutiques in whichever Masterson Hotel they were in and rack their purchases up to his account. 'And, yes, it is a token of appreciation—but there's nothing wrong with that.'

If a woman had given him the pleasure of her company and her body then it seemed reasonable to give her something back. Something that didn't cost him anything but money. After all he had more of that than he knew what to do with.

One thing he could thank his marriage for: in his lunatic attempt to prove he could settle down and reclaim the home of his childhood, he'd fallen into a career that he loved. And he'd made sure that Charlotte benefited; the alimony he paid was more than generous.

Heaven knew she deserved every red cent, because her pain had taught him the truth about himself: he couldn't do love, he couldn't do settling down. But that didn't mean he needed to condemn himself to celibacy. And if that meant a conveyor belt of beautiful women in his life, hell, he didn't have a problem with that. Not one.

'Olivia. I plead guilty to liking a moving line of beautiful women, but it's not for the kudos of having a trophy woman on my arm. I date women whose company I find enjoyable in the bedroom and out. And I make damn sure no one gets hurt.'

'How do you do that?'

'I have rules.'

She gave a small sigh. 'Of *course* you have rules. I can't believe I'm asking this, but please share.'

'Short-term, no expectations, no deep emotions, a good time had by all. That way everyone knows to jump off the conveyor belt when the ride is over. And no one gets hurt.' He hitched his shoulders. 'Works for me.'

'Not for me,' she said. 'In fact I'd rather poke myself in the eye than lose all my self-respect by even putting my toe on your conveyor belt. I refuse to be some interchangeable good-time girl, only valued for my looks and my understanding that all that's in it for me is just sex, expensive dinners and some goodbye jewellery.'

'Well, *I* refuse to be branded some rich Lothario who pays for his pleasures. And, for the record, I offer *hot* sex—not just sex.'

* * *

Hot sex.

The words lingered on the warm evening breeze alongside her own. Olivia's brain whirred a frantic calculation. Hot sex, expensive dinners and jewellery. And this was bad because…?

OK, she'd forego the latter two, but suddenly every molecule of her was asking what exactly was wrong with having hot sex with…say, Adam? In return for…hot sex with Adam.

Mutual pleasure.

So where exactly was the catch?

Oh, yeah, it was short-term. No love on offer.

She didn't want long-term. Definitely didn't want love.

So what exactly would she lose?

'Olivia?'

Her head snapped up from her unseeing contemplation of the table.

'You OK?' he asked, amusement lacing the deep voice. 'You look like you're having an internal debate on the meaning of life. And losing.'

'I am fine. Absolutely fine.'

And she was. Hot sex with Adam would mean loss of control and she would *not* go there. She'd want him more than he wanted her. She was interchangeable with any beautiful woman. The power would be all his. Bang would go her self-respect. Problem was, right now self-respect seemed highly overrated.

'Why don't we move inside?' she suggested. 'I'm sure you want to catch up with Saru and…'

'You looking for a chaperone, Olivia?'

She looked up at him, desperate to deny it, but seeing the glint of mischief and sympathy in his brown eyes she couldn't. 'Something like that.' Rallying, she managed a smile. 'I wouldn't want that bulldozed attraction to return.'

'Hell, honey, neither would I. I couldn't agree with you more. There's safety in numbers, so let's get ourselves inside.'

Rising to her feet, she picked up her empty glass and set off towards the bar, sandals crunching into the moon-dappled sand. She went up the rickety wooden steps that led to the interior of the bar and stopped on the threshold, air whooshing from her lungs.

'Wow!' The inside of the bar was a vibrant Mecca for reggae. Posters covered every millimetre of the walls, and the ceiling was looped with garlands of flags in bright red, yellow and green. Olivia absorbed the life-size cardboard Bob Marley in front of a small stage tucked into the corner. Tables half filled with customers were scattered over the wooden floor and there was a buzz of conversation against the beat of reggae music being emitted from the sophisticated sound system.

'Saru is a bit of a reggae fanatic,' Adam said. 'You should hear him and his cousin perform. They are amazing.'

'Hey, Adam,' Saru called from behind the bar. 'You want to play?'

Adam hesitated.

'Go on,' Olivia said, the urge to see this hitherto unseen side to Adam nigh on overwhelming. This was a different type of relaxed from his usual practised, laid-back charm and she wanted to witness it. 'Demonstrate your hot stuff.'

Just far away from me. Please. On the drums. Not on me. Please.

'You sure you don't mind?'

'Cross my heart.'

'Yes. Come on, Adam. Show Olivia what you can do,' Saru encouraged as he walked around the bar counter. 'Olivia, Adam has never brought a woman here before. We should mark the occasion. Sit here. I'll get you a beer.'

He tapped a man on the shoulder. 'And Marley, as he is known for obvious reasons, will sing.'

A totally stupid warmth melted over her as Adam ushered her to a table. He had never brought a woman here before. True, he hadn't exactly chosen to bring her, either, but that wasn't the point. She wasn't 100 per cent sure what the point actually was, but right now she didn't care.

Olivia watched as Adam strode to the stage and seated himself behind a pair of bongo drums. He stroked the top and drummed his fingers in a gentle experimental tattoo. Saru leapt up next to him and they had a quick whispered confab with Marley before the strains of one of the world's best-known reggae songs strummed from his guitar, the drums in perfect accompaniment as Marley started to sing.

He had a magnificent voice, but Olivia's eyes were riveted to Adam and a whole different level of desire swathed her. Utterly relaxed, lost in the moment and the music, he looked in his element. His large hands moved as if he and the instrument were one—as if he'd been born playing the bongos. When he and Saru chimed in for the chorus, Olivia picked out Adam's deep melodious voice and a shiver trembled over her spine.

Envy touched her. The idea of losing herself in something, really believing there was nothing to worry about, was alluring in the extreme. Maybe for a couple of hours tonight, though, she could do that. Be Olivia on holiday— actually be the Queen of Chill for real.

She drank another glug of beer and allowed her sandal-clad toes to tap the wooden floor. Like the rest of the clientele she found her body swaying as the set progressed. Her heart beat faster and faster as she watched Adam, his hands a blur now, his muscular forearms sheened with sweat, thick thighs pressed against the drums. He was so damn hot her insides twisted with the sheer wanting of him.

Marley bowed at the close of the song even as the clientele called for more.

Saru stood up. 'Anyone else want a go?'

A Thai man at an adjoining table jumped to his feet. 'I'll sing,' he said.

Saru plucked a guitar down from the selection hanging behind the stage. 'Elvis takes the stage,' he announced as he passed the instrument over. 'Olivia? You want to try the drums?'

It took Olivia a second to understand the question. 'Me?' she said. 'Um…I'm fine watching…but thanks all the same. I'm not really very musical.'

Then Adam looked up from the drums and made a *come hither* movement with his hand, and of their own volition her feet propelled her upward and onward. *Nooooooo!* This was the world's very worst idea. The last drum she'd played she'd been aged two and it had been saucepan-shaped. Yet she kept right on going to where Adam waited at the edge of the stage, his hand outstretched.

As his fingers clasped hers Olivia bit back a gasp even as she cursed her own imagination. Because that was all it could be. Electric currents could *not* be generated by desire; it was a scientific impossibility.

Once on stage Olivia looked around the bar, lit up by a scattering of red-, yellow-, and green-coloured paper lanterns, its relaxed patrons all chatting as 'Elvis' limbered up on the guitar. Saru drummed an impromptu solo, the haunting beat carrying on the night breeze wafting in through the open windows.

'I'm really not sure about this,' Olivia said.

'It'll be fun,' Adam said. 'Give it a go. Come on. The Queen of Chill would.'

'Ha ha!' Olivia hesitated for a moment and then pinned her shoulders back. What the hell? If she stepped off this stage now she'd regret it. After all, when would she ever get the chance to do something like this again?

It would be an experience, and it was worth the headiness provoked by Adam's proximity. He was buzzing; she could feel the vibe jumping off him. His scent assaulted her senses, the pure masculine tang of salt and his underlying woodsy scent sending her dizzy with longing.

'OK,' she said. 'I'll give it a go.'

She followed him to the bongos, dropped down onto the low stool behind them, and pulled the drums forward between her thighs. The leather was warm from Adam's body heat and Olivia shuddered.

And then she melted as he slid onto the stool behind her, the rock-solid wall of his chest against her back. A strange noise emerged from her mouth, half mewl, half groan, as his arms slipped round her waist and his big hands covered hers.

'Meep.'

'You need to sit on the edge of the seat,' he said softly, his breath tickling her ear. 'And position your legs at a ninety-degree angle.'

'Meep.'

Get a grip. He is positioning you to play the drums. Nothing else. This is not the time to channel Roadrunner.

'You OK?' Adam's voice held amusement and sin; the combination was lethal.

'Yup. Fine.'

'Good. You need the larger drum just below your right knee and nudge the smaller one to your left.'

If she focused really hard on the drums instead of the press of his body, she could do this.

'You comfy?'

'Just peachy.' Never mind that her muscles were in clench mode and it was nothing to do with drum-holding.

'Good. That's important. Make sure you've got the drum firmly in place between your legs.'

His voice was so low, so full of innuendo that Olivia was torn between a desire to elbow him or call him on it. She went for option two.

Wriggling her bottom backwards she grinned at the evidence of exactly what innuendo was doing to him. 'You sure you're talking about the drum?' she whispered.

His breath hitched and the solid muscle of his thigh convulsed against her leg. 'Excellent question. What would you *like* me to be talking about, Olivia?'

He pressed the edge of his erection against the small of her back and she moaned. She had to ground herself; she really did. They had agreed to bypass the attraction, so what exactly was Adam doing? Maybe he was being carried away by the music—in which case it was up to her to be the sane one.

'The drums,' she said hoarsely. 'That's what we're talking about here.'

'Anything you say, cupcake.' He caressed her hands, his thumbs stroking her index fingers until she couldn't think straight. 'In which case now you need to limber up,' he growled. 'You'll need to use your fingers and thumbs to do a lot of the work.'

'Meep. Meep.'

'This is what you'll need to get a beat going.' His nose brushed her cheek; he was so very close they were practically melded. Her entire body was on alert as his scent enveloped her.

Reality, Liv. Try to focus.

Saru had started playing now, and the singer strummed the first chord of the song.

'Just go with it, Olivia,' Adam murmured. 'Go with the rhythm. Lose yourself in it.'

For a second her body tensed against his and then something shifted inside her chest—a leaden block, pushed aside by the volcano of desire that was building up inside her like a fever. She closed her eyes and allowed her body to sway to the beat, encased by the strength of Adam's arms. She felt his body move with hers and dizziness soared. Her hands, still underneath his, moved instinctively to the rhythmic beat of the music until the singer sang a final harmonic refrain, the echo of his voice soaring into the warm glow of the bar.

Applause rang out and Olivia opened her eyes, suddenly aware of the insane grin on her face.

'That was amazing,' she breathed. And so was this: Adam's hard body pressed up against her, the high of having done something so out of character. She wondered if it was possible that aliens had abducted the real Olivia Evans.

'There's nothing like it,' Adam agreed.

Saru jumped down off the stage and after a long moment Adam released her waist and rose to his feet. Olivia gave a small shiver. Of cold, she reassured herself. Not loss, because that would be absurd.

Her heart still pounded, her head still spun, and desire still smouldered, desperate to erupt. Damn it, she wanted that physical connection to remain.

Without letting herself question it further she rose and twisted round, closed the gap between them in a single small step. She looped her arms round the solid column of his waist, curled her fingers into the waistband of his shorts and rocked right up against him.

CHAPTER TEN

ADAM STARED DOWN into her wide hazel eyes, saw her lush pink lips part. There was no way in heaven or hell he could resist her. One taste, one kiss—that was all he'd allow himself. After the glorious frustration of having her lush body so close, her apple scent intoxicating him whilst her sheer abandon in the music had stopped him short, a kiss was surely not too much to take?

'Adam? Please. This time I won't pull back.'

Whoa...

A kiss was one thing; Olivia was asking for more. *Huzzah.*

Somehow he had to think past the temptation to throw her over his shoulder, race back to the hotel, and take her at her word. Before she changed her mind.

'Damn it.' The words emerged from his throat hoarse and guttural. Twice they'd been carried away, and two times Olivia had hauled herself back. There must be reasons for that.

Complicated reasons.

So if she was surrendering herself now that was a huge deal for her.

Which further muddied the already swamp-like water.

About the only thing Adam was sure of now, apart from his body's urgent desire, was that complications were bad news.

For all concerned.

Olivia was vulnerable and that put her off-limits.

Digging deep into his reserves of willpower, he gently reached back to unclasp her grip and stepped backwards.

'No can do, Olivia.'

Her tongue peeped out as she moistened her lips. 'Why not?' A downward lingering glance and then her hazel eyes flicked back up to meet his. 'I can see that you're feeling this, too.'

'You'll get no argument there.' The thought that this hard-on now had nowhere to go was enough to make him weep. 'But we agreed. No explosion means no pieces to pick up. So help me, right now all I want to do is take you to my bed. But it's not a good idea. For either of us.'

No way was he taking that emotional journey with her. A fling with Olivia would necessarily involve more than hot sex, expensive dinners and a piece of jewellery. And he didn't want more because he had nothing more to give.

Olivia bit her lip, and his resolve faltered at the hurt that shadowed her eyes.

Then she blinked and pulled her hands from his grasp. 'Well, this is embarrassing,' she said finally, with a brittle attempt at a laugh.

'No. No embarrassment allowed,' he said firmly. 'Because there is nothing to feel awkward about. I promise. Now, come on. We deserve a beer, and after our excellent drumming performance there will be plenty of people who want to buy us one. Come on, Olivia. Let's party.'

She hesitated for a moment and then gave her small characteristic nod.

They descended the double steps leading off the stage and returned to their table where two beers already awaited them, the frosted glasses a welcome diversion from their conversation. Perhaps the ice-cold drink would cool him down. His body sizzled with disappointment at being short-changed. Whilst his libido was calling him every sort of fool.

'Cheers,' he said, raising his glass. 'To your first public performance.'

She clinked her glass against his. 'And likely to be my last.'

'Why?'

'I can't see me taking up drumming once I get back home.' There was an almost wistful note to her voice before she frowned and took another sip of beer. 'I'll buy a CD, though. That song—what sort of music was it? It didn't sound like reggae.'

'Calypso music,' Adam said. 'It's Afro-Carribean and the songs tend to represent the voice of the people. In the past the lyrics have been used politically and historically.'

This was ridiculous; the conversation was so stilted he might as well find some wooden sticks to prop it up.

It was a relief to see Saru arrive with two more beers in hand. 'Here you go. On the house, for a spectacular performance, Olivia.'

'Thank you, Saru. I enjoyed every minute.'

'Enjoy. I'll be back soon with some food for you both. Beef *phaenang*. You'll love it.'

Once he'd gone, silence loomed and Adam strained his brain to find any topic of conversation, drummed his fingers on the tabletop in time to the jiggle of her foot on the wooden planks of the floor.

She drained one beer and pulled the fresh one towards her. 'I've got an idea,' she said. 'To solve our conversational vacuum.'

'Go right ahead.'

'Let's play twenty questions.'

Good grief. Had it really come to this? The type of games he usually indulged in with his dates were more the kind you played in the bedroom. *Ah, but Olivia isn't your date. And you vetoed the bedroom. Idiot that you are.*

'Twenty questions it is.'

'Good. I'll go first.' Olivia wrinkled her nose in thought. 'What's your favourite colour?'

'Umm...' *Come on, Adam.* It was an easy question and the answer didn't even have to be true. 'Blue.'

'That's it?'

'Yup.'

'What type of blue? Navy? Royal? Turquoise? Aquamarine? Azure?'

'OK, OK. I get it. And that counted as an extra question. Navy blue.'

Olivia shook her head. 'Dull, Masterson. That's plain *dull.*'

Adam tried and failed to remember the last time a woman had dismissed him as being dull.

'Your turn,' she said.

'Where do you live?' Hard to believe that he didn't know, but he didn't.

'Bath. I love it. I moved there a few years ago and it's such a great city. It's steeped in history and it's got amazing shops, as well.'

'Where did you live before?'

'Oh, here and there. We moved around a lot. That's why I was so desperate to settle down properly. I think it's why I love my flat so much. It's not big, but it doubles as a work and home space and it's mine.' Animation lit her features, her skin taking on a luminosity that had nothing to do with the coloured lanterns. 'Do you want to see some photos?' she offered.

Guessing that it might well be Olivia's attempt to ground herself, to remind herself of home and work and the real world, Adam nodded. 'Love to.' Could be *his* resolve could do with a bit of focus, too.

Without preamble she stood up and moved her chair around so she was sitting adjacent to him instead of opposite, and he braced himself for what he was beginning to think of as The Olivia Effect.

'So, these are the "before" pictures,' she said, placing her tablet on the table between them. 'When I bought it the place needed a *whole* lot of work.'

She wasn't kidding. The pictures showed dilapidated, damp-ridden rooms. Floorboards pushed through the rotten wool of threadbare carpets, dingy wallpaper peeled off the walls.

'Now look at this. This is the work area.'

Adam let out a whistle as he saw how she had transformed the bay-fronted room. Originally meant as a lounge, it was now a professional office space. The walls were a bright, clean white, embellished with pictures of stylish fashions through the years and fabulous prints of Bath throughout the ages. Comfortable and homely overstuffed armchairs and a brightly upholstered sofa surrounded a table complete with fashion magazines. The wooden floor gleamed and the bright and cheerful rugs that littered the floor screamed *fun* along with good taste.

She beamed at him. 'And this is the kitchen.'

It was a fraction of the size of his but it looked way more personal. The blown-up photos showed a neatly put up shelf of eclectic cookbooks that covered the globe in cuisine, a row of brightly coloured mugs, and pottery jars labelled 'Tea', 'Coffee', and 'Sugar'.

'I'll bet your fridge is properly compartmentalised.'

'I'll let you into a secret.'

She leant forward confidentially, so close that he could see the light smattering of freckles on the end of her nose.

'I keep my spices in alphabetical order.'

'Whereas I don't own any spices at all.'

Which pretty much summed it up.

A stray strand of her strawberry hair tickled his cheek and lured his fingers as she shook her head.

'That's just wrong,' she declared slightly fuzzily as she picked up her glass.

'Hey! Not owning spices is hardly a crime.'

'It is from now. The Queen of Chill decrees it.'

Another shake of her head and Adam placed his hands on the table, out of temptation's way.

'Seriously, Adam, it's not right to live in a hotel room.'

'Penthouse suite,' he interpolated.

She waved a hand. 'Whatever. Point is, you never have to do anything *real*.'

'Such as?'

'Cooking. Cleaning. Dusting.'

Adam tipped his hands in the air. 'And this is a problem because...?'

'But that's what us normal everyday types have to do. I think it would be good for you to get down on your knees and scrub a bathroom floor.'

He couldn't resist. 'But I can think of so many more pleasurable activities to do on my knees. Can't you?'

Her face was tinged pink and her mouth smacked into a circle of surprised outrage, and Adam felt his lips quirk upwards into a smile.

'I can't believe you said that,' she said, before emitting a sudden snort of laughter and staring into her glass. 'Hey. It's empty. How did that happen?'

'I think you drank it.' Adam glanced up. 'Ah. Here comes our food.'

'And more beer,' Olivia said on a slight hiccup. 'Good man, Saru.' She beamed up at Saru as he placed two steaming plates in front of them. 'This looks incredible.'

Saru grinned. 'Thank you, Olivia. The ingredients are all fresh. I bought them myself from the market today.'

Leaning over the plate, Olivia inhaled. 'It smells as

good as it looks. What's in it? And do you mind if I take notes?' She indicated the napkin by her side.

Adam blinked; there was a certain fascination in watching the animation on her face as she listed all the ingredients, the tip of her tongue protruding at the corner of her mouth.

'Kaffir lime, coconut milk, palm sugar...'

Yet another first. Adam tried and failed to imagine any woman he'd dated taking recipe notes from a waiter.

'What?' she asked after Saru had left. 'I can't have sauce on my nose because I haven't started eating yet.'

'Nothing,' Adam said, shaking his head and pushing away the urge to tell her she was adorable. 'Just tuck in.'

'Don't mind if I do.'

Adam had never witnessed anyone demolish a plateful of food with such ladylike dedication. Within minutes her plate was wiped clean.

'That was amazing,' Olivia said, as she pulled her glass towards her. 'Now, where were we with twenty questions? Why don't you tell me your hobbies?'

To Adam's surprise, the next time he glanced around the bar had emptied, the music had been turned off, and he and Olivia had swapped a mountain of information. Favourite films—hers: *Breakfast at Tiffany's*; his: *The Great Escape*. Favourite book—hers: too many to count, so *Lord of the Rings* and all of Austen; his: *Lord of the Rings* and anything detective.

'I think it's time to go before Saru kicks us out,' Adam said.

Olivia nodded and then winced, placed her hands on the table and levered herself up. 'I may be ever so slightly... tipsy,' she announced. 'Not inebee...inebril...in...drunk, you understand. Just tiddly. Like in winks. That's what we should play next. Tiddlywinks.'

'Next time,' Adam said.

'Itsh a deal.' Olivia looked down and then dropped back onto the chair. 'We can't go.'

'Why not?'

'Cos I haven't got my...you know...my thingy. The thing that I wrote thingies down on.'

'The napkin?'

'Yup.' Olivia folded her arms on the table. 'Can't go without that. It's like a souvenir...you know?'

'I'll see what I can do.'

'You're a prince.'

Fifteen minutes later a diligent search had located the scrawled upon napkin and Olivia had very carefully folded it up and tucked it into her tablet case.

'Let's go,' she said, and wended her way towards the door.

There was nothing for it—no choice but to snake his arm around the slender span of her waist in order to steer her straight across the moonlit sand. His body reacted all too predictably as she tucked herself next to him, leant against him with a small, satisfied sigh.

'There we go. Easy does it, Olivia.'

'Call me Liv.'

'I'd be honoured.'

She looked up at the sky. 'So beautiful,' she said. 'All black and glittery and...and starry. Like your eyes.'

'Thank you.' Adam suppressed a grin; Olivia...no, *Liv* was going to regret this the next day.

'Adam?'

'Yes.'

'Can I ask you another question?'

'Question twenty-one? Sure.'

'What do you think about love?'

Ah. Talk about sliding in the knock-out punch right at the end. Glancing down at her, he acquitted her of intentionally wanting to catch him out. Her nose was simply crinkled in thought as she waited for his answer.

'I believe in it for other people but I know it's not for me.' He hitched his shoulders as she tilted her head, the movement casing a friction against his chest.

'Well, I don't like love. Because…'

She stumbled slightly and he tightened his grasp around her waist, his gut clenching with renewed desire.

'Because,' she continued, 'love is an illusion.'

If only the stirring of his body was a delusion. *Focus on the conversation, Adam.* Although it didn't really matter what they said because it was unlikely that Olivia would remember.

'Why do you say that?'

Olivia slid to a stop and turned to face him, held onto his arms as she peered up at his face. 'Cos it's true. Men cheat, dazzled by a beautiful face or the thrill of the forbidden, and they hop out of the marriage bed—' she snapped her fingers as she gave a little jump, scuffing up grains of moonlit sand '—just like that. Or they say they love you to get into your knickers. It's an illusion to romanticise sex.'

'Not all men are like that. Think of all the happily married people in the world.'

'Nah.' Her wave dismissed half the population. 'Another mirage. Most of them have compromised. For a lifestyle or a child. They'd all betray each other given the right price.' She heaved a great sigh. 'It's verrrry sad.'

'Would you compromise?'

'Never.' She slammed her shoulders back. 'Never give up. Never surrender. That's me. I'm not the compromising sort. And I know the truth. Remember the truth, Adam. Love is an illusion.'

'I'll remember, Liv. Now, let's get going. We're nearly at the hotel.'

Minutes later Adam surveyed the bedroom and gusted

out a sigh. Gan must have assumed they were sharing a room—more to the point that they were sharing a bed.

'I'll go and sort out another room.'

'No. Itsh OK. Really. We're past the attraction, remember? It's all over and done with.'

Clearly Olivia was suffering from selective memory and/or delusion.

She surveyed the bed. 'But just in case we'll build a barricade.'

With great precision she leant over the mattress and Adam's heart skipped a beat at the sight of her heart-shaped bottom.

Very carefully Olivia arranged an armful of pillows in a straight line down the middle of the bed. 'Easy-peasy, lemon-squeezy. Sleep well, Adam'

Somehow that seemed unlikely.

But it would be another first. Sharing a bed with a woman and a barricade; he must be losing his touch.

Olivia squeaked her eyelids open and hurriedly closed them again. Sunlight. That was definitely a clue. So was the whirr of air-conditioning.

Enough to tell her that she wasn't tucked up nice and safe and warm in her bedroom at home in the middle of a Bath winter.

Then there was the flower-sweet scent borne in on the sunlit breeze.

She was in Thailand.

Memories surfaced. Of a bar on the beach. Golden sand crunching underneath her toes. A fantastically beautiful sunset. Drums… A napkin scribbled with notes… And beer…lots of beer.

And there had been Adam.

'Rise and shine, Liv.'

'That's a joke, right? And who said you could call me Liv?'

'You did.' His deep tone was tinged with amusement. 'So, rise and shine, Liv.'

Olivia hauled her eyes open again and turned her head, wincing. 'Rising is a faint possibility. Shining, not so much.'

'I've brought tea,' he said, and stepped forward to place a steaming mug on the bedside table.

Bedside.

The word was ominous, opening the floodgates to the next wave of memory.

Olivia braced her hands on the mattress and hoisted herself up gingerly, wriggled backwards and leant against the padded headboard. She reached for the life-saving cup of tea, devoutly hoping that everything could be cured by a nice cuppa.

'Thank you,' she murmured, her tongue thick and fuzzy, but soothed by the strong brew, and her parched throat grateful as the reviving liquid slipped down her throat. 'So...' Gripping the folds of the blanket, she forced herself to meet his gaze. 'Hit me. How embarrassed should I be?'

'How embarrassed do you want to be?'

She very rarely got even so much as tipsy, and even then only if she was with someone like Suzi, whom she trusted implicitly. Alcohol was a known inhibition-destroyer and a sure-fire route to loss of control. So what had she been thinking last night? Somewhere along the line she had quite clearly dropped the ball.

Please let that be the only ball-associated activity that had gone on. What a crying waste it would be if she'd slept with Adam and didn't remember it. No. That wasn't possible. Every molecule of her would retain every second of the experience. This she knew.

'Just tell me, Adam. What did I do?'

'Nothing so terrible. Honest. I *like* sleeping with a barricade down the middle of the bed.'

His eyes glittered, and the glints of amusement were oddly reassuring. Adam was teasing her, and he wouldn't do that if she'd done anything spectacularly daft. Like climbing over the barricade and jumping his bones.

Trepidation returned and Olivia licked suddenly dry lips, heat shooting through her as his eyes followed the movement, snagged on her mouth 'Did it work?'

'Yes, it worked.' His face was suddenly unreadable.

For heaven's sake. She was being an idiot. Of course the barricade had worked; it hadn't even been necessary. Not only had she drunk enough beer to knock out a football team, she'd also passed out. That was enough to kill off any attraction.

And should any lingering tendrils have remained he'd now been treated to her in all her morning glory. A surreptitious glance down showed she was still in the grey top and trousers, now rumpled beyond repair. The strong tea had at least obliterated the fuzzy taste in her mouth, but Olivia could only imagine the state of her face. The remnants of yesterday's make-up; her hair back in bird's-nest mode. So one thing was for sure: any attraction Adam might still have retained for her would have been killed stone-cold dead.

Which was a good thing.

'Good. So now, if you leave me to it, I'll try and transform myself into something more human.'

'OK.' He nodded. 'I'll be in the foyer in half an hour.'

Thirty minutes later she surveyed herself in the mirror. This worked. Cool, calm, and the epitome of poised.

No one would believe the woman in the mirror capable of mad drunken exploits. The navy sleeveless dress had been chosen with a view to impressing Zeb with her professionalism, but it would now hopefully convey to both Adam and Olivia that she was a together person with a mortgage and a business. As opposed to a drunken idiot.

She tugged her freshly washed hair into a high pony-tail, slipped her feet into sensible plain flat navy sandals and made her way out of the bedroom.

Instinctively she turned right and headed towards the foyer, and slowed in an attempt to prepare for the impact of Adam. Now her hangover had receded she could take in his appearance with even more appreciation. Dark hair damp from the shower, a dark green version of the T-shirt that so admirably accentuated his chest, and beige knee-length shorts. Delectable.

But Olivia would be strong.

'Hey,' she said.

'Hey,' he replied.

Dark brown eyes swooped over her body and his lips quirked upward into what really could only be classified as a smirk. As if he knew exactly what her appearance de-noted and thought it was so much hooey.

'So what's the plan for the day?'

'I've got something to show you,' he said.

A boyish smile tilted his lips and against her will her heart did a hop, skip and a jump.

'But first I asked the chef to make you this.' He handed her a plastic container filled to the brim with thick red slush. 'It's a smoothie. Full of dragon fruit and watermelon. There should be enough vitamin C in that to zap the last of your hangover away.'

'Oh…' For an insane second tears prickled the back of her eyes—before common sense asserted itself. It was kind of Adam. Thoughtful of Adam. But it wasn't up there with Mother Teresa. 'Thank you.'

'No problem. Now, let's go.'

Olivia followed him outside, blinking in the brightness as he strode towards the vehicle, his canvas trainers puff-ing up clouds of dust from the path.

Climbing in behind him, she sipped her smoothie and

stared around, marvelling at the scenery, taking in the dark green leaves of the foliage of the palm trees that sprinkled the road. As Adam drove she saw the many scooters that zipped around at seemingly lethal speed and gripped her free hand around her seat belt.

A ten-minute drive and they pulled up outside a secluded villa, set back from the road and nestled within a mini-jungle of lush-leaved plants. Adam jumped down and came round to take her hand—a hand he retained as he led her towards the villa.

Its wooden structure was raised on posts, with an elegantly tapering roof and wide hanging eaves.

'Here we go,' Adam said. 'Our home for the week.'

'You serious?'

'Absolutely. Cooking, cleaning, dusting… Whatever you need doing, I'm your man.'

Whatever she needed? Hauling her mind out of the gutter she stared at him, sensing that for Adam this was a bigger deal than he was letting on.

'Why are you doing this? I have the feeling you want a home like you want a hole in the head.'

'Yeah, well. How much did *you* want to get up on stage and play the drums?'

'That would be hole-in-the-head level.'

'So fair's fair. Plus you issued a challenge—and real men don't refuse a dare.'

'Then lead on, Masterson, and show me the house.'

She followed him towards the front entrance, inhaling the earthy jungle smell of the lush, verdant foliage. 'It belongs to Gan's aunt,' Adam explained. 'She only lets it out to people recommended by Gan because she wants the house to retain its karma.'

Olivia could understand that; there was something personal about the villa that made it different from your average holiday let. Each room was clean and bright, with marble floors cool to the touch of her bare feet. Mismatching mahogany and teak furniture and a variety of Thai statues and tapestries were scattered around. There was also an enormous balcony with a view of the sea that stole her breath, complete with...

'A hammock! Adam, I have *always* wanted a hammock.' She turned to face him. 'Did you choose this place?' she asked. 'Or did Gan tell you about it?'

'I chose it,' he said. 'I saw a few others that were way more luxurious, but this one...well, I thought you'd like it.'

'I do.' But how on earth had he had time to do all this? She glanced at him and then at her watch. 'What time did you get up?'

'Early. Birds and worms and all that.' His expression was closed as he moved towards the sliding balcony door.

Oh, no. Maybe she'd been snoring. Just to add to the drunken, slovenly image. Little wonder if Adam had leapt out of bed and sprinted from the room to find alternative accommodation.

'Well, it was worth it. This place is amazing.' She tipped her palms in the air. 'Who knows? You may love having a home.'

'And maybe pigs will fly.' He smiled, but this time it was that practised smile of charm. 'Let the holiday begin.'

CHAPTER ELEVEN

'ARE WE NEARLY there yet?'

Adam braked to avoid a scooter that had swerved out of nowhere onto the dirt road, then gave Olivia a very swift, fleeting glance from the corner of his eye. 'Seven and a half minutes,' he said.

'Sorry. I'm stupidly excited about these caves. Especially as you won't tell me anything about them *and* you've made me promise not to research them online. So, yes, I am bouncing up and down like an overgrown child. I'll stop now.'

Three days in and this holiday was unlike any Adam had experienced. Truth be told, holidays for a man who had travelled the world and then built up a global empire of hotels had always been problematic.

This time it was different; it couldn't be compared to any of the most decadent, sex-filled sojourns in the penthouse suites of many of his hotels. And surprisingly enough not just because of the lack of any sex—decadent or otherwise.

Because, whilst frustration *was* his constant companion, putting lust aside, Adam was enjoying himself.

No doubt it was the novelty factor, but he loved Olivia's interest in everything—her relish of every bite of food, the way she had spent hours discussing music with Saru, turning his friend into her devoted admirer.

There was also her attitude to both shopping and money. Utterly appreciative when he had held a shop door open for her, she'd bristled into fury when he'd tried to pay for her holiday clothes.

'You're already paying for accommodation and you flew me out here. Our deal doesn't extend to new clothes. In fact I'll pay for *your* clothes. Seeing as I'm making you buy them.'

So for the first time since…well, the first time *ever*… Adam had stood back and watched someone else pull out a credit card. A novel experience, and not one he could see happening again in a hurry. It was hard to imagine his conveyor belt women going Dutch, let alone paying for him. As for purchasing him a selection of slogan-laden T-shirts—one depicting a reggae band, another saying 'Keep Calm and Play the Drums' and another blue number with an underwater sea scene and the caption 'I swim with the fish'—Adam knew that would never happen again, either.

Which was all fine. Predictability and decadent sex was definitely the way forward on future holidays. Unless, of course, frustration killed him first.

He pulled up at the side of the road. 'We're here.'

'And you're sure it's OK for us to do this by ourselves?'

'I'm sure. I know the family who runs the tours. I worked for them as a guide for a whole season, so they know I can do it safely. I've spoken to them. It's all good.'

Though for a moment Adam wondered why on earth he *hadn't* suggested they join a normal tour. Maybe because he wanted to see the wonder on her face when he introduced her to a place that was special to him? He really hoped not. Because that would be worrying. To say nothing of dumb.

A sudden shot of alarm zinged his synapses and he climbed out of the Jeep and inhaled deeply, sucked in the pure forest-scented air as he walked round to open Olivia's door.

He knew exactly what was going on. This was all about the frustration; he wasn't used to spending time with a woman he fancied the pants off and being unable actually to *remove* said pants. So all the lust had nowhere to go and it was affecting his brain. Big time.

Once she'd climbed out he looked her up and down. *Keep it clean, Adam.*

She gusted out a sigh. 'I've got comfortable, sturdy footwear, long sleeves and loose long trousers and I'm smothered in insect repellent. The only way a mozzie will come close to me is if all its nasal tubes have been extracted. Which isn't very likely. So can we go?'

Olivia entered the forest and breathed her appreciation as she looked around the vast canopy of verdant trees. The spectrum of green ranged from vibrant to dark, catching the dappled sunlight so that motes speckled the trailing fronds and leaves.

The path was gentle, almost meandering, and Olivia felt a peace and tranquillity that could only be exploded by... Crashing right bang into Adam's broad back. *Damn.* She'd been trying to hang back; the past few days had shown her all too well the disaster of getting too close. But in her gawping admiration of Mother Nature she'd taken her eye off the ball and now here she was. Back in the danger zone. Up close and personal with the breadth of his shoulders and his scent that won out even over that of the forest.

It took every ounce of her self-control to step backwards—especially as she was sure his body had given a small ripple of appreciation at her touch. *Delusional.*

Adam's face was inscrutable as he indicated what looked to Olivia like a sheer incline.

'Now the climb begins,' he said. 'You ready?'

'Bring it on.'

The harder the better; the more she exerted herself the less she'd desire Adam. That was the theory anyway. But there was something in the thickness of the air, the fertile thriving of this mangrove woodland, that clogged her throat with want.

'Off you go,' he said, and for a second she heard an echo of her own feeling in the depth of his voice. 'I'll be right behind you.'

She was imagining things; she must be. The past few days she'd kept a physical distance, avoided so much as a brush of their hands. As for Adam—Olivia was sure that he no longer wanted her at all. So it must be the magical atmosphere of the forest weaving some sort of hallucinatory spell on her.

Olivia hoisted herself up onto a rock, relieved to see a hanging rope suspended to help her continue the climb up the steep incline. It was an ascent that incorporated not just slippery rock but solid tree branches that jutted out at improbable angles. Thighs aching and calves protesting, Olivia felt sweat sheen her forehead over the twenty minutes it took to reach the cave entrance.

Or at least what Adam called the entrance.

'That's not an entrance. It's a crack in a rock. I'll never fit in there.'

He grinned suddenly. 'Sure you will. You fitted through that window a week ago. I watched you.'

'That feels like a lifetime ago.' Guilt smacked her; a flush rose to her skin. She'd barely given a thought to Zeb or her mum or the baby in the past days. 'Have you heard any news on when Zeb may get here?'

Adam glanced away from her and reached into his rucksack for a bottle of water. 'Gan called earlier. Friends of his met up with Zeb. He should be here tomorrow.'

'Tomorrow?'

Her dismay was embarrassingly apparent and shame coated her as actual disappointment weighed in her tummy. Meeting Zeb was her mission—surely she wasn't shallow enough to care that his arrival heralded the end of their holiday? Even worse, surely it couldn't have anything to do with Adam? She wouldn't, *couldn't* even contemplate that.

'That's great,' she said firmly, and plastered a smile on her face. 'Wonderful.'

'Isn't it?' he agreed, his tone so noncommittal Olivia had no idea what he was thinking. 'But why don't we discuss Zeb later? Negotiating the cave is quite tricky, so it's best if we concentrate on that right now.'

She nodded.

'It's pitch-dark in there, so you'll need this.'

Adam handed her a headlamp and Olivia put it on before watching him angle the breadth of his body into the sliver of darkness between two overhanging rocks.

Sucking her tummy in, she followed, glad of the flashlight as inky darkness enveloped them. The torch illuminated a bamboo ladder leading down into the midnight depths. 'Is there any lighting?' she asked.

'Nope. But your eyes will adjust. Once we get down the ladder make sure you stick close to me.'

'Not a problem.'

A cast-iron excuse to do what she'd longed to do for days, and this time she wasn't going to deny herself. Because tomorrow Zeb would arrive and this whole idyll would end; there would be no more opportunities to be anywhere near Adam after that. The chance of actually acting on this crazy, stupid attraction would definitely be over.

Life would return to normal.

Which was exactly what she wanted. Right? She would have accomplished what she came here for, made an attempt to ensure this baby had a father in his or her life. That was good, right?

Olivia waited for the anticipated buzz of enthusiasm and came up with a flat fizz of two-day-old champagne.

Ridiculous—she was being ridiculous.

'Liv? You OK?'

'I'm fine.' Of course she was. 'I just need to get my bearings.'

Truer words were never spoken.

Once down the ladder she looked round in awe, the light of her headlamp picking out the damp cave walls, the narrow passageways jutted with rocks.

'Follow me, and if you're worried, say,' Adam said. 'It's a bit difficult in places, but I'll be right here every step of the way.'

Olivia bit her lip and nodded. She had to stop reading double meanings into his words but somehow down here, in the very depths of a miracle of nature, every word seemed significant. It felt as though Adam were asking her to follow him somewhere else—or maybe that was wishful thinking on her part. She needed to get a grip; Adam was guiding her through a network of caves, not on some spiritual or sensual journey.

She needed to concentrate or she would fall into the abyss—both literally and metaphorically. Plus, no way should she miss out on an experience like this; these caves were a once in a lifetime... And there went her stupid brain again. Reinterpreting her every thought to bring her back to the idea of sleeping with Adam.

Consigning all such thoughts to perdition, Olivia edged along a bamboo plank, the rush of adrenaline adding to her already skittering nerves. She followed Adam along narrow passageways, scrambled over ancient rocks slippery with underground water and marvelled over a darkness that had never been so much as touched by sunlight.

And all the time the warm bulk of Adam's body both reassured and tantalised her. The whole journey was taking on a hidden depth of meaning as the heavy air of the cave made her dizzy. It wasn't only affecting her, either—she was sure of it. Adam was mostly silent, though always there, steadying her at the exact moment she needed it. But his face, dimly shadowed and dappled by torchlight, held a suppressed urgency, visible in the set of his jaw and the slant of his brows.

'Ooh…' Olivia gasped as she stepped through the narrowest of entrances into a cavernous chamber. It was magnificent; the domed ceilings must have been carved by some god of nature to create such a mystical vault.

Filled with awe, she trailed her fingers along the cold, damp stone.

'Look at these,' she said, and pointed up at the almost implausible stalagmite formations. 'I've never seen anything like them. That shape there—it looks like some sort of guardian…a gargoyle who guards the entrance. They must be ancient.'

Adam nodded. 'I used to stare at them for hours. If you look at them long enough they sizzle your brain.'

Olivia turned to him. 'I thought you were a tour guide.'

'I was. But my first foray into these caves was…' He shrugged. 'Unauthorised. This place—it's a great place to…' He shrugged, rocking back on the balls of his feet. 'Think.'

'I can see that,' Olivia said, and she could—could see an image of a younger, teenaged Adam, all gangly limbs and overlong dark hair, coming to these caves to brood. Perhaps to wish he could stay longer with the people who had been like family to him. Gan, Saru and his parents. That much she'd gleaned from snippets Saru had let slip over the past days—that and the fact that Zeb had been a pretty much absent parent, spending more time in retreat, leaving his son to his own devices until he was ready to move on again.

Olivia gulped, suddenly aware of the sear of his gaze. 'What are you thinking now?'

'You don't want to know.' A rueful smile tugged his lips as he turned his body away. 'Trust me.'

His words echoed through the air, bounced off the strata and into her consciousness. *Trust him.*

Pinning her shoulders back, she sucked in the musky air. 'Actually, I do want to know.'

He swivelled back round on one foot and studied her expression for a long moment. His brown eyes were dark and serious; his face was streaked with loam and age-old grime. 'I was thinking how very much I want you,' he said simply.

'You do?' Encrusted mud dislodged as she raised her eyebrows.

'Yes, Liv, I do. Bit of an open secret.'

Adam's velvet growl smoothed over her skin.

'I thought—' Olivia broke off.

'You thought what?'

'That we were past that. Especially after the other night.'

Adam frowned. 'What happened the other night?'

'Well, I fell asleep in all my clothes and probably snored the night away, the following morning I looked like a cross between a bird's nest and something the cat dragged in, and since then—well, we've shared a house.'

'And sharing a house kills attraction?' He dropped his mouth in mock horror. 'It's because you've seen me wielding a dustpan and brush, isn't it? My macho image is gone for ever.'

Her lips tipped up in a smile. 'Don't be ridiculous. It's me. The last few days I've wandered the house in scruffy pyjamas before I've even brushed my hair. And who knows what I look like now?'

Adam tilted his headlamp and studied her. 'Well, you have clay streaking your cheekbones like some sort of warrior markings and mud smudged across the freckles on your nose.'

'Great! I rest my case. You can't possibly want me looking like this.'

'You don't get it, do you?' He gestured at the air between them. 'This spark we have—it doesn't get cancelled out by tangled hair or rabbit pyjamas or mud. Trust me.'

Those damn words again, echoing round the walls as though the cave itself could pick which words to resonate. *Trust.* She didn't do trust; it wasn't in her make-up or her inclination.

Yet here and now, in this unspoiled place, it was difficult to see anything wrong with a primal, *natural* desire to mate. Adam wanted her and, boy, did she ever want him. Yet…

'We just have to ignore it. Stay in control,' she said, and her words disappeared into the dark currents of air, not deemed worthy of the smallest echo.

Olivia was right. Yet somehow her words didn't tie in with what her whole being was trying to tell him. It seemed clear to Adam that her brain was vying with her body and hanging on by a sliver of fingernail. Perhaps they were both being enchanted by the spirits of the cave? Eternal beings who had lived here for aeons and would be here for centuries more.

OK.

Something was messing with his head.

It was time to take control and regain perspective.

Adam understood exactly why *he* needed to keep the spark between them under control, but it occurred to him that he didn't know why Olivia had pulled back.

He moved towards her, stepping firmly on the slippery rock face.

'Why?' he asked softly. 'Why is it so important to you to not lose control?'

Another step and he was close enough that if she slipped he'd catch her. So near that her scent—loam, clay and that all-elusive apple—taunted him.

'Tell me, Liv.' *Trust me.*

Adam held his breath, lungs aching, not wanting to damage this moment as she hesitated, her teeth caught around her lower lip.

'I won't lose control,' she said. 'Because attraction is all a power game. Two people angling for what they want. Be it sex, money, or the upper hand.'

'You're assuming they are adversaries,' he said gently. 'It doesn't have to be that way.' Something must have happened to make her believe this. 'Did someone hurt you, Olivia? Cheat on you?' His mind scanned for possibilities as he pieced together the fragments she had let fall. 'Someone with money?' The thought of some scumbag breaking her heart and throwing her aside for a newer model balled his fists.

'No.' She shifted her weight and he placed a hand on her arm to steady her, saw indecision pool in her hazel eyes as if in internal debate about confiding in him.

'Why don't we sit down?' he suggested, and led her over the floor towards the corner of the cavern. 'I used to call this The Ledge.' He slipped his rucksack off his shoulder and unzipped it. 'It's where I used to sit and study the stalactites in the hope of achieving hallucinogenic effects.' Rummaging in the bag, he pulled out a waterproof sheet, shook it out and spread it on the ledge. 'Sit down and try it, if you like.'

Olivia sank down lithely and he followed suit, careful to sit close but without touching her. For a long moment she stared at the bulging mass of stalagmites, before clasping her hands on her lap and drawing in an audible breath.

'No one hurt *me*. But my mum—that's a different story.' Hazel eyes met his, clouded with a sadness that twisted his chest. 'When she was fourteen she was raped. By a so-called family friend. She never dared tell anyone.'

Revulsion wrenched Adam's chest, encased his body in steel-cold anger. 'I'm sorry, Olivia.'

'Her life fell apart; she turned into the quintessential rebel. When she was sixteen she met my dad and fell pregnant with me.'

Adam shifted closer to her and took her hand gently in his, and with a small sigh she folded her fingers around his.

'Mum had no qualifications, no family support, but she did have looks and she decided to use them. On her terms. Over the years she had affairs, mostly with rich, married men—men who enjoyed having a gorgeous trophy mistress. That's how we lived.' Her voice caught as she looked at him. 'I vowed that I would not let that happen to me. That I would never depend on anyone for money and I would never let lust control me.' A small shiver ran through her body.

So much made sense now and his heart ached. With Jodie as a tragic example, no wonder Olivia had such mixed feelings about her beauty, about control and power.

Olivia gave a small sniff and pushed away from his chest, swiped her palm across her eyes. 'I shouldn't have told you any of that. It's not fair on Mum.' Her hands clenched into fists. 'I know it looks bad, but I promise she did *not* target your father. I know that, Adam.'

Surprise reared in the hindmost part of his brain, his body stiffening. It hadn't so much as occurred to him to question Olivia's story; it was impossible to suspect that the woman he'd got to know was anything but legitimate.

'It's OK, Liv. *I* believe *you*,' he said. And should her

faith in Jodie prove to be misplaced—because after all they were all human, and old habits died hard—then Adam would not judge Olivia.

In all honesty it wasn't Jodie he was concerned about now—it was Olivia. Because, however cheesy it sounded, this had gone beyond lust; he might not do love or happy-ever-after, but he *wanted* to show her that sex could be a beautiful act between two people. That was well within his remit. They only had one night left. No harm could come of one night.

'I want you to think about something,' he said. 'Zeb arrives tomorrow. What happens after that is out of our control. But until then it's up to you, Olivia. If *you* want to explore this spark more then we can.'

She stared at him, hazel eyes wide. 'Why?' she asked. 'Why have you changed your mind?'

'Because I want to show you that you are a beautiful, desirable woman and that there is nothing wrong with that. I want to show you that losing control can be liberating.'

She shivered and desire flared in her eyes. Adam clenched his hand on his thigh. Because no matter how much he craved to kiss her, taste her, plunder her lush mouth until she felt nothing but burning arousal, this was *her* choice.

'Think about it,' he said, forcing his tone to remain light, as if his entire body *wasn't* seized with need. 'For one day only, I am on offer.'

A small huff of laughter emerged from her lips. 'Are you asking me to step on your conveyor belt for a one-night ride, Masterson?'

'Hell, yes, I am. And it'll be a ride to remember.'

CHAPTER TWELVE

ADAM STOOD ON the villa's balcony and stared out at the glow of the evening sunlight, at the sky streaked with spears of vivid orange as the sun began its glorious descent.

He turned. 'Liv,' he called. 'You're missing the sunset.'

And she loved the sunsets, would gaze mesmerised each evening as if she were etching every colour, every nuance, on the easel of her memory.

'Adam?'

The soft husk of her voice pulled him to the present and he turned away from the pink slivers of disappearing sun.

'Liv... You look—' He broke off and tilted his hands palms-up in the air. 'There are no words.'

The vibrant orange dress she wore was reminiscent of the sunset itself. Its simple off-the-shoulder style bared her sun-kissed skin then cleaved low to reveal the tantalising top of her firm breasts. The clinging material accentuated the slender span of her waist, then dipped to midthigh.

Adam leant against the railings, arms spread, fingers gripping the iron in an attempt to prevent himself from moving forward. His eyes skimmed down the lissom length of her legs, over the toned calves and down to the bejewelled flip-flops that glittered in the rays of the setting sun.

She smiled, her eyes holding a feminine appreciation

of his all too evident male approval. 'I thought we could go out for dinner tonight,' she said. 'On me. I know you can afford a thousand meals, but tonight…it's important to me that I pay.'

'Then I accept, with thanks,' Adam replied, his gaze riveted to her expression. His gut churned in anticipation. Every instinct was telling him that this was it. Olivia had made her decision and tonight would culminate in making all his and her fantasies reality.

Her skin was a touch pale, her oval face framed by the magnificent cascade of strawberry tresses. She wore minimal make-up, so far as he could tell, but her eyelids shimmered and her gorgeous lips were glossy. This was Olivia dressed to kill—and, yes, he was dying over here.

'Where are we going?' he asked, and almost laughed at the deeper meaning under the simple question.

An answering gleam lit her eyes. 'I booked us into Snapper Fish,' she said. 'After that we'll come home.'

And so to bed—or so he hoped. 'Sounds good to me,' he agreed. His gaze lingered on the dress as his brain whirred. 'So that's where you went when we came back? Shopping?'

Olivia nodded. 'I wanted a new dress for the evening. To mark the occasion,' she added with a siren smile.

It was the kind of smile that had his heart threatening to escape his ribcage, the tilt of her glossy lips teasing him.

'Shall we go?' she asked.

Adam nodded; Olivia had a plan and he needed to go along with it. Her choice. Ruining her timetable of seduction—and every atom of his body prayed that he was reading the schedule right—by turning Neanderthal, throwing her over his shoulder and storming to the bedroom, was not an option.

They left the villa and walked in easy silence in the fragrant Ko Lantan dusk. The sweet frangipani-scented air enveloped them, somehow merging with Olivia's under-lying apple scent to send his head awhirl.

The gaily lit restaurant rose out of the dusk and they followed a waiter onto the covered decking to a secluded teak table. Amber and orange paper lanterns slanted light onto the array of floating candles that ornamented the gleaming wood.

'Good evening, Olivia. Your champagne is on ice, as requested.'

Olivia nodded. 'Thank you, Kamon.' She turned to Adam and smiled. 'Thought it would be safer than beer! I promise not to disgrace myself. And I hope it's OK with you but I ordered our meal, as well. May as well put all my research to good use.' She pressed her lips together in a small smile. 'Sorry. I'm talking too much.'

'I don't mind,' he said. 'I like to hear you talk.'

Dark eyebrows rose as she slid along the wooden bench. 'You do? I kind of thought my chatter would have driven you nuts by now.'

'Well, you thought wrong.' The sound of her voice, her sheer enthusiasm and interest in myriad subjects, capti-vated him. The only thing that might well send him loop-the-loop would be frustrated desire. If he were reading her body language all wrong and the evening should culmi-nate in another night alone. But it was Olivia's choice; that was the deal they had made and he'd honour it. Even at the cost of his sanity, she had to come to him without regret.

Olivia reached out to the garland of flowers that had been draped round the edge of the table and smiled.

'I found out some facts about frangipani,' Olivia said. 'Did you know that in different countries they represent different things? Here in Thailand they were once taboo, because they were thought to bring sorrow. But now they are seen as special and worthy of offering to Buddha. In Vietnam ghosts were thought to live in frangipani trees, and in India the flower means loyalty.' She rubbed her finger against the petals; the innocent sensuality of the movement constricted his lungs. 'This must have been Kamon's idea,' she said. 'I told him I wanted the dinner to be special.'

Hope and a whole lot more reared its head. 'Any particular reason?' he asked.

Before she could answer, Kamon arrived with a bottle of champagne, two long-stemmed champagne flutes, and an aromatic platter of shrimp tempura. He was followed by another waiter with a further selection of dishes.

The time it took to open the bottle, pour out the fizzing liquid and exchange pleasantries was excruciatingly long. Adam clenched his hands into fists—the only way to stop himself from grabbing the bottle and plate from the obviously besotted Kamon and booting him on his way.

Eventually, after assuring Olivia that everything had been freshly prepared, Kamon wended his way back into the restaurant's interior. Where Adam devoutly hoped he'd stay.

'You didn't hear a word of that, did you?' Olivia asked, a lilt of laughter in her voice.

'Nope.'

'Well, in that case, as penance you'll have to listen to me tell you all about each dish. In detail.'

There was that smile again; pure seduction, it seemed to have a direct line to his pants.

'That's not a problem,' he said. Not if she was going to keep talking with that husk in her voice.

'OK. We have crabmeat and prawn spring rolls with the house special tamarind sauce. Herb-marinated stuffed chicken wings with fragrant lemongrass. Grilled aromatic beef wrapped in betelnut leaves. And lastly honey-marinated duck breast fried in pandan leaf.'

She leant forward in a deliberate movement and Adam nearly bit his tongue.

'Delicious,' he murmured, his eyes fixed without shame on the tops of her firm breasts.

'Then tuck in,' she said.

'I hope to,' he returned, and grinned at the shiver that goosebumped her skin as she hurriedly started to serve herself.

Adam followed suit. It felt good to eat in silence for a while and let the endless possibilities of the night ahead roam free in his brain.

It was only when Olivia gave the characteristic little huff that signified that she was ready to break from eating that he lifted his glass. 'To the rest of our holiday,' he toasted.

Without hesitation she clinked her champagne flute against his, her face glowing in the dappled moonlight just as the overhead lanterns went out.

'Ooh! That means it's time for the fire-dancing,' she said.

For a second Adam wished the dancers would disappear to the Outer Hebrides—before guilt zapped him. Olivia *should* have a chance to see the truly spectacular performance; this was their last night here.

He sipped his drink, the ice cold bubbles focusing him. This night was exactly as it should be. One magical night. And if he had his way the magic would continue straight into the bedroom. He glanced at Olivia, saw the small telltale crease on her forehead, and his gut wrenched at the thought that she might not have made her final decision.

'Oh!' Olivia drew in audible breath as the dancing started. 'How do they *do* that?' she breathed.

The two young Thai men, bare-chested, spun and dipped, twisted and swirled through the shadows of the night. The fire-tipped sticks created incredible patterns that lit up the air with eddies of orange; spirals of flame surrounded each dancer. Olivia gave a small cry and reached out across the table to grab Adam's hand; the heat of her touch on his skin rivalled the blaze of the dance.

'That was incredible,' Olivia breathed.

'They're moving farther down the beach,' Adam said levelly. 'We can go down later and see some more if you like?'

She shook her head, strawberry tresses ruffling round her oval face, releasing the scent of freshly washed hair to tantalise him.

'Crunch time,' she said, letting go of his hand and curling her fingers round the stem of her champagne glass.

Anticipation grapple-hooked his chest, caused his heart to hammer his ribcage.

'I've been thinking about what you said in the cave,' she said. 'About you being on offer for the night.' A small, nervous laugh escaped her lips. 'I've made you sound like a BOGOF supermarket deal.'

Adam tipped his hands upward. 'That doesn't sound like the impression I'm aiming for.' *Keep it light.* Unease prickled his skin at how important Olivia's decision was to him. It was a night. Important? Yes. Crucial to his entire well-being? No. Though it was fast becoming more and more critical to a rapidly growing part of his anatomy.

A welcome smile touched her lips even as she rolled her eyes. 'I was forgetting that you are above the echelons of those needing to shop for bargains. BOGOF means buy one, get one free.'

Adam grinned. 'There's only one of me, honey.'

'Don't I know it? Which is why I've decided to climb on that conveyor belt for the night.'

Relief washed over him in a warm wave even as he strove to remember the rules of the game. 'Welcome aboard.' He sucked in much needed air. 'But remember one thing, Liv. You're unique. Not interchangeable. This night is about *us*. OK?'

She gave a small nod, as if she had processed and approved his words, and then hers lips turned up in a shy smile. 'So what now?'

Adam returned the smile, aiming to project a whole lot of inner wolf. 'We are going to do whatever *you* want, Liv. Your choice. Your control. Your terms.'

Olivia tried to think over the exhilarated buzz that hummed through her body, turning her into a live wire of excitement. They were going to do it—assuage this crazy attraction. Any which way she wanted.

'Whatever I want?' she asked.

He nodded.

'OK. Don't laugh, but I want to go home and sit under the stars and make out.' She blurted the words out.

A smile tipped his lips and creased his eyes.

'Hey,' she protested, 'I said don't laugh.'

'I'm not laughing. I'm thinking that sounds about perfect.'

Light-headedness born of anticipation made her giddy as they rose together. Adam made to pull out his wallet and Olivia shook her head. 'My treat, remember? It's already paid for.'

'So we're all done here?'

'Check.'

'Then come on!'

Olivia's heart did a funny little flip at the huge grin on Adam's face as he held out his hand and she slipped hers into it.

Half running, half walking, both of them laughing in sudden exhilaration, they made it back to the villa. It was only when they stood on the threshold that Olivia felt the onset of faint panic, and an absurd shyness tugged across her chest as they stepped inside.

But diffidence loosened its hold as Adam reclaimed her hand and led the way onto the decking. Without breaking their connection they settled onto the woven bamboo swing chair.

Olivia curled her feet under her bottom on the white cushion as the chair rocked under their weight, feeling that strange shyness returning. It had been easier back in the day in the lift, or in the limo, where passion had simply overtaken them with no time for thought.

This was different. Adam had given her a choice.

She stared up at the inky black sky, coruscating with starlight, and turned to Adam. The half-moon dappled his profile with its beams.

'It's beautiful,' she said, meaning *You're beautiful*. But maybe that wasn't an appropriate thing to say to a man? Her tummy dipped with desire; this was *right*. How could it not be?

Stop overthinking, Liv.

She took a deep breath—infusing her senses with the calming frangipani aroma—and dropped a bare foot to the ground to act as a pivot, twisting herself onto his lap. Her knees straddled his lean hips, the core of her pressed against his hardness, and she exulted in the reaction.

The movement was a deliberate replay of their time in the limo—only this time she knew she wouldn't pull back. She would trust herself to Adam completely.

She pushed her fingers into the thick springiness of his hair and lowered her lips onto his.

As if her actions weren't enough, he growled against her mouth. His lips parted and his tongue touched hers, gently at first, each stroke teasing her, sending a stream of exquisite sensation rollicking through her body.

'More,' she breathed. And with a deep groan he gripped

her waist and rocked against her. Just like that warmth rushed through her lower abdomen and she wriggled in his lap.

Tilting his head, he deepened his kiss, his hands slipping from her waist to plunge downwards and smooth back up her thighs under the skirt of her dress. She writhed to give him room, and when his fingers curved around her bottom and he kneaded the soft flesh she seized in rapture.

Her whole body was alight—until Adam ended their lip-lock. When he pulled back she gave a mewl of protest.

'Liv…' he said, his breathing ragged. 'You need to decide what's next. Because soon we're going to gallop over the line of making out and I won't be able to stop.'

His gorgeous milk chocolate eyes were dark and dilated with raw, primal need and she tensed inwardly, waiting for the automatic reflex of shame. Adam had managed to stop, to call a halt, whereas she would have kept going without a thought. Out of control.

Not so much as a flicker. Instead she felt heady, exhilarated. As if she could swim the Channel doing the butterfly stroke.

Her lips curved upward as she braced her palms against his chest, felt the pounding of his heart beneath her fingers.

'Good,' she whispered. 'Because I don't want you to stop.'

In one lithe movement he stood up, and she wrapped her legs around the solidness of his waist, entwined her arms round his neck as he strode towards the sliding door leading back inside the villa.

She pressed her lips against his, desperate for another of his blissful kisses. Their tongues danced, the tempo increasing as they wended their way through the lounge. Olivia was faintly aware of knick-knacks tumbling in their wake as Adam bumped into a laden table.

They entered the bedroom and Adam halted; Olivia slid down his body and stared up at him, senses awhirl.

She stepped backwards, caught a glimpse of her reflection in the ornate gold-framed mirror. Eyes wide, pupils dilated, a fine sheen of desire glistening in her skin.

She wanted him.

A tight knot of anticipation tangled her tummy up as she slipped her dress off so it fell in a tangerine pool to the floor. She stood in front of him. Just her. Olivia Evans. Completely and utterly naked.

Mouth parched, she licked her lips as her throat clogged in sudden vulnerability. 'Adam...?'

The predatory glint in his eyes as they raked over her said it all. Had more of an effect—she felt hot and squirmy and exultant.

Careful, Olivia. Any beautiful woman standing here would make him react like this.

Really, Liv? You really believe that?

No, she didn't. Because the point was that it *wasn't* any woman standing here. It was her.

'Liv. You are gorgeous.'

He skimmed the back of his finger along her collarbone, followed the curve of her breast until it reached her tight nipple. One soft caress, one light flick with the pad of his thumb, and an electric flash of heat jolted through her body, turning her legs to jelly.

'So beautiful,' he murmured, and for the first time in her life she was glad of it. Wanted to be beautiful, to give pleasure.

'Tell me what you want,' Adam rumbled, the dark chocolate of his voice strumming her skin.

And suddenly it was all so simple 'I want *you*,' she said, and buzzed with exhilaration at the sinful smile that curved his lips and lit his eyes. 'Naked.'

'That's easily arranged.' He crossed his arms, his fingers gripped the bottom edge of his T-shirt and he tugged it over his head.

His chest was perfection: sculpted muscle with a light smattering of hair arrowing down over ripped abs, pointing in a sexy vee towards the ridge in his pants.

'Keep going,' she breathed.

'Patience,' he admonished in a mock growl, before deftly shucking off his shorts and boxers and kicking them unceremoniously to one side.

Holy Moly. Adam was…*magnificent*, was one adjective. *Bloody enormous* would be two.

Mine.

For this night Adam was *hers*.

Her skin felt taut with a yearning to be touched, but her greedy fingers were more interested in him and she wanted to stroke and caress and explore every inch of his muscular glory.

His chest felt hard under her fingertips, and when she smoothed her palms over his hot skin Adam reciprocated, cupping the weight of her breast in his palm, his thumb circling her nipple. Olivia whimpered for more.

Suddenly the backs of her knees hit the edge of the bed and Adam coaxed her down; her back hit the satin coverlet and she looked up at him, braced above her. His palms were either side of her head, his brown eyes so completely focused on her that she shivered from head to foot.

Rolling onto his side, he tiptoed his fingers across her sternum, over her tummy and downward, his eyes hot and heavy with delicious intent as they reached the very heart of her.

His fingers circled and teased and tantalised until she was burning for him, and when he finally slipped inside her she clenched around his fingers. 'Please, Adam,' she breathed, begging him to end the torment.

At her words his erection nudged her thigh and she

reached out to span and stroke the velvety thick length of him. He groaned long and low as she slid her hand to the tip of his hardness, circled the satiny head and glossed over the bead of moisture she found there. He felt amazing.

'You're killing me, Liv,' he gasped.

Not as much as he was killing her.

Olivia undulated on the bed, raised her hips, questing, needing release with a painful intensity as his skilful provoking ministrations pulled her to the brink and back; the pleasure was so excruciating her breath caught in her throat.

Then finally, with one, two, three deft strokes, he found her sweet spot and she cried out, shattered as she clenched around him in release.

It could have been seconds, it could have been minutes before she floated back down to earth to find him watching her, a thoroughly satisfied smile tilting his lips. She stroked his cheek, unable to think of anything to say except thank you—which felt wholly inadequate.

'That was incredible,' she said.

'That's just the starter,' he said. 'You're in luck. It's HOOGOF day.'

'You've lost me.'

'Have one orgasm, get one free,' he murmured, and Olivia burst into a peal of laughter.

'You want to take me up on it?'

'Absolutely, I do.' Hard to believe she could come again, but already her body tingled as he gently nudged her legs apart and knelt between them.

Adam lowered his head to kiss her tummy, then trailed a path of butterfly kisses upwards until he reached her breasts, where he laved first one nipple then the next. Exquisite sensations shot through her, and Olivia gripped his shoulders and scored her nails down the gorgeous supple length of his back.

Waves of pleasure swirled deep inside her and she thrust upward, desperate to have him inside her.

She watched him fist a condom down his length, his hands unsteady. '*Now*, Adam,' she whispered.

Then he was braced above her, sliding that long, hard thickness inside her so slowly that every gorgeous inch sparked a new and building tension, creating a maelstrom of pleasure until she couldn't bear it any more.

'Please...' she moaned, and he began to thrust faster, harder, the sensuous wonder so fierce Olivia thought she'd pass out. Then they reached the apex and she shattered beneath him, crying out his name as she soared to release. Distantly she heard Adam's deep, exultant roar and knew he'd followed her into the abyss.

Olivia opened her eyes to the lilting sound of birdsong and the knowledge that all was right in the world. A world where she lay cocooned in Adam's strong embrace, enclaved in a sanctuary of sheer bliss.

The night and the pre-dawn hours had fulfilled and exceeded any flight of fantasy, and had revealed to her a truth so blinding in its pure simplicity that she felt like an idiot for never realising it before.

Yet at a primal level she knew no one else could have shown her except Adam. He had demonstrated that a union of bodies was exactly that. A union. She and Adam had given and taken, shared a mingling of mutual need and fulfilment, soared on the waves of ecstasy to achieve communion.

Nothing she had experienced before could be compared—no more than she would liken the flickering light of a nearly dead torch to the hot blaze of a desert sun.

Very gently she shifted, not wanting to wake Adam but consumed by the need to see him, to study the planes and angles of his sleeping face. Too late; his eyes had opened and he surveyed her with drowsy, languorous contentment.

'Hey,' he said, and his sleep-roughened voice tugged her heart as he pulled the blanket over his head and pulled her back into the crook of his arm.

A sudden realisation shot through Olivia: she would never see him like this again. Dark hair mussed from her fingers, bare, smooth skin available for her caress. Never again would Olivia experience the magic of their bodies' union.

Zeb was arriving; the night was over. The portals of paradise were swinging closed and reality had to be faced. The irony of the situation struck her. A week ago all she had wanted was to locate Zeb Masterson. Now she wished she could put off his arrival for just one more day.

But that wasn't possible, so somehow she had to be all right. She'd known the rules—could hardly cavil now. Yet Adam had changed so much in her life. He'd smashed her notions of desire; he had shown her that a man could still desire a woman even if she didn't look perfect all the time. That sex could be a beautiful, consensual act, and that a little bit of power play could be fun. As long as there was trust.

That was it. Somehow over the past week she'd grown to trust him, to believe that he saw her as a unique individual and not a beautiful commodity.

And if he had changed *her* so fundamentally then maybe there was a chance that she had done the same for him. Turned his conveyor belt view of relationships topsy-turvy?

A furling tendril of hope took root. Later, after they had seen Zeb, she would talk to Adam. After all, there was nothing to stop them from exploring their feelings. This baby could be a shared bond between them; it didn't have to be a barrier.

Drowsily Olivia closed her eyes....

She woke later to the aroma of coffee teasing her nostrils and the realisation that Adam was no longer next to her.

No need to panic.

Today was about meeting Zeb. It was time for her to put all these new burgeoning feelings aside and focus on the baby. No way could she tell Adam anything about her epiphany. *Yet.*

CHAPTER THIRTEEN

ADAM DROPPED WATERMELON slices into the juicer and pushed the on button. Soon enough all these oddly domestic chores would end. No more preparing breakfast, or visiting the market for ingredients, or cooking with Olivia.

In fact reality dictated that within hours they might well be on their way back to the UK. Mission accomplished.

And it wasn't only household activities that would cease; there would be no more shared bedroom antics, either. His body gave a cold shiver that belied the blazing sunshine pouring through the open window. The shudder of protest was augmented by the fire of memory from the night before; his mind and body were still caught up in the flow and eddy of the most amazing sensual experience of his life.

He'd known that he and Olivia had a spark; he'd failed to realise it would be an ember that lit flames so intense he doubted they would ever bank.

Whatever they had shared last night had transcended sex; there had been a connection, a mutual bond that sent a bolt of panic straight down his spine. Definitely time to call it a day. He'd waded into the pots and pans, scrubbed a few floors. and now it was time to play the 'I'm a billionaire, get me out of here' card.

'How do I look?'

Olivia's soft voice broke his reverie and he turned from the kitchen counter.

His breath hitched in his throat; she was stunning.

She wore a fluorescent camisole top over white jeans, a jewelled clip held her hair in a knot on the top of her head, strawberry blonde tendrils escaped to frame her sun-kissed face.

A far cry from the muted dressed-in-grey girl who had arrived on Ko Lanta in her carefully chosen neutral outfit to meet Zeb.

This Olivia would meet Zeb on her own terms—as herself.

'You look perfect,' he said simply as he handed her a glass of smoothie.

'Thank you.' Sipping the vivid red drink, she shifted from foot to foot. 'So where are we meeting him?'

'Gan is taking him to Saru's bar. They should be getting there any minute now.'

'How are you feeling?' she asked.

A daft glow lit deep within him because she cared, even as instinct told him to dodge the question. This wasn't about him, and nor did he want to discuss Zeb in arbitrary detail. This new chapter in Zeb's life should not be influenced by the old.

'Fine,' he said.

Her lips pouted in a plump moue of disbelief. 'I want to know how you're *really* feeling.'

Trying not to focus on the mouth that had moved over his body with such devastating effect only hours ago, he hitched his shoulders. 'I'm not feeling anything. Best not to with Zeb, because you never know what to expect.'

'So there is no point having expectations?' she said softly as she moved towards him, surrounded him with a cloud of sheer Olivia. 'Does he know we're here?'

'He knows *I'm* here. But that's no guarantee that he'll

stick around. Zeb has a good nose for danger. He'll suspect that it has to be something pretty big to get me out here waiting for him for a week. So the sooner we get to him the better. But first tell me how *you're* feeling.'

'Nervous. I hope with all my heart that Zeb will step up and want to be a great father.' She wrapped a stray tendril of hair around her finger. 'But no matter what happens now, this week has been incredible.'

Suspicion pricked his thumbs; there was something in Olivia's expressive eyes that initiated unease. Ridiculous. Adam shoved the brooding thought aside. They had an agreement: one night. Olivia knew and concurred with the rules—and anyway she didn't believe in love and wasn't looking for a relationship.

Whatever bond had been formed would now be dissolved. Following this meeting with Zeb, he and Olivia would go their separate ways. If Zeb confirmed paternity then perhaps their paths would occasionally cross and the steeped banks of desire would give a little smoulder. But right now she deserved his support; she must be anxious about Zeb. *That* was the vibe he was picking up.

'Come on.' He held out his hand and braced himself for the shock of impact. This was a grasp of friendship, nothing more. 'Let's do this.'

Her small decisive nod betokened determination and she slipped her hand into his.

A ten-minute Jeep drive brought them to their destination and after a brief beach walk they stepped out of the bright morning sunlight into the cool interior of the bar. Adam scanned the room; only a few tables were occupied, and the muted hum of conversation blended with the low background beat of reggae music.

There was Zeb, and the familiar conflicted jumble of feelings knotted in Adam's gut. The leaden knowledge that this was the man who had moulded him genetically and by nurture had made him, for better or worse, into the man he was today. A massive chunk off the old block. Then there was gratitude that Zeb had done his duty, had swooped in to rescue Adam from the terror of the care system. And of course the thread of guilt that his father's much wanted arrival had come at the cost of his mother's death.

Too many emotions, added to the tumult of feelings generated by Olivia—who was rigid by his side as she stared at Zeb.

'Hey. It's going to be all right. We can do this,' he said, hoping it wasn't the biggest lie ever.

'OK…' she whispered.

They walked towards the table and Zeb looked up, his brown eyes glinting from Adam and then resting on Olivia.

'Adam. My boy. How's the hotel business?' The question was a standard one, the reply never listened to. 'More important, who is *this*?' Zeb turned directly to Olivia and stroked his chin. 'Whoever you are, you look familiar.'

'This is Olivia,' Adam said. 'Olivia, this is Zeb.'

Olivia stepped forward and leant across the table. 'I'm Jodie's daughter.'

For an agonising second a pang of guilt by association burned Adam's neck. He prayed that his father remembered Jodie—hadn't dismissed her from memory once she'd stepped off Zeb's conveyor belt.

'Hawaii,' Adam prompted.

'Of course.' Zeb nodded. 'Apologies, Olivia. Your mother seemed way too young to have a daughter your age, hence the confusion. Hawaii. What a wonderful place, as Adam can no doubt tell you. Sit down, both of you. I'm having a rather marvellous cocktail. Five days at sea on basic provisions, cleansing my body and soul, and I feel ready for one of these. Can I get you one?'

'No, thank you.' Olivia's opened her mouth to continue,

her expression glazed; no doubt she was looking for a polite way to turn the conversation.

Before she could utter a word Zeb launched into a lecture on cocktails of the world. Adam recognised the tactic all too well. Heaven help him, it was a strategy *he* had utilised in many a business meeting.

Behind the façade of bonhomie, even as his mouth poured forth a torrent of avuncular chat, Zeb's brain would be working overtime. Assessing and discarding the possible reasons for Olivia's presence in the same way he would evaluate the cards in a hand at a game of poker.

It was entirely feasible that any minute now Zeb would guess and quite simply do a runner before Olivia could break the news.

Adam moved to sit at the table, positioning himself between Zeb and the door. He wouldn't interfere in the conversation unless it became imperative, but neither would he let Zeb leave without being told about the baby.

After all, who knew? Maybe this time around Zeb would welcome impending fatherhood. Olivia's optimism might be well founded; no one was asking Zeb to be a single parent again. Olivia just wanted him to be a part of the baby's life. Surely *that* wouldn't cramp Zeb's style?

'So…' Olivia managed, slipping onto the seat next to Adam. 'Did you and my mother have any cocktails in Hawaii?'

'Ah, yes. Hawaii. I got distracted. Definitely an excellent place to holiday.'

'So *my mother* said.'

Zeb looked disconcerted, but only for a second. 'Indeed. And how *is* your beautiful mother? Do give her my best and…'

For goodness' sake.

Impatience snapped within Adam and he opened his mouth to intervene just as Olivia leant forward and thumped the table. Her small fist caused the cocktail to give a little jump, its paper umbrella falling to the tabletop.

'Jodie is pregnant,' she stated. 'And you're the father.'

Pallor stripped Zeb's face of its tan and rendered it blotchy. With one abrupt move he snatched the glass and drained it, before signalling to Saru for another one.

'Are you sure?' he demanded, all trace of bluff joviality vanishing

'Yes.'

'So why isn't Jodie here?' Zeb asked.

'Because she believes that you won't want to know; she thinks it's unfair to burden you with a child you hadn't bargained for.'

The colour returned to Zeb's face, along with a smile that creased his eyes but didn't reach it. 'Your mother is a wise lady,' he said.

As the impact of Zeb's words smashed into him Adam shifted his chair closer to Olivia and laid a hand on her denim-clad thigh. Anger and sadness vied inside him; clearly being a father to Adam had changed nothing for Zeb.

'Yes, she is,' Olivia said quietly. 'But I still thought that you would want to know. That you'd want to be a part of your baby's life.'

Saru brought the drink across; as he placed it in front of Zeb he shot Adam a quick glance. Instead of returning to the bar he sauntered towards the door, seemingly casually, effectively blocking Zeb's exit.

'It's better if I'm not,' Zeb said. 'I'm sure Adam has told you that I'm a wanderer. I'm not parent material. I've done my parenting stint and it's over. Of course I can send money—or if I can't Adam certainly can.' Zeb pushed his chair back and made to rise. 'Be sure to wish Jodie well.'

'Wait.' Olivia's voice was sharp. 'Please.'

'My dear girl, there is little point in trying to change my mind.'

Zeb stood and Adam mirrored the action.

'Sit,' he said. 'Olivia wants you to stay, so that is what is happening.'

Zeb hesitated and then threw his hands in the air. 'Very well, then.' He sank back down with a shake of his greying head.

'Don't you feel *anything* for your baby?' Olivia asked.

Adam flinched, wondering if Olivia was thinking of her own father. This must be her personal hell: to see the face of indifference in the flesh. Here was a man thinking only of himself, with never a thought for the child he had helped create.

'Of course I feel something,' Zeb said expansively. 'I accept a fiscal responsibility and I believe that I am doing the right thing for the child. Better that I don't raise any expectations that I know all too well I cannot come anywhere near fulfilling. The Mastersons don't like to be tied down, Olivia.' He waved a hand at Adam. 'Adam will vouch for that.'

Zeb's words sucker-punched Adam. They were no more than the truth and he would do well to remember it.

'So...' Zeb picked up his drink and glugged it down. 'Any more questions? Do I need to order another drink or am I free to go?'

Adam shot a glance at Olivia, who shook her head. She looked pale, her shoulders slumped, and his heart ached for her. For a second he was tempted to grab Zeb and force him to do what she wanted, make him grovel to Olivia for hurting her. But there was no use in walking that path. It would simply put off the inevitable. Zeb would always leave; that was what Mastersons did.

'Just go, Zeb.'

Weariness descended on Adam's shoulders as he watched Zeb bound to his feet.

For a second the older man hesitated. 'Adam, I am as I am.' He walked around the table and clapped an awkward hand on Adam's shoulder. 'I'll see you.' He nodded towards the door. 'You may want to let your friends know I'm good to go.'

Adam turned and nodded at Saru, knowing he'd pass the signal onto Gan, who was no doubt lurking in the vicinity.

'Ciao.'

With that, Zeb was gone.

'Olivia.' Despite knowing Zeb's actions weren't his fault, guilt jabbed at Adam. 'I'm sorry.'

She expelled a sigh and shook her head. 'Don't be. You didn't walk out through that door. I just can't believe that's how it went down.'

She reached across the table and picked up the paper umbrella, closing it carefully, smoothing the thin paper folds.

'I played it wrong. I should have tried harder. Asked more questions. Told him more about Mum. I should have done *something*. Asked you and Saru to keep him here locked up. Instead I let him leave.'

'It wasn't your fault.'

'Easy for you to say. *I'm* the one who stuffed it up.'

'You didn't stuff it up. Leaving is what Zeb does.'

No one knew that better than Adam, and he needed Olivia to believe that. To stop blaming herself.

'What do you mean?'

'I mean Zeb called it right. Mastersons aren't good at being tied down. There is nothing you can say or do to change that.'

'He looked after *you*,' Olivia said softly.

'Reluctantly.' The dark twist of knowledge wrenched

his insides. 'He looked into every other avenue first and he cut me loose at the first opportunity.'

'I don't understand.'

Adam ran a hand down his face and round the back of his neck; memory's bitter taste coated his very soul. A memory he'd never shared with anyone.

But here and now he could not let Olivia think that if she'd done something differently Zeb would have made a different decision. He'd hoped for her sake that Zeb would. Hell, he'd hoped it for his own sake. Wished that having Adam in his life, being a parent, had affected Zeb in some way. Clearly not. And Adam could see now what a foolish mirage *that* had been.

'It was my sixteenth birthday and we were celebrating.' Adam had been stupidly pleased; it had been the first time Zeb had marked his birthday in any way. 'Turned out we weren't celebrating my birthday.'

'What do you mean?'

'It was my send-off party.' He could feel the weight of Zeb's hand on his shoulder, hear his voice echo down the twelve years.

'You're old enough to fend for yourself.'

'I don't get it, Zeb. What does that mean?'

Zeb raised his champagne glass. 'Son, I'll be honest with you. Having a kid around is kind of cramping my style. I've done my duty by you and now it's time to cut you loose.' A hearty slap on the back. 'But no worries. We'll keep in touch.'

Then, 'Ciao!' and he'd upped and gone.

'But… That's awful,' Olivia whispered after Adam had given her a shortened version of their exchange.

'Zeb never wanted to be a father. But he did step up to bat when there was no other choice. I guess to him it seemed the right thing to do. He put in an eight-year sentence and figured he'd paid his debt to parenthood.'

'That sucks. It really sucks, Adam.' She shook her head. 'You should have told me.'

'Not fair. Zeb's relationship with me shouldn't have prejudiced you. Maybe if I'd been a different type of son things would have been different. It could have been he'd changed his opinion on parenthood over the past fourteen years.'

Foolish thoughts, really; Mastersons didn't change their spots.

Olivia stared down at the table and then whipped her head up, nostrils flaring. 'Then the baby is better off without him.' She swept a sideways glance at him. 'And so are you. Kudos to you. Zeb cut you loose and you forged a great life for yourself.'

Typical Olivia. Even in her own hurt she could find time to try and make him feel better. The least he could do was reciprocate in kind, with the truth. 'So will this baby. He or she will have you and that will make all the difference.'

She shook her head. 'No. It's Jodie who'll do that. I'll just do my best to help. Now I know the score, I need to get home and tell her.'

'You can fly back in the jet. Tell me when you want to go. I'll let the pilot know.'

'What about you?' Olivia asked.

'I'm going to stay in Thailand. Move around. Research some hotel options—maybe design a more "homey" type of hotel. With alphabetical spices.' The smile he could always summon at will just this once refused to comply. 'But I can ferry you across to the mainland today, if you're in a hurry to get back.'

Olivia's heart plummeted; it seemed more than clear that Adam was dead set on getting rid of her, *pronto*.

Perhaps she should go. After all, didn't Adam keep saying that he was a chip off the old block? And she'd just seen the old block in action. *No.* Adam wasn't like that. This she knew with a bone-deep certainty.

Pulling her shoulders back, she stood up to face him. 'That's really kind of you. But before you do that I'd like to talk. We haven't had a chance since last night, and... and so much has happened in the last twelve hours and... and... We need to talk.'

Colour angled over his cheekbones, though she wasn't sure if it was a flush of embarrassment or sheer irritation at her presumptuousness. Maybe conveyor belt women didn't require conversation. *Well, tough.*

'Of course,' he said. 'Why don't we sit out on the beach for a while?'

'Good idea.' Somehow it seemed preferable to have this discussion in the open air, with only the sea and sand as witness.

She blinked as they exited the bar; the dazzling sparkle of light hazed the sand golden, the soft grains scrunching under her toes. Adam maintained a distance, his hands jammed in his chino pockets, his withdrawal from her complete.

Hard to reconcile this grim man with *her* Adam, who had transported her to such heights of ecstasy.

They reached the edge of the sand and Olivia kept going into the waves, let the sun-warmed turquoise water wash over her toes. She stared out at the timeless horizon of blue, its brightness so intense, so still, it almost overwhelmed her. The blue of the cloudless sky was undisturbed by the swoop of even a solitary bird.

No courage to be found there; that would have to be dredged from somewhere within her, nurtured by the memory of what she and Adam had shared these past days. Their shared laughter and relaxed silences, their animated conversations about everything and nothing. The mind-blowing, incredible union of their bodies.

Turning, she moved towards him. He sat, long legs stretched out, palms down in the sand to brace his weight.

She sank down next to him, the heat of the sand permeating the white denim of her jeans, and pulled her knees up, hugging them to her.

'I—' She broke off. Where to begin? Maybe best to cut to the chase. Roll the dice...show her hand. 'I want to change the rules.'

His head snapped round with neck-cricking speed. 'Excuse me?'

'I'd like us to see each other again. Not as fling partners but as...'

'As what?' His voice was hoarse; the words rasped from his throat.

Olivia dug her fingers into the sand. 'As two people who want to spend time together and see what happens.'

A derisive snort indicated his opinion. 'I can tell you what would happen.'

'What? Suddenly you're the Delphi Oracle? You can't know what would happen.'

'Yes, I can. Someone would get hurt. Olivia.'

Not *Liv* any more—and, wow, that did hurt.

'It doesn't have to be like that.' Shifting in the sand, she wanted to reach out, but couldn't. She was too sure that he would flinch, and that would suck away the last bit of her courage. 'You've made me see that. A relationship doesn't have to be a power game. It can be a partnership, a give and take.'

His whole body stiffened, tension visibly rippling across his shoulderblades. 'You're mixing up a relationship with sex. We had crazy hot sex. That doesn't make a relationship.'

'We had more than that, Adam, and you know it.'

'In which case all the better to end it here and now.' Rooting in the sand, he pulled out a smooth, round stone and with a deft, angry flick of his wrist sent it cresting across the waves.

Olivia watched the pebble hop, skip, and jump before sinking into the watery depths. Indicative of where this conversation was going.

'Why?' she asked. 'Why won't you give us a chance to become something more? At least tell me that. Did I read it wrong?'

He twisted his torso and made a guttural sound, reminiscent of pain. 'You did nothing wrong, Olivia. It's me. I'm not relationship material. You just met Zeb—surely that gave you a clue?'

'You are not like Zeb,' If only she could get that through his thick, stubborn skull.

'I'm a carbon bloody copy.'

'That's not true. It doesn't even make sense. You're you. You make your own choices.'

'I do. And I choose to not hurt anyone else.'

He must be talking about his ex-wife. 'Did you hurt Charlotte?'

'Yes.' He uttered the syllable with a savage twist of self-derision. 'I married her and then two years later I left her.'

'Relationships break down. It happens.'

'Our marriage didn't break down, Olivia. I destroyed it. I promised Charlotte everything. A white picket fence, a family—the whole deal. When push came to shove I couldn't make good. It's the only deal I ever reneged on in my life.'

His large body was still rigid with a tautness she longed to soothe. The knowledge that he would reject her touch caused her to bury her hands in the warmth of the sand.

'What happened?' she asked instead.

'I blew it. Because every day the walls closed in a little more. I threw myself into work—anything to avoid returning to a place that had become like a prison. Eventually

I couldn't take it any more. So in true Masterson style I upped and left. I vowed to give Charlotte the rest of my life and I managed less than eight hundred days before I cracked and walked out of the door. Just like Zeb walked out of Saru's.'

His voice was so full of self-derision, so sure of his own guilt, it turned her thoughts topsy-turvy.

'So that's why we cannot take this any further. I hurt one woman in the pursuit of an impossible dream. I won't hurt another. You deserve better. A man who wants a home and a family. A man you can trust.'

His last five words stopped her in her tracks. Adam was right. If they took things further they would spend the whole time waiting for the sword to fall. Damocles would have nothing on them. Olivia loved her home; the thought of sitting in it, waiting and watching to see the walls close in on Adam, made her body shiver in revolt. All they could have was an interval until Adam left.

She had just witnessed what an utter coward Zeb was, and it was Zeb who had brought Adam up—Zeb whose genes he carried. Which explained why Adam still moved from place to place, had his moving line of beautiful women. What an idiot she was; she'd let mind-blowing sex blind her to all common sense. Looked through the filter of an amazing orgasm or three and made herself believe that Adam Masterson was something he wasn't.

Been willing to take a risk and trust him, let him in to her carefully constructed life. She couldn't even blame *him*—after all, Adam had never lied to her; he knew the kind of man he was and acknowledged it freely. He was a man who walked away. Like his father. Like her own father.

Idiot didn't begin to cover it. Because she'd broken all her own rules and now her poor exposed heart was shattering.

But, damn it, she'd chosen to jump on the conveyor belt and now she would climb off with her dignity and her self-respect intact. Hell, she'd even take him up on the private jet offer.

She gulped in the salty air before rising to her feet. 'You're right. I do deserve all of that. So if you wouldn't mind sorting out the jet I'll go back and pack. I can get a boat to the mainland, then a taxi to the airport—or I'm sure Gan or Saru would drive me. Good luck, Adam. And thanks for last night—it was fun. But you're right. Better to quit whilst we're ahead of the game.'

Turning, she walked away across the sand and didn't look back.

Didn't see Adam scramble to his feet and stretch out a hand.

Didn't hear his whispered, 'Liv...' before he slammed his hands into his pockets and stared out to sea.

CHAPTER FOURTEEN

OLIVIA DUCT-TAPED the cardboard box securely and hoisted herself up from her hunched crouch. Pressing one hand to the small of her back, she stretched and glanced around the packing-case-strewn floor of her mum's apartment.

'We're getting there,' she said, watching as Jodie carefully wrapped a delicate glass figurine in tissue paper.

Jodie smiled at her. 'And we'd get there a lot quicker if you stopped clucking over me and let me do more.'

'You've done loads. And you're six months pregnant, remember?'

'Well, second trimester or not, I can make my lovely daughter a cup of tea.'

'Thank you, Mum.'

Jodie glided across the thick-pile cream carpet, one hand circling her swollen belly with a reverent touch that filled Olivia with a strange yearning. Admiration and love mingled in her chest. Her mother had been completely unfazed by Zeb's attitude—had accepted his decision with a serene dignity. She hadn't let it affect her enjoyment in her pregnancy. Diet, yoga—anything Jodie could do to ensure the health of the baby she was doing. In spades.

'This way the baby will be healthy and so will I,' she'd explained. 'So I can look after her properly.' Reaching out, she'd laid a hand on Olivia's forearm. 'I know I made mistakes with you, Livvy. I want to make sure this time I get it right.'

'Oh, Mum. You did great with me. I couldn't have wished for a better mum.'

'That's sweet of you, darling, even if it's the most enormous fib. I do know that I love you more than anything else in my life. But it's time I stopped relying on you. This baby is a second chance for me. I have to learn to stand on my own two feet.' Jodie lifted an elegant hand to forestall Olivia's protest. 'It's true. I'm forty-two years old and I have spent my whole life depending on other people. I owe you an apology.'

'No. You don't.'

'Yes, I do. I am determined things are going to change. I've even got myself a job in the mother and baby store in town, and I love it.'

And over the two months since Olivia's return from the disastrous Masterson Mission she had come to see that Jodie meant every word.

Memories threatened. Adam's sinful smile—the real one that she had believed was for her and her alone. His eyes—shades of brown, glinting with mischief or dark with desire. His touch. When would her body stop craving it?

'Livvy? Tea's up.'

Olivia blinked the thoughts away and focused on the present, accepted the steaming mug with an attempt at a smile. She needed to banish Adam from her brain or at least wean herself off the man. Allow herself a hundred memories today and ninety-nine tomorrow.

Her mum's blue eyes studied her way too thoughtfully.

'How did last night go?' Olivia blurted. 'At antenatal class? I'm so sorry I couldn't make it, but—'

'Sweetheart, I told you—it's fine. I get that you needed

to see a client. It's no biggie. The class went well. Really well, in fact.'

Jodie opened her mouth and then closed it again, turned away so that her highlighted bob swung forward to hide her expression.

'Mum, are you sure everything is OK? You *do* know you don't have to move out of here?'

Jodie swung back round. 'Olivia Louisa Evans. We are *not* having this conversation again. I am appalled with myself for not realising long ago how wrong it was that you have been paying the extortionate rent on this place.' Her lips curved into a loving smile. 'Plus, I adore my new place. It's way more suitable for Bubs and me. There's a park. Local shops. It's a real community. Anyway, you're still contributing to the rent.'

'Mum. I've explained. I'm not *contributing*. You're earning the money. Consulting at Working Wardrobes counts as a job.'

It had turned out that whilst Olivia had been away her stand-in had gone AWOL. It had been Jodie who had stepped into the breach; Suzi, love her, had the clothes sense of a horse.

Her mother had done an amazing job.

There came a lash of guilt. If Jodie had been wrong to accept Olivia's help, Olivia had been wrong not to be honest with her mother. Had been wrong in so many of the assumptions she had made about Jodie. Turned out some people *did* change.

'Where are you going?' she asked as Jodie shrugged herself into her chic lime-green raincoat.

'Milk,' Jodie said. 'I've run out of milk. I'll just pop out.'

'I can go.'

'No. It's good exercise for me.' Jodie tied the belt loosely around her waist. 'See you later, Livvy.'

Five minutes after the door had clicked shut behind her mum the doorbell chimed. Sighing, Olivia switched the Hoover off. Many things had changed about Jodie, but housework still wasn't her forte. There was enough dust gathered behind the sofa to fill a skip. Olivia swiped a hand across her brow and grimaced as she glanced in the mirror. The postman was in for a bit of a shock.

She pulled the door open and shock impacted her, dropped her chin kneewards. 'What are you—?'

And why now? If ever she had been stupid enough to hallucinate Adam turning up unannounced, the vision had *not* included Olivia dressed in an old apron, with a scarf over her head, looking like a demented version of a fifties housewife.

Deep breath.

'Adam. What are you doing here?' She half closed the door and stepped forward, holding the handle behind her back.

'I'm here to see you. Didn't Jodie mention it?'

Just great. Maybe her mum was retaliating against Olivia's foolhardy jaunt across the world to find a man her mother had already identified as a waste of space.

'No. She didn't mention it.'

'Ah. Well, she knows I'm here. So can I come in?'

'No.' Just this glimpse of him was half killing her; no way was she letting him inside.

Dark blue jeans moulded to muscular thighs, and his reggae T-shirt stretched across the expanse of his chest and brought back a flood of memories she'd kept at bay for weeks. His dark hair was longer than she remembered, and it glinted with raindrops from the intermittent spring showers that were plaguing Bath.

Adam sighed. 'I'm not going anywhere, Olivia. So you have two choices. You can let me in. Or I can pick you up, sling you over my shoulder and carry you inside. Your choice. Three seconds.'

For an insane heartbeat Olivia was tempted to hold her ground; a tremor weakened her legs at the thought of being thrown over Adam's shoulder.

As if reading her mind, he raised an eyebrow and stepped forward.

She had to get a grip; if she let Adam touch her she would be lost. Stepping backwards, she sucked in a breath to avoid any such possibility. The downside of that strategy being that she got a lungful of his woodsy scent. Her head whirled as desire jolted through her.

'Let's make this quick. I don't care if Mum knows you're here. I want you gone before she gets back.'

'That's no problem. Jodie won't be back for a while.'

'Huh? What have you done? Where is she?'

'Liv, I'm not the mafia, and this isn't a mob movie. Jodie said she'd spend the day with her friend Juliette and go to the cinema.'

He'd called her Liv, and the fact spread warmth over her chest. A heat she had to fight.

'Hang on a minute.' Olivia slammed her hands onto her hips, tried to ignore the sudden predatory glint in his eyes as they rested on her body. 'Exactly when did Mum tell you all of this?'

'Yesterday. I called her and we met for a coffee. Or a herbal tea, in your mum's case.'

'You came to sort out the money?' Why else would he have turned up?

'Amongst other things,' he agreed calmly. 'Your mother strikes a hard bargain.'

'She took the money?' Confusion mixed with an obscure sense of disappointment.

'Why shouldn't she? The baby is my sister just as much as yours. I don't see why she shouldn't benefit. Jodie suggested I set up a trust fund for the baby, which is exactly what I've done. The money will be hers when she reaches the age of twenty-one—or before, if Jodie, you and I all agree. So if she wants to go to university, or go travelling, or set up a business, or buy a home she'll be able to.'

Adam smiled. *Her* smile—the one that warmed his eyes and curled her toes in the grubby trainers that currently adorned her feet.

'You and your mum are very alike. It took me a while to persuade her to accept anything from me.'

Olivia flexed her feet and attempted to pull her brain into gear. 'This is all very generous of you, Adam, but it's between you and Mum. Nothing to do with me. It doesn't explain why you're here. Unless you want my gratitude? If so, thanks very much, and the door is that way.'

Ungracious, she knew. But Adam must know that she couldn't be bought—though what he was trying to buy was anyone's guess. Another night? Heaven help her, her body melted at the thought. So the sooner he left, the better.

He stepped forwards, closing the space between them, and she moved backwards, manoeuvred herself behind the sofa.

'I'm not after your gratitude, Liv. I came here because I wanted to see you. I *needed* to see you.'

Her tummy fluttered with an anticipatory fizz that common sense instantly doused. There were loads of reasons for Adam to need to see her. She tucked a stray tendril of hair behind her ear, her fingers skimming the synthetic material of the utterly horrendous scarf. Her fingers itched with the feminine need to tug the damn thing off and she dropped her hands to grip the back of the sofa. She didn't care how she looked.

'If you need me to sign something to do with the trust fund leave the papers here. I'll get them back to you once I've read them.'

'That's not what I need.' Brown eyes looked at her with a hunger he made no effort to hide. 'Why didn't you tell your mum about us?'

Olivia narrowed her eyes. 'How do you know I didn't?'

'Because after I took her to her antenatal class last night we went for a drink, and until I explained the situation she seemed to think that I was just someone who'd helped you find Zeb.'

Olivia wasn't sure which bit of the sentence to tackle first. 'You went to her antenatal class?'

'Yes.'

Adam took another step closer to the sofa so that he stood at the corner, and her heart started flipping like a blueberry pancake in her chest.

'Why?'

'Because I want to be part of my sister's life.'

'You do?'

'Yes,' he said simply. 'Just because Zeb isn't choosing to feature it doesn't mean I can't. That's why I went to Jodie first, before coming to find you. I want you both to know that regardless of what happens between you and me I will always be involved. Not out of duty but out of love.'

His words swam around her mind, her brain circling and trying to come to terms with them. It focused finally on 'regardless of what happens between you and me'.

'You and me?' Clenching her nails into the palms of her hand, she straightened her shoulders. 'I don't understand. There *is* no you and me. And, whatever happened between us in the past, I'd never stand in the way of you being in the baby's life.'

'I want there to be a you and me.'

His words resurrected that tendril of hope—the very one she thought she'd uprooted and composted. *Careful, Olivia.* He'd cracked her barriers and her heart on a Thai beach two months ago. *Don't let him hurt you more.*

'You were pretty damn clear two months ago that that wasn't a possibility. Sure enough that you convinced me.'

He rubbed a hand over his face and back up and through his hair—such a familiar gesture that her heart ached.

'Two months ago I was an idiot.'

'And now?'

'Now I know that whilst I may still be an idiot I'm not my father. I don't want to walk away from the baby. And I don't want to walk away from you.'

Another step and he was behind the sofa with her. Her only method of escape was to scramble over the back. The problem was flight was the very last thing on her mind.

Wait, Olivia. Don't just fall into his arms.

Adhering her feet to the floor, she turned to face him. 'But you will. You walked away from Charlotte.'

'Yes, I did. But I've done a lot of thinking these past weeks.' He rubbed the back of his neck. 'After Zeb and I parted ways years ago I was adrift.'

Against her will she felt her heart smite her as she imagined the incredible hurt of that rejection. So much worse than being rejected as an unknown baby.

'I thought a home would ground me,' he continued. 'Then I met Charlotte. She was an army child; she'd never had real roots. She was desperate for a home, as well. We were so caught up in the idea of having a home we thought that was what marriage was all about. We were in love with an idea, not each other.' His forehead creased into a frown of confusion. 'Does that make sense? Because it makes perfect sense to me now that I've met you and I've understood what love really is.'

'What *is* love?'

'It's wanting be with the person you love all the time. It's feeling able to share anything and not be judged. It's loving the sound of their voice and the smell of their hair.' His huge body was rigid with tension as he closed the gap further. 'I love you, Olivia. I know I messed up, but please believe this: I love you. And I will spend the rest of my life proving it to you and winning your love.'

Joy exploded in a firework of happiness, sending her giddy as she took the final steps so that she was standing close enough to touch him.

'You don't have to win my love, Adam.' She placed her hand on his heart. 'You already have it.'

'I do?' His smile was blinding in its radiance as he spanned her waist and tugged her closer.

'You do. I love you, Adam. I love how you make me feel beautiful and how you make me *want* to feel beautiful. For you. I love how I trust you to protect me and care for me. I love how you make me smoothies. I love the way you give and I love the way you take. I just love you. With all my heart. And all my other vital organs, too.'

She grinned at him.

'And I mean *all*! Turns out love isn't an illusion after all. It's wanting to be with someone and not caring where you are. If you don't want to live in a house then we'll live in a hotel suite. We can live in a tent, if you like.'

Adam shook his head. 'Liv, that week in Ko Lanta with you in that house was magical. I get that it was only a week, but not once did the walls so much as move. I want more of that. I want to go shopping and fill a house with clutter, with souvenirs of our life together. Which reminds me…' He dug into his jeans pocket and handed over a small tissue-wrapped packet before looping his arms back round her.

Olivia opened it up and gave a small gasp. Nestled in the folds were three silver charms.

Pushing her sleeve up, she unclasped the bracelet he'd given her. 'I'll put them on now.'

'A beer bottle to remind you of our first night together, a frangipani flower, and a ring.'

'A ring?' Olivia stilled.

Adam nodded and dug into his pocket again. He hauled in a breath and pulled out a velvet jewellery box. He popped it open and sank to one knee.

'Will you marry me, Liv?'

Tears of sheer joy dewed her eyelashes and thrills of bliss trembled though her as she nodded. 'Yes, Adam, I will. With all my heart.'

Her fingers quivered as he slid the exquisite diamond band on. Then she tugged him to his feet and a bubble of laughter escaped her lips. In her wildest dreams she'd never imagined that she, Olivia Evans, would be proposed to looking like this!

The grubby scarf still encased her hair, dust and grime smeared her face, and she was wearing a flowered apron that had seen better days. And she didn't give a stuff.

Secure in Adam's love for ever, she stepped forward into the warmth of his embrace and tilted her face up to receive a blissful kiss.

* * * * *

MILLS & BOON®

Why shop at millsandboon.co.uk?

Each year, thousands of romance readers find their perfect read at millsandboon.co.uk. That's because we're passionate about bringing you the very best romantic fiction. Here are some of the advantages of shopping at www.millsandboon.co.uk:

* **Get new books first**—you'll be able to buy your favourite books one month before they hit the shops

* **Get exclusive discounts**—you'll also be able to buy our specially created monthly collections, with up to 50% off the RRP

* **Find your favourite authors**—latest news, interviews and new releases for all your favourite authors and series on our website, plus ideas for what to try next

* **Join in**—once you've bought your favourite books, don't forget to register with us to rate, review and join in the discussions

Visit **www.millsandboon.co.uk**
for all this and more today!